# Call It Quits

**Other Book**

## *Too Much Gold to Flush*

If you have not read *Too Much Gold to Flush*, you need to.
In it, Pat Grissom shares the story of her three-month
marriage ending in betrayal.
She fills *Too Much Gold to Flush* with quotes on every page along with
an honest self-evaluation of who she was when she married that creep.
By doing so, she found the courage and the
strength to shift from victim to living a vital life.
Plus, she gives half of the proceeds to women's shelters.

# Call It Quits

PAT GRISSOM

Permission requests should be directed to:
Patricia Ann Grissom
c/o Dedicated to Empowering Women, LLC.
P.O. Box 2235
Friendswood, Texas 77549
www.patgrissom.com

Dedicated to Empowering Women, LLC. (DEW)

Cover & Layout Design - Yvonne Vermillion

First Edition
ISBN 978-0-9853813-2-5
Library of Congress Control Number: 2018901735
Printed in the United States

For my children, Justin, Brandon, and Reagan.

Each of you has gifted me with your own version of love, which far exceeded what I had previously imagined possible.

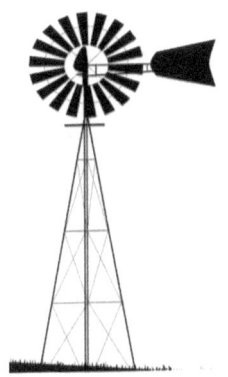

# Prologue

## December 8, 1972, Friday

The nurse standing over me adjusted my arm and asked, "Is that better?"

When you hurt like hell, 'better' is relative. I tried to speak, but what came out of my swollen mouth sounded like a muzzled dog's whimper. It had been a hell of a day, and all I wanted to do was sleep.

"Here's your call button," she said, slipping it into my hand. "You let me know if you need anything." She crossed her arms over her large breasts and gawked at my battered face. Then she clicked her tongue. "I wonder what a pretty little thing like you did to get beat up like that?"

In my current condition, I doubted that I looked like a 'pretty little thing,' but she was right about it being my fault. I had brought this upon myself. Like Vince says, I should be grateful for what I've got, instead of always wanting more.

The busty nurse's chest swelled like an angry horned-toad as she shook her head and walked out of the room. Her disgust with me rang loud and clear. I was equally fed up with myself. What made me constantly do and say things that aggravated the snot out of Vince? And why couldn't I learn to keep my big ideas to myself?

The pain killers were finally starting to kick in when footsteps stopped right outside my door. Someone who sounded like Papa Martin cleared their throat, which he did when he had something to say and didn't want to repeat himself. "We need to get square about this." It was him all right, and it was the tone he used with Vince when his only son had screwed up royally.

"I said it won't happen again." Vince paused, and I imagined them doing a stare-down. "You think I can't control myself?" he whined like he was five instead of thirty-five.

"Given the condition your wife is in, I doubt it." Papa Martin cleared his throat. "I meant about making this right, or at least trying to."

What was going on? Papa Martin had never gotten involved before, but if he hadn't I might be dead now. That was one advantage of living next door to your in-laws.

"Where do you stand on Abi going to school? Betty and Harold—well Betty says they want to pay for it. Are you gonna stand in Abi's way?" Papa Martin demanded.

I was stupefied—that Mama had offered to pay for me to go to school, in spite of what Daddy must have said. Did they even know about me being in the hospital? I would do just about anything to get to go to school. I'd even make a deal with the devil—or God, who ever was willing to negotiate. If I promised to make Vince happy, if I was the best wife possible, then maybe God would step in on my behalf. Since I did not consider myself pals with God, I decided I better show Him I was sincere, so I started speculating on what I needed to do. *God, if you make Vince say yes, I will do everything in my power to be the very best wife possible. I'll cook whatever he wants, I'll act like I'm enjoying sex no matter how often he wants it, I'll be. . .well, I'll be perfect*—whatever that meant. I held my breath and waited for Vince to reply, knowing in my heart that he wouldn't go along with this, but still wishing and praying, and desperately wanting to satisfy the yearning to go to school that had been eating at me for the last few years.

It was taking Vince too long to come up with an answer, which told me he was thinking of a way of backing out of whatever agreements had already been made. Papa Martin going to bat for me wasn't a huge surprise. Out of that whole family, he was the one person I could count on, which was why I had found the courage to mention my desire to go to school while we were eating peach cobbler after Sunday dinner a few weeks ago. It had taken me weeks to get brave enough to say something, but I figured it was the only way to gradually break the news to Vince about cleaning houses to earn money. I hadn't counted on him finding out before I got around to telling him. While my best friend Christi and I were cleaning Juanita Barn's house, Juanita happened to see Vince at the filling station, and told him she was on her way home to see how nice I had cleaned for her. He trailed her over there and dragged me out after saying a few choice words to Christi.

"Yeah," Vince finally breathed, so faint I could barely hear him, and by then it had been so long and my head was so foggy from the drugs that I wasn't sure what he was saying yes to.

"Yeah, what?" Papa Martin demanded, which I greatly appreciated.

"Yeah, she can go to that—"he stopped short, and I knew he would have said 'fucking' if he had been talking to anyone but Papa Martin. "She can go to her gol dern college."

I could not breathe. It felt too unreal to believe I was going to college. Then I remembered my deal with God. Maybe He was testing me to see if I could hold up my end of the bargain. It would take everything I could muster to be the best wife possible to Vince. But I would do it. A warm blanket of peace settled over me.

# Chapter One

*She's so nervous she has to thread her
needle with the sewing machine running.*

## January 15, 1973, Monday

*T*he radio clicked on. Carly Simon was in the middle of *You're
So Vain*. She finally got through reminding me that I "probly"
thought this song was about me, and the DJ started yammering, "Good
Monday morning, all you High Plains drifters. Y'all stay tuned for the
latest bulletins on the Watergate trial, scheduled to start up again this
morning. I hope you were one of the millions watching Elvis Presley's
televised concert in Hawaii last night. Supposedly, more people watched
that than saw the Apollo moon landing. Also in the entertainment world
yesterday, the Miami Dolphins defeated the Washington Redskins in
Super Bowl VII, completing the NFL's first perfect season.

"Zak Graham of John Deere Implement and Supplies in Flatland,
Texas brings the farm and weather report to you. Stop by Zak's this
morning and get a cup of coffee and chew the fat for a.. ."

While the disc jockey jabbered on in his thick nasal accent, I lay
perfectly still under the electric blanket, which was in itself a true miracle
because I had a bad case of the heebie-jeebies. Today, I would start college.

When Vince groaned, stretched his arm overhead, and then reached
for me, I knew what was coming next. "I need a poke, Abi-girl." He
rolled on top of me, his warm morning breath in my face.

5

Spreading my legs, I waited for Vince to work his tool inside me. As he probed my hole, I stiffened with every jab. A wave of nausea washed over me, which made me wish I was pregnant, but I dared not ask for that too since I was already overextended with the Lord. Vince kept prodding, and my stomach settled, so I figured it was only nerves.

"Talk about a dry hole," Vince muttered as he rolled off of me and turned on the bedside lamp. He rummaged through the nightstand until he found a nearly empty tube of KY Jelly. After working the last of it onto the tip of his large, stiff poker, he placed his calloused hands on either side of my head and made several more attempts at entering me. When his tool finally slipped into place, he began the familiar, steady, mechanical motion of sex. In the dimly lit room, his large, muscular frame reminded me of the oil pumps he worked on all day, constantly sucking, but never getting enough. Then I stopped myself, remembering how lucky I was that Vince was letting me go to school. Once more, my thoughts had strayed from that of the perfect wife. Hopefully, God wasn't listening.

After a few minutes, Vince's speed increased, and I knew he was getting close—thank goodness. He finished with a few hard, deep thrusts before his sweaty body collapsed on top of me. Anxious to get up before his juice slipped out of me and leaked all over the clean sheets, I lay there and waited. Finally, he stretched and rolled to his side of the bed. I turned the other direction and grabbed a tissue from the nightstand to plug my hole.

Before I got up, he slapped my butt and howled loud enough for Thelma and A.V. (Papa Martin) to hear him next door while he crawled out of bed. I trailed him to the bathroom, grabbed my housecoat from the hook on the back of the door, and slipped it on. Then I turned on the water to get it hot while Vince straddled the toilet and peed a steady stream. His sturdy, muscular hips reminded me of a horse's rump. When he stepped into the steamy shower, I lowered the seat and sat on the commode. As his juice dripped out of me, my thoughts returned to the day that lay ahead. I had dreamed of doing this for years, but now that it was here, I was as nervous as a cat in a room full of rockers. When Vince shut off the water, I jumped up and headed for the kitchen, scared he'd fling back the shower curtain and see me sitting there instead of making his breakfast and lunch.

I was filling a container with pecan pie when Vince walked into the kitchen, wearing his standard work clothes, a gray shirt and jeans. He sat and turned on the black and white TV that took up one end of the table. Because Vince loved to watch TV, we had three of them—one in every room of the house, except the bathroom.

He switched channels and a reporter began spouting the details of President Nixon terminating mandatory wage and price controls—which meant absolutely nothing to me. After the newsman predicted moderate temps and none of the snow that we had last week, Vince muttered, "It's about time we got some decent weather. You got any idea how hard it is to pull a line of pipe when you're freezing your ass off?"

"No, Vince, I don't." I made sure I had everything on the table for his usual breakfast—fried eggs, toast, bacon, coffee, and a glass of orange juice.

Satisfied he wouldn't need anything else, I hurried to the bathroom to dress in the clothes I picked out yesterday—bell-bottomed jeans and the red, white, and blue sweater Mama gave me for Christmas—a far cry from the dresses we wore every day to high school. As soon as Vince left, I'd high-tail it for Oaces since I didn't know how long it would take me to drive forty miles, park, and walk to my first class. I also didn't want to get Vince's tail-feathers in a knot by acting too eager to see him leave. He was already primed to have a conniption fit about me carrying through on what he repeatedly termed a "stupid goddamn idea."

Our tiny house shook as Vince approached me with his heavy work boots. Seeing the unmade bed, I started that direction, but Vince's six-foot three-inch frame filled the bathroom doorway before I cleared it.

A wave of panic rushed through me when I considered the possibility of Vince deciding at the last minute I didn't need to go to school. Frozen, I stood before him with my chin down.

Using his fingers like giant combs, he lifted my hair and let it fall to my shoulders. "Where you goin' all dressed up, Abi-girl?"

"I start school today." I looked into his pale blue eyes because I knew if I didn't it would make him mad.

Again he raked his fingers through my hair. "Abi-girl," he murmured. "I hate to see you crash and burn when those kids straight out of high school leave you in their dust."

"Thank you, Vince, for letting me do this." I dropped my gaze to the short, curly hair at the neck of his shirt and worried he had heard my words as smartass rather than grateful as I had intended them.

He sniffed. "It's gonna cause trouble," he warned, his voice gentle and coaxing, although his underlying message crystal clear—keep on being his Abi-girl.

"I'll only be gone while you're at work, and Mama's paying for everything." I counted the threads holding his top button in place and willed the calm that had claimed him while I was in the hospital would continue.

"And is your mama gonna keep every bastard there from feelin' you up with his eyes?" He cupped my chin with his vise-like grip, pinching my cheeks until my eyes watered. My heart raced with the dread of an explosion. While this version of Vince lacked charm and appeal, at least I was familiar with it.

"Nobody's going to look at me," I mumbled, my words slurred by his painful hold on me.

"Right," he growled. "I've seen the way men look at you, especially Buckie boy. He's always wanted you instead of that bitch he's married to."

"Buck's not interested in me" I protested weakly. It was insane for me to argue with Vince about whether or not my best friend's husband was interested in me. I needed to keep Vince happy—that was it.

"The hell he's not." He squeezed my cheeks tighter.

I closed my eyes to contain my tears—the Vince I knew well was still here, only temporarily squelched.

For whatever reason, his hold slackened, and he crooned, "Abi-girl, you're the prettiest girl in Texas. That's why I married you. And I don't plan on sharing you with nobody else."

A car horn honked outside; his dad was ready to go to work, and he was waiting on Vince.

"Just see to it that you keep them big brown eyes to yourself," he warned.

"Yes, sir," I whispered, which was stupid on my part. To Vince, 'sir' meant I was mocking him.

His expression turned hard, and he shouted, "I told you I don't want you goin' to school."

"But you said I could. You told Papa Martin –" Again, I had said too much.

He gave my face one last wrenching squeeze and stomped toward the back door, grabbing his heavy coat and cap from the hook on the wall.

In the kitchen, I spotted his lunchbox on the counter. There would be hell to pay if he got to work without it, so I hurried after him. "Don't forget your –"

He reeled around, yanked the metal box from my hand, and then shot back over his shoulder as he hurried down the concrete steps, "Mama said for you to carry her to the doctor today."

After pulling the backdoor closed, I slapped the knob to turn off the blaring kitchen TV. While I cleaned the kitchen, I dreaded calling Thelma. When I finally got up the gumption to dial her number, she answered on the first ring.

"Mama Martin, Vince said you need a ride to –"

"Yeah, I'm feeling so bad, I'd have to get better to die. Martha can't take me 'cause she just started a new job at that UP university."

"She did?" Thelma might think we should ride together, which I sure didn't want to do.

"Yeah, she's working as a secretary. We need to get to the doctor's early, so we don't have to sit and wait. You know how it is if you get behind a bunch of Mexicans. They bring in every one of their kids, and they've all got runny noses. They're on some kind of federal. . . ."

I tried to interrupt, but she was on a roll, so she carried on about Mexicans and the impossibility of a doctor curing her. While she talked, I thought about Martha working at UP. I'd probably never see her, but I wanted going to college to be my thing—without someone from Quits potentially keeping tabs on me.

When I noticed the time, I blurted out, "I can't take you to the doctor this morning."

"You can't? Well, why not? You should'a said so to begin with? Vince said you would."

"He forgot about my classes starting today."

"Oh, that. I still don't understand this silly notion you got. You don't need a college education. A.V. and me has been married thirty-seven years now, and I never needed any more than what I learned in high school and a lot of that was just stuff. Besides, Vince works steady."

"I know, he's always worked with Papa Martin, but I need some education in case he gets hurt." That was the most logical explanation I had concocted to explain my obsession with going to school.

"You're looking to be a schoolgirl again, Abi, but it's been too long."

"I'll take you to the clinic this afternoon if you like," I said, cutting her off before she got revved up again about how stupid it was for me to think I could go back to school.

"Get here early," she warned. "If we get there after two, we'll be there 'til six."

"We'll go as soon as I get back. I'm not sure when that will be. Bye."

Within ten minutes, I backed my black 1965 Volkswagen out of the dirt drive that separated our yard from Vince's parents'. In the street, the car coughed and sputtered. I hadn't warmed it up. If Vince were there, he'd ream me out. With no traffic in sight, I restarted it, shifted it to neutral, and studied the white stucco house that had been my home for eleven-and-a-half years. Vince's family lived there until he was three. When his sister Beatrice was born, they moved next-door to a similar house, but it had three bedrooms. Thelma's parents moved into the vacated house. Sixteen years later, about the time I met Vince, his grandparents moved into a nursing home, so it was only logical that he and I would live there. Shortly after our wedding, Papa Martin painted the trim on both houses with the same blue paint, which seemed to tell the world we were connected.

Thelma pushed her screen door open and hollered something at me, but rather than figure out what her questioning scowl meant, I drove past frantically waving and hoping she understood I did not have time to talk.

An hour-and-a-half later, I walked into an empty classroom at the University of the Panhandle. Arriving earlier than I had anticipated, even after I drove all over creation looking for a parking spot, I sat in the center of the front row. To calm my nerves, I leafed through the history text. The room filled, and a lady wearing a brown suit walked in carrying a book and a stack of papers. I figured she was the secretary helping the professor, but then she introduced herself as Dr. Horton, which surprised the heck out of me. She passed out what she called a syllabus, and then she launched into a lecture about the colonial days of America.

When some of the students grumbled as they got out paper and pen, she remarked, "I hope you didn't think I was going to cheat you out of what you paid for by letting you go early on the first day."

"I ain't paying for it," volunteered a man from the back of the room.

She leveled him with a look that could have hung icicles on careless weeds and said flatly, "That, sir, may end up being your biggest challenge."

Without giving him a chance to respond, Dr. Horton told us she was committed to telling both sides of the story—what men *and* women had done throughout America's history. According to her, history had traditionally focused on men's accomplishments, so she felt compelled to weigh in on the female perspective.

The same smart-aleck on the back row piped up again, "Isn't that reverse male chauvinism?"

"Actually, it's feminism," she countered, "which is quite different from a reversal of the self-righteous nature of male chauvinism you have so aptly portrayed."

"Are you saying I'm acting like a male chauvinist pig?" The satisfied look on his face said he thought he'd scored points, maybe not with her, but with the young women in the class who were snickering.

"If the oink fits, wear it." The class erupted with laughter, and the corners of Dr. Horton's lips twitched as if she was forcing herself not to smile.

The 'pig' emitted a series of grunts that sounded like a real porker, which further amused the class.

Apparently tired of his shenanigans, Dr. Horton said, "Should you want to pursue this topic, I suggest you make an appointment to see me in my office. You have my phone number on your syllabus." She went on to explain that during colonial times Lord Baltimore of Maryland offered tracks of land to attract both women as well as men to the new world; the British government offered female prisoners the option of becoming indentured servants in the colonies rather than serve out their sentences in British prison. Margaret Brent, who is known as the country's first feminist along with Anne Hutchinson, were both treated unfairly. Margaret was not allowed to participate in the legal system, although she had successfully handled numerous legal transactions, and Anne was "guilty" of being too strong as a religious leader. Margaret and Anne were both shunned, but Margaret moved on and avoided politics while Anne and her family also fled, but they met an untimely demise at the hands of the Native Americans.

"When you say Native American, do you mean Injuns?" Mr. Back-Row hollered.

"I mean Native Americans. Indians live in India." She flipped her book shut. "Read the first two chapters of our text by Wednesday, and be forewarned I am a fan of pop quizzes." She collected her notes, walked out of the room, and the class released a collective sigh.

Maybe Vince and Mama Martin were right; I might have bitten off more than I could chew. Before I headed for my next class, I glanced over my scrawled pages of notes. Dr. Horton must have said something about men, but none of that ended up on my paper. Most of what she said about women struck me as irreverent, especially the part about a female minister. Surely God knew what I was getting into, or He would not have accepted my deal and let me get into something like this.

In my second class, Basic Drawing, the instructor, Dr. Cole, spent most of the class talking about the syllabus and how important it is to come to class, do the outside assignments, and show up with the right materials—paper and pencils. Afterwards, I sat on the college bus, counted what remained of Mama's money, and prayed the bookstore still had used copies of the textbooks I needed for psychology and design. Neither Mama nor I could believe that books cost so much. Thinking of Vince's warning about not talking to anyone, I focused on the brightly painted plywood fences around construction sites with contradictory messages like 'Smile, Jesus Loves You', 'Nuke The Gooks', and 'Make Love Not War'.

Before entering the bookstore, I reluctantly left the canvas book bag Mama had made for me on the shelves just inside the door. It was forbidden to carry it past the turnstiles, but I worried about coming out and finding it gone or empty. Not sure how to find the books I needed, I began wandering up and down the aisles.

* * *

Already late for class, Garrett charged away from the counter where he had stood in line for thirty minutes only to find out they had lost his order. What good did it do to fill out their stupid forms if they were going to lose them? Garrett looked up just in time to see a woman step in front of him. Because he couldn't do anything else, he plowed into her. Miraculously, the pile of books he carried remained in his arms.

"Watch where you're going!" The words had not fully left his mouth when he wished he could pull them back. In front of him stood a groovy chick who was obviously as shocked as he was mad.

While straightening Garrett's jumbled stack of books, she muttered, "Holy shit. I'm so sorry. Oh, my god, holy shit." She looked to be about his age with eyes so dark that the pupils and irises blended together.

The term *holy shit* echoed in his head. How had something so graphic come out of such an innocent looking mouth? Unable to stop himself, he laughed. Her huge brown eyes flicked from his eyes, to his mouth, and back to his eyes while her words fizzled into a stony silence and terror replace her look of disbelief.

"Hey, no. My fault. No harm," he assured her, frustrated with himself for acting like such a hothead.

Apparently convinced he wasn't going to get physical, she nervously looked around the store, although her hands lingered on the books in his hands. "I'm really sorry. I don't have a clue where anything is."

"Can I help you?" he offered, hopeful she would look at him again with those gorgeous brown eyes.

"Do you work here?" She barely glanced at him.

"No, in fact, I was upset...." he trailed off, reluctant to admit what a jerk he had been.

"You were what?" she prompted, now leveling him once more with her gaze.

He shifted the books to his left side and extended his hand. "I'm –"

Before he could say his name, she quickly stepped back. "I need to go." She raced toward the door.

"Didn't you want some help?" he yelled after her.

She started out the double doors, but quickly backtracked and grabbed a cloth bag from the sea of backpacks on the shelves beyond the turnstiles.

Garrett moved toward the checkout line, and then he thought better of it. UP was large enough that he might never see her again. He set down the books he had spent an hour collecting and trailed her down the street, around the corner, and into the library. Keeping a safe distance, he moved at her pace, which was fast for a woman. The whole time, he refused to admit to himself what he was doing.

The woman looked around, headed toward the stairs, and hurried up them. Hoping she had not seen him, Garrett gave her time to reach the second floor before he followed her. By the time he got there, she was nowhere in sight. Before going to the third floor, he cautiously checked several secluded corners, finally spotting her red, white, and blue sweater. Thankfully she sat with her back to him and was preoccupied with pulling books out of her bag. Garrett sat close enough to watch her through an opening in a wall of bookcases. While he watched her study, he puzzled over why she had acted so weird when he tried to talk to her—and why he was doing what he was doing, which was equally strange.

Ignoring the fact that he should be in class, he studied the way her long brown hair followed the curve of her shoulders and stopped midway down her back. He chuckled when she discretely nibbled on something that she pulled from her bag. She was probably scared she would get in trouble for eating in the library. Working his dog tags back and forth on a chain around his neck, he thought of his wife, Trang, and his son, Loc.

When his mystery woman began packing her bag, the thought that he might not find her again sent him into a panic. He walked toward a woman he did not know, for reasons he could not explain. As he got even with her, he turned toward her as if suddenly recognizing her. "Aren't you the person I ran over in the bookstore?" Without waiting for her reply, he pulled out a chair. "May I sit here?"

She glanced at the empty tables on either side. "I, ahh…sure, I'm leaving." She kept her eyes trained on her book bag as she loaded it.

Garrett sat, took off his Clint Eastwood *The Good, The Bad, and the Ugly* leather hat, flopped it on the table, shook out his mane of long hair, and stuck out his hand. "Garrett Clay."

She looked at his hand and then at his hair. "Garrett," she repeated softly before she timidly put her hand in his for only a moment before she pulled it back.

"So what's your name?" Aiming for casual, he began emptying his backpack. When he decided she wasn't going to answer, he looked up at her. "You didn't tell me your name," he prodded as gently as he dared.

She glanced around like she was expecting someone. "I really shouldn't," she whispered.

Garrett had never worried about being overly quiet in a library, but clearly she believed it was important. When she scooted her chair back and began to rise, his hand involuntarily shot out and grabbed her arm. He was acting like a mad man, but he could not stop himself. "Don't go. You don't have to tell me your name. We'll just sit here and act like we've been friends forever."

Something akin to panic moved over her face right before it twisted with pain. "That hurts," she breathed, yielding to his grasp.

"Oh, my God. I'm sorry." He let her go. "Please forgive me. I didn't mean to hurt you."

She gave him an embarrassed smile, and then she whispered in a barely audible voice, "You must think I'm a baby. It—my arm—was broken. I just got it out of a cast a few days ago."

"Oh, what happened?" he asked, lowering his voice to a whisper as well.

"Just an accident," she answered softly, looking down at her arm and then up at him.

She lowered herself back into her seat, never breaking eye contact. Garrett remembered being ten or eleven and finding a baby bird in the grass. This woman reminded him of that bird. She had the same terrified and fragile look, but she also seemed to accept him even though she obviously did not want to.

"I apologize for acting weird, but I'm nervous. This is my first day of college," she confided.

Weird? Garrett was the one acting like a mad man. He studied her delicate nose, her high cheekbones, and the fine layer of new growth along her hairline. Again he thought of the baby bird, its downy covering, and how timid it had acted. "Bird," he whispered, not intending to say it out loud, but like everything he had done since he saw her in the bookstore, it just happened.

"What did you say?" she asked.

"You remind me of a bird, a baby bird," he explained.

Her lips parted into a dazzling smile. "Abi. My name is Abi Martin."

"Nice to meet you, Abi Martin. Would you like to go get some lunch over at the sub?"

"No thanks," she murmured diverting her eyes to her cloth bag. "But I have some cookies if you want them." She pulled out a small paper sack. "They're homemade, and they'll end up getting crushed in here."

Garrett peered inside the sack and pulled out a cookie. As he bit into it, nuggets of chocolate melted in his mouth, and he moaned that involuntarily sound that he emitted when he climaxed. "Did you make this?"

She nodded and ducked her head. Then she stood, picked up her cloth bag, and walked away from him. Her small round hips moved up and down slightly in rhythm with her steps.

"Bye, Bird," he called after her.

She turned and smiled at him.

Abi Martin, he repeated to himself. In spite of his bizarre behavior, she had trusted him. The baby bird had trusted him with her name, with her identity, with her cookies—he wished.

\*   \*   \*

As soon as Daddy pulled into the drive, Vince saw Mama through their living room window, sitting in her chair and waving. She held up the receiver to the phone, signaling she would call as soon as he got into the house. Inside, Abi scurried around the kitchen, frying chicken, stirring a pot, and checking something in the oven. Damn, she was pretty, even with her hair in a ponytail and her sleeves pushed up like she was working on a rig.

"Well, Abi-girl, how did the first day go?" He set his lunch pail in the sink.

"Just fine." She flashed him her heart-stopping smile.

"Did you meet anybody?" He hung up his coat and cap.

"No." She got a beer from the refrigerator and opened it, leaving it on the counter for him. "You know me. I'm too shy to say anything to anybody."

Vince saddled up behind Abi where she was frying chicken. Cupping her hips, one cheek in each hand, he said into the hollow of her neck, "Keep it that way." He gave her butt a squeeze and released his hold. Just holding her gave him a hard-on.

He grabbed the beer and walked to the living room, turning on the TV before he sat down. The announcer said that due to the peace talks President Nixon had ordered to halt all offensive action against North Vietnam. The phone rang, and Vince picked it up, sure it was Mama. She immediately launched into how put out she was that Abi had not taken her to the doctor until this afternoon. Vince grunted and stared at the TV. It was the same old song, second verse same as the first. Mama had tried to get along with Abi when Vince first married her, but it didn't take long for Abi to start rubbing Mama's fur the wrong direction. Abi brought him another beer about the time Mama confided that Abi said she wouldn't be able to carry her to the doctor anymore because of her schooling. Mama reasoned that if she was going to the doctor, she sure didn't feel like driving herself.

The news ended and Vince sauntered into the kitchen where Abi was pulling yeast rolls from the oven. He sat at the gray Formica-top table his parents had given them as a wedding gift. They lived here rent free, and every week they ate Sunday dinner with Daddy and Mama. Abi didn't seem to understand how much they owed his parents. Her parents had never done anything for them, except pay for her tuition, which aggravated the shit out of Vince.

Abi handed him the chicken platter. He took several pieces and finished filling his plate with mashed potatoes, rolls, gravy, and fried okra.

Biting into a leg, he immediately knew it was not done enough. "Goddamn it; this thing is still squawking." He threw it on his plate and shoved his chair back. This was how this schooling business would go—meals thrown together and half cooked, the chicken burned on the outside and practically raw in the middle.

And there she sat, cowering like a mistreated dog.

"What the hell do you have to say for yourself?" He kicked the table leg, sloshing tea out of the pitcher.

Abi jumped up and grabbed a towel. "I'm sorry. I'm sorry." She sopped up the mess, wrung the towel in the sink, and then returned to sop up more.

"Mama said you're refusing to take her to the doctor. You told me this schoolin' thing wasn't gonna be a problem, but you said something totally different to Mama."

"Do you want me to cook the chicken some more? The grease is still hot."

He pulled his chair back up to the table. "*Mama said* she's worried you won't take her to the doctor when she needs to go." When Abi reached for his plate, he shoved her hand away, determined to make her answer.

"I suggested she might drive herself, or get one of her friends to take her if I don't get back from class as early as she wants to go." Abi sat down and nibbled at a piece of chicken. "I'm sorry, Vince. I'll try to get her there sooner next time." She looked up at him with those pleading eyes of hers.

Later that evening, Vince lay in bed watching the news while Abi read. When it ended, he nudged Abi and pointed to the light. Otherwise, she would sit there and read all night.

As his eyes adjusted to the darkened room, Vince recalled the time Daddy tricked him into letting Abi go to school. He had sat Vince down in the hospital cafeteria and said he called Betty who said she agreed Abi should go to school, and she would pay for it. What he did not say, but it was a given, Abi going to school was Daddy's punishment for what he had done. Because the police had just read Vince the riot act about never muscling up on Abi again, Vince felt cornered into going along with all this, but everybody in the family knew this was the last thing Vince wanted her to do. He loved Abi, but damn it, he told her he didn't want her to work, which was exactly where this schooling business was going to take her. Why couldn't she understand he's the breadwinner in this family? That's his job, and her job is to take care of him. That's all she needs to do.

Horny from just thinking about the possibility of losing her, Vince climbed on top of Abi. He knew she didn't want him, but he needed her, more than he cared to admit. Surprisingly, his tool slipped into place with ease. While he settled into steady thrusting, he wondered what her wetness meant. Was she thinking about him, or had she already met someone else? She said she wouldn't talk to another man, but he had seen men ogling her. She was a looker, and any man that didn't think she was drop-dead gorgeous was a goddamn queer.

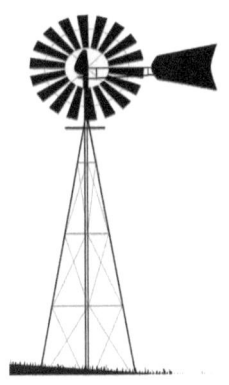

# Chapter Two

*A loose horse always
seeks new pastures.*

**January 16, 1973, Tuesday**

Garrett hurried to the second floor of the library and spotted Abi at the table where she sat yesterday. This told him she was going to school every day. He also surmised that she was either a creature of habit, or she hoped to see him again, which meant she had thought of him— like he had thought of her.

"Hey, how are you?" he asked, approaching her table and trying to sound casual yet surprised to see her.

Abi kept her gaze trained on her book and whispered, "Hi." Apparently, she wasn't thrilled to see him.

He took off his hat, lay it on the table, shook out his hair, and using both hands pulled it away from his face. "So, Bird, how was your second day of college?"

A smile twitched at the corners of her mouth, but she kept eyeballing her book. Then after a long pause, she peeked at him and whispered with proper library etiquette, "Fine. How are your classes going?"

"Okay, I guess," he said, leaning toward her and matching her hushed tone. "This is my last semester, so I just have a few oddball classes to finish up, statistics and anthropology. I'll do my internship in Houston in the fall." He decided not to share that he had skipped class yesterday while watching her, and he had barely heard anything his stats prof said

21

today because he was preoccupied with the possibility that he might see her again.

"Internship, in what?" she asked, finally making eye contact, but only briefly.

"Counseling," he said, wondering what stereotypes she associated with that profession.

"Really? I'm taking Introduction to Psychology. Our class met today. Dr. Posey is my professor." She looked up, saw him looking at her, and immediately returned her gaze to her book.

"Maybe I can help you—I mean with your psychology class. Mariam, or rather Dr. Posey, is great. It's been a few semesters since I took Intro, but I could dig out my notes. Most people think you have to be crazy to want to study psychology, but it helps me understand why people do the insane things they do." Like why he was irresistibly drawn to this stranger while he was married and would soon live elsewhere.

"Maybe that's why I'm taking it—to understand why I do what I do." She began scooting her chair back. "I really should go. This is crazy for me to sit here talking to you."

Needing to keep her talking, so she wouldn't leave, he gestured to the books beside her. "What classes are you taking—besides psychology, I mean?"

She glanced at the spines. "History and a couple of art classes, drawing and design."

Dying to peek at the ruffled pages of the sketchpad, he said, "So you're an artist, huh?"

"I like to draw, but I couldn't make a living at it." She glanced around the room nervously.

"What do you want to do?" he asked.

Her smile wavered slightly and her gaze shifted right and left as if checking to see if anyone was listening in. "I'm not sure, but I do know I want to do something that I pick out - not what my husband wants. Don't get me wrong, I want Vince to be proud of me, to see me as someone who's. . . well somebody who can do something besides cook and clean, but mostly I want to follow my heart."

He glanced down at the modest wedding set on the ring finger of her left hand. He was married, but he had never worn a ring. What an idiot he'd been to not even consider that possibility for her. "So what is your heart telling you to do?" he asked, marveling that he had missed something so obvious. Why wouldn't she be married? Most women her age were.

"I'm thinking along the lines of a degree in teaching, maybe elementary school," she said timidly.

"If you have kids, then you'll have the same hours," he said, angling to find out more about her.

"I can't have children." She folded and unfolded a small piece of paper.

"That's not the end of the world," he said, immediately regretting his callous comment.

"Maybe not for you, but Vince—well, that's all he wants." Her eyes glistened.

Vince was a lucky guy to have a wife who cared so much that talking about what she could not give him brought tears to her eyes. Trang's pregnancy was the reason they married. She had saved his life, but he had paid her back ten-fold by bringing her to the States and rescuing her from a life of poverty and struggle.

"What about you? Do you have children?" she asked.

"No, I'm not married." It shocked him how easily the lie had spilled out of his mouth.

"Oh," she answered, her brow knitted.

"Is that a problem?" Garrett asked. "I mean, should I be married to talk to you? Because if that's the case, I'll go out and find a wife." He crouched like he was ready to get up.

She chuckled. "It's just that my husband is terribly jealous. He doesn't want me to go to school because he thinks men will. . . well you know. Not that I think you'd do anything—I'm not saying I think you're—Oh

God, I'm putting my foot in my mouth." She bunched her eyebrows and made an exaggerated frown.

He laughed. "I had a friend in Nam who used to say when you see you're in a hole, quit digging."

"Vietnam? You were over there? For how long?"

"Two years, three months, and five days." He had spent six weeks of that lying in Trang's hut, unable to put weight on his broken leg.

"Were you a POW?" she asked eagerly.

"Not really, although I did spend nearly six weeks of that in a village when my helicopter went down and I broke my leg. Luckily, a ground troop finally found me. By then my broken leg was nearly healed." And he had dug his own hole by turning his primary caretaker into a lover.

"Wow, I've barely gotten out of Quits, Texas, and you've been all over the world. I'd love to travel."

"Quits?" he echoed, not sure he had heard her correctly.

"Yeah, Quits. It's a little place south of Flatland, you know that town due west of Oaces." He loved her Panhandle drawl, her timid way of speaking, and the childlike innocence and eagerness in her voice.

"I can't believe that—a town called Quits," he teased.

"Oh, yes, it really exists. I've lived there ever since I got married eleven years ago." She laughed again, but this time he detected a note of regret—probably because he wanted to hear it.

"How in the world did it get that name?" he asked.

"This is the story I've heard." She cleared her throat ceremoniously. "It's an oil town, and when it first sprang up, the people got together and argued all one day about what they should name it. Finally towards sundown, this old man, who hadn't had much to say until then, said," she continued, assuming a gruff voice and a scowling expression while imitating the old man, "'Well, let's just call it Quits and go home.' So they did."

She had been so animated in her presentation, so apparently pleased by his attention that Garrett had to stop himself from clapping. "That's great. Call it Quits and go home."

"Yeah, a lot of towns have a story about how they got their name. Like Oaces was supposedly named by a guy who had been traveling across the plains all day when he found this little spring, which he considered a real oasis, but since he was a poker player, he decided he would put an extra spin on it and spell it with the word ace in it. I like that story because I think Oaces is going to be my oasis, the place in the dessert where I find new life."

"I love both of your stories—an oasis in the dessert and call it quits. They are both perfect."

"I better call it quits and go home to my other oasis." Smiling to herself, she stood and pulled out a small paper sack from her bag like the one she had given him yesterday. She set it on the table and began putting her books in her bag.

Garrett watched her, wishing he could entice her to stay longer. "You're a good story teller."

"You should meet my mother's friend, Charlene. She's got a funny expression or a joke for every occasion. Like when she wants to say she's hungry, she'll say her belly and her backbone are bumping." She looked as pleased with herself as Loc did when he made a one-hundred on his practice spelling test.

"I love that." Garrett said, "Will you teach me more of those sayings?"

Her smile faded as she scooted the sack across the table to him. "These are left from my lunch if you want them." She had ignored his question, and her offering felt like a final good-bye.

"Thanks, Abi," he said, peeking into the sack at two generous-size brownies.

"Bye, Garrett," she whispered, back to her barely audible voice, although she *had* remembered his name.

"See you tomorrow?" he asked, trying to sound casual.

She hesitated and said without looking at him. "It would be better if we didn't talk. Like I said earlier—my husband's kind of jealous. He keeps telling me not to even speak to another man. In fact, he said not to even look at them." She barely glanced in his direction as she walked away.

"Bye, Bird," he called after her, thinking about what she had said. That guy had no right to tell her what she could and could not do.

Her smiling face glanced back over her shoulder, but she kept going. Garrett watched her hips moving gracefully within the confines of her jeans, her white sweater accentuating the indention of her waist, her long brown hair moving from side to side with the rhythm of her stride.

After she had disappeared, he pulled a brownie from the sack, took a large bite, and allowed the sweet richness to dissolve in his mouth. He had thought of little except Abi since he ran into her at the bookstore yesterday. Beyond her obvious beauty there was something mesmerizing about her. His attraction to her bordered on addictive behavior. From a psychological standpoint, he wondered if the neuroses he had studied were affecting him in a subliminal way.

* * *

Before I got in the door, the phone started ringing. Sure it was Thelma, I ignored it and sat down to read my history assignment. If Dr. Horton was serious about pop quizzes, I wanted to be ready. The first chapter contained none of the facts that Dr. Horton had given us about women's role in the colonies, so I wasn't sure whether to focus on the text or my notes. My mind kept drifting to Garrett, how he often worked the metal discs on the chain around his neck, his golden beard and long curly hair, his aqua green eyes. Was he thinking about me? I had no business thinking about anyone but Vince. Still, I could not get him off my mind.

When Vince got home two hours later, the phone immediately began ringing, no doubt Thelma calling Vince. From the kitchen, I heard Vince grunting one syllable replies. While we ate, Lucille Ball performed one crazy antic after another. I waited, sure that Vince was armed with complaints from Thelma. Right after Lucy revealed her sneaky scheme to Ethel, commercials took over.

Vince turned off the sound on the TV. "Mama says you ain't answering the phone again."

Examining my half-eaten steak, I wondered if he would accept the explanation that it hadn't rung. After glancing at his cold, blue eyes, I knew he wouldn't.

As he finished his plate, I got up to dip him a bowl of ice cream. I put it before Vince and sat down again. While he ate and watched the silent TV, his accusation hung in the air.

"I needed to study," I finally whispered.

He glared at me long and hard before slapping the table with his open palms and rattling the dishes. "You talk to my mama! She's good to you. Better than your own."

I watched him, clear his anger was about me going to college—not whether or not I talked to Thelma.

His clear blue eyes narrowed. "You quit ignoring her." He paused. "You understand?"

"Yes, sir." The 'sir' slipped out before I could stop it.

"And don't sass me." He finished his ice cream in silence before returning to the living room.

While clearing the table and washing the dishes, I thought about how normal Vince was acting, more like he had before he caught me working with Christi—not the nice guy who brought me home from the hospital. My starting school had slingshot him back to where we were before. Knowing I shouldn't go there, I wondered how Garrett would feel about his wife going to school—if he was married, which he obviously wasn't. Then I thought the unthinkable; I wished I was married to someone even half as nice as Garrett. As soon as the idea came into my head, I shooed it away. Vince had let me go to college, and I had promised God I would be the best wife possible. What kind of person was I to wash dishes with another man in my head while my hard-working husband sat in his chair waiting for me?

\* \* \*

By the time Abi finally sashayed her little butt into her chair, Vince was ready to go see what she was hung up on. Two days into this school business, and she already had Mama in an uproar. When Abi finally joined him, she immediately stuck her head in one of her damned books.

During a commercial, he flung an empty beer can at her.

She wiped drops from the page and hurried to the kitchen, leaving the book on the table between them. Curious, what was so damned interesting, Vince picked it up. It weighed a ton. If nothing else, she would build up her muscles carting it around. Vince hated books. They reminded him of school and feeling like the dumbest kid there. He had learned to read enough to get by, but not enough to read a contract or even the newspaper. In high school Vince begged Daddy to let him work with him on the rigs. Daddy finally agreed, probably figuring it was the only way Vince could ever make a decent living.

Vince opened the front cover of Abi's book and read where someone had written 'Jack Brown' followed by a phone number. It was not her handwriting, but that wouldn't keep her from calling him. He should have forbidden her to go to that goddamn school.

When she sauntered back into the living room, he demanded, "Why have you got some creep's name and phone number in your book?"

"I-I b-b-bought the book used. It was already there."

He threw it on the floor. "You get it out of there right now."

She scrambled to her hands and knees to get it. "Vince, these things cost a lot of money."

He was ready to burn it, and she was acting like it was the Holy Bible. "What about the rest? They got names, too?" She was not about to lug around books with men's names and phone numbers in them.

"I don't know." She stood and backed toward the bedroom like she wanted to shield them from him.

Vince followed her and watched while she dumped her book bag on the bed. He picked up the top one. "Read this," he demanded, not wanting to stumble on what it said.

She opened the front cover. "'Tom Sneed," she said just barely loud enough for him to hear.

"And this one!" He pointed to another one.

"Rick Voit," she said slightly louder.

He held up the last one. "Read it to where I can hear you."

"Gerald Atkins," she said in a normal tone of voice.

"Don't any women go there? What is it—a fucking man's school?"

"I wasn't looking at the inside covers—just what kind of shape they were in."

"Get rid of these names. I don't want to see any evidence that some man has even touched these books." He was ready to throw the whole goddamn mess in the trash can. He wanted to, but then she would go running to Daddy. Abi had him wrapped around her little finger.

When she did not respond, he leaned into her. "You hear me!"

"Yes...." she whispered, all but tacking on her sassy little 'sir.'"

She stacked the books on the kitchen table, sat in her chair, and then she began drawing a box around one of the names and numbers. Satisfied he could go back to watching television, Vince returned to his chair.

After a while, she sat the books on the table beside him. She watched while he checked each one. Without a word, he returned to his program. When she started to sit in her chair, he extended his arm and drew her into his lap. Vince had gotten so riled up over Abi's books, he didn't know what the show was about. He could tell by the look on Abi's face, her mind was forty miles away, probably on some bastard in one of her classes. No doubt a number of them found her hot as hell. They'd have to be blind not to. Vince toyed with her breasts while assuring himself that these were his, all his.

*   *   *

## January 18, 1973, Thursday

After his flight to Houston, Garrett took his time filling out the post-flight checklist. The idea of going to the Houston apartment had no appeal—except for seeing Loc. Garrett had never slept there, and he refused to think of it as home. Tuesday evening, after he finished his flight to Houston, he called and spoke to Loc while they reloaded his plane. Then he made the return flight that same night. Facing Trang and his lack of feeling for her had been too much to tackle. With a knot in the pit of his stomach, he picked up the office phone and dialed the phone number for the new apartment.

Trang answered in Vietnamese. She refused to speak what little English she knew, and he refused to speak Vietnamese. They understood each other's languages enough to communicate.

"This is Garrett. Can Vinh come and get me?" Since Trang refused to learn to drive, Garrett could either beg a ride from her crazy uncle or pay for a taxi, money he didn't have after buying books.

She said in a combination of English and Vietnamese that Vinh had gone to the grocery store, and she would ask him to pick up Garrett when he returned. Then she asked if Garrett was spending the night. That had been his plan, so he could eat breakfast with Loc before he went to school.

"Yeah, I'll sleep there and then take off early tomorrow." He started to ask her to make down the couch, but thought better of it. Why cross that bridge until he reached it?

While he waited for Vinh, he thought about sitting alone at the library table where he had talked with Abi on Monday and Tuesday. She had not shown up Wednesday or today, which was no surprise given her husband's jealousy. Still, he had hoped for a miracle. UP was so big that he doubted he'd see her again.

Over an hour after he called Trang, Vinh pulled up in a jalopy that would never again pass inspection. He honked before Garrett got out the office door. To be as bad a driver as he was, Garrett marveled that the little guy could find his way from the west side of town all the way to Hobby on the southeast side. Stevie Wonder blasted *Superstition* from the radio while Vinh darted in and out of traffic, and Garrett tried to keep his eyes shut and not think about Vinh's numerous tickets and accidents.

Garrett smelled Vietnamese cooking as soon as Trang opened the door and wrapped her short, thin frame around his.

She stepped back so he could come inside. "I cook food for you," she announced, her face beaming.

Loc ran into the room, wearing his pajamas. "Daddy, Daddy," he squealed, grabbing Garrett's legs.

Trang ran her finger through Loc's hair. "We glad to see you," she said, enunciating each word.

"I can see that. What's the occasion?" Garrett squatted and wrapped his arms around Loc.

"Just love you," she said.

"Yeah, Daddy, we love you," Loc echoed in Garrett's ear.

Boxes lined the walls of the tiny apartment, although a considerable amount of unpacking had been done. Ten days ago he drove the rental truck from Oaces to Houston. Vinh assured Garrett that he would unload it and turn it in after he took Garrett to the airport. When Trang first began campaigning to move here, Garrett had argued that they should wait until he was ready to start his internship. Trang kept saying, "Why wait?" In the end, he had given in. Seeing Loc only twice a week was the worst part.

Trang ushered him to the dining room table where she had prepared a feast of his favorite dishes, including a large bowl of stir-fry, spicy fish soup, fresh vegetables, and a plate of fresh fruit. Where and how had she bought all of the ingredients for these dishes? Vinh must have given her the money.

While they ate, Loc told Garrett about the new friends he had made and his first grade teacher. "Daddy, there's two things about this town— one I like, one I don't."

"What are those?" Garrett asked, both impressed and saddened by how grown up Loc sounded.

"You don't live here—I don't like, and it's green even in winter—I like."

Garrett laughed.

"Daddy, are you going to come live with us?" Loc asked.

"Not right now. I have to finish school. After that, I'll move to Houston." He had pointedly not said he would live with them. The idea of continuing to live in a separate apartment had taken root after he met Abi, which was irrational because Abi was married. Plus, he had not seen her since Tuesday.

After eating more than he should, Garrett fought to stay awake while he read to Loc. Slipping into a deep sleep, he snuggled up next to Loc rather than unfold the couch bed. He did not remember switching off the light, but sometime during the night he fought to make sense of what was going on around him. He dreamed that he was making love, not to Abi as he had fantasized every evening over the last few days, but instead to Trang.

He awoke to bright sunlight. Glancing at his watch, he noted the time, 9:30. Jesus Christ, Trans-Texas expected him to be nearing Oaces by now. Throwing back the covers, he saw that Trang lay next to him in Loc's bed, and Loc was not there. Neither Garrett nor Trang wore clothes. He immediately wondered about his weird dream, which didn't appear to have been a dream after all.

While scrambling to gather his clothes from the floor and dress, Garrett demanded, "Trang, wake up and call Vinh. I've got to go back to the airport. I need to leave."

She rolled over and pulled the covers over her shoulder.

"Trang, get up. I've got to go," he shouted in her ear.

She gave no response. She acted like she was drugged. And he had that fuzzy-headed feeling of having drunk too much. He wondered what she had put in his drink, or in the soup she had warned Loc in Vietnamese not to sample because it was only for Daddy.

\* \* \*

## January 19, 1973

Friday morning after I got out of class, I gave in to my overwhelming desire to return to the library table where I had talked with Garrett on

Monday and Tuesday. It was empty. A guy in graduate school who had been all over the world wasn't interested in being friends with a freshman from Quits, Texas. I knew that, but I couldn't stop myself from coming back to see if he might happen to be there.

Talking to Garrett felt wonderful. He seemed to be sincerely interested in me. Vince was like that at first, but with time, we had less and less to say to one another. I'd probably never see Garrett again, but it felt nice to sit at the table and rerun our previous conversations—just as I had countless times since I met him.

After I sat there for the better part of two hours, intermittently studying, sneaking chunks of my sandwich, and thinking about Garrett, I concluded that Vince had been right. He couldn't trust me. I was doing exactly what he had said I would do—getting all moony-eyed over someone else. What was I thinking—hoping to run into someone who had shown me an ounce of kindness? Disgusted with myself, I pulled out a sack of cookies and loaded my books into my canvas bag, leaving the sack in the center of the table. I sure didn't want to be reminded of how foolish I had been by taking it home with me.

I stood up and was collecting my things when Garrett raced toward me. Panting as though he have been running, he threw his books on the table and looked at me expectantly.

"Looks like I just caught you before you left." His flushed face filled with a beaming smile. Then he noticed the sack sitting in the middle of the table and peeked inside. "For me?"

Nodding, I sat down and folded my hands on the table in front of me. "I had those left from my lunch," I lied. My insane excitement at seeing him was fueled by the fact that he seemed pleased to see me as well, and he had purposely come looking for me.

As if he had done it thousands of times before, he rested his hand on top of mine. "Thanks, Abi. That's so sweet of you to bring this to me—I mean to share your *leftovers*."

Vince's warning to avoid even looking at a man echoed in my head, so I pulled my hands away and put them in my lap. Talking to Garrett was bad enough, but if someone saw a man touching me, and it got back to Vince—I didn't even want to think about what would happen next.

Garrett's green eyes danced with pleasure as he reached into the sack, pulled out a cookie, and ate it, the whole time making that deep moaning sound he had made before. Chewing, he said, "Thanks again, Bird." As if knowing that I had been waiting for him, he began explaining that his ride from the hotel in Houston had been delayed, and then he had to contend with weather problems. The whole time he worked the discs back and forth on a chain around his neck.

While he bit into another cookie, I asked something I had wandered about, "Why do you call me Bird?"

"You take me back to something that happened when I was a kid." He studied my face.

"Tell me about it," I pleaded, and when he looked down, I did too and saw that my hand was on his. Immediately, I jerked it back.

Probably thinking how silly I was acting, he smiled, more to himself than at me. "Let's see, I was about ten. Out in the backyard, I found a baby bird in the grass. Feeling like a real hero, I got a ladder out of the garage and managed to get it back into the nest that I figured it must have fallen out of." He stopped and looked at my hand that now rested on the table. He lightly touched his index finger to the tip of my nose.

"What happened to the bird?" My fate seemed to rest in an incident that happened decades ago—to something that wasn't even human.

"I want to think she lived, but I have no way of knowing."

"Why do I remind you of that bird?"

"I don't know. The incident just came to mind." He paused. "I used to think of it when I was in 'Nam, especially when I saw the innocent women and children whose lives were destroyed by that asinine war."

"What was that like, living there?"

He directed his gaze toward the now empty paper sack. From his pained expression, I knew I had touched a raw nerve. After some time, he said, "I used to leave bread on the lawn, thinking the mama bird would use it to feed her babies."

"How kind," I said. My words sounded hollow and corny.

"This time the bird is feeding me." His hand rested on the table with his fingers barely touching my arm that also lay on the table. I'm sure he didn't mean anything by it, but it was there nonetheless. Again, a valid reason in Vince's mind for flying into a jealous rage—one I probably would not live to tell about.

Garrett knew I was married, so he was simply being a friend, but I was playing with fire by maintaining any kind of relationship. I needed to promise myself I would never come to this part of the library again—certainly not with the intention of meeting Garrett. But needing and doing were two different things. With Garrett sitting next to me, I could not imagine doing the "right" thing by staying away. Wednesday and Thursday when I sat in my car rather than going home and dealing with Thelma's demands, I obsessively wondered if Garrett had come to the library hoping I would be there.

Unaware of the war going on inside me, Garrett said he had been reading articles in the paper about a case that the U.S. Supreme Court was deciding. He called it Roe v. Wade, and he said that if they ruled favorably, it would lift the ban on abortion. After he said women should have the right to end their pregnancies if they wanted to, I argued for the unborn child, thinking if I ever got pregnant, I'd never kill it, no matter what. Then I wondered what had given me the courage to say such a thing; I had never argued with a man - about anything. I started to apologize, but Garrett seemed so pleased by my response that I stopped myself.

"The important thing is that you think for yourself, Bird. Every time you let someone else do your thinking for you, you lose a piece of yourself. If you do it long enough, there's nothing left." He paused. "Believe me. I've been there."

"I can't imagine anyone thinking for you," I assured him.

"Thanks, Bird, for your vote of confidence, but I haven't always been particularly independent. In fact, I didn't really start standing up for myself until after I was out of the service. When my parents started treating me like I was still a kid, we had a major disagreement." I wanted to ask him about the conflict with his parents, but I wasn't even supposed to be talking to him.

"So, do you have big plans for the weekend?" he asked.

"Tonight we'll probably go bowling. Tomorrow Vince will sleep in, and I'll read since I feel like I'm already behind. Saturday afternoon we'll buy groceries together."

"That's nice he goes with you."

"Oh, he always does." I recalled a time years ago when Vince handed me the phone. Mr. Humphrey from the grocery store apologized all over himself for not giving me the ten dollars in cash I had added to my check. I tried to convince him that he didn't owe me any money. In spite of my objections, Mr. Humphrey ended the conversation by saying he would be right over with the cash. I met him at the door, trying to hide his visit from Vince. When I shut the door and turned around, I saw Vince waiting for me. The ten-dollar bill turned limp in my hand. I always got caught—just like I did when I cleaned houses with Christi.

"You look far away," Garrett said, raising his eyebrows. "Where'd you go?"

I met his gaze. "I need to leave."

He lightly touched my arm. "I'll see you Monday. Don't fly off without me before then."

We both laughed, but sadness lingered in his eyes. Or maybe I saw what I wanted to see. He couldn't be nearly as sad as I was at the prospect of not seeing him again. Vince and I had never talked like this. After I picked up my book bag and my purse, I gave Garrett a slight wave. I couldn't bear to tell him I would not come back. I just couldn't.

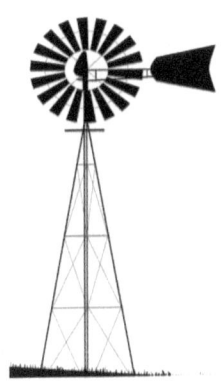

# Chapter Three

*She catches your eye*
*like a tin roof on a sunny day.*

**January 19, 1973**

Friday afternoon I barely got into the house and started supper when Thelma huffed her way onto my back porch and then into the house. She sat at the kitchen table, and neither of us spoke. I kept working.

After a few minutes, she shifted heavily. The chair creaked. "You too good to talk to me, Abi Martin?"

I hated the fact that she used my last name like we barely knew each other. When Vince and I got married, I tried to get along with my mother-in-law, but everything I said and did rubbed her fur the wrong way. "I'm cooking Vince's supper. I didn't mean to ignore you."

Anger lay beneath her thick eyelids. "You still ain't been getting home before supper time. You trying to avoid me?" She crossed her arms and rested them on her huge stomach. Mama Martin had hit the nail on the head; I did not come home because I knew she would do exactly what she was doing now.

"I'm studying, Mama Martin. Like Vince says, I'm way behind all the other students." I pounded a piece of round steak with a tenderizing mallet until it was paper-thin—just like Vince liked it.

She moved restlessly in her chair, and I grew nervous thinking about what she would say to Vince. "How about a glass of tea, Mama Martin?"

Her scowl melted into a fake smile. "That sounds nice."

I set the tea and a spoon in front of her and moved the sugar bowl within easy reach. While I filled a plate with homemade chocolate chip cookies, she scooped sugar into her glass until she had an inch worth settled in the bottom of the glass.

"Martha likes her job. Says they're real nice to her." She took several bites of a cookie. Still chewing, she said, "Between you and me, I suspect Jack's shop is falling on hard times. Why else would she drive all the way to Oaces every day?"

I shook my head as if to say I could not understand it either. Actually, I didn't give a rat's ass.

"Last night Martha said they been covered up the last couple of weeks, but she's gonna look for you now that things are slowing down."

Thank God, Martha had not happened onto me in the library. If she reported to Thelma that she saw me talking to a man, Vince would go ballistic. A cold sweat covered my back when I thought about Vince finding out about Garrett. "We probably won't see each other. I just go to class."

A car parked in the drive between our houses—probably Vince and Papa Martin home from work.

After refilling Thelma's glass, I grabbed for the empty cookie plate, thinking I wanted Vince to walk in and see that I was taking good care of his mama.

"Don't put any more out. They're a little dry. Besides, I'll spoil my supper." She pushed her chair back to make room for the folds of fat that had come to rest on top of the table.

Two car doors slammed shut outside.

The grease popped on the stove, calling me back to the chicken-fried steak.

"You're not in class all day, Abi. Even I know that." Thelma picked cookie crumbs from her chest.

"I usually study in the library." Realizing I had just told her where to look for me, I hurriedly added, "Sometimes I take a sandwich to eat in the cafeteria."

"They let you eat in there even if you don't buy a meal?" She studied me suspiciously.

"Nobody says I can't." That was the part about school that I loved. People didn't mind each other's business, not like here in Quits.

The back door swung open, and Vince walked in. He ambled into the kitchen and reached over the half wall to set his lunchbox in the sink. While he hung his coat on the hook, I looked back and forth between mother and son, struck by the similarity of their round faces and light blue eyes.

Mama Martin struggled to her feet. "Abi was just telling me how liberal they are at her new school."

Vince sniffed. "Bunch of goddamn hippies."

She chuckled and playfully swatted his arm before they gave each other a bear hug.

I checked the steak and wondered what he would say if he ever saw Garrett's long hair.

Thelma patted Vince's back as they separated. "I better get home." She waddled toward the back door.

Vince looked at me and jerked his head in her direction. Wiping my hands on a cup towel, I raced to catch up with her and open the door. Outside on the porch, she turned and raised her arms. I leaned into her pillow-like front and her distinct body odor.

"Don't let this school business start some crazy notions in your head," she said quietly in my ear.

As she eased herself down the steps, I wondered if she could read my thoughts.

*   *   *

Friday night Garrett rambled around his one-bedroom apartment. If he unpacked the dozen or more boxes, it might feel more like home. They had moved out of a two-bedroom rental on Twenty-First Street, which was close enough for Garrett to ride his bike to class. Plus, it had a bedroom for Loc and a small backyard where Garrett had constructed a swing and sandbox out of four-by-fours. He did all that knowing they would leave it when they moved, but he also knew Loc would enjoy it. And he had. There was a park in walking distance of the Houston apartment, although someone had to go with Loc. Trang might not feel safe taking him on her own.

Garrett needed to read. No telling what he missed in class this morning when he was scrambling to get the cargo plane back to Oaces. The real irony of that was that he elected to see if Abi was at the library rather than check in with his anthropology instructor, Dr. Moser, who just happened to also be his adviser. He would have the last word on whether or not Garrett was ready to start his internship. A week ago, Garrett could not wait for that to happen. Now, all he thought about was Abi. Today, when he saw her in the library, he was jubilant. Her return after a two-day absence, and the fact that she brought cookies and a brownie spoke volumes. He was not sure what it said, but it said a lot.

In the bedroom, where Garrett slept on a mattress on the floor, he set one box on top of another. From the weight of it, he guessed it contained books like most of the others. He pulled the flaps open and, lying on top, he found several envelopes of pictures. The first one contained family shots taken last summer: Loc in the park, Loc at the swimming pool, Loc on his swing, Garrett at his desk studying, Trang in the backyard nearly headless and off center. Loc must have taken that one. Garrett had not, and no one else would have.

The next envelope contained pictures of Garrett and Trang's wedding. They both wore traditional Vietnamese silk shifts. Trang's pregnant bulge made hers stand out in front. He would never forget six months after he was found by the ground troop looking up from his army cot and seeing her standing there with his dog-tags in her hand; they were her ticket to finding him. And her obvious pregnancy was her ticket to going home with him. He had seen other guys go through similar situations. Some of them accepted the responsibility and some of them denied even knowing the girl. While Garrett never thought he was in love with Trang, she had been instrumental in saving his life—and his leg. He got emergency leave, escorted her back to her family, and within two days went through the ceremony featured in the pictures he held.

Somehow he had ended up married with a family. He loved his son, and there is no way he would ever wish he had not come along, but he did not love Trang. Unfortunately, it was a package deal. He could mull it over all he wanted, but it was not going to change the situation. These pictures, slipped in by his wife, were a reminder of his legal obligations.

The rest of the pictures would further depress him, so Garrett set them aside and began emptying the texts into a makeshift bookcase made of boards and cement blocks. Midway through, he found his favorite book, a heavily marked up copy of *As a Man Thinketh*. He had expected to pick up a new copy at the bookstore the day he ran over Abi. While thumbing through it, he recalled how its simple message had deeply impacted him.

According to James Allen, a person's life reflected their thinking. If Garrett had positive thoughts, then good things would happen. If he had negative thoughts, then bad events would follow. It all sounded so easy, and in many instances, Garrett could see a direct correlation, but how did it fit with his marriage? What impact would his constant thoughts of Abi have on his life? Just because he could not get her off his mind would not make her feel the same way about him. Besides, it wasn't fair for him to try to undermine her marriage. She must love Vince, or she wouldn't be married to him. After all, this was the 70's. Women were standing up for themselves, and refusing to stay in unhappy marriages.

Abi had said Vince was jealous. Vince knew every man on campus would find Abi attractive—and he had warned his wife to stay away from them. Garrett couldn't fault him for that. How would he feel if he were in Vince's place?

Garrett shouldn't go back to the library on Monday. He shouldn't complicate his life—or Abi's.

*    *    *

When Vince finished supper, he got another beer. "You ready to go?"

Abi looked up from the sink filled with dishes and soapy water. "Why don't you go without me?"

Vince walked up behind her. "Abi-girl, you got that cast off, and it's time to get back in the swing of things." He grabbed her right wrist and pulled it back like she was bowling. "Now go get dressed."

After she dried her hands and hurried to the bedroom, Vince decided tonight was the perfect occasion to wear the outfit he bought her for Christmas. Abi was going through her side of the closet when he walked in, reached past her, and pulled out the purple blouse with a ruffle in front that showed off her knockers. He didn't like the idea of other men ogling her, but he did like the way it had looked on the mannequin. So far she had refused to wear it, saying she couldn't get it over the cast. Now that stupid thing was gone. Silently, she pulled off her sweater and put on the blouse.

Vince rifled her closet, looking for the pants he bought to go with it. "Where's the rest of that outfit?"

From the bottom drawer of the chest, she pulled out the bell-bottoms that the sales girl had described as crushed velvet. She made a point of telling him how lucky Abi would be to get something like that. It had cost him more than he wanted to spend, but she assured him he was making a great choice. While Abi got dressed, Vince rummaged through another drawer and found the gold sequin belt that completed his Christmas gift. He laid it on the bed and left to get a beer. Drinking a couple before he bowled helped him relax. When Vince returned to the bedroom, he saw that Abi had piled her hair on top of her head and left a few strands hanging down around her ears and neck.

Staring at herself in the mirror as she loaded on the mascara, she said to herself, "A Friday night whore if I ever saw one."

"Yeah, and she's mine, all mine," Vince assured himself—and her.

He met her in the center of the room and reached behind her to grab her hips while he kissed her. She didn't always kiss him back, but this time she did, so she must like the outfit. Vince stood back, inspecting his wife. Remembering, he snapped his fingers. "Put on those spiked heels that I got you for your birthday."

"I don't think they're appropriate for the bowling alley," she hedged.

"Appropriate. One week in school, and you're Miss High Fashion." He pointed to the closet.

She dug them out of the back of the closet and put them on.

Five minutes later, they were pealing out in Vince's 1972 black Ford pickup. After telling Vince no for six months, Daddy had finally loaned him the money to buy it.

Vince noticed Abi gazing out the window at the dots of light on the horizon. "Looking at your ground stars?" he asked, pleased he had remembered her saying that a while back.

"It's like God plucked them out of the sky and lined them up just for me." She gave him that smile that had made him decide she was his the night they met at the Quits vs. Dahlia high school basketball game. She was already dating Buck, but that didn't stop Vince from marrying Abi six months later.

They passed the city limits sign going seventy, and Vince took his foot off the gas. "When those bastards see you walk in there tonight, they're going to eat their hearts out."

"Let's go somewhere else tonight. I feel overdressed. Besides, my arm's still weak, so I can't bowl."

"You look fine." The light from an on-coming car's headlights lit up Abi's face, and the worry in her eyes. "Abi-girl, I got a right to show you off, don't I? And your arm needs exercise."

"Yeah, but —" she objected weakly.

"No, buts. We're going to have a good time." He could tell she was bothered about something, probably seeing that bitch, Christi, who she still called her best friend, even though she had done nothing but get Abi in trouble. They had not seen each other since Vince put an end to their shenanigans. While Abi's arm and her bruises were healing she had stayed home, rather than go to the bowling alley. This was her first week back.

Vince screeched to a halt in his regular spot—the space everybody knew to leave open for him.

Inside, they found the gang in their usual pit in the back of the building where the manager ignored the guys spiking their drinks from the whiskey bottle under their jacket. Steve and Sandy swung practice balls while Brent and Aleisa changed their shoes. Abi sat down without taking off her coat.

Vince sat next to her and began tugging at one of his western dress boots. They looked sharp, but they were a pain in the ass to get on and off. "Where's Mark and Cheryl?" he asked.

"They had to go see Cheryl's father in the hospital," Aleisa answered, always the one who kept up with everyone's business. She was so damn ugly, she needed some reason to justify being there. "Abi, aren't you going to bowl tonight? You've got your cast off don't you?" Over the last month when Vince showed up without Abi, Alesia asked about Abi, acting far too concerned—like she knew more than she was saying.

"No, my arm's too weak." Abi sat on the plastic bench seat with her arms crossed and her long coat covering most of her outfit. She was especially nice to Aleisa, probably because she felt sorry for her.

Aleisa was one of those people that Vince hated to be around. Her face was messed up in a car accident when she was in high school. Brent had been driving, and she came out looking like a freak with one side caved in and scars on the other side as well. Vince had to give Brent credit for marrying her even though she looked like she did, but damn it, Vince wondered how Brent could get a hard-on going to bed with something like that.

Vince glared at Abi. "Abi-girl, show off what I gave you for Christmas."

When she slowly stood up and slipped off her coat, everyone stopped and gawked at how damned good she looked. Shy as she was, Abi couldn't take all that attention, so she headed for the lady's room.

Before she got out of ear-shot, Vince called after her, "Abi-girl, get some drinks for everybody." He stood up, pulled his wallet from his back pocket, and handed her a $10 bill. The gang expected him to buy the first round of drinks, which sometimes pissed him off, but he figured that was the price of popularity.

After Abi hung out in the bathroom for way too long, Vince sent Sandy in there to check on her. They finally came out and walked to the snack bar. About the same time, Buck came out of nowhere and stood right behind Abi. When Abi turned around, the drinks she had in her hands spilled all over that asshole.

Buck started laughing and saying something, which sent Vince into a fury. That bastard was over there making the move on his woman—in front of everyone at the goddamn bowling alley. Outraged, Vince hightailed it to the snack bar, arriving just as Abi began mopping Buck's front and apologizing. They were both too preoccupied to see Vince standing there.

Buck grabbed her hand and held onto it. "Hey, I'm fine." He jerked his head toward the other end of the building. "Christi's over there. She asked me to see if you'd meet her in the bathroom."

"She's not meeting anybody anywhere, especially not your bitch!" Vince shouted.

Buck dropped Abi's hand and turned to face Vince.

"I accidentally spilled the drinks on Buck. I was just cleaning it up." Abi stepped to Vince's side and grabbed his hand.

"I see what you're doing with him," Vince demanded, as he glared at Buck.

"It's not what you think," Abi pleaded, which made Vince wonder what the hell was going on.

"Go sit down," he hissed through clenched teeth.

"Promise you won't do anything." She remained beside Vince.

"She's right. We had a little accident. Everything's cool." The yellow-belly started walking away.

Vince yelled after him, "You keep your hands and your woman away from my wife. You understand?"

Facing Vince, Buck said, "Unlike your wife, Christi can go anywhere she pleases."

"The hell she can." Vince charged Buck, in spite of Abi hanging onto his arm for all she was worth.

"Vince, please, don't do this," she begged.

A spooky silence filled the bowling alley. When Abi gave Buck a pleading look, he finally stepped back, raised his hands like he was calling a truce, and said, "I don't want to fight."

That made Vince madder than ever. He didn't need Abi or anyone else to intervene for him. "Stay away from me and my wife. You understand?"

"Perfectly." Buck gave Vince a shit-eating grin and walked away. Vince wanted to follow him and cold-cock the son-of-a-bitch, but he had promised Daddy he wouldn't get into any more trouble. Just this once, he'd let the little bastard think he had won.

Abi trailed Vince back to their pit and sat there like a zombie while he bowled three games. She'd never before refused to bowl, but since she was dressed up, and her arm was weak, he figured he would give her a break. It wasn't long before the Wild Turkey started to flow and everyone loosen up.

By the time they left the building, Vince was singing, "I want to hold your hand." It was his standard ballad when he was drunk. He hated the Beatles, but the words were easy for him to remember.

At the truck, he made several jabs before his key slipped into the lock. He figured Abi wanted to drive, but she had never driven his new truck, and she wasn't going to start tonight. As Vince screeched out of the parking lot, Abi fastened her seat belt, which made Vince laugh and press on the gas. Vince didn't remember what happened after that.

*       *       *

## January 20, 1973, Saturday, late morning

Garrett counted the ten empty boxes by the front door. It had taken him several hours last night and most of the morning to put away his books, the limited kitchen items, and hang up his clothes. Two boxes ended up in the floor of the closet to hold his underwear, socks, and tee shirts. All of the furniture had gone to Houston except for a mattress, a folding table, two folding chairs, a beat up coffee table, and a ratty old couch. The coffee table, mattress, and couch would end up in the trash when he moved. In the kitchen and living room, he had constructed bookcases like the one in the bedroom. All of them were full. He loved books and refused to sell them at the end of the semester, even though he could use the money.

It took two trips to get all of the empty boxes downstairs to the trash dumpster behind the apartments. On the way out the door the second time, he grabbed his keys and decided he should take a drive. The Charger would run better if he blew the rust out of the carburetor. Besides, he needed to get some fresh air.

He settled himself in the bucket seat. It had been an impractical vehicle with a family, but it had also been his dream to own a muscle car, one that would top out at 160 mph, one that had enough power to shut down anything else on the road. He cranked the engine, and the 440 roared to life. Pointing the car west, he drove toward the edge of town. Amidst the barren landscape of cotton fields laid to rest for the winter, he found a long, straight two-lane road. In less than a minute, he was able to top out the engine. He was coasting to a stop when he thought about Abi and the story she told him about the little town where she lived—Quits.

After pulling off the road, he rummaged in the glove box and found a Texas roadmap. He replayed what she had said, "South of Flatland." As if magnetically drawn to it, his finger pointed to Quits. Since he was headed that direction, why not check it out?

\*    \*    \*

Vince slept until nearly noon. Before he opened his eyes, he flopped his arm in Abi's direction and realized she was reading. They could be going through a tornado, and she would be sitting there gawking at a book. With his arm draped across her chest, he heard and felt her close the book and drop it on the floor. "Goddamn, I drank too much," he muttered.

"I'll make you some coffee." She began wriggling free.

"Oh, no you don't. You owe me for last night." He rolled on top of her, pulling her gown out of the way at the same time. She wasn't wearing panties, which pleased him. He had made it clear to her from the get-go that he did not want to deal with those things in his way. He lowered himself over her and jabbed his tool at her dry hole several times. The more he jabbed, the tighter it seemed to get.

"Let's use some KY," she suggested through clenched teeth.

Vince managed to get one more squeeze out of the tube. Then he threw it on the floor. They'd need to get some more at the grocery store today, although he hated to buy it because that just told Mr. Humphrey that Vince wasn't man enough to juice up Abi on his own.

As he mounted her again, Vince muttered, "You're so goddamn frigid."

She immediately seemed to go into a trance. Good thing it didn't take him long to make it because it turned him off to watch her zone out like that. "I never fucked a more frigid bitch." Vince dismounted and walked to the bathroom.

While he took a leak, he said, "Other women would die to have what you've got, a house and a man who busts his butt all week. When we were dating, you told me how jealous your friends were of you. I told myself how lucky I was to get a girl that hadn't been laid by every boy in the senior class. Little did I know the only reason you were a virgin was because you're ice cold. You've never enjoyed sex. From the very first night you've treated me like I had the clap or something."

He returned to the bedroom and began dressing in the clothes he had worn to the bowling alley. "It's like having sex with a dead body. I've heard there's perverts that get into that."

"It's called necrophilia," she said on her way to the bathroom.

"There you go, Miss Smarty Pants. You think I'm stupid, don't you?"

"No," she whispered.

Vince decided they would buy groceries now since he didn't feel like doing anything else. When they got in the truck, Abi snuggled up next to him like she had when they were dating and first married. Over the years, she had quit doing that, but after he checked her out of the hospital, she started doing it again. He backed out of the drive, thinking how much he liked it when she did things to please him. Still, he was pissed about last night and her making over Buck.

"You ain't had much to say to me," he remarked.

"What do you want to talk about?" she asked, right on the edge of being sassy.

"Last night—how you treated me at the bowling alley," he shot back, his left hand holding the steering wheel while he wrapped his right arm around her shoulders.

"I apologize for embarrassing you in front of your friends," she said half-heartedly.

"That's not all. As soon as some other man gets within reach, you're all over him." He couldn't stop thinking about Abi putting her hands on Buck's chest.

"I spilled the drinks on Buck. I was trying to clean it up."

"Right! And that crap he was feeding you about that bitch wanting to talk to you. That's bull. She wants to bring you down to her level—cleaning like some goddamn maid." He took a breath and snorted. "I can't believe you ever thought she was your friend."

"Christi is my friend. I asked her to let me work with her." She looked up at him.

God Almighty, he saw defiance in her angry face. Wouldn't she ever learn to respect him? "Don't I make enough money? Don't I provide everything you need?"

She shifted her gaze to the road. "Yes, you provide very well for me. You work hard." She said it like a robot, like she was only trying to get him off her case.

Vince thought for a few moments, and realized he was furious. "You treat me like shit. When we make love, you lay there like a dead fish. Instead of getting better, it's getting worse. Your blank face says you don't care a thing about having sex with me. It's just something you have to put up with."

"That's not true. It's just hard for me to relax. You're right. It's my fault. You're a wonderful husband. You provide everything I need—everything." Again, her words were flat and phony.

At the four-way stop on the edge of town, a lady with a head full of long blonde curly hair driving a shiny new red Charger pulled up and stopped. Vince wondered who the hell this hot babe was. He had never seen the car or the woman. When she—or rather *he* turned to see if Vince was stopping, Vince could not believe his eyes. On top of that, that bearded bastard looked like he was raising his hand to wave at them. The only way he was acknowledging that goddamn hippie was with his middle finger.

"Son-of-a-bitch," Vince muttered as he gunned his engine—no way he was stopping for the likes of that. "That's a goddamned man. He's got a beard." When they were through the intersection, Vince checked his rear view mirror and saw that he was still sitting there. "I ought to go back and punch his lights out. He's got some nerve showing up here."

"He's probably lost," Abi said with more life than anything else she had said all day.

"Lost? I just want to know what the fuck he's doing here." Not in the mood to deal with scum like that, he kept on driving toward Flatland. Realizing Abi wasn't going to carry on a conversation with him, Vince turned on the radio. Melanie sang that silly song that was so popular right now, *Brand New Key.* He never had figured out what that was supposed to mean about her having a brand new pair of roller skates. Must be some kind of reference to marijuana or LSD. Then Don McClean started in on his *American Pie.* It had something to do with assassinations that had taken place in the 60's—King and the Kennedys, but what the hell did that have to do with a dry levee? Goddamn, couldn't somebody come up with some lyrics that made sense?

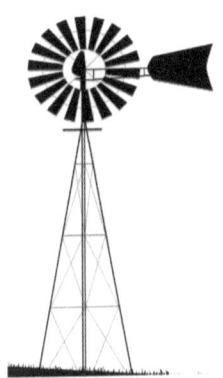

# Chapter Four

*Only a fool argues with a
skunk, a mule, or a cook.*

### January 21, 1973, Sunday morning

When the phone woke me from a sound sleep, my neck had a heavy-duty crick in it. At the same time, I realized I was still in my living room chair and not in bed with Vince. I jumped up and started breakfast, hoping it would appear I had been doing that before Papa Martin's usual Sunday morning wake-up call.

Twenty minutes later, Vince entered the kitchen wearing an undershirt and dress pants, his hair wet from a shower. We each sat, and he glanced at me as he diced his fried eggs.

"What did your daddy say?" I asked, trying to gauge his mood.

"He said to wear your heavy coat. They're forecasting snow flurries." He salted his eggs. "Why'd you sleep in the living room? You too good to sleep with me now?"

The eggs on my plate stared back at me. "I woke up in the night, and I couldn't get back to sleep, so I studied in my chair to keep from bothering you."

"You know I hate that." Chomping a slice of bacon, he locked his cold, blue eyes with mine. "You sleep with me."

"Okay," I whispered.

On the way to church, Harry Nilsson sang *Without You,* which brought Garrett to mind. I had not known him a week, and I already felt

51

the kind of friendship for him that I had with Christi. God, I missed her. It made me think of Vince when Nilsson sang the line about not being able to give any more. Then I remembered the deal I made with God about being the best wife possible and how Garrett did not fit into that picture at all. He was only a friend, but I didn't know if God understood that. Vince sure wouldn't.

We arrived midway through the first hymn and sat in our regular pew behind A.V. and Thelma. During the announcements and mission report, the seventy-year-old pianist on the stool in front of the old upright piano scrambled through her hymnals looking for the next song. Then we sang *Rock of Ages*, and after that Brother Sims started preaching. Immediately, my mind drifted to the second floor of the library forty miles away where I sat at a table talking with a long-haired, bearded man who held me captive with his aqua green eyes. He listened intently to every word I uttered, and he made me laugh. Somehow I had to muster the strength to never go there again. But if I did succumb to my need to see him, I better tell him, he sure better not come back to Quits.

* * *

His anthropology text lay open next to Garrett on the couch. He had tried all morning to at least get through the first chapter, but that scene from yesterday kept playing through his head. He couldn't stop thinking about stopping at an intersection just outside Quits. He looked one way and then turned around to check the other direction before he drove on and saw Abi sitting in a pickup truck next to a guy that had to be her husband. They were sitting close like couples do who are deeply in love, but she looked profoundly sad. That didn't fit the Abi he knew. Seeing her like that and immediately wanting to make her feel better had caused him to instinctively raise his hand. Luckily Vince plowed through the intersection before he saw what Garrett was doing.

Seeing her look so unhappy made his heart hurt. It had been wrong of him to drive to Quits, but Abi's distraught expression confirmed what

Garrett already suspected. She needed someone to tell her that it was okay to want more from life, and Garrett could do that for her.

With Trang and Loc in Houston, it was easy to pretend he had gotten out of a bad situation. He hadn't though. He was just as committed as he had ever been, and when he thought of getting a divorce, he also thought about the responsibility he had assumed by bringing Trang to Texas. After six years, she still did not speak enough English to take care of herself. Vinh could cart her around, but he was nearly as inept as she was at handling legal matters. Like it or not, Garrett had made his bed, and now he had to lie in it. Bed. Abi. Together. He needed to think about something else.

*      *      *

Brother Sims issued one alter call after another. Part of me wanted someone to troop down the center aisle, so we could get done with church, but that would also mean dragging it out some more to hear their testimony. When we finally sang the last verse the last time of *Just As I Am*, I scooted out to Vince's parents' Cadillac and waited for Thelma. They had owned this vehicle the whole time I had known them. Thelma drove it, on the rare occasions when she drove herself. Vince and his dad rode to work in a Ford Ranchero, a car with a pickup bed on it that A.V. bought new right before Vince and I got married.

Vince stood outside the church with three guys from his high school football team. They all wore identical letter jackets and bounced to ward off the cold while Vince amused them with a story that required huge sweeping arm gestures. Papa Martin would ride with Vince after he finished counting the offering and doing the books for the Quits First (and only) Baptist Church. Thelma visited on the porch with several other ladies for ten minutes, then she waddled to the car, where she let in a blast of frigid air while she huffed and puffed as she lowered herself into the front seat. She laid her Bible on the space between us.

As soon as she had her door closed, I began backing out.

"You remember Billy McNeil, that kid who was always picking a fight with Vince? His mother died last week on Monday, and they didn't have her service until Friday." She opened her enormous purse and rummaged through it. "That's just plain weird if you ask me."

"Maybe some of her family lived far away," I offered.

"Yeah, she's got that daughter who got pregnant while she was still in high school. She was engaged to some boy stationed over in Vietnam at the time." Thelma smeared cold rub inside her nose and on her lips. "Homecoming Queen and all that." She put the jar back in her purse. "She had a boy. That's one way to get a son to carry on the family name. Not the way I'd choose, but one way. Apparently she took something serious that was poked at her in fun." Thelma gave a phony laugh. "Isn't that one of your silly expressions?"

"Yeah," I whispered. Her question felt like a jab to my gut. I used that saying several years ago when Vince and I were talking about me not getting pregnant. Before I knew it, he had backhanded me. He must have thought I was laughing at him because he wanted a baby, and I couldn't give him one. That was about the time I decided I wanted to go to college. At first I wanted to make Vince proud of me, and then I had an overwhelming desire to do something for me—not for anybody else. Since I knew it would cost a lot and Vince wouldn't let me work, I started sneaking off and cleaning houses with Christi. At first it was just every once in a while, and then I got cocky and did it several times a week. My mind jumped to Garrett and guilt washed over me for hiding something else, which to Vince would be much worse than working.

"Elroys had a baby last week—a boy," Thelma said, bringing me back to the present moment. "Agnus Bean's daughter and son-in-law went to the doctor. They figured out she could take some hormones of some kind. Got pregnant almost immediately."

Several years ago, Vince came home with the results of the fertility tests we'd both endured. I could tell by his hangdog expression that I didn't want to hear the outcome. When I asked how it went, he muttered that the doctor was a quack. I suggested we go to someone else, and he shouted, "Drop it! There's no way you can get pregnant!" We have not discussed my infertility since then—except the time the conversation ended with him backhanding me after I made the remark about me not taking something serious that was poked at me in fun.

"What do you make of that?" Thelma asked.

"About somebody getting pregnant?" I asked, wondering where we were in the conversation.

"Keep up with what I'm saying. If you'd go to Sunday school, you'd know some of this already." Her eyes moved impatiently over the small, gray houses that made up Quits.

"Vince likes to sleep in late on Sunday," I answered.

"That doesn't keep you from getting up and going with me and A.V. God knows A.V. likes you better than his own daughter." She pulled a used tissue from her pocket and blew her nose. "Considering that no a 'count she married, it don't surprise me."

"Chuck's not so bad," I said.

"What kind of father is he?" she asked indignantly. "Don't even take those babies to church. And never comes to eat with us for Sunday dinner. He thinks just because his daddy set him up in some fancy job and built that house for them, he don't have to associate with the rest of us common folks."

I pulled into their drive, which ran parallel to ours.

"He'll get his comeuppance. You'll see," she declared.

She picked up her Bible and waited. I climbed out of the car, scurried around, and opened her door. Several years ago when Thelma's back started bothering her, we had started this routine of me taking her home from church, getting her into the house, and helping her finish Sunday dinner. That ailment had remained and other disorders had developed, solidifying the need for me to act as her personal chauffeur after church.

She pried herself from the white Cadillac. "You could at least visit after the service. Everybody knows you think you're too good for them."

"I'm just shy." Plus, I didn't want Thelma to make something out of everything I said.

Holding onto my arm, she walked to her backdoor. "You need a hobby, something like crochet or embroidery, so you'll have something to talk about. All you ever do is read and draw. What have you got after you've read a book or drawn a flower?"

"Not much," I said, trying to say what she wanted to hear.

"After dinner, we'll start you on a simple crochet pattern." She had been saying that for years.

I helped her up the back steps and opened the door. Like ours, it was never locked. Thelma took off her brown vinyl coat and handed it to me. I hung it in her bedroom closet, and I laid mine in the usual spot on the couch. Thelma continued her monologue from the kitchen while I spread her mother's hand-embroidered tablecloth on the large rectangular dining room table and then used the Sunday dishes to set the table.

When A.V. and Vince arrived, I stood at the stove stirring the gravy. "Hello, Papa Martin."

Wrapping his arm around me, he brushed his stubbly face against mine. "How's my Abi?"

"Fine." I hugged him back then pulled away teasingly.

Thelma scowled at us. "How much was the offering today?"

"Not enough. Christmas is catching up with everybody." He took off the only dress coat I had ever seen him wear. "Going to have to tell Brother Sims to pull out one of those pay-the-bills sermons."

A few minutes later, Vince's sister Bea arrived with her two children, a three-year-old boy, Chase, and a one-year-old girl, Tiffany. Bea took her kids to a church in Flatland that she claimed was progressive and open-minded, unlike the Baptist church she had attended growing up. That didn't set well with Thelma, but it was a subject on which they had agreed to disagree. Bea changed the kids from their stylish dress clothes into play clothes and helped us finish preparing lunch while Vince rough-housed with the kids on the living room floor.

We all sat down and A.V. lowered his head. Everyone followed suit. "Thank you, God, for these gifts, for bringing our family back together, and for your guidance in the past and in the future. Watch over us and keep us. Amen." His prayer had never varied. Everyone took a food dish, served their plate, and then passed it on until all the food had come full circle.

When Bea handed the gravy to Thelma, she passed it on. "Last week Abi salted this up so it made me sick. That's probably what sent my blood pressure soaring."

Bea fussed over her kids who were both wound up from playing with Vince. He sat between me and Chase who had begun feeding himself when Vince goosed him in the ribs. Chase erupted into laughter, spewing English peas all over the table.

"Vince, stop acting like a child." Bea picked up the peas and put them back on Chase's plate.

He smiled to himself and waited until everyone started eating again before he tickled Chase again.

Collecting peas for the second time, Bea exploded, "Vince Martin, you're a terrible influence."

"You know Vince just wants his own son." Mama Martin shot me an accusing look.

As if my inability to have children were part of the conversation, Bea announced, "Oh, Abi, I've got a bag of clothes for you—mostly maternity clothes. It's in the car."

"Thanks," I whispered.

"She don't need your hand-me-downs," Vince snarled, never missing a bite.

Bea knew how much Vince wanted children. Giving me maternity clothes was her way of gigging him. I still snuck them into the house when Vince wasn't looking. Mama was good at figuring out how to change the maternity outfits into regular clothes.

"Everything has designer labels. But they do remind me of being miserably pregnant. Abi can use them for around the house." Bea scooped green baby food into Tiffany's mouth as she spoke. "God knows she needs something besides what you'd have her wear—like that prostitute get up you gave her for Christmas."

Shock from Bea's remark settled over the room. She was prone to speaking her mind, but there were limits—even for her. Papa Martin cleared his throat. Vince stiffly chewed his food while the blood vessel on his temple pulsed. By the satisfied smirk on Bea's face, I guessed she had gotten the reaction she intended.

"How did school go, Abi?" Bea wiped Chase's face and hands and then helped him down.

"Just fine," I said, glad to change the subject.

"It's taking all her time. That's how it's going." Thelma stabbed another helping of meat and grabbed a yeast roll. "The very first day she promised to take me to the doctor. We got there late and ended up waiting for three hours behind a busload of Mexicans."

I wanted to set the record straight about Vince telling Thelma I'd take her to the doctor, but I figured it wasn't worth it, so I smiled and stared at my plate.

"It ain't funny." Thelma doused her meat with the gravy that caused her blood pressure to skyrocket.

Hoping the conversation would shift to something else, I hurried to the kitchen and retrieved the peach pie and dessert plates. Standing next to Papa Martin, I cut the pie and gave him the first and biggest piece. He grunted his acknowledgment.

"She's been coming in later every afternoon," Thelma announced, unwilling to let the subject die.

I handed the next piece to Vince, who did exactly his father had done when I gave him his pie. ThenI looked around the table as I handed Thelma her pie and saw everybody looking at me, so I ducked my head and said, "It's going to be hard to compete with other students who have a stronger academic background."

"Oh, listen to that. Already talking fancy-shmancy." Thelma crammed her mouth full of pie. "You could study at home, but no. Somebody like me might want to call and talk a bit."

"For Christ's sake, Mother, leave her alone!" Bea shouted. "Abi has a right to get out of this hell-hole—even if it's only a few hours at a time."

"A few hours!" Thelma shouted back. "She's gone as soon as Vince walks out the door, and she's not back until right before he gets home."

Vince opened his mouth to speak when Papa Martin cleared his throat. The room fell silent.

"All right, you two," Papa Martin said slowly. "Beatrice, you know we don't talk like that in this house. And, Mother, I think maybe you're being a little hard on Abi. She's just trying to better herself."

Thelma and Bea both sulked in silence. Vince glared at me as if I had instigated the whole thing, so I kept my head down and ate my pie.

After a long silence, Vince said, "I'm going out to the pit to shoot my gun, Daddy. You want to go?"

"No thanks. I hear my chair calling me." Papa Martin shoveled in his last bite of pie. "It's supposed to warm up some today, but I don't know how good it will be for target practice."

I pointed to the pie pan and gave Papa Martin a questioning look. "There's one more piece, and I think it's got your name on it."

He winked at me, scooted back from the table, and rubbed his bulging stomach. "Maybe after my nap. Right now, I'm as full as a tick."

"Why don't you take Abi? Isn't she the one who gave you that gun?" Bea quizzed.

"Abi's going to see her mother, or she'd be out there with me," Vince shot back.

Some Sunday afternoons, like today, I went to see Mama on my own since Vince hated sitting around my folks' house trying to make conversation. Truthfully, I liked going by myself, so that when Daddy left to drive around, which he nearly always did, Mama and I could talk privately. For the past several weeks, I had been trying to figure out how to tactfully ask how and why she was paying for my schooling, without getting into the particulars about my broken arm. Apparently, Papa Martin initiated the whole thing, but I know Mama had no idea I had been in the hospital because she didn't come to see me the two days I was there, and Vince had forbidden me to go over there until my bruises were gone, which over the years I had learned to hide from everyone. But the cast that had stayed on for six weeks had required a story about my clumsiness.

*     *     *

The phone rang three times before Trang picked up. "Hello?" While it did not sound natural, Garrett could tell she had been practicing.

"How's it going?" He called on Sunday because long distance was cheapest then. They had an unspoken agreement he would talk to her before she handed the phone to Loc. Unfortunately, their conversations were stilted at best and sometimes ended in misunderstandings due to their two different languages.

"Loc teach me reading," she said proudly.

"He's teaching you to read?" Garrett asked, not sure he had understood.

"Yes, read. Wait. I show." A thud indicated Trang had set down the phone. After a minute of background conversation and shifting of the receiver, Trang returned. "I read to you. Look, look. See the cat. See the dog. Look at the cat. Look at the dog...."

Clearly Loc had brought home his reader and was teaching her what he had learned in school. Garrett could have done as much. He should have done much more than that.

When she finished, Garrett said, "Great. How long have you been working on that?"

"Working?" she echoed.

"How long have you been reading?" he asked slowly.

She asked Loc in Vietnamese how long she had been reading. He answered in English, and she proudly parroted, "One week."

"That's really good. I'm proud of you." His heart tightened in response to her eagerness to please him. It reminded him of how she had acted when they first moved to Oaces. They had communicated in gestures. With time they learned enough of each other's language to dismiss the ongoing game of charades.

"You want talk to Loc?" she asked.

"Yes, please." He had to admit she was stretching toward him more than he had to her—lately.

After a series of thuds and bumps, Loc said, "Daddy, Daddy. I learned to count to one hundred. You want me to do that for you?"

Garrett laughed. "I'm sure you can, but let's wait until we get together. That will take a long time. I'd rather hear what you've been doing."

"Me and Sammy Tong started a club. No girls allowed. His sister wants to join, but we won't let her. We're gonna build a fort out in his backyard. He lives in a house real close to our apartment and his mom said we could use some of the boards that are piled up in the backyard." Loc rattled on, telling Garrett the rules of the club and how they planned to invite other neighbor kids, but none of them girls, he repeated.

Loc had begun building a life that Garrett was not privilege to. He missed his son. And he regretted that the relationship he had once had with Trang when their marriage was new no longer existed. He now associated that feeling of anticipation and excitement with hopefully seeing Abi tomorrow in the library. What if she didn't come? After the boner he pulled by driving out to Quits, she might avoid him like the plague. She might, but, God, he hoped she showed.

*       *       *

Mama's beauty shop, The Beauty Box, sat across the road from the house where I grew up. When I saw Charlene's car parked there, I figured Mama was there too. Sure enough, inside I found them giving each other perms. "Don't you get enough of this place during the week?" I asked.

Mama laughed and motioned me over for a hug.

"We're playing today. During the week, it's work," Charlene answered. "Abi, you got to tell us about your first week of school. Did the other kids play nice?"

Her reference to the other kids made me think of Garrett, who was, of course, a forbidden topic. "I figured out where I'm going, and I've gotten all my books—finally. I may have to buy a few more supplies for my art classes, but I've got enough money from what you've already given me, Mama." I hated for her to spend more than she already had. "I really appreciate what you've done for me."

Mama returned to gazing in the mirror and checking the curl by unwinding one of the rollers. "It's money well spent."

"Don't you worry about Betty," Charlene advised. "She's walking in high cotton. Just last week Gracie Dane gave her a twenty-five cent tip."

That made both of them erupt into laughter. Over the years, Gracie had been the butt of countless jokes due to her skinflint ways and her inability to get anywhere on time.

"Mama, will you have time to trim my hair?"

"Sure, Baby. This solution needs to work a little longer." Mama dabbed at a trickle running from one of the many curlers on her head.

I grabbed the latest issue of *Ladies Home Journal,* and sat in Mama's chair. I would love for her to cut it off to chin length but Vince would have a wall-eyed fit if I did that.

Charlene wrapped a plastic bag around Mama's head as they smiled at each other in the mirror. "Betty, I think we ought to tie Abi down and perm her, too," Charlene said with a mischievous grin.

Mama laughed. "I've tried. She won't hear of it."

"Vince doesn't want me to get a perm. Besides that's not in style for my age." I flipped the pages of the magazine, noting miniskirts and hot pants, thankful Vince hadn't bought either as my Christmas present. What did Garrett think of them? I wasn't suppose to care, but truthfully on the days I went to the library, I had picked out my outfit thinking about him.

"Come on, Baby, you're next." Mama tied the cape around my neck. "What will it be?"

I stared at the mirror, imagining my hair chin-length, which meant a whole lot less work. Relations with Vince were already strained enough without me pouring kerosene on the fire. "Just trim the dead ends."

As she began snipping, I wondered if she ever purposely pissed off Daddy, or if he just naturally stayed in a sour mood no matter what. Had she said anything to Daddy about paying for me to go to college, or had she done it without his approval, which was not like her at all? It was no secret he wished I had been a boy. As he often joked, God had forgotten to put a stem on my apple. Like me, Mama had tried to give her husband a son, but her other pregnancies ended in miscarriages—no doubt due to my dad beating the hell out of her, especially when he was drunk. Had he mellowed in the last ten years? Mama and I never talked about our marital relationships. We could talk about just about anything else, but husbands were forbidden territory.

"Betty and I are going to a seminar in a couple of weeks. We've got a room at the Holiday Inn in Amarillo. We're gonna' have a time that's finer than frog hairs split four ways." Charlene gave me a knowing wink. "You want to come?" She checked the tightness of the curl on one of her own permanent rods.

"Thanks, but I've got classes." Vince wouldn't let me spend the night even if I didn't have school.

I watched my beautiful mother as she concentrated on combing and cutting my hair. Even with a head full of curlers, she carried her fifty-four years well. Living with my father had not been easy, but they had been together for thirty-six years and would probably remain that way until one of them left this world. "Where's Daddy? I didn't see his pickup at the house."

"He went over to look at new trucks. You know how he likes to drool." She stood back to check her work. "With cotton prices so low and the crops so bad the last few years, we'll be lucky to stay afloat 'til next year's crop comes in." She paused. "Guess it doesn't cost to dream."

"Then how did you afford the money for me to go to school?" I asked, seizing the opening.

"Oh, I juggled the books a little. I figure what Harold don't know won't hurt him. It's our secret, Baby." She smiled at me in the mirror.

"Daddy knows you're paying my tuition, doesn't he?" I asked, not sure she would tell me the truth.

"Yes and no." She winked. "He knows, but he doesn't know how expensive it is."

"I feel bad about putting you two in a bind."

With a faraway look in her eyes, she brushed the length of my hair with strong sure hands like she did when I was little. "We'll always be in a bind, but you won't always have the chance to go to school. Enjoy it."

"Thanks, Mama, I am." My eyes filled with tears as I watched her admire my long auburn hair.

"Have you made any new friends, Baby?" she asked.

"I've met a few people. There's one friend I study with in the library." I didn't dare say he was a man—or that we weren't getting much studying done for yakking.

"Oh, is she in one of your classes?" Mama asked.

"No, we met at the bookstore. We seem to have a lot in common." I hated deceiving Mama, but I couldn't risk telling anybody about Garrett, not even Mama.

She pulled the cape from my shoulders. "Oh, I almost forgot. Christi's mother came in yesterday. She said Christi wants you to call the next time you're here."

I made a show of picking up the phone and calling her, except I didn't dial all of the numbers. After a while, I said, "I guess, she's not there." Returning to the magazine, I remembered the countless nights Christi and I had stayed at one another's houses since we found each other in fourth grade. How could a friendship that had lasted that long be destroyed in one day? She had been to me what Charlene had been to Mama over the years.

They worked on each other's perms, including me as if I was part of their circle, although I felt like an outsider. I didn't belong—not here or at Quits. Maybe it had to do with starting school, but I felt lonely and depressed. Realizing I needed to get home, so I could cook supper for Vince, I got up to go.

"Did Betty tell you she's branching out?" Charlene asked as she gave me a goodbye hug.

"What do you mean?" I asked.

"She's doing men's hair now." Charlene howled with laughter. "Did two this week."

I tried to imagine my mother trimming Vince's long sideburns or Garrett's flowing hair.

"Young guys." Charlene's eyes danced mischievously. "Betty likes them that way. Don't you?"

"Their money spends same as anybody else's," Mama said dismissively as she hugged my neck.

Before I left, I borrowed Mama's manual typewriter, so I could use it when I needed to write a paper.

Mama had given me an electric one when I graduated from high school, but Vince had thrown it across the room when he thought I was writing a letter to an old boyfriend. Number one, I didn't have any old boyfriends, and number two, why would I type him a letter? Actually, I was practicing my typing in case I found a secretarial job. After that, I gave up on that idea, which made me wonder how or why I had been brave enough to think I could go to school. But I had, and I was actually doing it.

All the way to Quits, I thought about whether or not I could keep myself from going to the library tomorrow. I knew I shouldn't because my friendship with Garrett was too dangerous for both of us. While my VW Beetle puttered along, Neil Young sang *Heart of Gold*, and I sang along. The line about searching for that heart of gold made me think of Garrett - even though I wasn't suppose to.

When I walked into the living room, I found Vince cleaning his new gun—the one I said I wanted to buy him for Christmas with the money I earned working with Christi. "How did target practice go?" I asked as I sank into my chair.

"Not too good. Let me see if my aim is better close up." He pointed the gun at my head and cocked the hammer with his finger resting on the trigger.

"That's not funny." My voice shook. He always kept his gun loaded. When he first got it, I had suggested he take the bullets out if he wasn't using it, but he told me an empty gun was a worthless gun.

"Oh, Abi-girl, you know I'm just kidding." His face turned hard and serious, and he kept the gun pointed at me. "But if I ever catch you touching another man again, it won't be a joke."

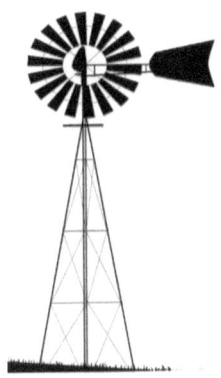

# Chapter Five

*Just because a chicken has*
*wings don't mean it can fly.*

**January 22, 1973, Monday**

S itting in class Monday morning, Garrett debated with himself whether or not to return to the library. Ethically, he shouldn't. He was married. Abi was married. Seeing her with Vince had convinced him she was miserable. She needed Garrett. Truthfully, Garrett needed Abi. He laughed out loud.

"Mr. Clay, do you have something to share?" Dr. Moser asked, his hand posed over the chalkboard.

"No, sir, except that I'm a total idiot," Garrett replied.

"What evidence have you found of that?" Moser quizzed, clearly amused by Garrett's observation.

"Just that I think I can save the world, and I haven't even gotten my own act together."

"A common dilemma of soon-to-be psychologists. Perhaps we can pursue this in my office after class," Moser suggested.

"Good idea," Garrett answered, determined to think about the lecture rather than Abi.

After class, Garrett and Dr. Moser walked to the professor's office. Moser sat at his desk and motioned for Garrett to sit on a metal framed chair that could have come from army surplus.

"Well, Mr. Clay, you seem to be preoccupied this semester. Last week you attended one class and today you might as well not have been here." He rolled a pencil on the desk. "Your remark in class leads me to think you may have personal problems."

Garrett didn't know where to start. "Last semester, I told you I was moving my family to Houston. I fly a cargo plane down there two days a week, so I get to see them then."

Moser steepled his fingers and touched them to his pursed lips. "Yes, you plan to do your internship there this fall—assuming, of course, you complete your classes."

"That's right. My wife, Trang, wanted to be closer to her uncle who lives in Houston. Friday I overslept at our Houston apartment. That's why I missed your class."

"You weren't there Monday either," Moser observed.

"No, sir. I lost track of time while I talked with a friend at the bookstore." Some of that was true.

"Unfortunately, that's the only time the class is offered, and there isn't anything else we can substitute."

"Getting there shouldn't be a problem—I mean not in the future. The thing is. . . You see I met this person who's not happy, but I'm not sure what I can do to help them."

"When you say *person*, do you really mean a woman?" Moser asked pointedly.

"Yes, sir," Garrett answered, wondering how obvious his thoughts were about Abi.

"And when you say she's not happy, what does that mean?"

"Well, she really hasn't said anything. It's more what I've read into the situation," Garrett explained.

"You think she's in an abusive situation?" Moser asked with genuine concern.

"Oh, no, nothing like that. She's just married to a really protective guy. The other day she said, he would be jealous if he knew she was even talking to me."

"But you *are* just talking." Moser shifted in his chair.

"Yes, sir, we met by chance last week. She's my age, but this is her first semester, and she seems nervous about it, so I've taken an interest in her."

"You've been sort of a pal to her," Moser suggested.

"Right." After seeing Abi and Vince together, he had daydreamed about being the husband to her that Vince obviously was not.

"Well, I don't see any harm in that; gives you an opportunity to practice your counseling skills." Moser turned to his desk and began shuffling through some papers.

"Thanks for talking to me." Garrett got up.

Moser glanced up at him. "Does that solve your problem; I mean the one about taking care of someone else's problem when you still are struggling with your own?"

Garrett was astounded at his adviser's keen memory. It had been over an hour since Garrett made that remark, and Moser remembered. "It's not resolved, but it gives me a little perspective."

"Sometimes that all we need." Moser paused with his pen in midair. "For what it's worth," he purposely met Garrett's gaze, "if you have any doubt about whether or not to do something—don't."

"Don't?" Garrett repeated, no sure he understood.

"Yes, don't. When you get that niggling voice that says don't think, say, or do something, then pay attention to it."

Nodding, Garrett left Moser's office. He checked his watch. Abi was at the library—if she had elected to come. If Garrett didn't show, he would be following Moser's advice. That niggling voice had offered one reason after another, including Loc and Trang, for why he should stop this thing while he still could. Abi was on the list as well. Clearly, she wasn't happy. He had seen that Saturday at the intersection. Fate had compelled him to drive to Quits. That undeniable force had pulled him like a magnet, willing him to see her. Moser was saying don't while Garrett heard an even stronger voice yelling *step forward and at least offer her a choice.*

Garrett thought of his favorite book, *As a Man Thinketh.* He would go by the bookstore and see if they had finally gotten it. If Abi read it, she would see she has a choice.

The bookstore had gotten it in, but by the time he paid for it and ran to the second floor of the library, Abi was nowhere in sight. In the center of their table sat a paper sack containing three large sugar cookies. He sat down and ate the cookies, pondering Dr. Moser's advice. Garrett examined *As a Man Thinketh.* How were his own thoughts helping or complicating his and/or Abi's life?

*       *       *

So Garrett would know I appreciated his kindness, but I just couldn't be friends, I left a sack of cookies where I usually sat in the library. Then I climbed the stairs to the third floor and put in a couple of study hours before I drove home and started supper. When the phone rang, I answered the kitchen wall phone because it had a long cord, and I could cook while Thelma talked. The men were due home soon, and then she'd talk to Vince.

Right after I said hello, Garrett said, "Bird, thanks for the cookies."

Hearing Garrett's voice sent a rush of excitement through me. "You're welcome."

"You left early. Where did you go?"

"I went up another floor." Like an idiot, I was telling him where to find me in the future.

"I got hung up talking to my adviser, and then I went by the bookstore to buy you something."

"You bought me something?" I was flattered, yet curious that he had not questioned my moving. Then a more obvious concern popped into my head. "How did you get my phone number?"

"Easy. I called the operator and told her I needed Vince Martin's number in Quits, Texas."

"There are two Alva Vince Martins." I stretched the phone cord to look out the bedroom window for Vince and Papa Martin. Hopefully, Thelma wasn't looking out her living room window. She'd see me. "You could have gotten my mother-in-law instead of me."

"Yeah, the operator said there were two, a junior and a senior. I figured yours would be the son."

"But it's long distance to call here," I protested.

"That's all right, Abi. I can spend a quarter on you. Don't I owe you for all the sweets?"

"I'm the one who owes you an apology for Saturday when Vince ran the stop sign." I had purposely not sat at our regular table, so I could end this thing, and now I was egging it on.

"I had no business in Quits, but I have to admit, I was curious."

"It surprised me to see you," I said, recalling Garrett's stunned expression.

Garrett laughed. "Me too. Like an idiot, I started to wave, so you know it caught me off guard."

"I'm glad Vince didn't see that." I checked the driveway again. "We can't study together anymore." The other end of the line was silent. "Are you still there?"

"Yeah, Bird, I'm here.… You left cookies for me, which means you like being friends, right?"

"I do enjoy our friendship. It's just that Vince wouldn't understand. And if anyone else I know saw me talking to you, and it got back to Vince.… Well, he's just really jealous." A popping sound in the kitchen made me realize I needed to turn off the fire under the grease. I ran to take care of it.

"Let's use one of the study carrels on the third floor of the library? Did you notice them when you were up there today?"

"I didn't. But someone might see me. My mother-in-law's best friend started working at UP this semester. If she saw me talking to you, she'd tell Thelma who couldn't wait to tell Vince." I turned off the fire under the skillet and looked for a lid to cover it since the grease was starting to smoke and smell up the house.

"Abi, we don't have anything to hide."

"I know we don't, but to other people.… I have to go. Vince will be home soon." I ran toward the window to see if the men were home yet.

"I'll meet you on the third floor," he said calmly.

"I shouldn't. It's not a –" As I approached the window, I saw Vince look up at me from outside. It scared the holy-bejesus out of me, and I froze.

Garrett must have heard the hesitation in my voice because he said, "See you tomorrow, Bird." He was gone before I could say another thing, and there was Vince staring at me.

\*     \*     \*

Vince couldn't wait to hear how Abi tried to snake her way out of this one. They both knew she was caught—probably talking to Christi. Why couldn't that bitch stay out of their lives?

He stepped into the house as Abi turned on the water in the kitchen sink. Vince sat his lunchbox on the counter and hung up his coat. While Abi fumbled with a sack of potatoes, he grabbed a beer out of the refrigerator and watched her squirm.

Impatient to get on with this, he asked, "Who was on the phone?"

"Nobody." She threw a handful of potatoes in the sink.

"Was it that bitch?" he asked dryly.

"If you're talking about Christi, it wasn't." She grabbed a paring knife and began peeling the potatoes.

"Who was it?" he demanded.

"A wrong number. That's all, just a wrong number." Her voice trembled.

He leaned against the counter with his legs crossed at the ankle while he drank his beer. "Let me see if I've got this straight. You talked for ten minutes to someone you don't know."

"It wasn't that long," she shot back.

"Long enough for you to be watching out the window for me," he countered.

"I knew you would be home soon, and I told them I needed to get supper ready, but they kept asking me to help them figure out what number they need," she spoke quickly and her voice had a higher pitch than usual, which meant she was lying.

Vince shifted and re-crossed his legs. "Why didn't you have the phone book out if you were trying to help them find a number?" he asked.

"I wasn't sure who he was trying to call."

"He!" Vince demanded. "Who the hell was this *he* bastard?"

"I don't know," she whined, sounding like she might start crying.

"Who did *he* want?" Vince demanded, again emphasizing the word he.

"Gerald Atkins," she answered too quickly.

"There's nobody in Quits by that name." Wasn't that one of the names in the front of her books?

"That's what I told him." She looked at Vince as if checking to see if he believed her.

Vince drained his beer, dropped the can in the sink, and turned Abi to face him. While kissing her hard on the lips, he grabbed her hips. He was not convinced that she wasn't talking to Christi, and she didn't want to admit it, but saying she was talking to a man as a cover up surprised him. One way or the other, she was lying. First, she got this crazy notion about working, and then she connived her way into going to school. Little by little she was getting more headstrong and cocky. He was not sure where this was going, but he did not like it.

He ground his lips into hers and squeezed her butt cheeks. "These are mine," he muttered between their clinched lips.

She returned his kiss, pressing her body against his, which wasn't typical for her. They separated, and he leaned against the counter again, giving her the once over. He did not know what to make of her, so he grabbed another beer and walked into the living room.

He turned on the TV and the anchorman said, "This news just in. Lyndon Baines Johnson has died. At 3:50 this afternoon he called the ranch switchboard requesting someone come immediately. By the time they reached him, it was too late."

"Good riddance," Vince muttered. Daddy liked the bastard because he was a Democrat, and he was Texas born and bred, but Vince didn't have any use for his yellow-belly stance on Vietnam. Johnson should have sent the troops in and bombed the hell out of those gooks instead of pulling our boys out of there.

\* \* \*

## January 23, 1973, Tuesday

The next morning, Garrett raced to the library as soon as he got out of his stats class. He wanted to claim a study carrel if there were any left. As a graduate student, he had first dibs, but by the second week of class, they could all be gone. One remained. He considered this a good omen. Garrett checked out the keys, grabbed a second chair, and struggled to get it in next to the one that was already there. Together they barely fit. Then he found a place to watch the elevator and the stairs to make sure he saw Abi when she got there.

He heard her trudging up the stairs before he saw her wearing the same red, white, and blue sweater she had worn last Monday when he met her. Before approaching him, she looked to her right and to her left. She was indeed paranoid that someone would see her. Garrett thought of Moser's inquiry as to whether she was in an abusive marriage. Surely not. She was too smart to stay in a situation like that.

Without saying a word, Garrett got up, motioned for her to follow, and walked to the study carrel in a back corner, making it unlikely that anyone would happen to look inside while they were walking past. He stood back to let her enter first, but she looked at the room and then at him.

"It's awfully small," she whispered.

"Neither one of us is very big," he offered hopefully.

She scanned him from head to feet with a growing grin on her face. "You're not much taller than me."

Her remark pleased him. After pulling back one of the chairs, she stepped in front of it and sat down. With barely enough room to shut the door, he pulled out the other chair and awkwardly climbed over it to sit down. For now, he had her trapped, although Abi might decide these cramped quarters were unacceptable.

She glanced at the small window on the door. "This is as about as private as possible, I guess."

Shifting back to his role as host of small spaces, he asked, "How was your weekend?"

"It was okay. How was yours?" She leaned against the sidewall and faced him.

"No fair, I asked you first." He gave her a smile that he hoped would relax her.

"Well, I went over to my mom's house Sunday afternoon."

"Tell me about your mother. I don't think you've ever mentioned her before."

"She lives about twenty miles from Quits in a little town called Dahlia. That's where I grew up."

"Does she work or have any hobbies?" Garrett became increasingly aware of the books stacked on the table and the reason they were there. Still, he had an insatiable need to know everything about Abi.

"She has a beauty shop, called the Beauty Box. Her best friend, Charlene, works with her. My dad's a farmer, but most years he doesn't make enough to pay all the bills, so they need what Mama makes. Plus, this year, she's paying my tuition."

Garrett stopped himself from asking why Vince wasn't paying it. "That's awfully nice of her."

Abi smiled. "In a few weeks she and Charlene are going to a hair seminar. They invited me."

"That sounds like fun. Are you going?"

"No, those things last through Monday." She emptied her bag and sorted through her books. "We better get busy, but first tell me about you."

"Well, let's see," he began, sorting through what he could say without divulging too much. "I was raised in Savannah, Georgia. We lived in a very old house that somehow survived the Civil War, my mother has been the running president of the DAR chapter since as long as I can remember."

Abi, who was listening attentively, bunched her eyebrows with confusion. "What's the DAR?"

"Daughters of the American Revolution. She takes great pride in knowing that some great-great-great uncle on her mother's side single-handedly saved this country from those damned British red-coats."

This made Abi smile. "So your mom's a real fighter?"

"Quite the opposite. She's extremely proper to the point of making passive aggressive behavior an art form—getting her way without openly saying what she wants." He spoke with an exaggerated southern bell's accent, trying to imitate his mother. "That may be why I haven't talked to her or my dad in over five years—not since I got back from Nam." Telling her they were at odds was a mistake because that left questions in her mind.

"Why haven't they spoken to you?" she asked—as he had anticipated.

"I came back a different man than the one who went over there. I didn't cut my hair, and I decided to live life by my terms instead of by theirs—or rather hers." He paused, again trying to tell her the truth without getting into dangerous territory. "I've made overtures, like at Christmas, I offered to visit, but I think they had a party scheduled, and they sure didn't want me to show up looking like this." He ran his hands through his hair. They had no idea what he looked like. Their issue was introducing Trang and Loc as Garrett's family.

"That's too bad. Can you celebrate Christmas with a brother or sister?"

"No, I'm an only child of two only children. I have no idea what it's like to have cousins or aunts and uncles. What about you? Any siblings?" he asked, eager to shift the conversation to her.

"I'm the only one that made it out alive," she said turning back to her books.

This remark concerned him. "What do you mean?"

"My mom had two miscarriages before me, and two after me. I guess I was meant to be an only child," she said as she opened her psychology book.

"Your parents must feel lucky to have you." He wanted to ask more questions, but that would lead to her wanting to know more about him.

"I guess so." Her somber tone contradicted her statement. "We better get busy studying."

"Yeah, we should." Garrett began blindly leafing through his statistics text, although he couldn't think about anything except Abi. She ran her finger along the text and then stopped to go back over it. Was his presence interfering with her concentration? Or maybe she was insecure about how to study after being out of school for so long.

For an hour, they sat elbow to elbow with neither of them saying a word. If Garrett asked her all the things that kept popping into his head, she might say she needed to study elsewhere.

When Abi began packing up, Garrett dug in his GI backpack, pulled out his gift for her, and laid it on the desk in front of her. "This is my present to you."

"*As a Man Thinketh*," she read aloud. She flipped through it. "I really can't take this."

"Remember the first day I met you? I was angry because the book store had lost my order, and I plowed into you. This is it. This is my special order."

She laughed. "Then I sure can't take that."

"Things happen for reasons we don't understand." He put his hand on her arm. "If they had given me this book then, I would have walked out of there and never seen you. But as it was, after I ran over you, I followed you and waited until enough time had passed so I could act like I had just seen you."

The intimacy of the room, his admission about following her, and his hand on her arm must have been too much; she attempted to stand up, but there wasn't room. "I can't accept it. I really can't."

His heart raced, but he remained seated, knowing she was trapped until he moved. "This book is special. I have an old copy that I've read a thousand times. It's kind of hard to get in print since it was written so long ago. The language is dated, but the ideas... Oh Abi, it has such a good message."

Her chocolate brown eyes met his gaze. "I can't take it, Garrett. Really, I can't."

"What if I give you my old copy," he suggested, refusing to let go of the idea. "It's covered with notes and falling apart. I started to give you that one, but I hated to with it in that shape."

"I guess that would be all right." She shoved her chair back.

"Take this one and read it tonight. I'll bring my old copy tomorrow." He began gathering his things. When she stared at the book, clearly reluctant to accept his gift, he slipped it into her cloth bag. "There's one thing I want you to promise me, Bird."

"What?" she asked.

"Read it through at least once every day. It won't take more than an hour, but you'll be amazed at the way it changes your thinking. Oh, and feel free to write in this copy. I want to know your reactions."

"I'll try." She looked pointedly at the door, obviously telling him she needed to go without saying so. "Thanks for getting this study room. I feel better here than in the open."

Garrett climbed out and pushed his chair in, so she could get out.

"Bye," she answered as she walked away.

"I'll see you tomorrow." He watched her go, already yearning to see her again.

*     *     *

As I drove the flat desolate miles back to Quits, Simon and Garfunkel sang *Bridge Over Troubled Waters.* A few years ago right after the song came out, I asked God to give me a bridge over my troubled waters. Was Garrett the answer to my prayers? In a little over a week, I had grown dependent on him. Today, we had said little, but sitting next to him gave me a sense of calm. I knew little about him except he and his folks didn't get along—and that I lived for the next time I saw him, which was insane since that went against my deal with God. Still, Garrett was the only person besides Christi who had ever truly listened to me.

After supper, Vince left to help his dad work on the Ranchero, so I hurriedly cleaned up the kitchen and then got out Garrett's book, *As a Man Thinketh* by James Allen. The poem at the beginning made me wonder what I had gotten into.

*"Mind is the Master power that moulds and makes,*
*And Man is Mind, and evermore he takes*
*The tool of Thought, and, shaping what he wills,*
*Brings forth a thousand joys, a thousand ills: --*
*He thinks in secret, and it comes to pass:*
*Environment is but his looking-glass. "*

Every word, every sentence seemed to have a message that was too big to wrap my mind around. It almost felt like I was reading something akin to the Bible because it was so powerful. Thinking that made me question if I was getting into dangerous territory—ideas and beliefs that went against Christianity. Even though I worried that I was dicing with the devil, I read it through just like Garrett had suggested. He asked me to write my thoughts in his book, but I couldn't. Using my own paper, I wrestled with the idea that mere thoughts had created my world. If I accepted the author's ideas, then I also had to take blame for my life and the things about it that I did not like. Wasn't God in charge of making things happen, and not what I thought or did not think?

When I heard Vince opening the door, I hid the book and my notes. After a bath and going through our regular nighttime ritual of having sex, I went to sleep with James Allen's words echoing through my head.

The next day when I got to the third floor of the library, Garrett was already there, his head bent over a book while he sat in our room. Once we had jockeyed around and both gotten seated, he suggested we go over my class notes, so I pulled out the ones I had taken in history that morning. Dr. Horton had talked about premarital sex among the colonist and how women were encouraged to be "fruitful." While I had written notes, there was no way I was showing them to Garrett. Instead, I went back to my earlier notes about the Salem Witch Trials and the two women who had acted as spies for the colonial army—Debroah Champion and Lydra Darragh. When Garrett acted intrigued, I told him about Abigail Adams asking her husband President John Adams to recognize the rights of women, but he had refused.

"How does it feel to know your namesake was a pioneer in seeking women's rights?" Garrett asked.

"I was too busy writing notes to think about that connection." Honestly hearing Dr. Horton's lectures on women's roles and our lack of recognition made me generally uncomfortable. What she said made sense, but these were ideas that contradicted everything I had grown up believing. "Dr. Horton spends more than half of the time talking about what women have done. She says we are way under recognized in the history books and in life in general." All I could do was parrot what she had said. It felt too intimidating to have my own opinion.

"She's right, you know," Garrett admitted.

I loved his response. I had never heard a man say that. Too many men were like the back-row jerk who persisted in saying something stupid during every lecture.

When we finished going through my notes, I suggested we discuss Garrett's classes. I knew I couldn't help him, but I felt selfish using up his study time on me.

"I'd rather talk about the book I gave you yesterday." He pulled a worn copy from his bag and handed it to me. "This copy is falling apart, but it does have my notes. I'm not sure if that will help or hinder you in finding your own truth."

The idea of finding my own truth echoed in my mind as I carefully examined the fragile copy. After leafing through the book and noting small, precise handwriting on every page, I flipped the front cover open and read 'Garrett Clay.' I should refuse his gift, but it felt like holding a piece of him—his thoughts, his writing, almost like having a picture of him, something I had fantasized about drawing, but had not been brave or stupid enough to attempt. If Vince saw it, he would recognize the hippie he saw at the intersection. His mind worked like that. I wanted desperately to take the book home with me, so I continued leafing through the pages telling myself that I could keep it hidden from Vince. It would be a secret, just like the person who gave it to me.

When I looked up and saw Garrett watching, I laid the book on the table and pulled the new copy and my comments from my bag. "I couldn't bring myself to write in your book, so I wrote on my own paper. I'm not sure I should let you read my thoughts, though. I probably didn't really get what he was saying." Reluctantly, I laid my notes on the desk.

Garrett began reading them, periodically looking up and staring into space. His brow furrowed, which made me think I had probably missed the point.

Unable to withstand the suspense any longer, I said, "I'm sure none of what I've written makes sense."

When I grabbed for my papers, he shifted the pages out of my reach.

"I'm intrigued by everything you've written." He smiled ruefully. "May I keep these for a few days?"

"Sure, but I...I don't know why you'd want –"

He silenced me by pressing his index finger to my lips. It was the most intimate thing he had ever done, and it stopped me cold. "Tell me how you felt when you read this book, when you wrote these words."

I looked at the notes that he still held.

"Tell me from here." He lightly touched my chest, which took my breath away. "Not from here." He softly tapped the side of my head.

My skin tingled where he had touched me and my mind whirled. "Honestly, reading that book made me uneasy. Allen talks about doing something I don't think I can do."

"What can't you do, Bird?" he asked gently.

I lifted my eyes to his. "How can I change what I think?"

"'*As a man thinketh in his heart, so is he,*'" Garrett quoted from the first page.

"So all the bad thoughts I have make me a terrible person?" Our eyes stayed locked.

"You're a good person, but refusing to take responsibility for your thinking makes you unhappy."

His words carried a truth I could not face, so I turned away and began stacking my books.

"I didn't mean that as criticism." He put his hand on my arm.

"I need to go," I whispered.

"First, tell me how you feel."

"Confused."

"Did you get all the way through the book?"

"I read all of it, but I'm not sure I have one ounce of that *serenity* he talked about in the last section."

"You must identify your tempest and conquer it," he said, referring to what Allen had said in the book as he climbed out of his chair, so I could get out.

"What's your tempest, Garrett?" I asked before I knew the words had left my mouth.

His face registered surprise. "I'm not sure."

I shoved past him, feeling more confused and unsure of myself than ever.

He grabbed my arm again. "See you tomorrow, Bird?"

I nodded and quickly walked away.

That night I waited until Vince was sound asleep before I crept out of bed to read Garrett's copy of *As a Man Thinketh*, the whole time aware of how mad Vince would be if he woke up and found me reading a book with Garrett's name in the front. I read every page, studying Garrett's notes on each one. His commandment to identify my tempest haunted me. The only tempest I could identify was me. I was the one who was breaking my promise to God by studying with a man while knowing it would infuriate Vince if he knew.

When I returned to bed, Vince slept soundly. After I slipped into the warm bed, I repeated over and over again the last phrase of the last page of the book, "Peace be still!" God, I wanted that. Going to school once seemed like the answer, but now that I was there, I felt farther from being at peace than I ever had.

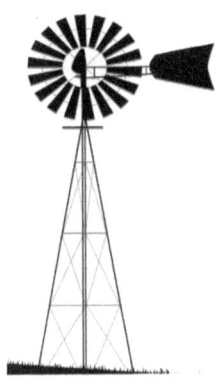

# Chapter Six

*The bigger the mouth,*
*the better it looks when shut.*

## January 31, 1973, Wednesday

*I* woke up with terrible menstrual cramps. Every month, my period seemed to get worse, like my body was punishing me for not getting pregnant. When I met Garrett at the library, I told him I needed to leave early since it was my time of the month, and I had terrible cramps. He fussed over me more than Vince had ever done—even when I was in the hospital. It felt strange to tell Garrett something so private, but I had crossed a line of intimacy with him that I never had with Vince. We talked about feelings and emotions, issues around women's rights, stuff Vince wouldn't have a clue about.

As we were packing up to leave, I said, "Dr. Cole asked me to model for the life drawing class. Plus, he said they would pay me." I wanted to. Of course, I couldn't tell Vince,

Garrett grinned wickedly. "Did Dr. Cole mention you'd be doing that in the nude?"

"Oh, my God, no. Vince would kill me if he found out I was even talking about something like that." I looked at Garrett to make sure he wasn't teasing me. "Are you pulling my leg?"

"No, I'm not. But if you decide to do that, I'll definitely sign up to audit the class." Then his face erupted in an ear to ear grin, and his aqua green eyes danced mischievously.

I took it as a complement that Garrett wanted to see me naked, but the idea of it was someplace I could not go—and be married to Vince.

When we parted ways, Garrett cautioned me to drive safely as thunder kept rumbling overhead. The rain beating on the roof of my VW made me hope Dahlia was getting their share. Daddy was a dry-land farmer, so whether or not he could make a crop always depended on how much rain he got.

At home, I put the beans on to cook that I had started soaking that morning. Then I lay in bed with a heating pad on my stomach and prayed that Thelma would not see I was home early and call, wanting to chat. I read Garrett's worn copy of *As a Man Thinketh*. Even though I had read this a dozen times, the idea that my environment would change when I changed my thoughts struck me as both disturbing and intriguing.

When I got up to cook the rest of Vince's supper, I began looking around, wondering if I could somehow see my world differently. Above our bed, I studied the loaded gun that rested in a rack Papa Martin had given Vince for Christmas. A.V. made the rack as a young man, and the gun was my way of appeasing Vince for defying him. Early in our maid business, I told Christi I wanted to earn money to go to school, so I could make Vince proud, which was sort of true along with simply wanting to do what I wanted to do for a change. She said I needed to buy a bus ticket to a place as far away from Vince as I could get since there was no way to please him. Right after Vince and I married, I made the mistake of telling her that he had hit me when he thought I had sassed him. Because that upset her, I never told her about the other times he hit me, but I figure she assumed the worst.

Still wandering aimlessly through the house, I examined Vince's bowling trophies, the football from his last high school game, and the Bible that lay open on a stand in the living room. Even that somehow belonged to Vince more than me since his parents had given it to us for Christmas several years ago. There seemed to be nothing that I could call my own, except my clothes, my textbooks, and my sketchpad. When we married, I moved in with little more than my clothes. None of my drawings were on the walls. My current sketchbook, which Mama gave me for Christmas, was the first I had owned. All the rest of my drawings were done on scrap paper, which Vince threw out by mistake when he was looking for something and found them stacked on the top shelf in our coat closet. According to James Allen, I had created all this—my life and everything in it. If I was in charge, why did it seem so one-sided—so all about Vince?

During supper, Vince watched television while I rearranged the food on my plate. When a commercial came on, he stopped chewing and asked stiffly, "You back on the rag?" He had seen the heating pad on the bed.

"Yeah," I admitted, unable to meet his gaze.

He snorted in response. "These beans aren't done." He returned to his food and a special news feature on how the recent signing of the cease-fire accord ending the Vietnam conflict would play out. "Damn gooks," Vince snarled. "We're pulling out just like a bunch of yellow-bellies."

Vince judged the decision to withdraw from the war as if he were directly involved, yet he had lied about a football injury to avoid the draft. What right did he have to say anything?

That night when I turned off the light by the bed, Vince immediately began mounting me.

I put my hands on his chest. "I'm flowing heavily. I'll make a mess."

"Goddamn it," he muttered and rolled away from me.

Even though my cramps still kept me doubled into a tight ball, I went to sleep feeling powerful. For the first time in my life, I had declined sex with Vince.

The next morning, Vince said little as he watched TV and ate breakfast. The weather man predicted thunderstorms all day. As Vince put on his heavy coat, I waited close by, holding his lunch box.

Still thinking about the power of thought, I decided to plant a seed. "Vince," I said softly.

"What?"

"We could adopt a child. There are kids out there who would love to have you as a daddy."

"I don't want some bastard kid." After grabbing his lunch box, he started past me, but then he hesitated and rested his hand on my shoulder. "Look, Abi-girl, you got to understand, I want my own son, not some kid that nobody else wanted."

I considered arguing that an adopted child could be that son, but I knew it would only make him mad, so I kissed him quickly on the lips. He turned and left.

*  *  *

## February 1, 1973, Thursday

Garrett made a game out of seeing how fast he could cover Abi's notes. The whole time they were volleying questions and answers back and forth, Garrett mentally debated the wisdom of what he had planned to suggest once they got through studying. Dr. Moser's advice to 'don't' when in doubt kept running through his head. Still, he couldn't stop himself from silently rehearsing what he intended to say. For the second day in a row, they finished an hour early—just as he had hoped.

When he noted Abi stalling as she put her books away, like maybe she was disappointed they were stopping so soon, it gave him the impetus to say what he had been practicing in his head. "I have some books I'd like to lend you. They're too heavy to carry around, so you can come by my apartment and get them."

Abi wistfully smiled. "That's awfully nice of you, but I don't have the time. Besides, I don't know where you live." She stood up.

He looked at his watch like he hadn't already checked the time. "It's just now 2:30, and I got a great parking spot close by." Thunder rumbled outside, as if on cue. He wasn't about to tell her he had parked illegally, using an expired permit from last semester. Hopefully, the campus police wouldn't check it and ticket him - again.

"I'm sorry, I really can't," she said.

Again the thunder rumbled. "I'll at least take you to your car. You don't want to get caught in that." He pointed skyward. When he saw hesitation on her face, he began climbing over his chair.

"But, I –" she objected as he manipulated his way out of the closet-size room.

Grabbing her book bag out of her hands, Garrett raced down the stairs rather than taking the elevator where she might debate whether or not she should go to his place. When he turned and saw her trailing him by several steps, he smiled at her.

Outside, he guided Abi to his Charger where he unlocked and opened the passenger door. Once they were both seated, and he had returned her book bag, she reluctantly gave him directions to her car.

After he stopped behind her car, and while she got out, he said with as much nonchalance as he could muster, "Just follow me. I'll go slow."

"I still don't think –"

"I live five minutes from campus. Don't worry, you won't get lost."

Opening the driver's door on her VW, she gave Garrett a look that said she could not believe she was doing this. He smiled and gave her a thumbs up. She halfheartedly waved and climbed into her car. Driving slowly, he checked his rearview mirror and saw her dally far behind him. When he pulled into the apartment parking lot, she parked several spaces away from his Charger.

Apparently, still paranoid about someone seeing her, but remarkably still going along with his plan, she walked several yards behind him as they approached his apartment building. On the balcony landing while he fumbled with the key and opened the door, she scanned the parking lot. When he stepped aside, she shot past him into his sparsely furnished living room.

Garrett walked to the bar that separated the kitchen from the living room and put his hand on a stack of books. "These are the ones I want to lend you."

Abi opened the cover of the top book, revealing his name and phone number. Immediately, she shut it and began checking the rest in the same efficient way. Turning to face him, she said. "I can't take them."

Based on what she had said about her jealous husband, he understood. Vince would go bonkers if he saw them right now, only inches apart and staring into each other's eyes. Garrett's hands moved of their own volition toward her waist while he slowly leaned toward her.

Before he could press his lips to hers, she bolted toward the door. "I've got to go."

Garrett grabbed her arm. "Bird, just use the books while you're here."

Like a trapped animal, she glanced around the room. "I-I guess I can do that."

He motioned to the rickety card table next to the kitchen, and while she seated herself, he moved the books to sit in front of her. Abi made notes on Karl Jung, and he sat in the other folding chair, trying to act like he was reading one of the books, but actually taking advantage of watching her when she was not looking at him. As she worked, he marveled that she was actually there. Plus, he cursed himself for trying to kiss her. But, damn, she had an overpowering effect on him. He thought of her constantly, and when they were together it was all he could do to keep his hands off of her.

Garrett noted Loc's drawing covering his refrigerator. Most of them were labeled, "Mommy, Daddy, and Loc" below the stick figures. He had spent yesterday evening straightening with the anticipation of hopefully luring Abi over here. How had he forgotten something so obvious as the drawings on the refrigerator?

At one point, she raised her head and glanced toward the kitchen, but thankfully she quickly returned to the books.

When she flipped her notebook shut and pushed her chair back, he mentally scrambled for a way to keep her there. "Bird, would you like some water?"

"No." She cleared her throat. "I really need to go. Thanks for the use of your books."

"I wish you wouldn't leave." Standing between her and the door, he backed his way to it.

Her book bag on her shoulder, she approached him. Their gazes met. Again, unable to stop himself, he grabbed her arms, and gently pulled her to him. This time she did not resist, so he lightly pressed his lips to hers.

She wasn't responding, but she also was not pushing him away. When they separated, she stared at him without moving. Fueled by her lack of resistance, he solidly kissed her. Initially she squirmed, but then she relaxed. Desperate to read her face, he pulled away, and looked deeply into those hypnotic brown eyes that had initially captivated him. When he leaned toward her a third time, she seemed to come out of her trance and broke away. Reaching past him, she began frantically struggling with the locked door.

Hoping to calm her, Garrett covered her hand with his. "Don't you feel something for me as well?"

Focused on their overlapping hands, she stammered, "I-I-I d-d-don't know what I feel."

"Let's talk," he pleaded.

"I need to go." She pulled her hand away and stepped back.

Once he had unlocked the door and opened it, she raced past him.

"Bird, please don't go," he called after her.

Abi sprinted all the way to her car. Garrett watched from the doorway where she ignored his raised hand as she backed out and hastily drove away. His stupid, insatiable need to follow his instincts had backfired on him. As Moser had warned, he should have listened to that niggling voice.

*   *   *

All the way home, I cursed myself for being such an idiot. Why had I gone there? What did I hope to accomplish by going to a single man's apartment? How had I been so dumb, so absolutely stupid?

America was singing *A Horse with No Name* on the radio. The lyrics seemed to fit perfectly. It was raining in a land that was typically a desert, and there were all kinds of things going on under the surface of my friendship with Garrett. I had tried to believe that we were just friends, but when Garrett kissed me, I couldn't help but kiss him back. Like an idiot, I had gone to a man's apartment who I wasn't even supposed to be talking to—much less kissing. Not only was I not the best wife in the world, I had in record time become the worst one.

Once I got home, I flung my bag and purse on the bed and vowed to somehow regain my footing in this situation. From the refrigerator, I pulled out hamburger meat, potatoes, ketchup, and the under cooked beans—the ones Vince had complained about yesterday. I grabbed the grease can from the cupboard, and when I turned to put the heavy iron skillet on the stove, it hit the grease can, sending it flying across the room. Dropping to my hands and knees to clean it up, I thought how fair this all seemed. I had gotten myself into this mess; and I would pay, in more ways than this. Yes, I would pay.

After cleaning up the grease, I began slicing potatoes. Then I thought of the beans. I still had an hour before we ate, so I decided to put them in the pressure cooker. Grabbing them, I turned quickly, slipped on a grease spot, and lost my balance. The bean pot and I ended up in the floor. Scooping up the brown, jelled mass and plopping it back into the bowl, I muttered, "I mopped Saturday; he'll never know the difference." As I lit the fire under the beans, my words and their underlying meaning came back to me—what Vince didn't know wouldn't hurt him—or me. That kind of thinking had gotten me into this mess.

I returned to the potatoes and began frantically trying to make up for lost time. On the third stroke, my hand slipped and the knife cut deep into the side of my left thumb. Fearful of what I might see, I pressed a cup towel around the wound and began pacing a circle that included the kitchen and living room. All I could think of was Garrett's lips on mine. I had to stop thinking about him. I had to get him out of my mind.

Instead of calming my pounding heart, the walking seemed to agitate it. An answer. I had to find an answer, some way of keeping my sanity. My thumb throbbed, and I hesitated in the living room. The open Bible on the chest of drawers in the corner caught my eye. I pressed the towel tighter around my thumb and muttered, "God, tell me what to do. Tell me."

I leafed through the pages of the huge Bible. Unseen forces located Matthew 5:28 where I read: "But I say unto you, that whosoever looketh on a woman to lust after her hath committed adultery with her already in his heart. If your right eye causes you to sin, tear it out and throw it away; it is better for you to lose one of your members than for your whole body to be thrown into hell."

Remembering Garrett's lips on mine and the warmth that swept through me every time I thought of him, my eyes focused on the words again. A drop of blood fell from the saturated towel onto the printed page, marking the passage I had just read. I froze with horror. The blood on that exact spot spoke volumes about the guilt in my heart that grew enormously with every second that passed. Then I heard the back door opening.

*Don't tell him. Oh, God, don't tell him.* I raced to the kitchen for a wet dishrag to clean up the blood and had barely reached the sink when Vince stepped inside the house. Our eyes locked.

\* \* \*

"Abi-girl, what's the matter?" Vince lumbered toward Abi. He had never seen her look so scared.

Her gaze dropped to the sink where she held a towel saturated with blood. "I cut my thumb."

Vince peeled the cloth back to expose a bone-deep cut. "You got it good."

While he took off his coat, she remained at the sink, holding the wrist of the hand she had cut.

Pretty damned sure she was glad he had gotten home when he did, he ran cold water over her thumb and then studied it for a few seconds. "We can get Mama to sew it up for you."

"It's not that bad is it?" she asked, sounding like she'd rather do anything but let Mama sew it.

"It's pretty deep." He turned her hand at the wrist to get a different vantage point.

"Don't you think a bandage would be enough?" she urged.

"Okay, but it'll probably take longer to heal." He found the bandages in the cabinet about the stove and tore the wrapper off of one he thought would fit. "I can't understand why you're so accident-prone. Didn't we just pay a big hospital bill?"

She didn't respond. Vince figured she was thinking about whose fault it was that she was there.

While he applied the bandage, Vince mulled over Abi's hospital stay. Granted he had lost his cool, and in the process gotten in deep shit with Daddy. Plus, a couple of cops had sat him down and given him a talking to about what he could and couldn't do with his wife—like it was any of their business. He had been clear with Abi that he did not want her working, especially not something like cleaning someone else's house. She may as well have put an ad in the paper saying he wasn't a good provider.

"There. You're all done." He kissed her forehead, feeling more like her dad than her husband. Then he got a beer from the box and went into the living room. He heard Abi cooking and thought about helping her, but he also needed to let her know who was boss. Plus, she needed to see that doing stupid things like cutting her thumb was not going to get her any breaks from doing her part, which was cooking and taking care of him.

The news was halfway over when Abi walked into the living room and set a fresh beer on the end table between their chairs. Then she walked across the living room and shut the Bible.

"Why did you do that?" he asked, wondering what was making her act so damned weird.

"D-d-dust. It gets so dusty in here." She ran a finger along the edge of the coffee table.

"Next, you'll be putting it in the drawer. You don't like it 'cause Mama gave it to us." He shifted in his chair as he took a long drink from the fresh beer.

"I read the other day it's hard on a book to lay open like that. It breaks the stitches and weakens the glue." She edged toward the door, still looking like a cat in a room full of rockers.

The television caught his eye, and he saw her quietly slip into the kitchen. When Abi didn't call him for supper at the usual time, he went ahead and took a shower, giving her more time to get everything done. While they ate, Abi kept looking at Vince. He was glad to see her interested in him for a change, but he also wondered what was going on because she kept giving him that deer-in-the-headlights look.

"You sure are moony-eyed," Vince remarked during a commercial. When she stared at her plate instead of him, Vince shoveled beans into his mouth and grunted. "These are better. What did you do to them?"

"Cooked them, like you said." Unable to use her knife, she tried to cut her steak with her fork.

"Let me do that." He cut her meat into bite-size pieces, glad she needed him.

\* \* \*

That night, Garrett made his second run of the week to Houston. The weather cleared and the plane performed like a champ, which left his mind free to think about what an idiot he had been. If he had not kissed Abi, she would have been okay with the whole thing. Christ, he could see she was already nervous about being there. Why had he crossed that boundary? She had told him time and time again that she was married. And he was married, even if he had lied to her about that. He didn't feel guilty, except he did. If he was any kind of a man, he would tell Trang that he wanted a divorce, and he would tell Abi about Trang.

Then he thought of Loc, his sweet, sweet boy. He could not hurt him, nor could he put him through the torture of growing up without a dad. Sure, Garrett could see him as much as he wanted, but Loc would never live with him again if Trang and Garrett divorced. They did not have the ideal marriage, but she was a good mother, and Garrett would never try to separate her and Loc. They needed one another, just like Garrett needed Loc.

After he landed, Garrett called Vinh and asked for a ride. He showed up about the time Garrett finished his paperwork, a new record.

As Vinh drove toward West Houston, he said, "I start classes at church down street."

"Really, what kind of classes are they?" Garrett asked, more concerned about the back end of the Ford Mustang they were approaching too quickly than how Vinh answered.

"We learn plenty about English." He stopped inches short of hitting the car. "Read, write, speak."

Garrett closed his eyes and vowed not to open them until they got there. "So you're learning how to communicate better."

"Yes, com-mun-i-cate. We learn listen. We learn talk."

"Is Trang going with you?" Unable to keep his eyes shut, he looked out the side window.

"Nobody stay home with Loc."

Apparently, they had talked about it. She would never think of leaving their son home alone, and she probably didn't know her neighbors well enough to ask for their help. "Exactly when is your class?"

"Tuesday and Thursday. Day before the day before and today." He gave Garrett a snaggle-tooth grin.

Garrett liked his fresh approach to indicating the days. "What time does your class meet?" It was already after 10:00, and Vinh had been at his house when he called.

"Class start seven. Stop at nine."

If he left Oaces at 3:00, he could get to Houston in time to stay with Loc, so Trang could go with Vinh. He and Abi usually studied until 4:00, but he doubted she would have anything to do with him after today.

*       *       *

Friday after I got out of class, I drove to the Beauty Box. I didn't dare go to the library, and I didn't want to get home early again or Thelma would start thinking I should keep that schedule every day. Plus, being there reminded me of how miserably I had failed as a wife. All the way to Dahlia, I thought of Garrett and how wrong I had been to let things get out of hand, how guilty I was for sending him the silent message that it was okay to kiss me. I enjoyed it, but I shouldn't have. Oh, God, I knew I was playing with fire from the first day I met

Garrett, but I had pursued the friendship like an idiot, telling myself nothing was wrong with it.

At the Beauty Box Charlene laughed and kidded with her customers, including me in all her stories—like the time we killed a rattlesnake when I was twelve. "Now she's our sweet little school girl."

That made me feel even guiltier. Not only was I not innocent, I was downright sinful.

"How are your classes going? What kind of things are you learning?" Mama asked as she backcombed Freda Gainer's mop of silver-colored hair.

"My drawing class is fun, although I'm not crazy about the crazy stuff I see displayed in the gallery." I had tried to see it from a creative point of view, but piles of junk were piles of junk, whether someone spray-painted it red or not. I wasn't about to mention that Dr. Cole had suggested I could model for the life drawing class—not after Garrett told me that the models pose in the nude. That was right up there with having an affair—sort of like kissing a man in his apartment.

"Modern art, huh?" Charlene chomped on a mouthful of gum. "Those artist types can get really weird." She pointed to my bandaged thumb. "Say, what did you do to yourself?"

I explained that I had cut it while cooking supper. Then I changed the subject by telling them about Dr. Horton and how she gave the female perspective on history. I gave that day's lecture on Harriet Tubman, who led over three-hundred slaves to freedom using the Underground Railroad, as an example.

When I said some of my classmates complained before class about Dr. Horton focusing on women so much in her lectures, Charlene said it was about time women got some recognition. She sounded like Garrett.

While Charlene and Mama worked, I sat in one of the unoccupied drier seats and read my history text, trying to not think about Garrett, but that was like trying to not miss a best friend, which is what he was before he kissed me. What had I done to encourage him? Truthfully, it had felt nice—gentle and sweet. Stop! I had no business thinking like that. Those were the very ideas that had gotten me to that apartment and caused him to think it was what I wanted.

At home, I started supper and had it on the table right after the news ended, just like Vince liked it. During the commercials, I commented on the news stories I had overheard from the kitchen, but Vince wasn't interested in talking about the news, so I asked him about his day.

"Good. It's Friday." He watched Goldie Hawn on *Laugh In*—the program that had just come on.

That meant we would go to the bowling alley, which was the last thing I wanted to do, but I decided to throw myself into the occasion, so I dressed in the outfit that Vince had given me for Christmas. When I stepped into the living room and twirled in front of him, he beamed happily, got up, and slapped my bottom playfully.

A picture of Garrett seeing me like this flashed through my mind, and I cringed.

On the way to the pickup, Vince wrapped an arm around my shoulders. "This is my old Abi-girl."

At the bowling alley, I used my thumb and my outfit as reasons why I wasn't bowling. Instead, I chatted with the other women when it was not their turn. Occasionally, I glanced toward the far side of the room to look for Christi and Buck, feeling relieved that I did not see them.

"That's some get-up," Cheryl remarked.

"Vince gave it to me for Christmas," I answered while watching Vince approach the line and deliver a ball slightly off-center for an easy strike. "I wore it a couple of weeks ago when you weren't here."

"Yeah, we've been gone the last two weeks. I heard you guys really put on a show with that Buck guy." Her expression said she wanted to hear my version of what happened.

"It was just a misunderstanding."

She lit a cigarette and blew her smoke over her shoulder. "Alecia said Vince wanted to punch Buck's lights out for touching you."

"Yeah, something like that," I agreed.

Cheryl said Vince had a right to protect what was his, but Alesia said Vince was being a bully. As Vince's wife, I should defend him, but I secretly agreed with Alesia, so I didn't say anything.

When Cheryl got up to bowl, leaving Alesia and me sitting by ourselves, Alesia asked, "Don't you think Vince gets a little pushy at times?"

"That's just him." As much as she was right, I didn't want to say something that would come back to haunt me.

"You really think it's okay for big guys like him to throw their weight around?" she pressed.

"Like I said; that's just him." Every time I saw her since I had been in the hospital, her comments all sounded critical of Vince. Her sister works at the hospital, and she came by to see me while I was there. No doubt Candy had said something to Alesia. "Tell Candy I appreciate her visiting me when I was in the hospital."

Alesia smiled like she appreciated the fact that I was connecting the dots between now and December. No good could come of this, though, so I shifted my attention to Cheryl who was rejoining us.

When they finished bowling, Vince bought another round of drinks, and we went outside. After Vince got a fresh bottle from the truck, we all sat in Steve and Sandy's van. Vince claimed the back seat, so Alesia and Brent sat on the bench in the middle. Steve and Sandy were in the front.

Vince passed the bottle forward, saying, "Make sure there's some of this left when it gets back to me."

When Brent handed it to me, I started to pour whiskey in my cup, but Vince grabbed the bottle from me. "Hey, what do you think you're doing?" he asked.

"I just thought I'd try some." Vince still believed I was his sweet little Abi-girl, not a woman who would kiss another man. I could not stop thinking about Garrett or how sinful I had been.

Vince emptied the bottle into his glass. "You know better than that."

He guzzled his drink, and then he wrapped his arms around me and began grinding his lips and teeth into mine, filling my mouth with the taste of whiskey. The other two couples talked casually about their children and work while Vince moved his hands up and down my body. Determined to redeem myself, I tried to return his passion. Right away, he reached inside my low cut blouse and roughly massaged my breasts.

When his hand moved to my zipper, I put my hand over his and whispered, "Let's wait."

Vince continued kissing me. The car gradually grew quiet, except for the sounds Vince and I made in the backseat, which probably came across as full-fledged sex. Actually, I was trying to avoid aggravating Vince while stopping him from undressing me.

Finally, Steve said awkwardly, "Vince, you're steaming up the windows. We better call it a night."

Then Brent chimed in, "Yeah, Vince, it's getting late."

"We've got babysitters to relieve," Alesia added in a sing-song.

Vince didn't like being told what to do, especially by a woman who repulsed him. Plus, he was drunk, and she had reminded him that he did not have a son. While awkwardly sitting up, Vince snarled, "Brent, you're just jealous because you don't have a looker like my Abi-girl." I thought he was going to stop there, which was bad enough, but then he added, "You got that dog ugly woman to sleep –"

"Vince," I shouted, trying too late to stop him.

After a few seconds of painful silence, Alesia erupted with, "Did you hear that? Brent did you hear what that ass-hole said about me?" She was mad, and I could not blame her.

I wanted to assure her that Vince did not know what he had said since he was so trashed, but doing so would get me in trouble with Vince. He had often remarked about Alesia's face, but I never imagined him being drunk or stupid enough to say something when she could hear him.

When she repeated her outrage, Brent replied in a soothing tone, "He's soused." He opened the side door and held out his hand to Alesia who was still muttering about how pissed off she was.

We climbed into Vince's truck with Alesia glaring at us from their pickup that sat nearby. I could tell by her moving lips and the angry expression on her face that she was still talking about what an asshole Vince had been. I didn't blame her, but there was no way I could cram the words back in his mouth.

Vince roared out of the parking lot, turning the corner on two wheels. Then as he gunned the motor and raced down the street. A screaming siren and flashing lights immediately appeared behind us.

"Mother fucker," Vince muttered and slowed to a stop.

The policeman gave Vince a speeding ticket and told him he'd let him off with a verbal warning for intoxication if I drove home. We changed places, but I had never driven Vince's truck, so I fumbled awkwardly as I started it and headed for Quits.

After we walked into the house, Vince slammed the backdoor shut and immediately reached for another beer. He was ready to explode, and I was scared. I had gotten in his way before when he was angry.

After Vince came out of the bathroom, I went in and shut the door, stalling for time.

In a few minutes, Vince bellowed from the bedroom, "Get your ass out here."

I crept to the bed and whispered a lie, "I'm still flowing heavily, Vince."

"If you can't give me a son," he snarled, "you can at least help me out. Strip."

I pulled my long flannel gown over my head.

He held up his hand. "Stand there. I want to look."

I stood erect, as I had been instructed to do in the past. My body turned to goose flesh from the frigid night air while I focused on the gun mounted on the wall behind him. Vince's body reduced to a blur as his shallow even breathing and the sound of steady rhythmic movements told me he had started jerking off. I thought of Garrett, wondering if he ever did this when he was sexually frustrated. As a single man, surely he did. Then I wondered if he had ever jerked off while he thought of me. The thought had not fully formed when I scolded myself for having it. *As a Man Thinketh* came to mind. I had created this whole mess, by throwing myself at Garrett and then ignoring the warning that God gave me in the Bible. I was the guilty party.

"Look at me!" Vince shouted like he could read my mind.

If he knew what I had done and what I was still thinking about, he would make what he had done to me in December seem minor in comparison. While he beat me that time, Vince accused me of screwing Buck, the only other guy I ever dated. Then it was a crazy accusation, but now I truly was guilty of lusting after another man. I was a sinner—in my eyes, in God's eyes, and certainly in Vince's eyes—if he ever found out.

Sweat ran from Vince's red, angry face. When he finished, I ran to get a washcloth to clean up his juice. I let the water run until it was warm, but not long enough to further rile Vince. When I returned to the bedroom, he had fallen asleep.

For an hour or more I lay awake. Thoughts of Garrett and the words from the Bible burned in my heart. But regardless of the words, the yearning I had vowed to destroy grew stronger with each tick of the clock. Why couldn't I get Garrett out of my head? I was sinful for what I had done, and continuing to think about him only compounded my crime.

In the middle of the night, I woke from a deep sleep to find Vince mounting me. My fog lifted as Vince began franticly pumping. He moved faster and drove his poker into me with more force than he had ever used. I tried to push him away, but I could not budge him. "You're hurting me," I managed between gritted teeth.

He pumped still harder and faster.

A part of me hated him, but I also knew he was justified for anything he did. When I couldn't take it any longer, I cried out. He responded with even stronger and deeper thrusts. Then he growled like an animal before he climaxed and collapsed on top of me. Tears leaked from my eyes. I deserved what I had gotten. I had been unfaithful, and on some level, Vince knew it.

# Chapter Seven

*Nervous as a whore in church.*

**February 3, 1973, Saturday**

Garrett stood on one side of a deep chasm. On the opposite ridge, Abi, bent and frail, leaned toward him. He struggled with his footing on the soft, crumbling edge of the gorge that separated them. A thick sea of blood red ooze filled the void between them. She reached out to him, her mouth open, but silent. While he helplessly watched, her body slipped into the quagmire, her arms still reaching toward him as she sank deeper. He needed to help her, but he could not reach her.

Gasping for breath, Garrett bolted upright in bed, panting with the horrific scene still vividly etched in his mind. Guilt washed over him anew as he relived his inability to save Abi. His nightmare had been so realistic. He could not rid himself of the awful feeling that Abi was in grave danger, and he could do nothing to save her.

After untangling his sweaty legs from the wet, clinging sheet, Garrett plodded to the bathroom where he stood in the shower that shifted gradually from ice cold to steaming hot as he unsuccessfully tried to rid himself of the anguish that had ridden him throughout the night. He knew when he kissed Abi that he should not—for her sake as well as his own. Seeing her mortified expression as she drove away set the tone for the feelings that had saddled him since then. Her absence at the library the following day validated what he already knew in his heart. He had to let her go. It was unfair of him to ask her to do something she did not want to do.

Without a doubt, he was enamored with her looks and innocent, bubbly personality, yet what he found irresistible went beyond what he could see, hear, and touch to the essence of who she was. He had tried, but he could not convince himself that what he wanted and what she needed were two different things.

With a cup of tea and a bowl of cereal at his side, Garrett opened his statistics book, determined to read rather than obsess about Abi. The image of her face, the sound of her voice, the music of her laughter surfaced, blurring the words and once more taking over his thoughts.

*   *   *

In excruciating pain, I tried to move when Vince got up to answer the phone. Blood-stained sheets clung to my legs. Seeing the blood reminded me of the dream that had left me trembling and sweating. In my nightmare, I stood on one shore and Garrett stood across the way on another. A sea of thick, red, soupy goop separated us. I had a choice—I could stay on my side with Vince, or I could struggle across to Garrett. Right before I awoke from my nightmare, I was up to my chin in the thick liquid. In my heart, I had chosen Garrett; I had been unfaithful. I had dared to cross the chasm, and I was paying for it.

In the bathroom, I held onto the sink to keep from falling over while I wiped dried blood from the inside of my thighs and my buttocks. Knowing Vince expected breakfast, I fumbled through slipping on my robe and panties and putting a pad in place to absorb the blood that continued to flow. After making my way to the kitchen, I started frying bacon and making coffee. Feeling something wet on my leg, I looked down and saw a rivulet of blood. I had overflowed my pad, and I felt dizzy, like I might pass out. I turned the fire off beneath the skillet where bacon was sizzling and stumbled back to my blood-stained bed. This was my doings. My thoughts had created this mess—now I must lie in it.

Through the fog that surrounded me, I sensed Vince's presence, his mouth moving as he chewed the toast he held. He silently assessed the situation and then left.

I drifted back to sleep, clear I should get up and finish breakfast, but unable to do so. Vince would want to know who I thought I was lying in bed all day. The phone rang and rang before I found the strength to crawl out of bed and stagger to the wall phone in the kitchen. Glancing at the clock as I mumbled "Hello," I was shocked to see I had slept all morning.

"We're eating over here," Thelma announced.

Vince's plate from breakfast sat on the table. Guilt washed over me when I realized he had finish cooking for himself. "You don't have to feed Vince." Even as I said this, I realized I was useless at that point.

"Him and A.V. been fixing my car, so they're eating here." She sounded putout, as usual.

I had just started to hang up, when she said, "We're waiting grace on you."

"I'm not well. Go ahead without me." After several clumsy attempts, I finally got the phone back on the wall cradle. Once I had changed another blood-soaked pad, I started back to bed and saw my school bag lying on the floor. I blindly fished inside it until my hand rested on the small book that I now recognized by touch. Garrett's directions to read *As a Man Thinketh* every day came back to me. I should not obey him, but I felt powerless to do otherwise. Hadn't following his lead gotten me into this mess? Falling into bed, I began devouring the eloquent phrases, even though I knew Vince might walk in any minute. As my eyes traveled over the text, Garrett's gentle voice seemed to be reading to me, and thinking of him, I fell into a deep sleep.

\*   \*   \*

After lunch, Vince went back to helping Daddy fix Mama's car. He liked doing this, which was different than out in the oilfields. They had been on the same crew for nearly thirteen years. Daddy expected more from Vince than the other roughnecks, chewing his butt when he made a simple mistake, telling him he might have to find another job if he couldn't get his head together for this one.

The sun was getting low in the sky, and he still needed to take Abi to the grocery store. She hadn't looked like going anywhere this morning when he left the house. Having already jacked off before he went to sleep, and then dealing with the alcohol on top of that, he had busted his butt to make it a second time in one night.

Thinking he might need to wake her, Vince stomped across the kitchen floor and through the bedroom on the way to the bathroom where he washed the black motor crud from his hands. "We better get to town. It's getting late," he hollered over his shoulder.

When she didn't answer, he walked to the bedroom door and saw that she was sitting on the edge of the bed, not at all awake or ready to go anywhere. "I'm going alone," he announced.

"Okay," she whispered and fell back on the bed.

Vince drove to town and bought the usual groceries. When Abi was in the hospital and recuperating at home, Mama had fed him, so all he needed was a weekly run to the bootlegger in Flatland for beer. Early in their marriage, Abi shopped alone - until she started writing the check for more than the total, so she could get cash, which pissed the hell out of him. He'd give her what she needed.

At home, he carried the paper sacks in, making two trips instead of one since Abi wasn't there to help.

Finished, he stood in the bedroom door and looked at her still lying in bed.

She lifted her head. "Vince?"

"Who the hell were you expecting?" What a stupid question—unless she was thinking of someone else?

She started struggling to sit up, but clearly wasn't going anywhere.

Vince flipped on the bathroom light and took a piss. "I'm out of here. I'll find something to eat while I'm gone." He had seen her feel bad with her period, but she usually didn't stay in bed like this. Granted, he had gotten a little rough during the night, but he was still drunk, and she had it coming for being so damned frigid.

He drove over to the Chat and Chew in Flatland and saw Brent's pickup in the parking lot. Looking for anyone else to sit with, he circled the parking lot. He didn't recognize anyone else's vehicle, so he decided he was stuck with joining them. He hated to look at Alesia's messed up face, but he also hated for people to stare at him while he sat alone. He'd had enough of that when Abi was in the hospital.

When Vince sauntered up to their table, he said, "Hey, Brent, Alesia, fancy seeing you two here."

Alesia stared at the salt and pepper while Brent avoided looking at him as well. Vince wondered what had crawled up their asses', particularly Alesia's. If possible, she looked worse than usual.

Finally Brent muttered, "Hey." But he still wasn't looking at him.

Brent still thought of him as that creep from high school that dropped out to work for a living while the rest of the gang finished up and went off to college. Nearly every one of them, including Brent, had ended up back in Quits running the family business or working next to their dads—no better than Vince.

Vince scooted into the seat on the other side of their booth. He wasn't going to slink off and act like he was cool with being treated like some no-account. "Two nights out in a row? Hey, Brent, you got something going with the babysitter?" That one was for Alesia. Teach her to sit there and be so damned anti-social. She should feel lucky to have anyone even stop at their table considering how damned ugly she was.

Apparently his remark hit the spot because she shot Vince a go-to-hell look and then pointedly turned those steely eyes on her husband.

Brent gave her a half smile, except Alesia wasn't returning it. Then he glanced up at Vince. "Alesia's upset about what you said last night—about you thinking I'd be jealous because she doesn't look like Abi." Brent snuck a peek at his bitch like he was checking to see if he said it right, and then he added, "And the part about—what you said about her face. She—we'd like for you to apologize."

Vince weighed the situation. He had no idea what the hell he'd said, but from what Brent was saying, it had something to do with her ugly mug, which was probably too close to what Vince thought. Damn he had been drunk. He could tell them both to fuck themselves, which is what he wanted to do, or he could make a stab at smoothing the whole thing over, but hell would freeze over before he apologized.

"Well, I don't know, Brent. Are you jealous? I mean, I look at my wife, and I think everyone must be jealous of me." That was as close as he would ever come to back peddling on whatever he had said. From the looks of Alesia's scowl, she didn't appreciate what he had just said any more than what he said last night.

When Brent shrugged his shoulders and gave her a bitch-whooped expression, Alesia leveled her angry glare at Vince. "How can you say my husband would be jealous of you? We are both sorry for Abi—not jealous of anything about you." She slapped a menu on the table as if trying to draw attention. "We know why Abi ended up in the hospital. You beat her. That's what kind of man you are, picking on a woman half your size."

If Vince could have gotten away with it, he would have pulled that little cunt across the table, rearranged her face so that both sides were equally messed up, and then choked the living daylights out of her. Lucky for her, she said that crap out in public. Otherwise, he would have killed her. But he wasn't about to walk away with his tail between his legs. Instead, he stood up, looked down on the two of them, Alesia glaring back at him and Brent too lily-livered to look at Vince.

Then Vince announced loud enough for the whole goddamn room to hear, "Gee, Alesia, I'm sorry to hear that Brent gave you the clap by sleeping around with that tramp from Dahlia. What was her name— Christi? But, hey, a penicillin shot will fix that right up." Vince walked toward the exit, satisfied he had fixed their little red wagon.

Vince had his hand on the door when Alesia screamed, "Vince Martin, you are one sorry bastard. You better start treating me and every woman you come in contact with, including your poor wife, a whole lot better." She paused, and Vince figured she was through, but then she added, "You broke her arm and her ribs, and you left bruises on seventy-five percent of her body. The police have your number, asshole. They're just waiting for you to screw up again."

"Nobody tells me what to do, and you better shut that ugly trap before I shut it for you." He walked out, glad he had restrained himself from beating the crap out of her. The worst part about it was she was right. Doing something would only invite trouble. Vince flexed his fingers in and out. Just one solid punch at her ugly face.

He got in and started his truck, but hesitated where to go. The bowling alley was out. Based on what just happened, he didn't know if he would ever go there again. Not knowing anywhere else, he decided to get a burger at the Hi-D-Ho. If it was anything like it used to be, it would be crawling with high school kids—guys looking to get a little pussy and girls pretending they wanted to get laid, but at the end of the night hoping to go home with their cherry intact—still a good girl—just like Abi had been when he found her.

*   *   *

### February 4, 1973, Sunday

I wanted to stay in bed, but Vince would not tolerate a second day of laziness, so I struggled to the commode, where it burned like hell while I peed. After filling the tub with hot water, I slowly lowered myself into it. My bath water turned pink, a not too subtle reminder from God of the wrath I had brought upon myself by attempting to cross the chasm. I must have fallen asleep in the tub because Vince walked into the bathroom and announced that it was time to go. After climbing out, toweling off, and awkwardly dressing, I walked to the kitchen where dirty dishes sat on the table. In a daze, I considered cooking Vince's breakfast, but then I heard him honking outside. I needed to get my ass out there.

At church Brother Sims, whom I usually found easy to tune out, spoke directly to me when he announced the title of his sermon, "Being Faithful". Several times during the service, I felt Vince's eyes on me, like he knew about my betrayal. Even though I found it hard to stay awake, the sermon poured kerosene on the fire of guilt that was already burning inside me. Throughout the three alter calls, I fought to remain in my pew, rather than march to the front and throw myself at Brother Sims' feet, begging for forgiveness.

After church I hurried to Thelma's car, exhausted and anxious to escape Brother Sims' words that still echoed in my mind. When Thelma finally got in the car, I sped away without a word.

"What's wrong with you?" she asked, drilling her beady eyes into me.

"Nothing," I snapped, trying to focus my blurring vision.

Folding her arms over her chest, she swelled like a provoked horned toad. Her silence filled the car.

"I'm sorry," I said. "I haven't been feeling well. Yesterday I stayed in bed all day."

"Sounds like you..." she hesitated, "...you might be..."

I knew she wanted me to say I had morning sickness. "No, it's just my period," I offered lamely.

She harrumphed like she usually did when I said anything about my period, which meant she knew perfectly well whose fault it was that Vince did not have a son.

Years of practice helped me get through the routine tasks of Sunday dinner, but Bea arrived later than usual. While we waited, the distorted haze that surrounded me grew thicker. When Bea and her brood finally hurried in the door, we sat down, Papa Martin said grace, and everyone filled their plates.

We were busy eating when Bea asked, "Abi, do you feel okay?"

I looked at her too weak to answer.

"She's got a touch of the flu," Thelma volunteered.

My fork froze on the way to my mouth. The room swam around me, so I rested my hand on the table and lowered my head, hoping to avoid passing out.

"Abi's fainted," Bea shrieked.

"Get a wet rag," Papa Martin directed.

The haze that surrounded me grew thicker. An icy cloth bathed my face, and Vince picked me up and carried me like a child across the yard to our house.

"Look at this. She's still got breakfast dishes on the table," Thelma announced indignantly.

"My God, these sheets are covered with blood," Bea exclaimed as Vince lowered me to the bed.

With me lying on top of the sheets, Thelma began stripping the bed around me and scolding, "This won't do. This just won't do."

Trying to accommodate her, I rolled from side to side and shivered with my arms wrapped around my chest. Thelma grunted and tugged at the sheets while Bea helped her.

Bea said in a panicky voice, "Look how she's shaking. We need to take her to the hospital."

"Nonsense. She's just having her period. She told me on the way home from church." Thelma plodded to the bathroom, probably looking for fresh sheets in the linen closet.

Lying on my side, I studied the large circle of dried blood on the mattress pad. If it had gone through to the new mattress Vince bought several years ago, he would be pissed. Bea and Thelma worked together to remake the bed, rolling me from one side to the other as they needed to. I was so out of it, I didn't care.

"Mama, I don't know about this. Look at her shake," Bea said uneasily. She spread several blankets over me then sat on the bed and stroked my cheek. "She shouldn't lose this much blood. And she's so pale."

I was drifting in and out when Vince said, "She'll be all right." He sounded so sure. I wanted to believe him, but he did not know what I had done, how far I had strayed.

*   *   *

## February 5, 1973, Monday

When Garrett got out of class, he told himself to stay away from Abi, to avoid the library all together, but he could not keep himself from going there—simply to check. She was not in the third floor study carrel, or in their regular spot on the second floor. When he darted into the restroom on the first floor, he spotted her red, white and blue sweater. She sat in a remote corner with her back to him. He quietly took a seat at a nearby table. Over the next hour, he saw her gradually go from hunched over her books to finally lying her head on her arm that rested on the table and closing her eyes. She was either sick or sleep deprived.

When she roused and gathered her things, he slipped behind a bookshelf, waiting until she left, so he could follow her. He stayed far enough behind that anyone who saw them walking would not think they were together. As she slowly trudged along, he rushed ahead, making a wide arc and finding her car before she got there. It was not locked, so when she eased herself behind the steering wheel, he already sat in the passenger seat.

She stuck her key in the ignition and stared into space. "You need to get out," she said flatly.

"Look at me, Abi. Please, just look at me," he pleaded.

Tears rolled down her face. She gripped the steering wheel and sat up straight, her eyes closed, her face pale and bordering on ashen.

"Abi, look at me!" he shouted.

She shot him a hurried glance, her eyes alive with what might be fear or anger or a mixture of both. Her gaze softened before she bent her neck toward her chest. She held up her left hand and her wedding ring glistened in the sun. Given who she was, she could not cross that chasm.

"Abi, you're so washed out." He put his hand under her chin and gentle lifted her face toward him.

"I've been sick. I need to go home and rest," she whispered and closed her eyes.

Dear God, he'd been right. It had not been his imagination. Incapable of stopping himself, his fingers lightly traced her jaw-line. The softness of her skin and being close enough to smell her sent chills through him. "Are you sick because I kissed you?"

She brushed his hand away from her face. "Please leave me alone."

"Tell me one thing," he said gently.

She looked at him.

"Are you happy?" he demanded.

"What do you mean?" Her eyebrows crinkled with confusion.

"It's your responsibility." He lightly traced the tracks of her tears. "Your happiness, that is."

"I'm married. Don't you understand?" she pleaded.

He closed his eyes and nodded. Now would be the time to tell her that he was as well. He wanted to, but the words would not come out of his mouth. "You deserve happiness, and I don't think you have that," he said, as much to himself as to her.

When she didn't answer, he opened the door. "Abi, I care for you deeply. Don't ever forget that. I'm always available, to be your friend—just your friend—if that's what you want."

Walking away, he realized he had gone way past crossing boundaries. As a therapist he had to get a handle on himself. As a friend, he had to let her go. Being able to do that felt absolutely, irrevocably impossible.

\* \* \*

I sat for a long time, looking at nothing while Garrett's words, 'You deserve happiness, and I don't think you have that,' echoed through my mind. An hour later, I drove home without seeing the flat horizon or occasional farmhouse along the way. Instead I saw Garrett's small frame with his long hair coming out from beneath his leather hat. He wore his vest, and as he walked away the leather fringe flowed in the wind. The image of his hunched shoulders and his hands crammed into his jean pockets stayed with me. I waited to see him turn and wave to me again, but he didn't.

As I drove, Roberta Flack sang *The First Time Ever*, and when she got to the part about lying in bed together and feeling his heart close to mine, I switched off the radio. That was the kind of thing that had gotten me into this mess. At first, I convinced myself that Garrett was simply a friend, but then I started comparing Garrett to Vince. I had wondered more than once how Garrett would treat me in bed, whether he would be the gentle lover I had always wanted, but never experienced with Vince. I had imagined him holding me close and saying sweet things to me. Holy shit, who did I think I was? Some teenager looking for a boyfriend?

That evening I played the role of Vince's wife, but a part of me still sat in the parking lot at UP struggling with my feelings for Garrett and the challenge he had posed. Was I happy? I was going to college; I was living my dream, but I was far from being the perfect wife. Instead, I was consumed with thinking of Garrett, even though I knew it was wrong. When we went to bed, Vince stayed on his side, thank God. If he expected sex, I would not resist no matter how bad it hurt. I needed to redeem myself.

By Thursday, I felt stronger, and my classes helped me think about something besides Garrett. Dr. Posey gave us a writing assignment based on locus of control and learned helplessness, two topics she had explored in previous lectures. She reminded the class about experiments done with dogs in which they shocked the animal and rang a bell. The experimenters expected the dogs to jump the short petition and move to the "safe" side of the cage away from the shock, but surprisingly the animal had given up and did not try to escape the shock.

Our task was to explore whether individual will or environment was the stronger force? To illustrate she cited the proposed annihilation of the entire Jewish race during the Holocaust. In contrast, she gave Viktor Frankl as an example of someone who survived war and said it made him stronger. She asked us to relate what we had learned thus far about psychology. This was far more than I expected to tackle in a freshman psychology class, but it gave me something on which to concentrate.

As I walked out the door, I thought how James Allen and Garrett Clay would side with the power of the individual. When I looked up, I saw Garrett moving toward me, so I lowered my gaze and walked faster as we got closer. When he walked past without looking at me, I felt disappointed. I had asked him to leave me alone, so he was honoring my wishes, but that didn't erase my undeniable and desperate need to speak to him.

Without going to the library, I drove home and did several sketches for my drawing class, and then I studied my history and psychology notes. For comfort, I read from *As a Man Thinketh*. My eyes glided over the now familiar phrases, and I considered how I would argue my position for Dr. Posey's assignment. Garrett's notes in the margins haunted my thoughts with points I wanted to make. Then I fell asleep. When Vince dropped his lunch box in the sink, he woke me, so I slipped the forbidden book into my bag and got up to cook supper.

After we got in bed that night, Vince reached for me, and I pulled up my gown, waiting for him to proceed. He hesitated slightly before mounting me. It was the first time he had initiated sex since he did it so fiercely in the middle of the night. It took him only a minute to make it, but in that short time I almost fainted from the pain.

\*   \*   \*

### February 9, 1973, Friday

Garrett walked to the building where Abi had her first class. He knew where it was because Wednesday he waited in her usual parking lot until he saw her park, and then he tracked her as she walked to class. Today, as she exited the class, he fell in step next to her. At first she ignored him, but when she did look his direction, she briefly made eye contact. In that instance, he seized his opportunity and handed her the folded note he had labored over the past four days, the short message he had settled on after dozens of failed attempts.

Reluctantly, he veered away from her, and then slowly trailed her until she reached the art building where she took a seat on the brick planter box at the entrance. She pulled the note from her pocket and unfolded it. As he imagined her reading it, he said aloud what he had written, "Aristotle said a true friend is two bodies sharing one soul. Bird, I need to talk to my other half. G. C." He had added a P.S., his phone number and a plea for her to, "Call me—collect."

# Chapter Eight

*He wouldn't be happy if they
hung him with a new rope.*

## February 11, 1973, Sunday afternoon

*I* was finishing up making cookies for Vince's lunches when he walked
to the bedroom from the living room where he had been sleeping off
Thelma's Sunday dinner in his chair. Right after that, he ambled into the
kitchen carrying his gun.

"Let's get out of this fucking house," he announced. "We haven't
been out all weekend."

When he made no move to leave Friday night, I didn't say anything,
but since he brought it up, I asked, "Why didn't we go bowling? You
usually seem pretty set on doing that."

"I thought you hated to bowl." He walked out the back door, leaving
it ajar for me to close.

What I liked or did not like had never mattered to Vince. There had
to be more to this than what he was saying. We drove to an open pasture
west of Quits. Vince balanced a board between two fence posts then set
six beer cans on the platform. He took ten long strides toward the pickup
where I stood. Turning to face his makeshift shooting gallery, he raised
the gun to his shoulder and settled it into place.

With the first shot, I jumped and plugged my ears with my fingers.

He grinned. "Abi-girl, you're acting like a scared rabbit. Ain't you
ever been around a gun before?"

"I've shot my dad's twenty-two." I leaned against the wheel-well of the truck with my arms crossed and studied the rifle in his arms. The day Vince brought me home from the hospital, he stopped at the gun shop in Flatland and insisted that I help him pick out his Christmas present, the one I said I wanted to buy him with my cleaning money, the one I wrapped and put under the tree.

"Twenty-two," Vince scoffed. "That's a sissy's gun. Now this thirty-thirty has kick." Once more, he put the gun against his shoulder, took aim, and shot. All six cans remained.

Plugging my ears with every shot, I watched him miss three more times. He walked two long steps closer. His last bullet finally sent a can flying.

After reloading the gun, he thrust it at me. "Let's see if you can hit one."

Standing where Vince had stood initially, I drew the gun to my shoulder and squinted down the sight. My dad's voice speaking in a slow and methodical cadence surfaced from my memories, "Squint to use your good eye; make sure you got the hair dead-center; draw a slow breath; then squeeze." On that rare father/daughter outing, Daddy had congratulated me for hitting the target as often as he did. Compliments weren't common coming from him.

"Do you know how to line it up?" Vince asked doubtfully.

I took a breath and squeezed the trigger. The gun kicked, deeply bruising my shoulder. The blast still rang in my ears, but when I realized only four cans remained, I smiled and took aim again.

My next two bullets also found their mark. Before I could continue, Vince put his hand on the stock and pushed it down. "That's enough," he warned.

With my ears still ringing, I climbed in the pickup, delighted about beating Vince at his own game, happy to sit in the truck out of the cold and wind, and glad to be removed from the gun blasts. Vince shot a full box of shells, rarely hitting his target, and with each miss his comments grew louder and more profane. I hated that because more often than not he turned his anger on me.

While I studied the straight line of the horizon, I remembered Thelma confiding on the way home from church that several of Vince's teachers throughout the years had said he could not see what was written on the board. She had taken him against his will to get his eyes tested, but he refused to wear the glasses she bought. When A.V. insisted he do so, the glasses had mysteriously gotten broken in gym class.

With his poor vision, he probably never learned to read, or at least not enough to make sense of it. He wouldn't take the paper, saying he heard all he needed to know from the television. Whenever we had to deal with paperwork, he told me to take care of it. How had he passed the written test or the eye exam to drive? He had read the men's names in the front of my textbooks, or had he? Remembering that night, I heard Vince demanding that I read the names to him. He recognized the items we bought at the grocery store, but that was probably from seeing the commercials. He refused to buy something unless he had seen it advertised, saying it probably wasn't any good.

The western sky turned pink as we drove home. I wanted to tell Garrett about hitting all three cans I shot at, but I would never have the chance. I could not get him out of my mind. The Bible said I was sinful just because I thought of him, and James Allen agreed. How could I argue with either one? But still Garrett's image haunted me. Again, I fantasized drawing his portrait, thinking it might free me from his magnetic hold. Although, doing that was suicidal since Vince would kill me if he ever saw it.

\*   \*   \*

### February 12, 1973, Monday

A sharp, cold wind cut through Garrett as he carried two bags of groceries up the stairs to his apartment. Inside, he turned up the wall heater and put away the groceries, except for a can of chicken noodle soup, which he warmed in his one huge sauce pan. His mother's scolding voice from childhood reminded him to take his boots off in the house, which he reluctantly did, even though his feet were cold.

Abi was probably at the library, hiding in one of her back corners and diligently reading the notes she had taken in class. Garrett ate spoonful after spoonful of the hot soup. It hit the spot. He had woken up late and raced out the door without grabbing what little there was to eat. With his initial hunger gone, he opened his anthropology book, planning to leisurely finish the soup while he read.

Garrett felt a creepy sensation like someone was watching him, so he glanced around the empty living room. When the feeling would not go away, he got up and walked around the apartment. At the picture window that looked out on the parking lot, he peeked through the curtains. A black bug just like Abi's car sat next to his Charger. Careful to leave the drapes closed as much as possible, he studied the VW and began to make out the details of Abi sitting in the driver's seat. She repeatedly looked up at his apartment and then down.

He wanted to run downstairs and beg her to come inside, but that would scare her off. Not daring to move, Garrett watched her as she continued. Several times, she flipped the page of a large white book—her sketchbook. He had asked to see her drawings, but she had declined, saying she was embarrassed to show him.

He recalled Abi telling him Dr. Cole wanted her to model for the life drawing class. Smiling, he remembered Abi blushing ten shades of scarlet when he told her that the life drawing class models posed nude. Vince had reason to be jealous—and possessive. Abi was beautiful—inside and out.

Garrett grew stiff from standing perfectly still next to the bone chilling window and straining to watch her through the slit in the curtain, but he dared not move. He wanted to see her as long as he could even if it was from a distance. She must be cold sitting in her car with the wind whipping around it, but she kept working, every twenty minutes or so flipping the page and starting again. He would give anything to see what she was drawing.

When she checked her watch, he did too. It was time for her to drive home. She tore the pages out of her sketchpad, and then she climbed out of the car. He held his breath, praying she would come running up the stairs with her drawings. It would be so childlike and innocent, which fit her perfectly. Turning to his car, she tried the passenger door and then peering through the window at the driver's side, she apparently realized he had locked it too. When she spun back to her own car, he refrained from running outside to stop her.

Miraculously, she spun back around and tucked the drawings facedown under his car's windshield wiper. She got back in her car, backed up, and then started forward. When she stopped and looked up at his apartment, he could not stop himself; Garrett pushed back the drapes and waved at her. He could not see whether she had seen him or not, although she immediately drove away.

Abi was turning onto the street when he reached his car. He pulled the drawings from under the wipers. Shock washed over him as he stood in his sock feet on the ice-cold asphalt and examined the uncanny likenesses of himself. It was like looking in a mirror, but each one was different. She had captured him laughing, playing with his dog tags, and looking serious. She had even drawn him with his mouth open as if he was in mid-sentence—probably how she thought of him since he talked non-stop while they were together. In one picture, he wore his floppy hat and the leather vest Loc had given him for Christmas. Each one was from the chest up, and each one was incredible. He had no idea she was so talented. How had she recalled the minute details?

He walked back to his apartment and spent the next several hours examining the drawings. Why had she done this? Was this her attempt at opening the door between them? What should he do, reach out or wait for her to make the next move?

*   *   *

### February 13, 1973, Tuesday

Going to Garrett's apartment parking lot yesterday and drawing the images that kept lurking in my head had only made matters worse. While I debated whether or not I should actually be doing this, Garrett in various poses had surfaced in my sketchbook without me consciously drawing him. I longed to draw him again because it felt so satisfying, and it connected me to him, but I dared not for fear of Vince seeing the results, and I knew I wasn't strong enough to throw them away or burn them like I had the note he had given me—after I memorized his telephone number. What started out as a method of releasing him had solidified him into my thoughts. Plus, it surely sent him the wrong message. We could not continue the relationship, and it was unfair of me to dangle that carrot in front of him—or me.

*    *    *

### February 14, 1973, Wednesday

Vince shoveled fried eggs into his mouth while the morning talk show host yammered on about Valentine's Day. What Alesia said about him treating Abi nicer shot through his head. He still wanted to punch out Alesia's lights for badmouthing him, and Brent was a chicken shit for not stopping her. No telling what they said to the bowling group. Not one of them had bothered to call and ask why they had not shown up Friday night.

When the commercials started, Vince said to Abi, "I gotta go pay that speeding ticket." He scooped in another mouthful of eggs. "It's your fault, you know?"

Abi gave him one of her blank stares.

"I wouldn't have got it if I wasn't so pissed off with you." He swigged his coffee and sniffed. "Ever since that schooling thing started, you've been too busy to take Mama to the doctor or do the stuff you used to do like starch my jeans. You're not the sweet little girl I married."

"You're right, I'm not a *sweet little girl*," she shot back. She immediately looked like she had stepped in something and regretted it. Not a full month in school, and she was acting like some damned women's libber.

He pointed at her. "Just like that. I said one thing, and you tried to start a fight."

"I'm sorry. I'll try harder," she said dryly, and without much conviction.

"So who's your valentine?" Vince asked, getting up from the table.

It took Abi too long to answer, "Why—you are, of course."

Vince walked to the bedroom closet and pulled a box of candy from the top shelf. As usual, he got the biggest one he could find. The sales clerk had observed that she hoped whoever received this had sense enough to appreciate it. When he set it on the table in front of Abi, she glanced up at him and then back at the box.

"Thanks," she said, fingering the red, plastic rose on the front of the heart-shaped box.

"You don't act very happy," he observed. Usually, she at least kissed him.

She looked him squarely in the eye. "I wish I could buy you a valentine."

"Not this again. You don't need to mess with money. That's my department." He put on his cap.

She grabbed his lunch pail from the kitchen counter. "But I want to be like other women and have a little money to spend. That's not too much to ask."

Hell would freeze over first. He earned the money, and he intended to spend it the way he saw fit. "You don't need to worry about things like that." He jerked his lunch pail from her and started toward the back door. He turned back to her, intending to say he would take her out for supper tonight, when he saw her angry face. Cocking his head to the side, he demanded, "You got something else you want to say?"

With the half-wall and the kitchen sink between them, she shouted, "You treat me like a child."

He could not believe his ears. Daddy tooted the horn. Vince hesitated. With their eyes still locked, he charged in her direction, intent on straightening her out before he left. Abi stood there, defiantly staring up at him. He set the lunch pail on the bar, Daddy's warning about not hitting her again ran through his head. Somehow she knew what had been said, and she counted on that to protect her. Probably thinking she was safe, she smiled to herself as she turned back to the dirty dishes. Vince could not stop himself. He grabbed her arm and spun Abi around, flinging the plates in her hands onto the floor. To make sure he had her goddamned attention, he swept the remaining dishes off the counter, filling the floor with food scraps and broken glass.

Fueled by her insolence, he started to grab her face to hold it while he told her what for, but then she gave him a look that went from boldness to scorn, and without really meaning to, he reared back and slapped her with his open palm. She fell back in the mess.

Daddy tooted the horn again. Once more interfering in their business just like he did back in December. Vince respected his dad, but at times like this, he also hated him. Drawing his boot back, he aimed it at Abi who scrambled to her feet, sliding in the coffee and orange juice. Gripping the counter for support, Abi backed away from him while she stroked her cheek. Bright red blood trickled from her nose and mouth.

He had not meant to hit her that hard. He had not meant to hit her at all. It just happened - like before. It always just happens. But damn her, she started it by provoking him with all this talk about money. "You're learning to be a smart mouth at that school of yours. Now watch it." He turned on his heels and muttered every curse word he could think of at her and at his dad as he walked toward the door, shaking the house with every step.

*   *   *

I closed the back door that Vince had left open and waited until Papa Martin's car puttered down the street before I screamed, "I hate you," over and over again until my throat was too hoarse to speak. On the bar, sat Vince's lunch pail. He had forgotten it. I hoped he went hungry for lunch. In the bathroom, I spat into the bathroom sink then studied the blood-stained swirling pattern of my saliva. It reminded me of my blood stains on our sheets and on the Bible passage about faithfulness. How much did God expect from me?

In history class, I sat next to an older student, Lucille, who I often chatted with when we both got there before Dr. Horton started her lecture. Immediately, she asked me what was going on with my face. I explained that the puffiness was a reaction to a new medicine.

"Strange how it left a bruise the shape of someone's hand on your cheek?" She gave me a knowing look. "I used to be married, but I finally figured out the only cure was to get rid of him."

I smiled wistfully. "You got a divorce?"

"No, I tried to kill him." She sniffed. "But the sorry bastard wouldn't die." Her gaze locked with mine.

I wanted to ask her what she meant, but Dr. Horton walked in and started class. While part of me was taking notes on the lecture, another part of my brain was consumed with Lucille's courage.

After Dr. Horton left the room, I turned to Lucille and whispered, "How did you try to kill him?"

"Opened him up with a butcher knife, but then I chickened out and called an ambulance. Good thing about it was he finally got the message and left. I haven't heard from him in five years, but I never stop being afraid he's gonna show up again." She paused. "I should'a never called that ambulance."

As I walked across campus, I couldn't shake the image of Lucille gripping a butcher knife over a gutted man. It didn't take much to imagine Vince and me in the same scene with me holding the knife. I wondered if I would be strong enough to wait until I was sure he was dead before I called the ambulance. Then I thought about my deal with God. He had honored His part of the deal, but I sure wasn't upholding my end of the bargain, especially the last few days when my mind seemed to have developed a will of its own.

*   *   *

Standing beside Abi's bug, Garrett reread the heart shaped piece of paper in his hand.

"'The world is your kaleidoscope, and the varying combinations of colors which at every succeeding moment it presents to you are the exquisitely adjusted pictures of your ever moving thoughts.' Surely you recognize Allen's poetry. Forgive the childish valentine. I think of you always. Your friend, Garrett"

He had used the red construction paper background from a card Loc made for Garrett. Somehow it felt fitting to use part of that childish expression of love to convey how Garrett felt about Abi. Garrett folded the card, opened the door, and dropped it in Abi's seat, wishing he could wait to see how she reacted. As he walked to his car several rows over, he glanced over his shoulder, hoping and praying he might catch a glimpse of her. Sitting in his Charger, he checked his watch, determined to get to Houston in time for Trang to attend her English class. More often than not since he had promised to care for Loc, he had been late. Usually he was thinking about Abi and lost track of time.

He was about to crank the motor when he saw a woman wearing a red sweater walk across the parking lot toward Abi's car. She was about Abi's size and she walked with Abi's slightly bobbing gait. When she got into the black bug, he released his breath with a sigh.

*    *    *

Vince's lunch still sat on the bar where he had left it. On the kitchen table, lay the heart-shaped box he had given me that morning. Somehow, Garrett's handmade card fueled my growing anger about what happened that morning. Right before I dumped the candy into the trash along with the mess I had cleaned up from the floor, I had a better idea. In the past, Vince ate every piece of my valentine candy. This year was going to be different.

Determined to act before I lost my courage, I drove to the nursing home where I had volunteered in the past. After clearing it with the nurse, I passed out candy in all the common areas, and then I walked from room to room, delivering a smile with every piece of chocolate until they were gone.

While cooking supper, I sliced potatoes and noticed the scar left from when I cut myself after Garrett had kissed me. I thought how gentle and soft his touch had been. I thought about how much I admired Lucille's courage. After waiting as long as I dared, I used the gas stove to set fire to Garrett's valentine. Fully aware that I might be biting off more than I could chew, I set the empty heart-shaped box on the table next to Vince's plate.

When Vince got home, he did not mention the lunch box that still sat on the bar, which was his version of apologizing for slapping me. As soon as I said supper was ready, he sat down and eagerly ate the steak and potatoes I had cooked, and then filled his plate with seconds. During a commercial, he held his loaded fork ready to take another bite and asked, "What did you burn?"

"A napkin. I got it too close to the skillet." I smiled to myself, pleased that Garrett's valentine lingered.

When Vince finished eating, he shoved his plate to the center of the table. Then he reached for the candy box. "I see you took the plastic off of it. Does that mean you're sorry for acting like a baby this morning?"

Rather than answer, I waited for his reaction. As Vince pulled the box toward him, a quizzical expression crossed his face. He could tell by the weight there was nothing in it. After lifting the lid, he stirred the brown, ruffled papers. "Where's my chocolates? I know you didn't eat them all."

I met his gaze. "I gave them to my friends at the nursing home."

"Why the hell did you do that?" he demanded.

"I don't even like chocolate. I've never eaten any of the valentine candy you gave me in the past."

His eyes narrowed, and he threw the lid at the box. "Goddamn it, Abigale Martin. Those old coots can't even chew." He got a beer and leaned against the cabinet as he drank it. "You did that to get back at me."

I resumed eating, knowing there was no right response.

He drained his beer then got another one before leaving the room. I felt a rush of satisfaction as he walked away. While my actions could not compare with Lucille's, it was as far as I dared go.

*   *   *

Friday afternoon I worked on my paper for Dr. Posey—my fifth draft. When I finished writing this version, I re-read it, realizing it lacked the sincerity and conviction I knew Garrett might inspire. I wanted to call him, but Vince would see the long distance charge. Plus, any overture on my part would fling open a door I had left ajar by drawing Garrett's portrait while I sat outside his apartment. As I started supper, I returned again and again to my paper, reading bits of it in between coating the chicken and frying it, peeling, cutting up, and boiling the potatoes, and while I stirred the gravy. Just prior to Vince's arrival, I cleared the table of my school work.

When Vince walked in, he set his lunch pail in the sink and announced, "We're going out to eat?" The last time he sounded this happy was the last time we went bowling, which had been a couple of weeks ago.

I told him I had supper ready, and he said to stick it in the refrigerator. On the way to the bedroom, he slapped my bottom. He whistled as he stripped, showered, and dressed. During the drive to town, he turned the radio up to full volume while Elton John sang *Crocodile Rock*. It made my ears hurt, but at least I didn't have to talk to Vince. He drove to Tyler's, a small family-style restaurant. Inside, he led me to a back table where a couple in their fifties sat next to each other, filling the bench seat with their large bodies.

Vince extended his hand to the man. "Hey, Fred, hope we didn't keep you waiting."

"Naw, me and Alma been chewin' the fat." He nodded to the woman beside him who wore a faded Hawaiian muumuu style dress.

Vince pointed to the bench-seat across from Fred and Alma where maroon vinyl peeked out from beneath a crisscross of gray duct-tape. I gingerly scooted over it, wary of snagging my pants on a loose spring.

"What did you think of those boll weevils they brought out today?" Fred asked, referring to the young new-hires on the oil rig.

"One or two of them will last." Vince reached across me for a grease-stained menu. "We was greenhorns once." This kinder version of Vince surprised me. I wondered how different he was at work.

"Yeah, but you're just as good as any hand out there, even your dad," Fred elbowed Alma and pointed to the menus, and she handed him one. "When we did that work over last week, you were the one that knew what to do. You could have taken your dad's place at any time." Clearly, this guy knew how to butter up to Vince.

Vince smiled with satisfaction as he studied the menu.

Alma and Fred had large, round faces framed by folds of fat and oily hair. Although they looked enough alike to be brother and sister, they seemed to be worlds apart. Like Vince and me, neither one spoke or looked at the other. I pulled out the remaining menus and handed one to Alma. As the men continued discussing the oil field, Alma and I mutely looked over the limited choices.

A waitress wearing an abundance of make-up and a shortage of fabric approached our table. "Did y'all make up your minds yet?" She surveyed the room and steadily popped her gum, clearly in a hurry.

"I'd like a chef salad," I said, thinking this was a chance to eat fresh vegetables for a change.

Vince scowled but did not look up. "That ain't what you want, Abi-girl."

Returning to my menu, I considered holding out for salad, but we had the whole weekend ahead of us.

"You don't come to a restaurant and order rabbit food," Vince chided.

Fred laughed as if Vince had told a real knee-slapper.

I closed the yellowing, plastic folder and replaced it. "Just order for me then."

The waitress popped her gum and shifted her hips in her tight skirt. "So what'll it be?"

"Give us two chicken fries," Vince said with command as he handed his menu to me.

Taking Vince's lead, Fred ordered the same for him and Alma and handed her his menu. Fred pulled out a pack of cigarettes from his breast shirt pocket and offered it to Vince, who turned it down. Without offering me one, Fred lit one while Alma stared blankly. Then it occurred to me that Alma and I had not been introduced.

I extended my hand to her. "I don't think we've formally met. I'm Abi."

With a puzzled look, she took my hand, and then her face brightened. "Alma."

Determined to make her talk, I asked, "What do you do?"

She clawed at her short, oily hair. "You mean work?"

"Well, anything—work, hobbies." My head itched in sympathy, but I refused to scratch it.

Her face returned to her previous blank stare.

"How do you spend your days?" I prodded.

"I watch my soaps. Which ones do you watch?" she asked.

Not knowing the names of any of them, I said, "I don't really have a favorite. Tell me about yours."

While she gave me a detailed account of her top three, her volume and enthusiasm grew to the point that Fred gave her a disapproving scowl. Shortly after that, the food arrived and everyone began eating. Alma and Fred grunted sounds of approval back and forth between them as they ate.

Halfway through the greasy chicken fried steak, a rock formed in my stomach. I checked Vince's plate and saw he had nearly finished, so I slid my plate next to his. "Would you like the rest of mine?"

He nodded and continued eating.

I looked at the woman across the table from me. Alma's tired, spiritless eyes could be mine someday. Or did I already look like that? I thought of my paper for Dr. Posey's class and her lecture on learned helplessness. Alma was the human version of those dogs who had given up and no longer attempted to escape the ongoing electric shocks they had learned to consider normal. Mama was as well. And I was on my way. Then I thought of *As a Man Thinketh*. James Allen would tell me to choose my own thoughts if I wanted to be free. The idea of it sounded perfectly logical. The actual doing of it, of defying what I was raised to think and do was akin to sorting fly specks from pepper—damn near impossible.

*   *   *

## February 20, 1973, Tuesday

Before putting my paper on the top of the stack that had been passed forward, I said a prayer that it would be good enough. Over the weekend while Vince worked with his dad, I had re-written it and began typing it. It took all of my study time yesterday to finish typing the ten-page paper with Mama's typewriter.

When Dr. Posey's lecture ended, I approached her podium. "How soon will we get our papers back?"

She set our assignments on top of her books. "I'll try to get them back by Thursday. Is there something you need to tell me about yours?"

"No, I just wondered. This is my first semester, and I'm kind of nervous about how I'm doing."

"Mrs. Martin, you're the only one that made an A on last week's quiz. That's a strong indicator."

I smiled, pleased that she remembered my grade. "A friend has helped me study some this semester. You might know him, Garrett Clay?" I shouldn't tell anybody about our friendship, but I also needed to give him credit for teaching me how to study my notes and figure out ways to remember things.

Dr. Posey's face registered recognition. "You couldn't have chosen a better study partner."

"Thanks." I had not chosen him. He had chosen me.

"I'll grade yours first," she promised, turning to go.

Sitting at a library table, I snuck bites of my sandwich out of my lunch sack while I thought about showing Garrett my paper, which felt like a crazy idea given my determination to end our relationship. Then a memory popped into my head of him sitting in my car only a few days after we kissed and telling me he was willing to be only friends. Was that possible? If I approached him with the intent of accepting his offer of friendship, did I have the wherewithal to keep it limited to that? Where did God stand with all this? I had reneged on my original end of the bargain, but maybe this was a test to see if I could maintain a friendship and a marriage at the same time. I wanted to discuss the situation with someone, which again made me think of Garrett.

# Chapter Nine

*It's better to die on your feet
than live on your knees.*

**February 22, 1973, Thursday**

*I* sat with the rest of the psychology class waiting for Dr. Posey who
was uncharacteristically late.

"We'll give her five minutes," said a guy who was usually late himself.
"Then we're walking."

Right after that, Dr. Posey hurried in and launched into a lecture.
An hour later, she flipped her book shut, having made her final point.
I wanted to ask if she had graded my paper, but I was too chicken, so I
walked toward the door.

"Mrs. Martin," Dr. Posey said from the podium. "Do you have time
to meet with me?"

"Sure." I saw the other students glance at one another.

Dr. Posey and I walked to her tiny office crammed with books and
furniture. On the way to my art class, I had stopped by to say hi when
I cut through the social science building, but I had never been there for
an official meeting. She cleared a chair and motioned for me to sit. From
one of the piles on her desk, she extracted my paper and handed it to me.

Conscious of her watching me, I scanned the red, scrawled comments
in the margins, which noted other theories and texts. On the last page,
I read, "I see Garrett on every page. It's hard for me to objectively grade
this since I am suspicious that he wrote it for you. Convince me he did
not. M. Posey."

My stomach knotted. "I can show you my rough draft and my notes. I haven't spoken with Garrett in several weeks—actually not since you made this assignment." I paused. "I can explain the paper if you like."

She pressed her lips together and took a deep breath as she took the paper from me and silently read through it. "On page three you reference a source, *As a Man Thinketh*. Tell me about that."

"It's a book Garrett gave me that I believe is relevant to this topic."

She nodded encouragingly.

"James Allen, the author, says a person creates the world they live in by the thoughts they choose. Whatever we think and believe will eventually happen—good or bad."

She returned to the paper and flipped a few pages. "On page seven you reference a quote from that book. 'The thoughtless, the ignorant, and the indolent, seeing only the apparent effects of things and not the things themselves, talk of luck, of fortune, and chance.' Explain how that fits."

"People use things going on around them as an excuse for not doing or getting the things they want. They blame somebody else for their unhappiness rather than accept responsibility for creating their lives."

She raffled through her disheveled desk drawer, pulled out a pen, marked a red A on the paper, and then handed it back to me. "I thought it was yours, but I had to be sure."

I wanted to hug her, but I figured that wasn't proper, so instead I said, "I'm glad you believe me. I thought about what Garrett and I had talked about, but I wrote it—every word."

She gave me an assuring nod.

This seemed like the perfect opportunity to find someone to talk to about my mixed up feelings. "Could I ask you, about the counseling service?"

"Sure, what do you want to know?" She leaned toward me.

That's when my courage left me. What if Dr. Posey thought I was emotionally disturbed? "I have this friend, in one of my other classes, who said she'd like to speak to a counselor, but she didn't know where to go."

"Tell your friend the counseling office is on the second floor of this building." She gave me a knowing wink. "Tell her it's confidential, so she needn't worry about anyone knowing she's talking to a counselor."

I figured she saw through my 'friend' routine. After thanking Dr. Posey, I climbed the stairs to the second floor and found the counseling office. The receptionist asked me to fill out pages of questions about my family history, which took me at least thirty minutes to complete. Writing down personal stuff made me worry about Vince finding out I was talking to someone. He'd be madder than a wet hen, especially if he knew I told someone about what had happened that finally got me into college.

When I finally finished the paperwork, I turned it in. Then I sat in the waiting room and carefully read Dr. Posey's comments on my paper. She cited theorists and used terminology that seemed directed toward someone who knew a lot more about psychology than I did. I wanted to know what she meant, and I knew someone who could tell me. A part of me wanted more than anything to show it to Garrett, and another part of me knew that I was dancing with the devil if I did.

The receptionist came out to the waiting room and said it would be next week before I could see anyone—unless it was an emergency, and then she would see what she could do. I could tell by the way she said the emergency part that she hoped like hell I didn't think it fell into that category.

*   *   *

Garrett sat next to the small, dirty apartment pool at his complex. He studied the picture Loc had handed him as he left Houston on his last trip there. It was of their family. Garrett knew it was a child's plea to end the growing tension between his parents. Even though he had not labeled it with names, it clearly expressed his son's desire to remain together as all of them were holding hands. Garrett needed to get to the airport, but first he would enjoy some sunshine. If he left in the next thirty minutes, he could get to Houston in time for Trang to attend her English class. He glanced at his watch.

Like always, he had thought about waiting outside the social sciences building, so he could just happen to run into Abi. She would know their meeting wasn't happenstance. The one good thing that had come of Abi ending the relationship was that Garrett no longer felt tortured with the idea that he should tell Abi about Loc and Trang. If he had it to do all over again, he would tell Abi. He should have been honest from the beginning. Abi, Loc, and Trang deserved that much.

When he heard someone walk toward him, Garrett didn't look up in case it was Jeff, the maintenance man who had a bad habit of chewing Garrett's ear for an hour or more about absolutely nothing. He loved to kid Garrett about looking like a girl with a beard. While Garrett had initially gone along with him, the joke had gotten old. The approaching footsteps did not sound like a man's; they were lighter and each one more tentative than the previous one. A crazy idea popped into Garrett's head. What if it was Abi? He wanted that more than anything, but hoping it and then seeing it wasn't her would make him miserable, so he watched a faded beach ball roll with a gust of wind and fall into the brown water of the half-full pool.

Miraculously, a pair of black shoes identical to Abi's stood next to his chaise lounge chair. The jean-clad legs sat in a chair next to his. When he stared into her chocolate-brown eyes, his breath caught in his throat. It still amazed him the way her pupils and irises blended, creating a void that sucked him in. The set of her jaw and the crease between her eyes spoke of serious matters.

"I can't believe you're here," he whispered, scared of breaking the spell that had brought her to him.

She smiled her sweet innocent smile. "You don't have to whisper," she whispered back. "We're not in the library." She looked down at the papers that rested in her lap.

He didn't know what to say.

She glanced up at him as if to make sure he was still there. "Does your offer still stand?"

"Offer?" he repeated, intent on not screwing up again.

"To be friends. Do you think we can do that? I mean just be friends."

"If that's what you want, Abi, that's all we will be to one another." Even as he said this, he knew she would always be more to him than a friend. "Did you get my valentine?"

"Yes, thank you. It was sweet. And it helped a lot." Her voice shook.

"With what?" he asked, genuinely confused.

"To write my psychology paper." She held up the paper. "And to make up my mind."

"About what?"

"About you and about me."

"So what did you decide—about you and me?" Given another chance, he had committed to tell Abi about his family, and here she sat, only seconds after he had made that promise to himself.

Rather than respond, she watched Garrett, her brown eyes following his slightest movement.

"I meant what I wrote on the valentine, Bird. I think about you all the time." He paused, fully aware that he was not getting any closer to conveying the truth about Loc and Trang's existence. Still, if they were *only* friends, maybe she didn't need to know about them.

"It was very sweet, and it reminded me of how much I miss our friendship."

Garrett recalled watching her draw his portrait. Surely, that said something about what was going on in her head. If she missed him one percent as much as he had longed for her, she had been absolutely miserable.

She played with the papers in her lap. "I'm married, which is why I left before." She glanced up at him for only a moment. "I don't want to do something I can't live with, but…but I couldn't stop myself from coming here. I even went to the counseling center, thinking they would talk me out of it. Isn't what I'm doing right on the edge of …" Her eyes locked with his.

"The edge of what, Abi?" he prodded, wondering if she would say what they both likely were thinking.

She returned her gaze to her lap.

Unable to stop himself, Garrett lifted her chin. "I don't want you to do something you can't live with." Alluding to her marriage might open the door to him saying something about his.

"No one forced me to come here." She gestured with her paper. "That's what I said in my essay. People create their own existence."

"James Allen would be proud." He laughed, but when she looked hurt, he added, "You got it, Abi. You understand his message. I'm laughing because it takes most people, like me, a lifetime to figure that out."

She smiled and returned her gaze to the safety of the papers in her lap.

"I'm scared," he admitted. It seemed like a decent way of easing into the truth. "It's as though a giant magnet is pulling me toward you. I feel like I've found my other half, a part of me that I never knew existed." He needed to tell her. Now. This minute. "It's just that, well, I don't know how to say this except to..."

Abi looked at him with the same expectant and vulnerable expression Loc had used when he asked if Santa was really real.

"You are married, and I sure don't want you to do something that you couldn't live with...down the road I mean." God, he had screwed up. He knew making it all about her was a shitty thing to do. "Not that I'm implying you want to have sex." But that was exactly what he wanted, whether he said it out loud or not. Was she also dancing around the issue of intimacy, or did she really want a purely platonic relationship?

Disappointment and disillusionment filled her eyes, and she nodded acceptingly. "I understand. I'm putting you in a tough situation. I shouldn't have come here today."

"No, Abi, it's not you. It's just..." Working the dog tags at his neck, he told himself this was it; he had to be honest. If he was going to do it, now was the time. Now was the time.

"I guess I should go." Abi leaned forward as if to get up.

"You said you wanted to show me your paper. And I'd love to see it." Garrett purposely lay his book on top of Loc's picture, and took

Abi's paper from her. As he leafed through the essay impressed with the length of it, he scolded himself for covering up what could have been an avenue for bringing up Loc and Trang. Then he willed himself to focus on Abi's paper. Posey had given her an A, which meant it was good since she was known for being a tough grader. At the end, he read the note that questioned whether he had written it. Mariam obviously knew of his connection to Abi. Abi must have told her as much. He flipped to the first page, now curious to read it and determine why Mariam had doubted Abi's authorship.

"Who's the artist?" Abi slipped Loc's picture from beneath his book and smiled as she looked at Loc's drawing of a long-haired man and a boy and woman with black hair, all holding hands. If he had labeled them as he often did, there would be no way out of this. Abi's questioning gaze met his.

"That's my—my nephew did that for me." Even as the words left his mouth, Garrett regretted them. Desperate to shift his thoughts away from Loc and Trang, he jabbed at Mariam's note on the last page. "Does this bother you, what she wrote here?"

"No, I explained it. She seemed satisfied. She didn't put the grade on until after we talked."

"Posey's tough. You must have deserved it."

"I worked really hard on it," Abi agreed.

"You must have." Trying to act nonchalant, yet unnerved by her holding Loc's picture, Garrett took it from her, folded it, and stuck it inside his book, careful to lay it on the other side of him out of her sight. Realizing he was literally holding a means of getting her back here, Garrett said with forced casualness, "Would you mind leaving your paper here until tomorrow. I'd love to have a chance to really digest it."

She hesitated. "I guess so, if that means you want to be just friends."

There it was again—the terms of their truce. They were to be friends. Between the two of them, Abi had been the forthright and honest one, so she had a right to set the rules they operated under. She did, and yet he wondered how he could keep his hands off of her. He knew one way to guarantee their relationship stopped at friendship—tell her the truth, but he could not make the words come out of his mouth.

*   *   *

Garrett got to Houston two hours late. Savoring the moments with Abi, he had kept their conversation going until she finally said she absolutely had to leave. Yet, she had promised she would return the next day to get her paper. As he walked from the plane to the Trans-Texas office, he saw Vinh's rusted-out jalopy sitting where he always parked. Vinh must be pissed. Garrett strode into the office to fill out the post flight paperwork.

When he finally opened Vinh's passenger door, the little man turned on him. "Why you not come? Trang say you be here long time ago." Vinh pointed to his watch.

"I know, I know. I'm sorry." Garrett had spent the entire flight concocting one lame excuse after another. In the end, none of them felt worth offering to appease the little man.

"We miss class. She fix food for you." He looked at Garrett with those riveting, black eyes.

"I said I was sorry. I'll teach you the goddamn lessons myself. We'll go –" He stopped himself. Vinh was right. He had been a jerk, not just to him and Trang, but to Abi for continuing to lie by omission.

Neither one of them talked as they drove to the west side of Houston. When they got to the apartment that smelled of chicken and cabbage, Garrett was greeted by another wall of silence. Loc lay on the floor staring at a mindless sitcom and Trang sat at the kitchen table, focused on the workbook before her. Neither one of them acknowledged his presence.

"Hey, Loc, is this all I get from my best buddy?" Garrett crouched, so Loc could run into his arms.

Instead, Loc glanced his direction and then returned to his program. "You're late. We already ate."

"I got tied up." Garrett stood. His heart felt empty and heavy at the same time.

"That's what you always say." Loc kept staring at the TV.

When he walked into the kitchen, Trang got up and began filling a plate from the pot on the stove.

"If you want me to, I'll go over the lesson you and Vinh missed," he offered.

Without looking at him, Trang set the plate on the table, filled another one, set it on the table for Vinh, and then resumed her place at the table, hunched over her English workbook. After Garrett and Vinh ate, Garrett went through their lesson about when to put an s on the end of a verb.

Close to ten o'clock, Garrett got up from the kitchen table. "I'll put Loc in bed. It's past his bedtime."

He was still sprawled in the living room floor.

"Time for bed." Garrett bent to scoop him up.

Loc, smelling of sweat, stiffened his arm and shoved Garrett away. "I'm still watching."

"I said it's time to go to bed. You haven't even had a bath." When Loc didn't respond, Garrett turned off the TV. "Now!" he shouted, louder than necessary.

Looking like he might cry, Loc ducked his head and plodded into his bedroom. He slammed the door behind him. Vinh and Trang silently watched from the kitchen. Garrett plopped down in the recliner he once thought of as his chair, a place to study, to read to Loc, to nap on a Sunday afternoon. Now it sat in a place he no longer called home, and it somehow represented a family he would never again call his own. His son was slipping away from him. He wanted to reason that Trang's desire to move to Houston while he lived in Oaces was the problem, but he had to admit he was responsible. He had created this mess.

After giving Loc enough time to change for bed, Garrett knocked on his bedroom door. He did not answer, so Garrett opened the door and found Loc still wearing his jeans and t-shirt while playing with army men in the floor. Rather than resume the battle, Garrett picked up Loc and set him in bed.

"Hey, I can't sleep like this," Loc protested.

"Why not? I do it all the time." Garrett thumbed through Loc's books and found *Alexander and the Terrible, Horrible, No Good, Very Bad Day* by Judith Vorst, a book that Garrett had given Loc for Christmas. Garrett lay down next to Loc and read until his son fell asleep. It had been both a horrible, yet very good day.

# Chapter Ten

*It takes more to plow a field
than turning it over in your mind.*

**February 23, 1973, Friday**

*A*s soon as my knuckles hit Garrett's door, it flew open.

"I couldn't wait for you to get here." He stepped back for me to enter.

"Hello, to you too," I said, hurrying past him and dumping my books on the coffee table.

He laughed. "Sorry, Bird. Hi, how are you?"

"Frazzled," I admitted. "Dr. Horton is giving us a test on Monday, and I haven't even started studying." As I straightened and took a deep breath, I saw my drawings of him. They were thumb-tacked to the kitchen wall behind the table where I sat when I was writing illegible notes and trying to figure out how to leave gracefully. Yet, here I was back again. I walked to the drawings to get a closer look, amazed by their likeness to Garrett. It felt like someone else had drawn these. They were that good.

Garrett followed me. "I love having your artwork, Bird, but I'd rather have pictures of you."

Ignoring his comment, I turned to the kitchen/card table where my psychology paper lay next to the book Garrett had with him yesterday at the pool. Yesterday when he said his nephew had drawn the picture, I was hesitant to challenge him as I recalled him saying soon after we met he was an only child of two only children. Today I wondered if I had the

141

courage to do that. As I slipped the child's drawing out of the book, I vaguely recalled seeing a child's drawing on the refrigerator when I was here before. There were none there now. "Why don't you display your nephew's drawing?"

He took the drawing from me and laid it on the counter out of my sight. "Great idea. That would give the place a bit of ambiance." He used his hoity-toity voice, which I guessed was supposed to be his mother.

"That is your nephew's drawing?" I asked, unable to resist. When he stared back at me, I prodded, "You said right after we met that you are an only child."

"I—I am. That's actually my cousin's kid, but he calls me his uncle since his dad and I are so close." Garrett opened the refrigerator door.

I was thinking he must be referring to a distant relative as a cousin when Garrett held a can of beer in one hand and a half empty bottle of white wine in the other. "What's your pleasure?"

"Could I have some water?" I asked, amazed had Garrett offered me an alcoholic drink. Still, his actions suggested we had slipped back into a space of ease with one another. If Vince knew I was here, he would shoot me and ask questions later, although coming home with alcohol on my breath would be the same as putting a gun in my mouth and pulling the trigger.

The idea of Vince killing me made me think about his gun and the time we went out to shoot cans.

"I haven't told you what a good shot I am, have I?"

He looked up from the sink where he was filling glasses with water. "No you haven't."

"Vince and I went out shooting a while back, and I hit the target three times in a row." Somehow bringing my husband into the room made what I was doing more okay.

Garrett gave me a quizzical look. "What made you think of that?"

"Just the idea of what would happen if Vince found me here."

"What he doesn't know won't hurt him, right?" Garrett carried two glasses of water to the table. He nodded toward my essay on the table. "I made some notes on your paper. I hope you don't mind."

I sat down and read through Garrett's comments. Most of what he said agreed with what I had written. His final words struck me. "Now start living it, Bird. Take off and fly."

I picked up my water and tapped my glass to his. "Here's to living it."

"To living it," he repeated and once more clinked our glasses together.

When I started to drink, he held up his hand, motioned for me to stand up, and then threaded his glass through my uplifted arm before bringing it back to his mouth. With our arms intertwined, we smiled at one another and drank long and deep. This felt too intimate, too much like something couples do. We both laughed as we unlocked our arms. While it thrilled me to do something playful and silly, I also worried that I had inadvertently given Garrett the wrong message by clinking our glasses—and by being there. Had that afternoon when we kissed weeks ago destroyed the option of simply being friends?

Stepping back, I clumsily bumped the table. "Like I said earlier. I've got a major test coming up."

"Right, right," Garrett muttered, still staring at me like he was in a trance.

Just like in the library, we sat next to each other, but we weren't jammed up against one another, which should have felt less intimate, except the privacy of his home felt even more blatantly wrong. As Garrett drilled me about my notes, I stumbled over my responses—even if I knew the answers. When it was his turn to go over his notes, he told me in detail about his classes, and I realized it was his way of prolonging me being there.

Noticing the time, I said I had to leave, so he helped me pack up my books. As his hand brushed mine, I felt a surge of energy, but it wasn't static electricity. It was the same charge I felt the night I met Vince. He had sat next to me and casually held my hand at the high school basketball game. Looking back on that night, I remember feeling thrilled that a man wanted me. I had the same feelings for Garrett. He wanted me, and while he was gracious enough to say we could be simply friends, that was a cover up for his real feelings. And my feelings... I wanted to believe I could be Garrett's friend and at the same time keep my deal with God.

At the door, I turned to say good-bye and Garrett gave me that soulful look that he had worn all afternoon. He was saying things with his eyes that weren't coming out of his mouth. Smiling, he lifted his hands as if to embrace me. "How about a hug since I won't see you again until Monday?"

I had a hard time telling anyone no—especially a man—so saying it to Garrett was twice as hard. Knowing I shouldn't, I leaned forward and cocked my head to the side. He held me a little too long, and honestly, I loved feeling his warm body against mine.

When we separated, he kept his arms around me with his gaze intimately holding me. "Oh, Abi," he whispered, and tears filled his eyes. He shut them and hugged me again.

I pushed away from him and stepped back. "I'm sorry, Garrett. I shouldn't have come."

Forcing a laugh, he dried his tears with his sleeve. "Don't say that, you'll really get me bawling."

Not sure how to make him understand what was going on with me, I looked around Garrett's sparse apartment. "This may not make sense to you, but I made a deal with God that I would be the best wife in the world if He would let me go to school. Being here with you does not fit into fulfilling my end of the bargain."

Confusion crossed his face. "You're right, I don't understand. I'm no authority on God, but I can't imagine God wants you to be miserable."

"What makes you think I'm miserable?" I feared he had somehow found out about Vince's temper.

"I saw you in that pickup, sitting there looking so dejected. It was written all over your face. You were truly unhappy." Then he sighed deeply. "It's not my place to jump to conclusions. What I do know is that I treasure our time together. I was thrilled when you showed up here yesterday."

I grabbed the doorknob. "I can't come back." His description of how I felt when I was with Vince rang true. He wasn't even in the same vehicle, and he understood by seeing my face.

"Is it because I hugged you?" He sounded like a little boy who needed to understand why I was punishing him.

Knowing it would be our last time together, I savored the feeling of calm that swept over me while I looked into his aqua green eyes. "It's because I hugged you back. It's because I felt all tingly when our hands brushed while you were helping me with my books. It's because I kissed you back when I was here before. What we have is more than friendship, and I'm torturing both of us by trying to pretend it isn't. We can't be *just friends*. I was stupid to think we could."

I opened the door, stepped out, and then seeing Garrett on the verge of following me, I said, "Please don't. This is hard enough as it is." By then I was crying, and I knew if he tried to hug me again or even kiss me, I would not have the strength to say no.

*   *   *

"See you," Vince said to Daddy as he got out of the Ranchero.

Walking toward the house, he thought about how glad he was to have a weekend, but he was also pissed that it was Friday night, and he did not feel welcome at the bowling alley, which was Alesia's fault. She should have kept her trap shut. He had no use for her or Brent. She was god-awful ugly, and he was so pussy-whipped he barely knew how to wipe his own butt without checking with her first.

On his lunch break, Vince overheard one of the guys talking about going bowling in Flatland. He had said the gossip was that the Friday night league had ousted one couple and was recruiting another one. He and Abi were getting booted, but who was taking their place? Buck and Christi? That sounded like Alesia's doings.

In the kitchen, Vince dropped his lunch pail in the sink and waited for Abi to ask about his day, but she just set a beer on the cabinet, opened it, and went back to frying potatoes. He wondered what was going on in that pretty little head of hers. She obviously wasn't thinking of him.

After supper Vince toyed with the idea of heading on over to Flatland and showing up at the bowling alley just to see what the old gang would do. No one had ever called, and it had been a month. Brent and the other chicken shits had avoided him at church. Vince took his gun down from the rack and walked around the house. It didn't take much for him to imagine emptying it into ole Buckie-boy, Christi, Alesia, and Brent as well. They all deserved it for making his life miserable. Some kind of friends those losers had turned out to be. While watching TV, Vince cleaned his gun. He didn't want to use it, but if he had to, he would.

\* \* \*

### February 24, 1973, Saturday

Right after breakfast, Vince went next door to help Papa Martin with a broken water pipe, so I pulled out my design book and began thumbing through it looking for ideas for my midterm design project—a better mouse trap. I didn't have a clue what to do. Plus, I needed to study for my history test, but all I could think about was my last conversation with Garrett.

Without meaning to, I had admitted to him and to myself that I was crazy about him. Whether or not I saw Garrett again, I could not change how I felt about him. Repeatedly, I toyed with how to rewrite my contract with God, toying with every possibility, except me quitting school. I was married, and I owed it to Vince and to God to be faithful. Nothing and nobody was going to change that. Besides, Garrett was moving to Houston at the end of the semester, although I could not imagine my life without him.

What had I ever seen in Vince? I married him because he said we would. At the time, it felt right, so I went along with the idea. I never once asked myself whether this was what I really wanted. Until I met Garrett, I didn't know what falling in love felt like. But what if Garrett proposed to me? I laughed out loud with the realization that I was jumping back and forth between wanting to honor my deal with God and hoping Garrett wanted to marry me and get me out of this mess.

\*   \*   \*

Sunday afternoon, I asked Vince if he wanted to go to Dahlia, which was my way of asking permission to go see Mama since I knew he wouldn't go with me, but he probably wouldn't stop me from going alone.

"Why don't we just stay here and watch TV, Abi-girl," he said, not taking his eyes off the television.

"They'd like to see both of us," I said, worried he would insist on me staying home.

He pulled me into his lap. "We'll think of something to do." He began playing with my breasts.

"I started my period this morning." I knew he wouldn't want to deal with that.

"Goddamn it," he muttered, his hold on me slackening as he stared at the television.

All the way to Dahlia, I thought about my parting words to Garrett. I had vowed I would never go back there. It felt like the only logical thing to do, but at the same time, I could not imagine never seeing or talking to him again. I kept remembering Garrett saying he doubted God wanted me to stay in an unhappy situation, which almost felt to me like he wanted to offer me an option.

When I let myself in my parent's front door, I saw Daddy asleep on the couch. Trying not to wake him, I walked quietly through the house and found Mama in her sewing room, my old bedroom. She was sitting in the middle of the floor, sorting through a box of fabric scraps. I joined her, and we dug through remnants left over from sewing mostly for me while I was growing up. Every piece of material had a story to tell.

"Do you remember us making this prom dress?" Mama smiled wistfully as she handed me a picture torn from a *Sixteen* magazine.

My mind returned to the night of my senior prom and waiting for Vince to show up, which he never did. "Too bad I never got to wear it in public." I handed the picture back to her.

While she stared at the picture, her expression shifted from puzzlement to remorse. Then she tossed it into the trash. "You could have gone by yourself, or Daddy would have taken you."

"What I should have done is call off the marriage." It was something I had never given myself permission to think, much less say.

She looked stunned. "You don't think he was out with someone else, do you?"

"I don't know what he was doing. He said he was working, but in the eleven years I've been married to him, he and his dad have never gotten home after 5:30. Besides, it doesn't matter what he was doing. He didn't call and tell me he wasn't coming, and he never apologized."

She took a deep breath and let it out. "Well, every man has his faults."

We both went back to sorting through the fabric. All of my life she had made excuses for my father/her husband, and now she was including mine. The last time I said anything negative to her about Vince was a month into my marriage when I asked if I could move home. At that time, Mama and then Daddy told me that marriage was for keeps, and I had made my bed, so now I needed to lie in it.

My parent's marriage had been far from perfect. I blamed Daddy for Mama's miscarriages, and I was certain he had been unfaithful to her. Once in high school, I was in a restroom stall when a group of girls started talking about who was cheating on who and one of them said that Harold Barker *as usual* was dipping his wick where it did not belong. Plus, I had overheard Charlene scold Mama about putting up with Daddy's shenanigans. Then it hit me—I had not slept with Garrett, but I had lusted after him in my heart, which according to the Bible was just as bad. And just like Mama, I had stayed with a man I did not love. Without even realizing it, I had managed to copy both of them.

Someone knocked on the front door, so I ran to get it, hoping to keep from disturbing Daddy. Too late—he was sitting up and rubbing his eyes as I hurried past him. When I opened the door, there was Christi.

"Hey," I said.

"You want to go get something to drink?" she asked like nothing had happened between us.

"Yeah, let me go tell Mama." Leaving Christi on the porch, I hurried back to Mama. "How did Christi know I would be here?" I hissed in a loud whisper.

"She was in the shop yesterday, and I told her you'd probably come over today." She looked up from her box of material scraps. "Talk to her. She said she really misses you."

I walked back to the living room. "Hey, Daddy. Sorry we woke you."

He had gotten up and was grabbing his Stetson from the rack. "I need to go see a man about a horse anyway." It was his standard goodbye before he aimlessly drove his pickup down one turn-road after another, this time of year looking at where crops would eventually grow.

Outside, I saw that Christi had gotten into her Mustang, so I got in with her. Christi and I had been best friends for twenty years, but I had not spoken to her since the day Vince dragged me away by the arm he eventually broke. Now we felt like strangers. "How are Buck and the kids?"

"Fine," she answered curtly as she backed out of the drive. "I won't ask about Vince." She paused and met my gaze. "I know how he is—still as much of an ass-hole as ever."

At one time, I would have laughed at her comment; now it felt like criticism for marrying Vince. "I'm sorry about what happened with the housecleaning business. And I'm sorry about the thing at the bowling alley with Buck. I hate that I've—well, I'm just sorry."

"That's who you are just sorry little Abi," she said, obviously pissed off. She parked at the volunteer fire station, got out, and fed change into the drink machine by the front door. When she returned, she handed me a Dr. Pepper, my drink of choice, although I never drank them any more because Vince did not buy them.

We stayed parked under the shade of the elm tree.

Christi opened her Coke. "Remember what Vince said he'd do when he caught us working together?"

I nodded. As he dragged me away, he threatened to kill both of us if he ever saw us talking to one another again. Yet, here we were, although not doing a lot of conversing.

"Are you willing to throw away a twenty-year friendship because your chicken shit husband thinks he owns you?" she demanded.

"No, but I also know I have to live with Vince," I shot back.

"Really? You're stuck with someone who would treat you the way he has?" I felt her glaring at me.

"He loves me, and he's—he's protective," I reasoned while working at a hole in the knee of my jeans.

"Breaking your arm and leaving deep bruises over most of your body is *protective?*" she challenged.

No longer able to avoid her, I searched her face for how she knew what Vince had done that landed me in the hospital.

"Alesia told me. She's told everyone who will listen to her, certainly everyone at the bowling alley. Her sister works at the hospital, so she knows what she's talking about. Besides, she hates Vince. You've seen the way he treats her. Not everyone is willing to make excuses for Vince the way you do."

Her accusations brought me back to my conversation with Mama when I was thinking the same thing about her. Plus, now I understood what was going on with the bowling league.

"No one has the right to treat you like that," she insisted.

I bent the tab from my drink can back and forth, toying with the idea of telling her about Garrett. Christi had known every secret of my life since the day we became best friends in elementary school. I wanted to share this one with her as well, but telling Christi about Garrett was suicidal. Somehow it would get back to Vince, or out of her need to save me from myself, she would threaten to tell Vince if I didn't leave him. Either way, I lost. She couldn't know. Then I thought of the one thing I could tell her since she knew about my injuries.

"When I was in the hospital, I overheard Vince and his dad talking just outside my door. I was pretty dopey from the pain shots, so I'm not clear about everything, but I do remember Papa Martin asking Vince about me going to school. Apparently something had been said to Mama about it, and she had said she would pay for it. I was sure Vince would say no, so I made this deal with God—if Vince said yes, then I'd be the best wife in the world. So when Vince said I could go, I decided God was telling me we had an agreement."

Christi looked at me long and hard with an expression of bewilderment mixed with understanding. "I wondered how you pulled that off - going to school and all. I knew Vince wouldn't just let you go out of the kindness of his heart."

I sat there thinking about how long it would take me to get through school. If I hunkered down and managed to make it through this semester, then I could do the same thing in the fall and eventually finish.

Apparently while I was lost in thought, Christi was festering because she exploded with, "That is the most ridiculous thing I've ever heard. What kind of God do you believe in?"

I was surprised by her outburst, but even more than that, I didn't know how to answer her question. We had gone to Sunday school together and believed in the same God she did, or, at least, I thought we agreed on that.

"What if God wants you to go to school, and She also wants you to learn how to take care of yourself and get strong enough to walk away from your loveless marriage?" Christi grilled.

"I can't believe you just referred to God as a woman." It felt blasphemous to say such a thing, but more than that, exactly what Dr. Horton would have said if she'd been there.

"That's right, I think God is a female." Christi put her finger on the center of my chest. "Abi, She's right here. She's not out in the sky somewhere. She's the one that made you want to have a job and go to school and do something with your life besides serve as Vince's punching bag."

"You think so?" My eyes misted up, thinking there could be a force within me that wanted the best for me. Then I came back to reality. "But I can't leave Vince. There's no way I can support myself."

"You don't know that. You've never been on your own," she argued. "It sure as hell would beat what you're living with now."

She was right, but I felt powerless to change anything. Plus, talking to her like this was only fueling a fire I could not allow to burn. "I better get back. Mama and I have some things to do before I go home."

She released an exasperated sigh and started her car. We sat in silence all the way back to Mama's house. As soon as she stopped in the drive, I opened the door and got out.

"Thanks for the Dr. Pepper," I said, and started to shut the door.

"Ab," she said softly.

I met her gaze.

"I love you, Abi. You'll always be my best friend."

"I love you, too." I shut the door and walked to the house, not daring to look back and show her my tears.

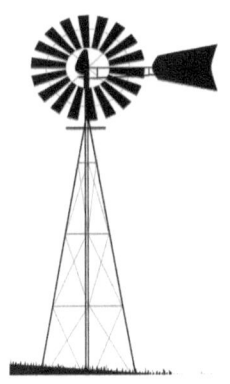

# Chapter Eleven

*Don't hang your wash
on someone else's line.*

**February 26, 1973, Monday**

*L*eafless elm trees swayed overhead as Garrett sat on his faded
bedspread—the only thing between him and the dead grass and
rock-hard ground. He was in the only city park he could find within
a few blocks of UP. While he watched the street and listened for Abi's
VW bug, he prayed she would show up in response to the note and map
he left in her car. Given her mood the last time he had seen her, this
neutral setting felt like a possible alternative. When he saw her black
Beetle round the corner, his heart began pounding. He stood up and
began waving his arms overhead. She parked and slowly got out, her
predictable reluctance obvious.

Before she reached him, he sat down, keeping his hands to himself.
He wanted to touch her, but he had already made enough screw ups in
that department. When she approached him, he patted the floral cloth
next to him. "Would you like to share my blanket?" As soon as the words
were out, he realized the innuendos.

"Sure." She lowered herself to hands and knees and then onto her
seat a few feet away from him.

"Thanks for coming. I wasn't sure you would." He felt incredibly
awkward.

Quiet as usual, she ran her hand over the loose threads of the quilted spread.

He reached inside his cooler and pulled out two Cokes. "Would you like something to drink?"

"Sure," she answered again, taking one from him.

He lay on his back, rested his drink on his chest, and closing his eyes, debated with himself how to ease into talking about their last conversation. "How was your weekend?"

"Not so good. I needed to study for my history test, but I couldn't focus. I have no idea how I did."

He opened one eye against the sunshine that peeked through the limbs and fell on his face. "I'm guessing you did fine without studying. You take good notes, and you remember what you've written down."

"I kept thinking about what I said to you Friday at your apartment." She opened her Coke.

Glad she had brought up their last conversation, he said, "I liked what you said. It made me think you might come here today, that maybe I had not totally messed up by letting you know I care for you."

"I care for you too, or I wouldn't be here." She took a drink. "But I am married, and I do have this deal with God that I told you about."

"Yeah, about that, I've been thinking about that too. Do you believe God wants you to be unhappy?" It was a question that came up every time he thought about her ludicrous proposition with the Almighty.

"That's funny you asked me that because yesterday a friend asked me the same question."

"I wish I knew your friend. I'd conspire with her on how to talk some sense into your head."

Abi drank her Coke.

Needing to look her in the eye before he said what he had thought about all weekend, he sat up. "Bird, do you love Vince? Because if you do, we should agree to never see each other again, but if you don't.... Well, if you're willing, I'd like to have more than a friendship." She might get up and walk away, which put him back where he started. But if he hadn't said it, they were finished. He had to at least try.

When she didn't answer, he tried to lighten the mood by giving her a hopeful grin.

She reluctantly smiled back at him and began pulling dead grass through a hole in the bedspread. "When you say more than friendship, you mean you want to have sex, right?" She gave him her sideways questioning look she used when she needed clarification while they were studying.

"I prefer to call it 'making love,' but, yes, I'd very much like to have a physically intimate relationship."

"I can't believe we are sitting her talking about this." She shook her head.

"And I can't believe that you've turned your life over to some mythical power in the sky," he chided.

"That's another area where you and Christi seem to agree. She says God is inside me, not out there somewhere." She looked toward the sky as if she might see some evidence that he and Christi were wrong. Abruptly, she turned to Garrett with her wide-eyed childlike expression. "And she thinks God is female. Well, I guess she thinks that God is whatever sex we are because She or He is inside of us. It seems pretty crazy to me, but it's also kind of nice—like there's someone or something inside me giving me directions or ideas. I'd never thought about God that way before Christi said that. What do you think?"

"I don't know. I hadn't thought about God that way either, but it makes sense. I sure like her version of God better than the judgmental God that I grew up hearing about," Garrett admitted, curious how they had gotten so far away from what he had set out to talk about.

"Me too. It seems odd to think of God as a friend rather than some old man who is eager to punish me when I don't make the *right* choice." Her eyes moved slowly over Garrett's face. "You asked me if I love Vince; I don't know. But I do know that I love you. That much I am sure of."

Garrett wanted to respond that he loved her as well, but how could he do that before he told her about Loc and Trang. That was the other part of the script that he had rehearsed, praying that a perfect opportunity would avail itself. Was this it? Returning her expectant gaze, he whispered, "Oh, Abi, I can't believe you said that." Unable to stop himself, he folded her into his arms.

As they held one another, he felt her heart beat against his own. He buried his face in her hair and wished to stay there in that embrace. Little by little he let go of her.

They sat for several minutes with neither of them speaking. She sipped her Coke, and when she emptied it, he offered her another one. She shook her head, so he lay on his back again.

"Where do we go from here?" she asked.

He smiled, thinking there was an obvious answer for him. "Let's get a few things straight, okay?"

"Such as?" she asked, raising one eyebrow.

"Promise me something," he urged.

Laughing, she shook her head. "I haven't even told you I'll make love to you, and you're already adding conditions. What do you want me to promise?"

"That you will do what is good for you—not what you think Vince or I want you to do. Do what makes your heart sing. Remember your paper? 'Start living it.'"

"I'll try, but I'm not so sure I can do that." She gave him a tentative smile.

When Abi smoothed her hair back, Garrett remembered his desire to take her picture. He reached behind the cooler and pulled out his camera. "I want some pictures of you, so I can look at you all the time."

"I'm not really photogenic." She skeptically watched him play with the settings on the camera.

"We'll see." He cocked the camera and began focusing it. "Talk to me. I want some natural shots."

"Get me started." Abi stared at the lens like it was the barrel of a gun.

"Tell me about something you did this weekend," he suggested.

"I went over to see my parents. My mom was sorting stuff in the sewing room. She keeps all —"

He pressed the shutter, and she stopped talking. "Go ahead, Bird."

She looked up at the tree limbs swaying in the breeze. When he shot another picture, she flinched.

"My mom keeps fabric scraps and every so often goes through them, but she never throws any away."

"Did you see your dad?" Garrett asked, pressing the shutter again.

"Yeah, I saw him." A heaviness moved over her face.

"What did you talk about?" He wondered about her mood shift, but he was too eager to photograph her to ask questions that required him to stop shooting and really listen.

"I think you have enough pictures," she said, raising her hand to block the lens.

"Just a few more." Garrett wanted at least one of her smiling. "Tell me the story about how they named that little town of yours."

She told the story and as she began relaxing, she did smile—beautifully.

When she said she needed to go, he walked Abi to her car. After he opened the door for her, she stood looking at him. Their eyes were on the same level, which was something he had immediately liked about her.

"You never really gave me an answer, Bird, about whether you'd like to be more than friends." Again, he knew he was stepping into a landmine of emotions, but he also sensed willingness on her part.

She placed her hands on either side of his face and drew his lips to hers, kissing him slowly and with clear intent. When they parted, she looked into his eyes. "I'll see you tomorrow at your place." Then she got into her car, started it, and as she drove away, she looked at him in her rearview mirror and waved.

Waving back, he said, "I'll take that as a definite yes."

\*   \*   \*

During the commercial, I returned my gaze to my plate, fearful that what I was thinking would show on my face. Everything Vince did irritated me—like breathing heavily through his nose while he ate and constantly watching the TV rather than looking at me, even when he said something to me like, "Pass the bread." As much as I tried, I could not recall why I had married him, except that I feared no one else would want me. When I thought of Garrett and how much I wanted to spend the rest of my life with him, I reminded myself that he had never even said he loved me—much less that he wanted to marry me. How could he? I was married to the man who was staring at an idiot box while he mechanically chewed fried potatoes. Then another thought struck me. Garrett did not have a television—at least not in his living room. This concept felt like a telling revelation. It said more about their differences than I could begin to sort out.

In bed Vince mounted me, even though I told him I was still having my period. Garrett would never do that, or at least I hoped he never would. While Vince pumped away at me, I recalled my meeting with Garrett at the park that afternoon, marveling that Garrett had asked me to become his lover, and I had in essence agreed. I had opened myself to Garrett while closing myself to my husband, the man I had at one time vowed to please to the best of my ability. Were Christi and Garrett right? Was God that force inside me that kept nudging me to grow beyond what I had known for the last twelve years? Was He or She the inner voice that kept drawing me back to Garrett, or was I using these ideas to justify what I wanted to do?

Since meeting Garrett, I had become increasingly better at completely tuning out Vince while we had sex—just like I was doing now. Could I turn off this habit when Garrett and I made love? Vince constantly harped on my frigidity. Garrett might think the same even if he was kind enough not to say so. It seemed insane that I was thinking these thoughts while my husband was finishing up and rolling off of me.

I got up, sat on the commode to let Vince's juice drain out of me, and worried about meeting Garrett's expectations as a lover. Then I thought about my promise to be true to myself and not worry about what others wanted from me. It felt as close to impossible as anything I had ever attempted in my life, sort of like changing my thinking—or bending over backwards and stacking BBs.

\* \* \*

## February 27, 1973, Tuesday

I knocked on Garrett's door that stood ajar, and after a few seconds, Garrett opened it.

"You should have come on in; I left it open for you." He stepped back so I could enter.

"I guess that would indicate I was totally at ease with coming here, which I'm not—yet." I looked around his apartment and wondered what it would feel like to live there.

"Because of what we talked about yesterday?" He slipped my book bag off my shoulder.

"It's a big step. I'm doing a one-eighty, going from wanting to be the perfect wife to agreeing to—to being your lover. It feels pretty scary."

"I understand. What if we study for an hour or so, and then we can decide what we want to do next. If you're ready, we might kiss or just lie down together. I certainly don't think we should strip and make mad passionate sex." He laughed, and then he got really still. "Unless you want to," he added expectantly.

"That sounds like a plan—the one about studying first," I said, glad he understood my hesitation.

Garrett set a timer on the stove, so "we wouldn't forget." While I started reading my history notes, he sat next to me with his statistics book open, but every time I glanced over at him, he was checking his watch.

Finally, I said, "You're more interested in *smooching* than in either one of us making good grades."

He kissed the tip of my nose. "Keep that honesty up when we get in bed."

As I returned to my studies, his hand found mine and rested in my lap.

When the stove buzzer sounded, he turned it off and looked at me. "What do you say?"

"I'd like to lie down together," I admitted.

Garrett smiled and grabbed my hand again.

He reset the timer for one hour, and then he led me to the bedroom. I took off my shoes before facing each other on his bed, which was a mattress on the floor. Lying on our sides, he gently kissed me. One kiss led to the next, and little by little our bodies became intertwined with our arms wrapped around one another and our legs woven together. When the buzzer went off again, I was amazed by how comfortable I had become in such a short time. It did not take much for me to imagine sharing Garrett's bed on a full time basis. While he helped me put on my shoes, I studied the golden locks at the crown of his head. He looked, acted, and thought so different than Vince. Maybe that wasn't the best reason for loving someone, but it worked for me.

\* \* \*

As soon as Abi was out of the parking lot, Garrett grabbed his keys and ran to his car. He wouldn't be there as early as he had promised Trang, but if the winds were right, she and Vinh might make the class. After Garrett landed, did the post flight paperwork, and opened the door to Vinh's waiting car, the little man shifted into gear, barely giving Garrett time to get in before he sped away. Both jovial for their own reasons, they practiced Vinh's broken English as they raced across town.

At the apartment, Garrett ran inside. "Vinh is waiting for you. I think you can just make it."

After a sandwich, Garrett asked Loc to take a walk with him. He grudgingly agreed, although *Charlie's Angels* beckoned from the TV. A few blocks down the street, they saw a convenience store and went inside. When Loc spotted a kite, he begged his dad to buy it. Garrett doubted it would fly, plus it was dusk, yet it struck him as better entertainment than a cheesy television show.

A nearby park surrounded with busy traffic offered an open area in which to try out their hastily constructed kite. As hard as Garrett ran, he could not manufacture enough lift to get the plastic and balsa wood airborne. Nearly faint from exertion, he collapsed on a cement bench next to a table. "It's getting dark. We need to go home." Panting, he marveled at how out of shape he had become.

"Let me try it." Loc grabbed the kite and began running across the grassy area toward a busy street.

It took Garrett a second to realize that Loc wasn't watching where he was going. Instead, he was looking back at the barely visible kite trailing behind him.

Garrett bolted for his son shouting, "Stop! Stop!"

Still preoccupied with the kite, Loc kept running.

Right before Loc ran into the oncoming headlights, Garrett grabbed him by the arm and spun him around to face him. Panting, he demanded, "Do you realize what you nearly did?"

A street light highlighted the same green eyes that stared back at him in the mirror. They filled with tears. "I nearly got it up, Daddy."

"You nearly killed yourself. Look at that traffic." Struggling to catch his breath, he pointed to the cars whizzing past. "You'd be dead if I hadn't stopped you."

Realizing the truth of what he had said, Garrett wrapped his arms around Loc and held him against his heaving chest. Their hearts pounded in unison. No matter what else happened, he could not lose this child. He loved him more than life itself. Once more he looked into his son's green eyes. "I love you. I could not live without you."

"I love you too, Daddy. I'm sorry I scared you."

Garrett hugged him again.

As they walked home hand in hand, Garrett thought about the kite and how it would not fly, probably because the temperatures had changed with nightfall, which caused the air to cool off and the winds to die. He knew a lot about flying that he had never shared with Loc. His son had always been too young to appreciate the information, and before long he would be too old to want to listen. Garrett struggled with the concept of timing and father/son relationships. In no time, Loc would be grown, whether Garrett stayed with Trang or not. If they did part ways, Garrett would spend even less time with his son.

He thought of Abi and how much he wanted to be with her. Their relationship felt so threatening to what he had with Loc, not that she had asked for any commitments from him, except when she expectantly said she loved him. Plus, there was an implied obligation that came with intimacy, especially with someone like Abi who obviously did not take it lightly. What would happen to his tie to Loc if Abi did leave Vince? If she did, he would divorce Trang and marry Abi, but first he had to tell Abi about Loc and Trang. When she found out about his family, he expected to lose Abi, and he could not imagine life without her any more than he could picture himself giving up Loc—or at least the right to see him anytime he wanted.

*   *   *

### February 28, 1973, Wednesday

While sitting on the side of Garrett's mattress and taking off my shoes, it occurred to me that the old Abi would never consider intimacy with anyone besides Vince—and even then, Vince always started it. Today, I had let myself in Garrett's partially open door without knocking and immediately walked to the bedroom where I now sat on his mattress. Who was I? What had happened to me? At this moment in this place, I was someone I did not know, and yet I liked the new me. Garrett knelt and began helping me with my shoes.

When we turned to face one another, he began ardently kissing me. Our lips remained fused together as he pushed me onto my back. My feet still hung over the edge. Unlike yesterday, things had escalated in a hurry.

Maybe this was because I had skipped our study time and gone straight to Garrett's bedroom.

For the first time in my life, I was glad to be barren. A family would tie me to Vince and my marriage, but I also wondered if Garrett would want kids if we ended up together—and if he would resent the fact that I couldn't give him any. That was if he actually enjoyed making love to me, if I wasn't truly frigid like Vince said.

Abruptly he stopped kissing me. "What are you thinking, Bird? I hear your mind spinning."

I started to tell him exactly what was going on in my head, but then I stopped myself. If I said I was thinking about what life would be like if we got married, he might panic. Garrett lay on his side patiently waiting for my response. When he playfully smiled, I responded in kind.

"You owe me another kiss," he said with mock seriousness, clearly giving me an out.

"Is that the price of freedom around here?" I teased.

"You got it."

Slowly I moved my lips toward his, thinking the whole time how impossibly wonderful this all seemed. When I got within an inch of his lips, he slipped his hands under my back and drew me to him. Garrett's tongue gently probed my lips. When he sucked my tongue into his mouth, I drew back in surprise.

He laughed, almost childlike. I moved my lips back to Garrett's and playfully sucked his tongue into my mouth. We both laughed and moved together again, kissing passionately. His hands slid over my back and shoulders in a gentle circular motion. How different this was than when I was with Vince.

Garrett and I kissed and massaged each other's back. The longer we stayed pressed together, the more confident I felt. We parted every few minutes to exchange a comment, but each time we quickly returned to kissing. As Garrett inched his hands over my breasts and massaged lightly, a feeling of warmth washed over me. When Vince and I were first married, I felt aroused, but it had been a long time since I felt this way.

Garrett laid his head back on the pillow. "Bird, you never told me."

"What?"

"What you're thinking?"

I ran my fingers through his thick beard before meeting his gaze. Then I carefully chose my words based on the note he had given me outside Dr. Horton's classroom. "I see the other half of me staring back, and I feel scared that I'll never understand what draws that half to me."

He pulled me to him and pecked my lips. "I'm so glad you're here."

While I loved that he approved of me being there, it occurred to me that he had not volunteered his feelings for me. I wanted to ask him to respond in kind, but that was equivalent to asking him to tell me what I had just said, but, of course, I would expect him to up the ante by saying he loved me.

Garrett slowly unbuttoned my blouse, kissing and nibbling my skin as he moved from my chin to my belly-button. My need to make him happy swept me along, although I sensed some part of me was preparing to bolt and run. He slipped his hands behind my back and unfastened my bra. Wanting to believe he would not expect more of me than I was ready to give, I watched like a bystander as he lifted my bra and exposed my breasts. He cupped one breast and sucked the hardened nipple. Then he cupped the other one and sucked with more force. The fact that my nipples were responding made me think that the rest of me must be on board with this—on some level. At the same time, a growing tide of fear began sweeping over me.

At war with myself, I tried to stop the pounding that started in my chest and slowly moved toward my brain, but it continued its steady beat, getting louder and stronger as it moved through me. A paralyzing shadow followed closely behind the marching wave that had seized me. As Garrett removed my blouse and bra, I slipped into a zombielike state of helplessness. My ears buzzed while a numbing haze moved over me as he eased off my jeans and panties. I wanted to return to my body, to be back in control of my thoughts, but I could not.

Naked and shivering, I lay paralyzed, and watched Garrett undress. Body-wise, he was half the size of Vince, but when he slipped his underwear off, his poker stuck straight out, and all I saw was that—no particular man, simply a red throbbing penis. A picture came into my mind of a time when I was very young, not even in school yet, and my dad stood over me in my bedroom. His pants were down around his knees and a hard thing was sticking straight out in front of him. He put his hand on it and stroked it like he was petting a snake, a mad snake. I remembered fearing something terrible had happened to Daddy, but he didn't seem to realize it. In fact, he looked pleased, which wasn't his usual expression.

"What's wrong, Abi?" Garrett asked, jerking me back to the present moment.

I needed to stop thinking about the picture in my head, but it wouldn't leave me. Now that it had found its way to the surface of my brain, I couldn't make it go away. I looked down at my exposed body. Memories of me touching my dad's poker and him smiling in response left me feeling covered in slime. If I stayed here, Garrett would somehow force me to tell him about my memories, which felt as terrifying as the memories themselves. I had to get out of there. I had to leave.

"I need to go." My skin prickled with goose flesh. I felt trapped inside my four-year-old self.

"Abi, what's wrong?" Garrett demanded.

While I scrambled to collect my clothes and then jerk them on, I muttered repeatedly, "I need to go."

Garrett followed me to the door where I left him naked and clearly dumbfounded.

*   *   *

Lying in bed that night, the scene of me as a child and my father standing over me with his poker sticking straight out repeated itself over and over again. Once I had opened the door and allowed the memory to come out, I could not think about anything else. That scene had been there while I drove home, cooked dinner, and ate with Vince. Even as I watched TV and most especially later while Vince and I had sex, I thought of how scared I had been when Daddy placed my hand on his erect penis and said, "Pet my poker." That's where I had gotten that name. Prior to allowing myself to remember this event, I had always thought of it as the slang Vince used, but he never said that. I was the one that thought of his penis as that—a poker.

When Daddy forced my hand to his terrible deformity, he gave me a leering grin. I started crying and my father's face turned hard and cold as he grabbed me by the arms and squeezed, which made me cry louder. Shaking me, he hissed, "Shut up, shut up!"

The venom in his voice made me freeze. I tried to stop crying, but squelched sobs came out anyway.

He shoved me back on the bed. "Don't say anything to your mother about this. If you do, I'll make you wish you'd never been born. You understand me?"

I nodded that I did.

"You forget it happened," he commanded and walked out of my room, closing the door behind him.

Of course, I had never told Mama, and as Daddy ordered me to, I had forgotten the incident. At least, I had put it away and managed not to think about it until today. That same slimy feeling washed over me again and again when I imagined what Garrett would think of me if he knew what had happened between my dad and me. I stayed awake most of the night trying to erase the awful memory from my thoughts.

The next day, I felt like I had been drugged. I got to school, but I fell asleep during Dr. Posey's lecture.

Afterwards, as I plodded down the hall, Dr. Posey walked up beside me. "I need to beef up my lecture; I saw you nodding off. What's going on?"

"I had a hard time sleeping last night." I wondered if my slimy feelings showed.

"What's wrong?" she asked with genuine concern.

"I can't talk about it." It felt too disgusting to share with anyone, much less one of my teachers.

"Let me remind you that there is counseling available," she suggested.

"Oh, I couldn't do that," I said.

"Why not?" Dr. Posey demanded.

"I just couldn't," I hedged.

She looked at me compassionately. "Nearly everyone at some point in their life needs to talk to someone who is not involved in the situation, someone they can trust."

"Thanks, I'll keep that in mind." I tried to smile.

She touched my arm. "Do."

Later, as I walked up the stairs to Garrett's apartment, I thought about Dr. Posey's advice. I should talk to someone besides Garrett because he was too involved. Still, he had asked me to tell him what I was thinking. This would test whether he was capable of accepting the real me, or it might completely repulse him.

Rather than let myself in, I knocked. When he pulled the door open, his smile shifted to concern. Grabbing my hand, he pulled me inside. "Abi, you look terrible."

"Gee thanks," I answered and laughed.

"Does this have to do with yesterday?" He led me to the couch. After we sat down, he studied my face. "What's going on?"

I shook my head, unable to put my shameful feelings into words.

"Was it something I said or did?" he asked. "You seemed to react to me taking my clothes off."

Wishing I had gone to the library rather than come here, I rubbed my throbbing temples. Desperate to somehow get a grip on the situation, I decided to risk it. "You said I should tell you what I'm thinking."

Garrett nodded, although one brow shot up like he wasn't sure he wanted to hear what I might say.

"Yesterday when we were together, I started thinking about something that happened to me when I was a kid." I checked his face to see if I dared go on.

Again, he gave me an encouraging nod, although his facial expression looked guarded and wary.

"Well, it's stupid really." It seemed like such a small thing, yet still repulsive at the same time.

He put his hand on my shoulder. "It's clearly upsetting you, so it must be something significant."

That slimy feeling washed over me again, and I decided not to tell him. I didn't want to risk losing him because of some silly thing that happened so long ago. "Garrett, can we lay down together. No kissing, just lay next to each other."

"Sure." He took my hand and led me to his bedroom where he slipped off my shoes and then lay beside me on the mattress. "You started to tell me something," Garrett prompted.

"It's nothing really. I just need to lie here for a while. Our fingers interlocked and rested on the bed between us. The anxious feeling that had been with me since yesterday slowly faded away.

Before I knew it, he was gently shaking my arm and telling me it was time for me to go home. I had slept so soundly that I had a hard time remembering where I was. As I slipped on my shoes, I told myself that the memories had gone back where they belonged, in that corner of my mind where I had stored them long ago.

*   *   *

Vince was standing in line to get his time sheet initialed by Daddy. It was ridiculous that the head honchos made them jump through hoops like this. Everybody knew they were here from eight to five. Last year, some no-account said he was at work when he wasn't, and now everybody had to go through this stupid routine of getting the boss' signature every day before they left the drilling site.

Behind him in line, several men back, Vince overheard a new hire named Ramon, talking to Trent, a guy who had been working this crew as long as Vince. What chapped Vince was that if Daddy had to leave the drilling site, he always left Trent in charge, instead of his own son. Daddy didn't give Vince an inch. In fact, he expected more from Vince than he did any man on the crew.

Ramon was the guy Vince had overheard talking about the Friday night bowling league. Ten minutes into their conversation, he started laughing and swinging his arm like he had an imaginary bowling ball. Vince wondered if he was talking about him.

Slapping his leg, Ramon said between snickers, "You should have seen it, man. He was retarded."

That did it. Vince knew this little pipsqueak was making fun of him bowling. Probably something he'd heard at the alley. Before Vince realized he was doing it, he broke line, grabbed Ramon by the jacket, and lifted him off the ground while shouting in his face, "Whatever you got to say, you say it to me."

Ramon looked back at him, with his lips trembling and his beady little eyes bugging out of his head.

Trent laid a hand on Vince's arm. "Hey, man, he wasn't talking about you. He was telling me about a movie he saw over the weekend."

Vince glanced at Trent.

Then Daddy was beside Vince, his clipboard in his hand. "Put Ramon down."

Realizing he had no other choice, Vince lowered Ramon. He needed to save face, but Vince had gone past the point of making it look like a stupid practical joke. Smoothing Ramon's bunched jacket, Vince mumbled, "Sorry, man, I misunderstood what you said." Daddy would still be pissed, but it was the best Vince could do.

Vince walked to the end of the line while all the men gawked at him. This was Alesia's fault. If she hadn't opened her big mouth, he wouldn't be thinking that everyone was talking about him. And maybe Ramon was talking about him, but Trent had covered his ass. Guys were like that, especially ones in line to be boss.

They were halfway home before Daddy said, "You want to explain yourself?"

"I thought Ramon was talking about me." Vince remembered the times he was sent home for fighting at school. Mama understood, but Daddy always made him apologize to the other kid. Vince hated that worse than taking a licking. If he got into a fight with some kid, they deserved it.

"If you can't work with the other men and settle your differences peacefully, I'll be forced to replace you with someone else. Because I asked, the big bosses allow you and me to work together—against the company policy." He paused, probably giving Vince time to think about how lucky he was to have a dad who would go to bat for him. "If this happens again, you'll be off the crew."

Vince opened his mouth to say that Ramon had it coming, when Daddy gave him that look.

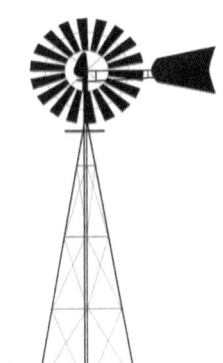

# Chapter Twelve

*A closed mouth catches no flies.*

### March 2, 1973, Friday

*A*s Garrett passed Mariam's office, it occurred to him that she might offer some insight into what was going on with Abi, although he couldn't say anything specifically about her. At Mariam's open door, he saw her bent over her desk, scrawling something, probably a note on a student's paper.

"Do you ever get caught up?" he asked.

She finished what she was writing, and then marked her place with the pen. "Never. Come in and sit."

Garrett cleared a chair by offloading a stack of papers onto the floor. "How is your semester going?"

"I'm behind, but that's nothing new. Care for a cup of coffee?" She sipped from a nearly full cup.

"Never touch the stuff." He would give anything for a strong cup of tea since he hadn't slept much the last couple of nights.

She smiled. "What brings you around these parts?"

"I'm worried about a friend." He hated being vague, but he didn't want to start creating bogus names.

"Why's that?" Mariam set her coffee aside.

"She seems troubled, but she won't tell me what's going on, so there's not much I can do to help."

"Is it because you're a therapist in training, or do you think she's not telling anyone?"

"I doubt she's telling anybody. She's sort of private, keeps her cards close to her chest so to speak." The reference to Abi's chest sent his mind spinning in a direction he did not want to go, so he reeled it in.

Mariam laced her hands in front of her and rested her chin on her steepled index fingers. "How's your situation going? Last time we talked, you were in the middle of moving your family to Houston."

Garrett cleared his throat. Mariam was savvy. She may have surmised he was talking about Abi. "Loc and Trang are fine. With my job, I fly down two nights a week, so I get to see them regularly."

"Has she started learning English? You voiced concern that she might isolate herself within the Vietnamese community there." She had a steel-trap mind for details.

"She and her uncle go to class the two nights that I'm there to stay with Loc."

Mariam smiled. "That's nice that you spend time with your son." She lowered her hands to her lap. "Now about your friend, how does she fit into all this?"

"What are you getting at?" He wondered if Abi could had spoken to Mariam before she came to his apartment yesterday.

"Garrett, don't try to shit me. If your friend has an emotional problem, you advise her to go to the counseling center. You don't play therapist. You know better than that." She gave him one of her *let's be professional about all this* looks. "Now, who are we talking about?"

"It seems you've already decided," Garrett answered, meeting her bluff with one of his own. Two could play psychological warfare, but he doubted his ability to keep up with her.

Taking a deep breath, she flicked one thumbnail with the other. "From the front of the classroom, I see things in people's eyes. I go over my students' papers, and I read between the lines, not that I'm trying to pry into their lives, but often their issues are crystal clear."

"What are you saying?" Garrett demanded, his voice louder than he had intended.

She leveled him with her steely gaze. "Abi Martin is married."

Garrett wondered how much Abi had said to her. He stared at Mariam, hoping to detect a chink in her armor. When she continued to flick her thumbnails, he gave in. "What have you two talked about?"

"Nothing really. Yesterday I spoke with her after class because she looked tired and worried." She seemed to be assessing Garrett's reaction. "Because I know you two are friends, and I know both of you are married, I put two and two together. Maybe I'm way off base. It won't be the first time."

"Are you saying I'm responsible for what Abi's going through?" Likely, he was, although Garrett did know what that was. He wished for Mariam's incredible insight.

She did not answer for the longest, and then she said, "I advised her to go to the counseling center, and that is what I would encourage you to do as well."

"Advise Abi to go, or go myself?"

"Both. It would benefit both of you." She sat back, and her chair creaked.

"You know all the crap I've waded through," Garrett argued, recalling the many sessions they had spent with him telling her about his pretentious mother and his emotionally absent father.

"When a therapist thinks he's through working on his stuff, it's time for him to quit." She picked up her pen. "In your case, you haven't even started—working on your stuff or practicing as a therapist."

He got up and walked away, more troubled than before he had darkened her door.

*   *   *

At Garrett's apartment, he set the timer, and we actually studied until it went off. Then he grabbed my hand and led me to the couch where I sat down, both surprised and pleased. This was much less intimidating than his bed.

Then he took off his tee-shirt, sat down facing me, and held both of my hands. "Abi, are you okay?"

"Yes, I guess. It surprised me when I saw you undressing."

He stroked the fingers on both of my hands. "We won't do anything until you're ready," he assured me.

I nodded, and leaned against the cushion, still facing him.

"You want me to put my shirt back on?"

"No," I said, although I sure didn't want him to take anything else off.

Starting at his navel, I ran my index finger along the center of his abdomen where the muscles came together in a small valley. At the center of his hairy chest, I stopped and examined the dog tags he always wore.

"CLAY, GARRETT M. What's your middle name?" There was too much about him I did not know.

"Morgan. What's yours?"

"Marie," I answered.

"Same middle initials," he observed.

Then I read a series of numbers followed by AF. "What does AF mean—awfully fine?"

He smiled. "Air force, although I like 'awfully fine' better."

He scooped me into his arms and held me against his bare chest.

"When's your birthday?" he asked. His lips against my ear sent shivers up my spine.

"The sixth of March." Then I remembered how close it was. "Next Tuesday, I think."

"You're kidding." He drew back and gave me a look of astonishment. "March sixth is my birthday. What year were you born?"

"You tell me first," I challenged, as amazed as he seemed to be.

"Nineteen-forty-three," he answered.

Flabbergasted, I said, "That's the year I was born."

"Really? We were born on the same day of the same year. Do you know what time of day?" His delight and surprise were too genuine for him to be putting me on.

"The way my mom tells the story it was mid-afternoon, around 2:30." I studied his green eyes, sharing his wonder. This seemed too remarkable to be possible.

"That's what's on my birth certificate—you know the one you get from the hospital." He cradled my face in his hands. "What are the odds of that? We were twins, separated at birth. Hey, wait a minute; that makes all this a bit kinky—like I'm attracted to my sister." He laughed.

I had always had a sense of rightness about our relationship, but this revelation felt like a final stamp of approval—if in fact it was true. But how could he make that up?

He kissed me so slowly and gently barely touching my lips, face, and neck with his lips, whispering my name over and over again, and lightly stroking my back, but steering away from anything more personal. I figured he was guarding against what happened before, and since I wasn't feeling anxious yet, I thought about taking my blouse off, but I worried that would trigger another panic attack.

As he nuzzled my ear, Garrett whispered, "Tell me, Abi, if you're okay."

"I feel good," I said, surprised that I could say that with perfect honesty.

We clung to each other and kissed until it was time for me to go.

At the door, I admitted, "I could have gone farther today. I wanted to, but I was scared."

"Don't push yourself. When the time is right, you'll know it." He kissed me lightly on the lips. "I have this fantasy, Abi."

"What is it?" I worried it would be something way beyond my comfort level.

He smiled. "I'd like to wake up next to you."

*Sort of like we were married,* I finished in my head. Waking up beside him was out of the question, but maybe I would be able to make love to him by our birthday. Since I had no money, it was all I could give him.

On the way home, I marveled at the fact that Garrett and I had a common birth date and time. It made me think of his note with Aristotle's quote about our friendship being one soul in two bodies.

\* \* \*

That night Vince and I met Fred and Alma at the restaurant where we met before, and like a rerun of a boring movie, we sat in the same places and carried on similar conversations. Fred and Vince retreated into their world of oil wells and pumpers while Alma gave me an update on her soaps, and I thought about Garrett.

The childhood memories of my dad in my bedroom still haunted me, but I escaped them by focusing on Garrett. In the time since we resumed our relationship, I had replaced the consuming guilt that once plagued me with thoughts of eventually being Garrett's wife. He had gone from being my partner in sin to the person who would free me from Vince. While we never talked of marriage or me leaving Vince, I knew that Garrett cared about me, and we would in time be husband and wife.

He still had not said he loved me, though, and this bothered me. As nice as it was to feel his gentle kisses and know that he enjoyed being with me, I wanted to hear those magical words roll off his lips. I needed some kind of commitment. The end of the semester would come too quickly.

\* \* \*

## March 5, 1973, Monday

Monday started mid-term week at school. The week after that was Spring Break. Before I got out of my car at Garrett's apartment, I rehearsed aloud a speech about studying more and smooching less, at least for today. Tomorrow was our birthdays, and I had already decided I would try to get to his apartment early and immediately suggest we go to bed.

As I stepped onto the balcony outside his door, Garrett opened it dressed in a silky robe. "What were you doing out in your car?"

Perplexed by his attire, but too shy to say anything about it, I said, "I was preparing my speech."

"This sounds serious. Is there a problem, Bird?"

I shifted my load of books onto my hip and looked into his questioning green eyes. "I need to study."

His face reflected confusion and relief at the same time. "That's it?"

"It's important, Garrett. I have to do well this semester. If I don't, I won't be able to go to school next semester." Then I caught a whiff of an unusual floral smell. "Garrett, what—"

Before I could finish my question, he grabbed my hand and led me to the kitchen. "We won't set a timer. You tell me when you feel we've studied enough. Then maybe we can. . .do whatever you want to do."

"You sure you're okay with that?" I asked, laying my books out in the order I needed to study them.

"Of course," he said, although not convincingly.

As had become our custom, I got two glasses of water and took them to the table. When Garrett reached for his, it slipped out of my hand and spilled all over my books. Not seeing a towel in the kitchen, I took off for the bathroom.

Garrett was right behind me. "Abi, wait."

Upon entering the bathroom, I knew why he had tried to stop me—and I understood where the floral smell had come from. The small windowless room wavered with the light from large pillar candles at the corners of the tub filled with a steamy bubble bath. A white, floor-length silky negligee hung from a hanger hooked over the shower curtain rod. I ran my hand over the white satin material. Lace trimmed the front opening and around the bottom. Within the thickly gathered lace, I saw birds with open wings.

While I examined the negligee, Garrett grabbed a bath towel and disappeared.

Thinking I would help Garrett clean up the mess, I stepped out of the bathroom and noticed beyond the partially closed bedroom door the same flickering candlelight as in the bathroom. I stepped inside and recognized the scent I had smelled upon entering the apartment. Two glasses of wine and a plate of cheese and crackers sat on the cardboard box nightstand. Instead of the worn, floral spread, black, satin sheets covered the bed. A red rose lay on the pillow. I walked over and picked it up.

From behind me Garrett said, "We still have time."

With my back to him, I smelled the rose. "What's the fragrance in here?"

"Frangipani, it's a flower that grows in Vietnam. It's coming from that candle." He rested his hands on my shoulders and drew me closer. "The bath water should still be hot."

"The robe is beautiful. And I see the birds in it." I could not begin to tell him how special this was—and how much I wanted to save it for the next day—our birthdays.

He turned me to face him. "I want to teach you to fly."

"If anyone can do it, you can." He was talking about sexual intimacy, which I wanted more for him than for myself. What I treasured was his kindness, not just for this wonderful surprise, but in general.

We kissed, and I thought about telling him I would study tomorrow since he had gone to so much trouble. Then I thought about the significance of having intercourse for the first time on our birthday, and I remembered Garrett's encouragement to be honest with him. Plus, I feared freezing under pressure.

"Tomorrow is our birthdays. Let's save all this for then," I suggested.

"I'm supposed to go to Houston early tomorrow. I promised my nephew I'd be there."

There it was again, that piece that did not fit. "When we first met, you said you were an only kid of two only kids. How can you have a nephew?"

Garrett hesitated as if he was puzzled, then he said, "Oh, I'm sorry. I bet I totally confused you. His dad, Gary, and I were in Nam together.

We're like family, and I stay with them in Houston a lot. Gary married a woman from over there, Trang. They have a little boy named Loc who calls me Uncle Garrett." He laughed. "Why didn't you say something about that earlier? Knowing you, I bet that's been eating at you."

"Yeah, I guess it has." He knew me so well—better than I knew myself.

It was the first time he had said I should not come to his apartment, and it was our birthdays. Plus, he was more interested in seeing this so called nephew. I met his expectant gaze. "Well, then Wednesday."

He wrapped his arms around me. "I'm not sure I can wait that long."

"You have to." I slid out of his grasp and returned to the kitchen where I checked my textbooks for water damage. Flipping through the pages, I tried to hide the pain I felt for playing second fiddle to a child who wasn't even related to Garrett.

*   *   *

"Open mine first." Loc thrust a crudely wrapped present into Garrett's hands.

Garrett examined the shoebox size package haphazardly covered in colored newspaper funnies and an abundance of clear tape. "Did you wrap this yourself?"

Loc nodded excitedly. "And I made your gift."

"That's nice." Garrett paused to survey the remains of a fantastic Vietnamese meal, sour soup and swordfish. Trang who sat across the table from him had baked a cake with chocolate frosting on which Loc had written, "Happy 30 Birthday to Daddy," with white icing.

"Hurry, Daddy, hurry." Loc bounced up and down.

Garrett shook the lightweight box. "Is it a book?" he asked, eager to sustain Loc's exuberance.

"I can't make a book," Loc scolded.

"So you made this yourself, huh?" Garrett tore off the paper and lifted the lid. Inside he found three woven rag potholders. He picked them up and examined them closely. There were a few flaws, but for a six-year-old this was a major accomplishment.

"They're for your apartment, Daddy. You use them when you cook—to hold onto the handle." Loc took one and demonstrated with an imaginary pan.

Garrett caught Trang's sad expression out of the corner of his eye. He did not want to think about how much work she had put into preparing all this for him. She obviously cared for him. Yet, his love for Abi was keeping him from being present with his family. And Trang knew it. He could see it in her eyes.

\*   \*   \*

Vince, Mama and Papa Martin, and I sat around their kitchen table.

Papa Martin lit the candles on my cake before he scooted it in front of me. "Make a wish."

I stared into the flames and then up at the faces around the table. What I wanted was to be Garrett's wife, to live with him, and to share his life. After taking a huge breath, I blew as if my life depended on it.

"Well, that one ought to take," Papa Martin said, plucking the candles from the frosting.

Mama Martin cut generous slices of cake for everyone, and we ate them while we played dominoes. At ten o'clock, I said Vince and I should go home and get to bed. Papa Martin said he guessed a little beauty sleep wouldn't hurt him. As Vince and I walked across the yard toward our backdoor, he slipped his arm around my shoulders and drew me close. Not that long ago I would have been thrilled by this simple gesture of affection. Now I wanted to pull away, but I didn't.

\*   \*   \*

Following his birthday celebration with Loc, Trang, and Vinh, Garrett stayed up all night studying for his statistics test, which he took as soon as he got back to Oaces. Then he came home and crashed.

Still half asleep, Garrett knew someone was in bed with him. He roused enough to realize this female body snuggling up to him was naked. Had he told Abi his fantasy, hoping she would do exactly what she had done? Would she be okay, or was this going to be a repeat of the last time they were naked together?

His arm glided beneath the satin sheet as he pulled her to him. "Bird," he said, his voice thick with sleep. "I missed the show." He nuzzled her neck and moved his hands over her bare buttocks.

She wrapped her arms around him, and pressed her flesh against his. "What a great wakeup call." He lightly kissed her. "Maybe I'm still asleep." He kissed her again and then pulled back to check her face. "You haven't said anything yet, so maybe I'm dreaming."

Their heads lay on the pillow facing each other. He felt closer to her in that moment than he had ever felt to another human being. They didn't have to have sex, except he wanted the connection that only physical intimacy could provide.

She took a deep breath and said softly, "I think I'm ready."

Questioning the wisdom in accepting her offer, but unable to refuse what he had wanted for so long, he reached across her to his cardboard box nightstand. There he found the condoms he had bought in anticipation of this moment. He handed one to her. "Would you like to do the honors?"

"We won't need this." She handed it back to him.

"What if you get pregnant?" He caressed her cheek.

She heaved a huge sigh, whispered, "I know I can't," and burrowed her head against his chest.

He held her and thought about Trang getting pregnant because they had not used precautions. He almost hoped Abi got pregnant; that would force him to tell both women the truth. Plus, it would make him more of a man than Vince had been. It was insane logic, but Garrett could not stop himself from going there.

Wanting this to be good for her, rather than another traumatizing experience, he began peppering her with kisses. As their lovemaking intensified, she held him tight, racking her fingernails across his back in what he hoped was her own climax. When he got around to slipping himself inside her, he was too close to making it. After only a few slow, gentle thrusts, Garrett said between gritted teeth, "Abi, I can't wait."

"It's fine. I'm okay," she assured him.

He lay on top of her. They had lain still for several minutes when Garrett stroked her cheek and said, "You didn't make it, did you, Abi?"

"I did," she said proudly. "I stayed with you all the way."

With her admission, he immediately understood that he and Abi were worlds apart concerning their expectations about intimacy. If he read her right, sex was an endurance test, not a means of giving and receiving pleasure. His heart ached for her. "I meant, you didn't climax."

"I don't even know what that means," she said dismissively and squeezed him. "Happy birthday."

"Thank you." He stroked her back. "You're the best present ever."

# Chapter Thirteen

*A drought usually ends with a flood.*

**March 9, 1973, Friday**

When Vince walked in the house, he didn't smell anything cooking. Then he recalled telling Abi they were going to eat with Alma and Fred again, but he had changed his mind. Abi stood at the kitchen table, working on something for her art class—a better mousetrap. He didn't understand how this could be art.

"Is that the rat trap you were designing?" he asked as he set his lunchbox on the counter.

Up to her elbows in white goop, she glanced at him. "Yes, this is my new and improved mouse captivation device." Abi stood back and looked at what had once been a large cardboard box. It was now a wedge with round cut-outs all over it. "What do you think?"

"It's all right." It actually was pretty darned clever. "What are you slathering it with?"

"Papier-mâché, newspaper strips stuck on with flour and water. When it's dry, I'm going to paint it orange."

"How does it work?" He was impressed that she created it out of nothing. When she mentioned buying plywood and getting him to cut it, he told her he wasn't spending money on crap like that.

She moved to the side and pointed to a small arched opening. "Inside, I'm hanging a mirror, which will draw him in to see himself. When he

183

goes in, it trips the support that holds this door up. Then, he's caught. See?" She used her hand as the mouse and demonstrated.

He had not seen her so excited or alive in a very long time. "That's good, Abi-girl. The next time we have a rat infestation, we'll know how to handle it." He rested his arms on her shoulders.

Abi looked up at him. He remembered her doing this when they first started dating. At that time, she gave him a moony-eyed expression that hardened his cock. Now she looked happy, but it wasn't about him.

"Get cleaned up; we're going to the bowling alley," he said, trying to sound like it was no big deal.

She picked at her hands where the paste had dried. "I thought we were going out with Alma and Fred."

"Nah, it's Friday night. We're going bowling." He wanted to sound natural as well as in charge.

Before she had time to object, he walked to the bathroom and stripped off his work clothes. He couldn't stop his onetime friends from asking Christi and Buck to take his and Abi's place on the bowling league, but he sure as hell was not going to give them the satisfaction of thinking they had run him off. He and Abi would bowl—right next to the old gang.

Finished with his shower, Vince walked to the kitchen with his pants in hand, thinking he needed to get Abi moving. Sure enough, he found her at the sink washing her hands.

She glanced at him. "Maybe we should do something besides bowl. We could go to a movie."

"No, I want to bowl." He stepped into a pair of jeans that weren't starched or ironed. She used to do both before she started going to school.

"But if we go over there, I'm afraid you'll get upset," she whined.

"We can bowl on our own. Those chicken shits don't own that place." Realizing she had forgotten to get him a beer, he pulled one from the refrigerator.

She trailed him with her eyes, clearly not eager to go along with him.

"Why don't you warm up something to eat?" He opened his beer.

She went back to looking at her art project. "You want a sandwich?"

"If that's the best you got to offer." This schooling business was getting to be a real pain.

Vince got his gun off the rack and carried it to the living room where he planned to clean it while Abi made his supper and got ready. He'd put it in the pickup just in case there was a problem.

Abi brought him a sandwich made of cold meatloaf. She watched him run the rag in and out of the barrel. "Getting ready for Sunday afternoon target practice?" she asked hopefully.

He sighted down the barrel. "No, I'm taking it with us." He drained his beer, and then he shook the empty can at her.

She took it and disappeared into the kitchen. Two minutes later, she came back with a slice of apple pie. "Vince, let's just stay here tonight. We could go to bed early."

"We'll do that when we get home." He took the pie from her. "You forgot my beer."

She didn't say anything, just walked to the bedroom. He'd fetch his own goddamn beer.

Vince took his time getting ready. He'd give the gang time to get there and have everyone in place, including Buck and Christi. The lane next to the gang would be empty. No one wanted it because the regulars were so damn loud. Vince grabbed his gun on the way out the door, and Abi gave him a look, but she didn't say anything. He rested his loaded gun in the rack that hung over the back window and sat a box of ammo on the seat between him and Abi. There was plenty of room since Abi had quit sitting next him like she had when she first got out of the hospital.

On the way to town, Abi silently stared at the horizon, and Vicki Lawrence sang *The Night the Lights Went Out* about some innocent man getting hurt. That wouldn't be the case tonight.

At the bowling alley, Vince stood at the front desk, renting their shoes. He could see the old gang in their regular pit, plus a couple with their backs to him. That had to be Buck and Christi. When Abi muttered something about going to the ladies' room, Vince grabbed her wrist.

"Let's don't play tonight," she pleaded as they walked to the pit next to their old one.

He pushed her down on the bench and threw the rental shoes into her lap. Sitting next to her, he jerked off his boots. "We're going to show those sons of bitches a thing or two."

Abi changed her shoes, although Vince could tell she wasn't going to go along with this as he had hoped. At work, he had mentally rehearsed bowling better than ever, laughing with Abi like they used to, and pretending those sons-of-bitches weren't there. If one of them said anything, he'd let them have it.

Vince found balls for him and Abi. He set both of them in the ball return, powdered his hands, and then drew his ball to that perfect spot right in front of his nose. He couldn't make out the individual pins, but he knew to aim slightly off center. Taking his first step, he levered his arm out, back, and then forward, knowing when the ball left his hand he had a strike.

He turned and smiled triumphantly at Abi. "Too bad that's just the practice round."

She gave him a twisted little grin like she was sick at her stomach. As soon as his ball came back to him, he bowled again and made another strike. On her practice round, Abi knocked down two outside pins and the second ball guttered before it reached the halfway point.

Vince stood at the line, psyching himself up when Alesia hollered, "Vince, you're so full of hot air—just blow 'em down."

The whole group laughed and yelped.

Vince finished his delivery, but the ball curved sharply, barely catching an outside pin. With his next ball, he overcorrected and took out three pins on the other side.

Their neighbors erupted with laughter and jeers of, "Way to go," and, "Groovy, man."

"Put your money where your mouth is," Vince hollered back. "How about a bowl-off?"

The six regulars drew their heads together while Buck and Christi stood to the side. Then Brent, Alesia's pussy-whipped husband, approached Vince. "We decided on Buck since he's taking your place."

Vince smiled, having seen this coming. "That's fine as long as we do it here. It stinks over there."

\* \* \*

Once Buck and Vince were well into their bowl off, I changed my shoes and grabbed my jacket along with the pickup keys out of Vince's coat. I had to do something with that gun before someone got killed. Rather than go straight outside, I detoured by the restroom so as not to raise Vince's suspicions. Christi walked in close behind me. I was glad to see her, but I didn't have time to talk.

"We never meant to hurt you," Christi pleaded. "You haven't been here in a month. This is the first time we've bowled with them. Honest."

"Like you said the last time we talked, Vince and I aren't welcome any more." A crowd cheered outside—Vince wasn't doing well. "I'm not blaming you, but I am scared of what Vince will do if he loses."

Knowing I had to do something with Vince's gun, I gave Christi a quick hug. "We'll talk later."

I bolted out of the restroom and saw everyone in the alley had gathered around the bowl-off. Heart pounding, I raced to the pickup and unlocked the door. I climbed inside and grabbed for the gun, but my knee slipped off the slick vinyl seat, and I fell, bringing the gun down on the bridge of my nose. Still holding the gun, I scrambled out of the truck. Blood was dripping out of my nostrils and onto the gun.

Just then the wind caught the truck door and slammed it shut. I had to fit these pieces into a workable story. The idea of a robbery sprang into my mind, and I looked around the parking lot. When I didn't see anyone, I frantically pounded the butt of the gun into the passenger window. The glass cracked into a thousand pieces but it clung together. I kept hammering until I managed to make an opening big enough for someone to reach through and unlock the door.

Shouts grew louder from inside the bowling alley. I had to get rid of the gun. As I bolted around the corner of the building, I saw the front door fly open.

Rushing into the darkness as hard and fast as I could go, I moved in a zigzag pattern up and down several streets until I collapsed in an overgrown vacant lot. Panting and exhausted, I lay in the weeds and tried to think. Only a few feet away, people talked in their backyard. A dog barked and a cat howled in return. My hands moved over the smooth, wooden stock of the gun as I tried to think what to do next.

*       *       *

The words Garrett was reading blurred, and he saw Abi's face. Her eyes were wild, and she breathed heavily. A shiver moved over him, and he checked to see if the front door had somehow blown open. Even if it had, it was mid-March and the weather had turned mild. The door was shut and locked. Still, something felt terribly wrong concerning Abi. Had Vince found out about their affair?

He ambled around the apartment. His anxiety reminded him of the dream he had about the chasm between them. Later when he saw her at school, she had been sick. In the bedroom, he ran his hands over Abi's negligee. She wore it Thursday and Friday when she came to the apartment. Their lovemaking had been incredible, although he could tell Abi never climaxed—even though she said she enjoyed it. Monday he would change up things—maybe take a daytrip because it was Spring Break.

Studying his portraits on the kitchen wall, he longed to have drawings of her, so he retrieved the photos he had taken of her at the park. Monday, he would ask her again to draw herself, and when she said she couldn't, he'd suggest she use these pictures. He removed the pictures of Loc and Trang taken at Christmas and laid the envelope on the bar. Seeing them there when she arrived would remind him to ask her.

He poured himself a beer, and sat down to read, determined to study. As he struggled to focus on the page, concerned thoughts about Abi clouded his mind.

*       *       *

A police car turned the corner and started toward me, sweeping its spotlight back and forth across the road. When the light shown in my eyes, I raised my hands as a shield. The car stopped abruptly.

A policeman jumped out of the car and ran toward me. "Mrs. Martin, is that you?"

"Yes," I answered, still concocting my story about what had happened. He cautiously approached me. "You've been hurt."

My trembling hands lightly touched my swollen nose and the blood on my upper lip and chin. His eyes traveled down my body where blood stains had blotched my jeans and shirt.

"I tried to stop him," I said weakly.

"The important thing is that we found you." He led me to the car and helped me into the backseat. "Your husband is beside himself with worry." As he pulled back on the street, he turned on the siren and raced away. Feeling sick at my stomach and dizzy, I lowered my head between my knees to keep from passing out. I hadn't eaten any supper for fretting about what Vince would do after we got to the bowling alley. When we pulled into the parking lot next to Vince's truck, I raised my head and saw Vince standing next to a police officer.

As soon as we stopped, Vince opened the door, grabbed my outstretched hand, and pulled me out of the car. "Abi-girl, I thought he'd killed you." He held me in a tight bear-hug, kissing my neck.

"I'm okay, Vince," I murmured.

He examined the bridge of my nose where the gun had fallen on it. "When I saw the truck had been broke into and the blood…. Abi-girl, I thought I'd lost you."

"I tried to stop him, but he was crazy," I lied. "He threatened to shoot me if I didn't go with him."

Vince protectively put his arm around my shoulders while the policemen who had found me asked question after question. Amazed by my ability to ad lib, I rattled off a story about a white male attacker pounding in the window of the truck where I sat inside.

"He was breaking in the window with a rock, so I grabbed the gun for protection. Once he got the window broken out, we wrestled and that's when I got hit in the face with the gun. He dragged me with him, but I guess I was too slow, so he made me lie down in the grass. Then he went on without me."

The policemen agreed with Vince that I was lucky he had not shot me since I could easily identify him. After I declined their offer to take me to the hospital, the policemen insisted I come to the station where they filled out forms and took our fingerprints, so they could distinguish our prints from those of the attacker. Around midnight, we headed for Quits.

All weekend the house was alive with calls and visits from people—some nearly strangers—who wanted to know the details of what happened Friday night. Besides making Vince the center of attention, it also gave him something to think about besides the bowling group. By the time I had told and retold the story what felt like a hundred times, it started feeling so real that I began believing it. Every time I walked into the bedroom and saw the empty gun rack, I smiled to myself and felt proud of how things had worked out.

\* \* \*

### March 12, 1973, Monday

Garrett was crouched on the kitchen floor packing a cooler when Abi arrived and let herself in the open door. Holding a soda in one hand and a loaf of bread in the other, he called out, "We need to celebrate Spring Break by doing something different. Let's take a road trip." He focused on getting the remaining items in the already full ice chest.

"Sounds good." She walked toward him.

He glanced up at her and saw her swollen nose. "My God what happened?"

Abi touched her nose like she was making sure it was still attached. "It was just a silly accident."

"A car?" he asked, remembering how worried he had been Friday night.

"No, actually it involved Vince's gun."

He stood up. "What happened?"

"Well, it's kind of a long story. Don't you want to go ahead and leave?"

"Yes, and I want every detail while we're driving." He ran to the bedroom to get the old blue spread.

In the car, she told him about Vince taking a gun to the bowling alley because he was angry at some people they used to bowl with. Abi explained Vince was doing a bowl off when she ran outside to hide the gun because she was afraid Vince would end up shooting someone. She hurt herself while getting the gun out of the pickup, so she made it look like someone had broken into the pickup before she ran with it. Not knowing what else to do with it, she had left it in a vacant lot. Then she lied to the police and Vince about someone stealing the gun out of the pickup.

"That worries me, Bird; that you lied to the police," he said, alternating his gaze from her to the road.

"The good thing is I kept Vince from doing something crazy. You don't know him; he gets so riled up over stupid stuff, he might have shot someone."

"What if the police realize you're the one who took it?" As soon as the words left his mouth, he regretted them. Debating this would only ruin their day together, and there was nothing she could do now.

"My biggest fear is that some kid will find that loaded gun." She stared out the car window.

He could tell by the worried look on her face that she now shared his concern.

"I'm sure it will be okay. If someone finds the gun, they'll probably just consider themselves lucky and hold onto it." He hoped that happened, but the Panhandle seemed too full of do-gooders who couldn't wait to step in and make things right in a case like this. The gun would surface. It was simply a matter of time.

Garrett shifted the conversation to how well Abi had done on her midterm tests. While they talked, Garrett drove north to Palo Dura State Park, two hours away. They hiked the steep bluffs and ate a picnic lunch of wine, sliced meat, and bread off the blue floral spread that lay over the red, brick-hard dirt of the canyon.

They laughed and sang along with the radio all the way home. It was 4:00 when they arrived back at his place, so she hurriedly helped him carry his things up to the apartment and started for the door.

Garrett caught her arm and pulled her to him. "Bird, I guess I didn't plan this very well. I had hoped to be home in time to make love." He pulled her to him and kissed her.

"We'll stay in bed all day tomorrow." She kissed him again before heading for the door.

"Just a minute." He grabbed the photo envelope off the bar. "Would you do me a huge favor and draw your portrait? These are the pictures I took of you at the park. I want them back, but it would be such a gift to me. It could be a second birthday present."

She flipped through the pictures. "I'm not very good at drawing people."

"You're a magician. You made me look good." He lightly squeezed her arm. "Please," he added.

She gave him a lingering look. "I drew you the way I see you in my mind." She gave him another quick peck on the lips and called back to him as she hurried out the door, "I'll try."

*   *   *

That night a solemn-faced policeman knocked at our door and introduced himself as Officer Fowler. He wanted to know if he might ask me some routine questions about Friday night. Vince turned off the TV and sat in his chair. After Officer Fowler declined a glass of tea, he and I sat on the couch.

He poised his pen over a notebook. "Mrs. Martin, exactly how long were you in the pickup before this man began pounding on the window?"

"Only a few seconds," I said thoughtfully.

He didn't write anything. "Do you think he could have seen you get in the truck?"

"Yes, I'm sure he did. It seemed like he immediately started pounding on the window." My hands shook, so I clasped them together and rested them on my knees.

"Why did you lock your door? Were you afraid someone might attack you?"

"Damn right she was afraid," Vince interjected. "You know better than anybody about the perverts out there." A weekend of discussing the criminal side of society had fueled Vince's conviction.

Officer Fowler set his steady gaze on Vince. "Mr. Martin, please allow Mrs. Martin to answer."

Vince sat back, suddenly silent and sullen.

"What was the question?" I asked, uncomfortable with Officer Fowler's formality and the way he seemed to be steering the questions in a direction I didn't want to go.

"Were you afraid?" Officer Fowler repeated patiently.

My eyes traced the in and out pattern of my laced fingers. "I don't know why I locked it. I guess because Vince had it locked to begin with."

"Does he usually lock it?"

"No, but he had his gun in there."

"Why did he have his gun that particular night?"

Vince shifted in his seat and cleared his throat.

I didn't look at him. "He wanted to show it to a friend," I said.

"What's his friend's name?" Officer Fowler asked.

My mind went blank. "Buck. Buck Wilson," I said because I couldn't think of anyone else.

"Weren't he and your husband engaged in some sort of competition?"

"I think so," I murmured, keeping my eyes on my hands.

"Some of the people at the bowling alley have reported that there seems to be a little rivalry going on between them. Is that true?"

"We're all just friends." I looked into the officer's eyes and silently begged him to stop before he offered Vince too much to think about.

"One witness said she saw you run out of the building several minutes before a fight erupted between Buck and Vince. Where were you going? Why were you running, Mrs. Martin?"

I hesitated choosing my words carefully. "I was afraid they might fight, so I went out to the truck. I didn't want to be a part of that." Refusing to look at either set of eyes fixed upon me, I focused on the blank television screen and wished that the damned thing was running as usual.

After what seemed like an eternity, Officer Fowler finally got up and slipped his pen back in his shirt pocket. He slapped the blank tablet against his leg. "Thank you for your time, Mrs. Martin."

I looked up at him, and he reached his hand out to me. I shook it. He offered his hand to Vince who shook it.

When Officer Fowler got to the door, he said to Vince, "You've got a brave little woman there."

"Yep, she's a keeper," Vince said gravely.

After Vince watched the policeman get in his car, he turned to me and asked, "Did you take my gun?"

"What makes you ask such a silly question?" My voice sounded tight and forced.

He worked his bottom jaw from side to side and watched me thoughtfully. "I didn't think you'd be stupid enough to do that." His words carried an unmistakable warning.

The following morning, I waited until my standard time to leave the house, but instead of going straight to Garrett's, I drove to Flatland. Starting at the bowling alley, I drove along back streets looking for the vacant lot where I had left the gun. Everything looked different in the light of day. I couldn't be sure how far I ran before I turned or how often. Several times, I went back to the bowling alley parking lot, trying to retrace my steps. I walked several vacant lots, but I found no gun.

\* \* \*

## March 13, 1973, Tuesday

Two hours later than he had anticipated her, Abi finally parked her VW bug next to his Charger. Garrett waited for her on the balcony landing. He could tell by the expression on her face that she was worried.

Intercepting her at the head of the stairs, he asked, "What's wrong?"

"Nothing," she said dismissively and walked past him.

He followed her into the apartment. "Where have you been? I expected you two hours ago."

"I got off to a late start," she said dismissively.

"But I called your house and no one answered," he challenged.

Her dark, anxious eyes locked with his. "What if my mother-in-law or someone else had picked up?"

"Look, I'm not an idiot. I know how to call and pretend to be a siding salesman."

She pressed her fingers to her temples like she had a headache. "It terrifies me to think about Vince finding out about you."

"He won't." Garrett grabbed her and kissed her neck.

She tilted her head, exposing more skin to him. While he gently nibbled her earlobes and lightly kissed her warm skin, she purred and ran her fingers through his hair.

He was ready to pick her up and carry her to the bedroom when she asked, "What's cooking?"

"It's my one and only recipe." He led her to the stove where he stirred the large pot. "It's fish soup. I learned how to make it in Vietnam. It's kind of spicy; you may not like it." He offered her a spoonful.

She sipped it and immediately coughed. "It is spicy. What did you put in it?"

"Most of the spices come from Vietnam." Remembering the lie he had told her about his friend Gary, he added, "Gary and Trang get them from her Vietnamese relatives in Houston." Garrett threw the spoon into the sink and grabbed her hand. "Come on. We're behind schedule. You promised me a day of lovemaking."

Abi laughed and playfully raced him to the bedroom. They made a contest of who could get the other person's clothes off first. Totally naked, they fell into bed, panting and laughing like children.

Slowly their laughter died, and she lay on her side, studying him with a satisfied smile. "You're wearing cologne."

"Yeah, Gary's family gave it to me for my birthday." He kissed her nose, wishing he had not been so heavy-handed with Trang's gift when he put it on this morning in anticipation of Abi's arrival.

"You see them a lot, don't you?" She gave him a look that made him wonder if she questioned the integrity of his story, or if she was toying with the pieces and did not like how the puzzle fit together.

"Yes, nearly every time I go to Houston." He worked his dog tags back and forth on the chain.

"Do you wish you had a child? Is that what draws you to him?" she asked.

"Are you asking if I wish you could give me a child?" He had been so relieved to steer the conversation away from Loc that the question spilled out before he considered how hurtful it might be.

She nodded and bowed her head.

He lifted her chin to look into her chocolate brown eyes. "Bird, you've given me more than that. You've given me yourself."

"Oh, Garrett, I love you." An expectant look lingered on her face.

A hush fell over the room, and he knew she wanted him to respond in kind. But he couldn't. It would only make the hole he stood in deeper. "You know I care deeply for you. And I know you want me to make a commitment to you, but I can't."

Tears filled her eyes.

"Abi, you're married. There's no way around that."

She played with his dog tags. "I don't have to stay married."

"No, you don't." He needed to tell her. He needed to be honest with her. He fully intended to leave Trang, but he couldn't right now, not with Loc so young and impressionable.

She didn't respond, so he charged ahead, "Abi, you've really changed this semester. I've seen you grow from a shy little girl to a beautiful, sensuous woman." Stroking her hair away from her face, he kissed her.

When they parted, he said, "Oh, God, Abi, you are so special to me." He held her tight, desperately wanting to say the words she yearned to hear.

They made love, got up and ate, went back to bed, made love again, and slept. When Abi awoke, it was an hour past time for her to leave. She pulled on her clothes and hurried toward the door without giving Garrett a good-bye kiss.

"See you tomorrow?" he called after her.

"Yes, tomorrow," she yelled back and ran for the car.

\*   \*   \*

All the way to Quits, I played with various explanations I might offer Vince. When I slipped in the backdoor, I heard Vince speaking in a hushed and serious tone, no doubt on the phone with his mother. I hurriedly pulled food from the refrigerator, not thinking about what I set on the counter while trying to look as if I had been there all along. Vince was still on the phone when someone knocked at the door, so I hurried to get it. A policeman stood on the porch with a gun in his hands. I opened the door and saw the damaged butt where I knocked out the pickup window. It had dark stains on it, probably my dried blood.

"Mrs. Martin?" the policeman asked.

I nodded because I felt too weak to speak.

Vince hung up the phone and strode to the door. "So you found it?"

"Yes, but it didn't give us much to go on. The only prints are yours, your wife's, and the guy who turned it in." He handed the rifle to Vince.

Vince examined the rifle. "These look like blood stains."

"We think that must be Mrs. Martin's blood."

"Where'd you find it?" Vince asked.

"Someone found it in the weeds. They turned it in Saturday morning. We had to run some test on it, or we would have gotten it back sooner." He tugged on the bill of his hat and stepped off of the porch.

I wanted to go with him or beg him to stay, anything but face Vince by myself. Vince followed him out to his car, chatting about the weather and asking why Officer Fowler hadn't mentioned the gun when he came yesterday. I retreated to the kitchen and supper, trying to make things look normal.

Vince walked straight to the kitchen upon entering the house. He got a cold beer and leaned against the cabinet, watching every move I made.

Enough time passed that I began thinking Vince wasn't going to explode after all. Although, it seemed impossible to hope that he had not figured out my hoax.

He drank the last of his beer then crushed the can against the counter. "You're a lying little bitch."

# Chapter Fourteen

*A pat on the back
don't cure saddle sores.*

**March 13, 1973, Tuesday**

*V*ince was so mad he could not see straight. Mama had just told him it was Spring Break, and here she was getting home late from wherever she'd gone, and whoever she'd been with. Probably Buck. Abi, Christi, and that bastard husband of hers had one of those open marriage things going, except Vince wasn't part of the game. Plus, there were no one else's prints on the rifle, so she lied about a guy making her go with him at gun point. What else was she lying about?

"I don't know why you think I'm lying." She opened a can of corn and dumped it into a pan. As she moved past him, he caught a whiff of a man's cologne and…cum.

"Where have you been?" he demanded.

This seemed to catch her off guard. She was probably thinking of a story to cover her ass about the gun. "S-s-studying. I lost track of the time. There's not a clock in the library."

"Mama said school's out." He started toward her. "She and Martha spent the day together."

As he neared her, she raised her arm in front of her face.

"You weren't in any goddamn library!" He caught her forearm and jerked it behind her, which made her yelp. Pulling it to the middle of her back, he said in her ear, "Where were you?" Again, he caught a whiff of

199

cum mixed with a man's cologne and her unique body odor, the smell of hot sweaty sex.

"I was studying," she insisted, although he could tell she was hurting.

"Without your books?" He pulled her arm higher as he pictured seeing her school bag beside the bed when he got home.

"Vince, you're hurting me," she cried.

"You're gonna hurt real bad before this is over." He increased the pressure on her arm.

She flailed at him with her free arm, so he grabbed it too.

"You think I'm stupid, don't you?" He emphasized each syllable with a separate jerk on her wrist that he held between her shoulder blades.

"I don't. Please, Vince, don't, please," she begged.

"Please, what? Let you go, so you can run off and do whatever you been doing all week." He loosened his hold slightly to give her a chance to confess. "Who you been fucking," he demanded, his lips in the small of her neck. Again, he smelled the results of some bastard fucking his wife.

"Nobody. I swear. Nobody," she pleaded.

The smell of cum on her seemed to get stronger, and he jerked her arm up in a tighter hold. "You're lying!" he shouted in her ear. "I can smell him on you. He's a pretty boy, ain't he? "

"I-I-I went went sh-shopping," she managed to get out. "That's just—that's just samples I tried on. I –I wanted to buy—to buy you a gift."

"With what? Where'd you get any money?" Vince demanded, slightly easing his hold to get her to talk.

"I don't have any. I was looking, just looking."

Vince pictured her in bed with Buck. "Who is he?" Vince demanded. The idea of it made him madder than ever, and he wrenched her arm as tight as he dared.

"Nobody!" she cried out defiantly.

"Where you been all week?" he shouted in her ear.

"The library."

"Without your books?" Still holding her arm behind her, he shoved Abi into the cabinet and penned his body against her. "You're lying. Just like you lied about the gun." He lifted himself above her and slammed his body against hers. "There wasn't an *attacker*. You're nothing but a lying little bitch."

"I was afraid you'd kill somebody." She gasped for breath. "I did it for you."

He forced Abi's cheek against the counter. "You did it for Buck. That's who you're fucking."

"I'm not. I'm not *fucking* anybody," she said amazingly sassy for someone so goddamn guilty.

Vince dragged her down the counter, shoving cans, pans of food, and dishes on the linoleum. When they got to the end, he released her and shoved her to the floor. "Take your clothes off." In one motion, he unbuckled his belt and whisked it from his pants.

She began scrambling toward the back door, no doubt thinking Daddy would help her.

Grabbing her hair, he jerked Abi to her feet. "I said take your clothes off."

Abi backed toward the door. "You can't do this again. You promised you wouldn't."

"And you promised you wouldn't lie to me again. Now get your clothes off."

She turned and bolted for the door, but Vince grabbed her shirt and dragged her screaming and kicking into the bedroom. He shut her up with a fist to her face, but she managed to duck, so he barely caught her jaw. It was enough to quieten her down, though. If she made enough noise, Daddy would be over here to see what was going on, so he grabbed her hair, held her face, and hammered it with his knuckles. It only took two hard licks before she passed out.

He ripped her clothes off, shirt buttons flying in every direction, and her jeans stubbornly clung to her hips and legs. Finding it impossible to get them off, he left them wrapped around her ankles along with her panties. When he finally had her back, butt, and legs exposed, he threw her face down on the bed.

While he bent to pick up his belt, he noticed Abi wiping at the blood that flowed from her lip and nose. Good. She needed to be awake for this. He stood over the bed, breathing heavily but not saying a word.

She rolled over to face him. "Vince, please don't. Please. I'll do anything you say."

"Too late for that."

She lay on her stomach, burying her face in a pillow. The first strike landed on her butt, causing her to flinch. She gripped the pillow with both hands. The next lash landed in the same spot. This time she cried out.

He lashed her three more times. "I'm going to kill that son of a bitch. I'm going to kill that mother-fucking bastard." The smell of cum and cologne and her sweat filled the room, and he was livid with the idea of another man touching his wife. As his rage built, his blows gradually struck in a wider range from her back all the way down her legs. With every few blows, he repeated his intentions, each time feeling more determined to make good on his vow. He would kill that sorry bastard. Nobody or nothing would stop him.

He stopped out of exhaustion—and if he kept going, he would kill her. Vince dealt one final lash, which made her yelp, assuring him she was still alive. But ole' Buckie-boy wasn't going to live much longer.

"I'm going to kill that bastard." He grabbed a box of ammunition from his night stand. Someone might have emptied his gun, and he wanted to make sure he had plenty of ammo to settle this score once and for all. His heavy steps shook the wooden floor as he staggered unsteadily toward the living room to get his blood-stained gun. He stopped in the kitchen long enough to grab a few cold ones out of the refrigerator before he marched out the back door. The tires on his pickup screeched as he peeled out. He didn't care if Daddy heard him or not. Nothing was going to stop him.

*     *     *

I could not feel my body. Nor could I see for the thick haze that surrounded me. Vince's threat to kill Buck kept echoing in my ears. I had to call Christi and warn her. Realizing my feet were bound together with my pants, I tried to pull out one foot and found it impossible. Somehow I had to get to the wall phone in the kitchen. Taking small hops, I slowly moved toward the doorway. Finally, I had the phone in my hand, and I stuck my finger in the rotary dial, hoping it was the zero hole. If I could only get an operator on the phone, she would connect me to Christi. Vince would be mad when he saw the charge on the phone bill. Funny, how my mind worked. Vince had all but killed me, and I still worried about what would piss him off next.

* * *

Garrett sat in his chair in the Houston apartment. About an hour ago, he began worrying about Abi—again. This was getting to be a pattern, although the churning in his gut told him this time was far worse.

Remarkably, he had gotten to Houston in record time, although he was still too late for Vinh and Trang to go to class. With Garrett there, Trang had asked Vinh to take her to the grocery store. Loc sat in the floor, constructing an airplane with the Erector set Trang had bought at a garage sale. He loved building models, especially of things that he could relate to like the airplane that his daddy flew. Garrett's statistics book lay open in his lap, but he had not read a word of it.

"Time for bed." Garrett closed his book and set it aside.

"No, Daddy, ten more minutes." It was the same most nights Garrett stayed with him, ten more minutes, and ten more minutes, until finally Garrett had to pick up Loc and forcefully put him in bed.

"Now, Loc. Mama will not be happy if she comes home and sees you are still awake." Garrett began gathering up the metal strips, nuts, and washers.

"She's not happy already. Every day you tell her you will be here in time for her to go to school, and every day you are later than the time before. She says she knows you will not come when you say you will."

Trang was right, but where did she get off criticizing him in front of their son?

"Why are you always late daddy? Mama told Uncle Vinh that she thinks you have a girlfriend." Loc lined up two holes and carefully worked a bolt through it.

Plus, she had no right to ruin his relationship with his son.

"Do you have a girlfriend, Daddy?" Loc asked matter-of-factly.

There was no way to make his son understand because Garrett didn't. "No, Loc. I don't have a girlfriend." He scooped his son up and carried him down the hallway to Loc's bedroom.

"Mama says the scratches on your back were made by another woman. That's what she told Uncle Vinh." Loc looked at him with eyes that begged him to disprove his mother's words.

Garrett had noticed when Vinh picked him up at the airport that the little man would not look him in the eye. "I got some mosquito bites, and I scratched them." He wondered when he had been careless enough to let Trang see his bare back, or if she was actively looking for evidence to support her suspicions.

After they settled down to read a book, Loc asked, "You won't quit coming to see me, will you, Daddy? You won't get another family, will you?"

"No, Loc. You're my only son. I love you more than there are seconds in the day."

"More than there are fish in the sea," Loc chimed in, repeating a phrase that Garrett had often used.

"More than there are stars in the sky." Garrett did love him—that much and more.

\*   \*   \*

It was dark outside, and I was in my own bed rather than the kitchen floor. People were in the room, but I couldn't make out anything except blurred images. When someone tried to roll me over, a sharp pain radiated from my shoulder socket, and I cried out.

"That side is bruised and swollen. Let's go the other way." It was Christi, calm and in charge. She had understood what I said on the phone, and Buck was okay, or she wouldn't be here.

"Let's cover her up," Thelma said. "She's indecent. Daddy, you should go back in the kitchen."

"Stay," Christi demanded. "You both need to see what kind of an animal your son is."

"That girl's bringing everything on herself, acting like a she-dog," Thelma spat back at her.

"Now, Mother," A.V. said, his voice thick with worry. "We may have coddled Vince a bit too much."

"Coddled!" Christi repeated indignantly. "Your son's not spoiled, he's insane. Look what he's done to her!" Christi shouted. "You can't just sit back and allow this to go on. This isn't the first time."

"Well now, missy, let's not go jumping to conclusions," Thelma said indignantly.

"Conclusions!" Christi exploded. "You and I both know Vince put her in the hospital back in December. There's no telling how many times he beat her before that."

"Vince wouldn't do anything to her that she didn't deserve," Thelma shouted back.

The room went silent, and I figured Christi had decided reasoning with Thelma was futile.

"Mr. Martin," Christi said with forced calmness, "I really think you should let Vince cool off in jail for a few days. If you bail him out tomorrow, he'll come home and kill Abi."

A.V. didn't answer. He liked to think things over and come to his own conclusions.

"You can't do that, Daddy," Thelma whined. "You've got to get him out as soon as they'll let you. What will people say if you leave him there, especially with you being a deacon at the church and all?"

"We should take Abi to the hospital." Christi adjusted the ice pack next to my face.

I needed to tell her I appreciated her being there, but I didn't feel strong enough to utter a word.

"We'll leave Vince where he is for the time being," A.V. bent close, his quiet breathing hummed in my ear, and I imagined him looking at my back. "Mother, go get that bag balm. We'll put that on tonight and see what these whelps look like in the morning."

Thelma let out a deep sigh before she waddled out of the room.

"And get those pain pills Dr. Cannon gave me last month for that toothache," A.V. called after Thelma.

The screen door slammed shut.

"If Abi's not better by morning, we'll take her in. You best go home to your family now," A.V. said.

"I'd rather stay here, Mr. Martin. Buck will want me to," Christi said decisively.

After a long pause, A.V. said, "We'll come over early in the morning and check on you." He moved toward the door. "Thelma will help you find anything you need." He walked out, his steps slower than usual.

Christi sat on the bed and stroked my arm. Then she walked to the kitchen phone and called an operator, telling her she needed to place a long distance call to her phone number. When Vince saw the charges—both for me calling Christi and now that she was calling Buck—he would be mad all over again.

After the operator made the connection, Christi said in a ragged voice, "Oh, Buck, Abi's face looks like he used her for a punching bag, and her back and legs are covered with huge whelps and bruises where he lashed her. He's crazy, Buck. I'm afraid of what he will do when his dad bails him out."

Several times she repeated how glad she was that the police had gotten to their house immediately after Vince arrived. She kept saying she hated to think what might have happened if I had not warned them, so they could call the police.

The back door opened, probably Thelma returning.

"They won't let me take Abi to the hospital, which is where she belongs, so I'm staying here tonight. I'll call you in the morning. I love you." Christi hung up.

"I've got the salve and painkillers," Thelma said as soon as Christi hung up the phone.

She and Christi applied the sticky ointment to my back, butt, and legs. Still lying on my side, Christi covered me with a sheet. She held my head up, so I could sip some water from a glass she held. Then Thelma poked two pills in my mouth. I tried to swallow, but a wave of nausea overcame me, my stomach wrenched, and I spewed the dark blood that had coagulated in my stomach all over Thelma and the bed.

"Well, I never," Thelma shrieked, her hands in the air as she looked down at the jelly-like globs clinging to the bodice of her dress.

Christi began helping me sit up, so I could get out of the mess. When she saw that Thelma was standing there doing nothing, Christi shouted, "Go get something to clean this up."

"To clean me up," Thelma harrumphed and lumbered into the bathroom.

"Good job, Ab," Christi muttered.

I wanted to laugh, but the swollen muscles of my face would not flex enough to form a smile, much less laugh. By the time Thelma got back from the bathroom, Christi had gotten me out of bed and positioned me so that I could steady myself with the dresser. After changing the sheets, they cleaned me up, helped me back in bed, and gave me more pills, which I managed to swallow and keep down.

"I'll leave my phone number on the kitchen table," Thelma said. "If Vince calls, you let me know."

Christi didn't respond, and I imagined my friend thinking Hell would freeze over before she did anything for Thelma, especially something to do with Vince.

Thelma left, and Christi lay beside me, my hands in hers. I thought of the many nights we had slept together, lying awake talking until the early morning hours. That was so long ago, and yet with her there beside me it could have been yesterday.

"Thanks," I whispered, drifting into a drugged sleep.

*   *   *

Garrett woke with a start. That same heavy feeling that he had gone to sleep with felt even more pronounced. Something was terribly wrong with Abi. Loc lay next to him, sleeping soundly. After slipping out of bed, he tiptoed down the hall to the living room. Vinh was sleeping on the couch, his bed when Garrett needed a ride to the airport the next morning. The glow of a streetlight shone through the window onto his gaunt face.

Shaking his shoulder, Garrett whispered in his ear, "I need to go. Can you take me?"

Vinh rolled over and muttered something unintelligible.

Garrett shook him harder. "I need to go to the airport."

Staggering to his feet, the little man began buttoning his open shirt. Trang appeared in the doorway of her bedroom. She wore a silk, formfitting robe. At one time it would have tempted him.

"Why you go now?" she demanded.

"I need to get back. I told my boss I would get the plane back in time for an early flight to Dallas."

"You go to hussy," Trang spat, her black eyes squinted.

The term hussy almost made him laugh, but he dared not make light of her accusation. Like it or not, she was the mother of his son, and she could use her wrath beyond what she had already done. "I'm not going to fight with you. You live here, and I live in Oaces. You knew it would be hard to be separated."

"Sep-ar-a-ted?" she said, pronouncing each syllable as she approached him. "You act like we divorced. You act like I not your wife, like I did not save your life."

"I will always be grateful, but I can't turn my emotions on and off like a faucet." He wasn't making sense, but he had to say something to get out of there. He grabbed his backpack by the door.

"I pregnant," she announced, loud enough to wake Loc.

Stunned, Garrett gawked at her. He shook his head. "That's impossible."

"I go to doctor today."

"But how? We haven't. . . ."

Tears stood in her eyes. At least six weeks ago, he had woken up next to her. She had tricked him into having sex with her. Once more she had trapped him.

As they drove, Vinh snuck peeks at Garrett. "Trang not happy you don't come when you say."

"She's not happy no matter what I do," Garrett shot back.

"You say you come Houston in plenty of time for class. We late every night. Teacher get mad."

"I'll try to do better," Garrett promised.

"You always say that." Vinh's gaze was riveted to the beam of the headlight. "Trang beautiful woman. She get new husband, new father for Loc. Different daddy for new baby."

Garrett wanted to grab his skinny little neck and squeeze. This bastard didn't have the right to threaten him with losing Loc. But first he had to get back to Oaces. That weight of concern that he had gone to bed with grew heavier by the second.

*   *   *

In the morning, I focused my blurred vision and saw Christi staring back at me.

"How do you feel, Abi?"

I raised my fingers from my pillow and rubbed my thumb and index finger together in a circular motion, answering the way we had as teenagers.

She laughed and held my hand. "Better, apparently. How about a bath?"

"Not too hot," I said weakly.

While Christi ran the water, I moved like a ninety-year-old toward the bathroom. After I emptied my bladder, Christi steadied me while I stepped into the tub and slowly sat down. The warm water felt good, but every part of me still hurt.

Christi was working in the kitchen when A.V. let himself in the back door. Through the open doorways between the bathroom and the kitchen, I heard him ask how I was doing. She said I was soaking in the tub, and she still thought they should take me to the hospital. The time for him to leave for work had passed. A.V. might be on his way to bail out Vince. I had to talk to A.V. before he left.

I called for Christi while I struggled to get up. When she got there, I told her I needed to talk to Papa Martin. She relayed the message to him and then helped me out of the tub and gently dried me.

After slipping on a housecoat, I walked slowly into the kitchen where I found A.V. seated at the head of the table where Vince usually sat. His shoulders were hunched, and his head sagged.

"Papa Martin," I said as I entered the kitchen.

He looked at me with sad eyes and a face that had aged twenty years overnight. "You feeling better?"

"Some." I carefully lowered myself onto a pillow that Christi had laid in my chair.

My legs and butt were so sore, I could barely stand to rest my weight on them, but I also felt too weak to stand, and I desperately needed to sort things out with Papa Martin. Christi scrambled eggs while Papa Martin and I sipped coffee and stared at the gray Formica table top. He was too private to talk in front of Christi, although that seemed ridiculous considering her part in all of this.

After preparing three plates, she sat two of them in front of us. "I'll leave you two to talk in private." She carried a plate and a cup of coffee out the back door, shutting it behind her.

A.V. bowed his head mumbled a few words and then he looked up at me. When our eyes met, I realized he was praying, whether it was his standard prayer or one specific to his current needs, I did not know.

"I'm scared—of Vince," I admitted, needing to know where Papa Martin stood with all this.

"You must be. I saw what he did in December. Is that the only time before this?" he asked.

I shook my head and dropped my gaze to the scrambled eggs. "No. He started hitting me not long after we married, but lately he's gotten a lot worse."

"He's always had a temper." He picked up his fork. "What set him off last night?"

"I was the one who stole the gun." Thankfully, I could tell him something that was true.

He bunched his brow and cocked his head to the side. "Why?"

"Vince took it to the bowling alley because he was mad at the people we used to bowl with. I was scared he would kill somebody, so I made it look like the gun had been stolen out of the truck. Then I left it in a vacant lot. Someone turned it in and the police brought it back last night."

A.V. nodded. "Who did he intend to use the gun on at the bowling alley?"

"Christi's husband. Vince thinks Buck and I are having an affair. He's always been jealous of him."

"But you're not?" A.V. held his coffee cup to his lips.

"Of course not; Christi's my best friend." Again, I was glad I could answer without lying.

"She said you called her last night, apparently after Vince left here." I nodded.

"I was surprised you could—considering the shape you were in."

"He left here saying he was going to kill Buck, and I believed him."

A dog down the street barked and the old refrigerator hummed. The phone rang.

Papa Martin answered it. After a short exchange, he hung up. "Siding salesman. Pretty early in the day for that."

It had been Garrett. Knowing my father-in-law had spoken to my lover gave me the willies.

After some time, Papa Martin cleared his throat. "If you'll agree to stay with Vince, I'll make him understand he can't do this again."

The idea that I could actually leave Vince had not occurred to me. If Garrett proposed, I would, but I couldn't count on that, especially with me looking as I did. For now, I needed the assurance that Vince wasn't going to kill me, and A.V. was the one person who could halfway guarantee that. I studied his downcast face for several seconds before I realized I was in a bargaining position. Given our track record, Vince would do this again, which told me I needed to be better equipped to leave in the future—no matter what happened with Garrett. "I want to finish school."

"I'll make sure you have the money for that," he promised, sounding relieved I would settle for so little.

"The money is important, but make Vince promise he won't try to stop me every time he gets mad."

He nodded, got up, having barely eaten anything, and left after lightly touching me on the shoulder.

Christi immediately came back inside.

She set her plate in the sink and sat down where A.V. had been. "Ab, come home with me."

"I can't. Vince will probably come back today."

"All the more reason. You can't stay here!"

"If I left Vince, he'd kill me."

"He'll kill you if you don't leave." She paused. "When Buck heard what he did to you in December, he wanted to do the same thing to him, but I convinced him it would only backfire on you. Now look at you."

I must look awful. What would Garrett think if he saw me? A part of me wanted to tell Christi about Garrett, but that would only fuel her conviction that I needed to leave.

"Come home with me." she repeated.

I loved that she thought we could fix things by resorting to our childhood strategy of going to one another's houses. "Where do I go after that?" I couldn't mooch off her and Buck indefinitely.

"I'll help you find an apartment. We can work together again," she said energetically.

Her optimism was both contagious as well as exhausting. "I can't. I'm not strong enough."

The faucet dripped and the refrigerator started up again. Christi had opened her mouth and was about to say something when the phone rang. She got up to answer it.

"It's Dr. Posey." She handed me the phone.

"Hello," I answered, puzzled that Dr. Posey had called me.

"Bird, are you okay? You sound funny," Garrett said, clearly frantic.

"I'm fine." My heart raced at the sound of his voice. I couldn't believe he had called a second time.

"Can you talk?"

"No," I said, aware of every word I uttered in front of Christi.

"Abi, something's happened, and I'm worried about you. Call me when you can. Please call me."

"I'm not sure I can."

"Abi, I have to talk to you. Call me collect when you're alone."

My hands sweated, and I stalled, trying to think of some way to tell him I couldn't. "My group will try to schedule a time when everyone can get together next week."

"I can't wait until next week, Abi. Call me collect before then," he demanded anxiously.

"Good-bye," I said, trying to sound impersonal.

I tried to get up to hang up the phone, but Christi took it from me. Her gaze shifted to the receiver and the tiny, agitated voice we both heard coming out of it. She started to put the phone to her ear, but I put my hand on it and shook my head.

Christi sighed deeply and returned the phone to the cradle on the wall next to the bedroom door. She sat down and watched me, waiting for an explanation. When I failed to offer one, she asked, "Was that Garrett?"

Dumbfounded by her question, I stared at her.

"You said his name over and over again last night. Was that him?" she demanded.

"He's just a friend," I said, my voice wavering.

"A really good friend?" she asked with insinuation.

"Yes, he's been very good to me."

"What's going to happen when you say his name when Vince is lying where I was last night?" She paused. "You think he's going to buy that crap about a study group."

"I don't usually talk in my sleep."

"It won't take but once, Abi."

The phone rang again. I held my breath while she answered. She immediately told Buck about her concern for me and that I was stubbornly refusing to go home with her. She finished, saying she'd be home soon.

After Christi hung up from talking to Buck, she helped me back to bed where she applied fresh ointment. "Do you know this is that stuff they put on cow's udders?" she asked as she gingerly dabbed it on.

"Yeah, the Martins use it for everything from smashed thumbs to mosquito bites."

We both laughed, although that made my ribs and even my back hurt.

After she finished, she moved to the other side of the bed and lay facing me like she had last night. Taking my hands in hers, she asked, "Will you go home with me?"

"I can't."

Christi heaved a heavy sigh. "You know how to reach me." She got up and kissed me on the cheek before letting herself out the back door.

As I listened to her car back out of the drive, the first tears escaped. After that, I cried with deep racking sobs until I fell asleep, exhausted.

# Chapter Fifteen

*The wolf loses his teeth,*
*not his nature.*

## March 15, 1973, Thursday

A t noon the next day, Thelma brought over beef stew. Without a word, she situated me at the table and left. What had she told A.V. about me going somewhere besides class and how would that influence him? Watching the kitchen clock, I thought about whether or not Vince was out of jail, me talking in my sleep, and what Christi had said about him eventually killing me. If he found out about Garrett, he would murder both of us.

By the time I tried the first spoonful, the soup had turned cold. Besides, my mouth was too sore to chew. When I washed my hands, I looked in the bathroom mirror at a hideous face staring back at me. My lips, swollen to twice their normal size, hurt to even move. After awkwardly brushing my teeth, I wiggled my front teeth to see if they were loose, which they were. My eyes were bloodshot and encircled with purple and blue blotches. Anyone, including Garrett, would be repulsed.

I returned to bed and slept all afternoon. The phone woke me to late afternoon shadows. Fearing—yet hoping—it would be Garrett, I struggled out of bed and staggered to the kitchen wall phone.

"You eating over here or you want room service?" Thelma snarled. A.V. had probably told her to call.

"Would you mind sending something? I'm not dressed."

"Fine," she retorted and hung up.

In the kitchen, I dumped the soup from lunch into the garbage can under the sink and poured myself a glass of milk. Easing onto the chair with the pillow, I wondered who would show up—A.V. or Thelma, or maybe even Vince. From the length of time that passed, I figured they were debating the issue. Finally, I heard someone on the back porch. A.V. walked into the kitchen carrying a bowl of peach cobbler and a plate of steak, mashed potatoes, and green beans. He sat them on the table in front of me and then took Vince's chair.

Thinking I needed silverware, but knowing I wasn't about to eat in front of him, I said, "Thanks for bringing this over."

"You're welcome." He cleared his throat. "Vince is at the house."

I studied the Sunday dinner meal and wondered if this was Vince's welcome home meal.

"He'll be staying there tonight." He paused. "We discussed what you and I talked about yesterday."

I nodded.

A.V. cleared his throat. "He's still really mad."

"I'm sure he is. Spending two nights in jail can't be fun." Of course, that was not what had him pissed.

"It's been a while since I took a vacation, so we decided to take off for a week or so. He needs the time to cool down…and I need to get to know him again." His eyes watered, and he blinked several times.

Papa Martin was a caring man, but I had never given him much credit in the sensitivity department. His haggard face spoke volumes about how he felt about Vince's actions. I couldn't imagine how he'd react if he knew what I had done.

"We're going down country to do a little fishing." He spoke lighter now, almost like it was something he had been wanting to do for a long time. "Mother will stay here."

"If she wants to go with you, she doesn't need to babysit me," I said.

"Vince and I need time to talk—alone. We got some things to work on." He quickly glanced at me.

I nodded. Neither one of us had to say it would be easier to talk without Thelma there. When he got up to go, I put my hand on his sleeve. "Thanks for helping me, Papa Martin."

He patted my hand and his face twisted into a grimace as he looked at me. "I still can't believe my son could do such a thing—and not have an ounce of regret. That's what we got to work on." His steps were slow and heavy as he walked out of the house.

His final comment summarized where Vince was with all of this. That night I slept fitfully, waking every thirty minutes or so with a start, fearful that Vince had returned to finish the job.

In the morning, while I soaked in a hot bath, the phone rang three different times. I had just gotten out when I heard Vince's heavy footsteps through the open bathroom door. He pulled our suitcase from beneath the bed and began filling it. I stood naked in the bathroom, trying to muster the courage to go into the bedroom and dress. Finally, I wrapped the towel around me and inched my way to the dresser where his drawers stood open. He slammed the suitcase shut. When it did not latch, he cursed and hammered it closed. Jerking it up, he walked toward the kitchen.

In the doorway Vince stopped, but did not face me. "We'll be back, not this Sunday but the next." After a pause, he added, "I'm sorry for hurting you."

"You're not sorry. You don't even know what you did to me. And you're too scared to look." I marveled at the fact that I had found the courage to talk to him that way.

He slowly turned. Realizing my opportunity, I looked him square in the eye, so he could see my face. After a few seconds, I turned my back to him and dropped the towel.

We stood frozen for what seemed like an eternity.

The sound of him swallowing reached me through the silence that separated us. "Are you screwing somebody else?"

"No," I answered, afraid to face him for fear that the truth would show on my face.

"I don't believe you." He marched out of the house.

\*   \*   \*

Sick with worry, Garrett drove to Quits Friday afternoon. He cruised the streets of the little town, looking for Abi's car and finally spotting it parked next to a white, stucco house. Abi's in-laws lived next door in the house with the same blue trim—close enough to eavesdrop on their dinner conversation, according to Abi. Two cars sat in their driveway, an older Cadillac and a Ranchero pickup, the car Abi said the two men drove to work. Apparently they were already home, which didn't feel right. Abi never left Oaces until about this time—even on Friday. The large, black truck that he had seen Abi and Vince in at the intersection outside of town was not there. Either Vince went somewhere alone in it or Abi was with him. More than anything, Garrett wanted to check on Abi, but he wasn't about to risk going to her door, pretending to be a salesman or someone looking for directions, and risk finding Vince at home.

Still, he needed a way to contact her or at least talk to someone who knew her and could make sure she was okay. While the overwhelming feeling of worry had subsided some, it had not disappeared. Who would know about Abi? Then he thought about Abi's mom, who Abi had said lived in Dahlia, not far from Quits. He pulled out his map, found it, and drove that direction.

After driving up and down Main Street, Garrett pulled in at a gas station. Careful to hide his hair under his wide-brimmed leather hat, he stepped inside and said to the old man behind the counter, "I'm looking for a hair salon in this area? It's owned by a local lady, but I can't remember the name of it."

"Hair salon? Looks like you need a barber," the old man said skeptically.

Garrett smiled, eager to get along, but not leave too much of an impression.

"Oh, you mean Betty Barker's place." He pointed. "Go down this road until you're just outside of town. It's that white house-looking building on the south side of the road. There will be a bunch of cars parked around it, ladies getting ready from Saturday night fun and Sunday morning repenting."

Garrett thanked him and drove to a house he must have passed several times. It was adjacent to a cotton field, probably the one Abi's father farmed. Elm trees surrounded it. Garrett parked his Charger next to a brand new Chevrolet. He walked up the cracked and undulating sidewalk, probably the result of all the elm roots that veined the grass-less yard. Next to the door, he saw a faded sign that read Beauty Box. As he stepped up the crumbling cement steps, he released his hair from his hat. That gave him an obvious reason for being here.

A tall, red-head flashed him a toothy smile as soon as he stepped inside. "Well, put on your sittin' britches, and come on in." From Abi's description, Garrett figured she was Charlene, the outspoken cutup who had worked with Abi's mom for a couple of decades.

Garrett nodded. "Hello." He looked around the small room for an empty chair, but there were none.

Charlene held her comb poised over a head of hair that stood out a foot in every direction. "Betty, wouldn't you kill to have hair like that?" She stared at Garrett as she spoke to the lady who worked next to her.

Betty who was winding silver-colored hair around small rods glanced at Garrett. She looked too much like Abi not to be her mother. "Too much trouble," she answered dryly.

"We gonna cut those lovely locks?" Charlene asked, looking at Garrett.

"Yes, ma'am, I want a trim." Primarily, he wanted to talk to Abi's mom. "A friend of mine said Betty cut his hair." He looked at Betty. "Could you work me in this afternoon?"

Betty glanced at a woman sitting under a hairdryer, at another one leafing through a magazine, and then at her watch. It was close to five. "You'll have to wait a while."

"That's fine." He grabbed a two-year-old copy of *Lady's Home Journal* from an overflowing magazine rack and began scanning it as he leaned against a free wall next to the shampoo sink. If he stood around long enough someone might mention Abi.

Bernice talked about her gall bladder operation, and Helen filled everyone in on her trip to Hawaii.

Garrett was dozing off behind the magazine when Betty's customer asked her, "Didn't your daughter marry that Martin boy from Quits? I saw in the paper about him having a run-in with the law."

Betty focused on the curls she was layering in a dome on top of the woman's head. "He probably got a speeding ticket, and they needed filler for the newspaper. You know how they blow that stuff up."

The customer held up her finger and started to say something else when Betty asked Garrett, "Who did you say sent you over here?"

"I don't know his name—just a guy in my class who said you did a really good job on his hair." Garrett couldn't risk getting creative since Betty probably knew every customer by name.

"Where do you go to school?" she asked.

"UP," he answered, hoping she would mention that her daughter was going to school there as well.

She nodded and returned to the dome of flattened curls.

"So how's Abi doing?" Charlene asked Betty, her question following too closely to be coincidental after the comment from Betty's customer as well as him mentioning UP.

"Last we talked she had midterm exams coming up. She's been off this week for Spring Break."

"And you haven't heard from her all week?" Charlene asked.

"Nope," Betty answered. She dropped her comb, picked it up, and pitched it on the counter. Getting another one from a drawer, she glanced at Garrett. "I can't think of anyone I've cut that goes to UP."

"He said it had been a while. And it might have even been last semester that I talked to him." Garrett needed to shift the conversation back to Abi and the newspaper article.

"Betty, I'm done for the day. Let me give Goldilocks here a trim while you finish up." Charlene winked at Garrett and snipped her scissors open and shut a few times. "What's your name?"

"Gary," he said, sticking with the one he'd given Abi. Too many aliases, and he'd trip himself up.

Charlene sat him in her chair and tied a vinyl cape around his neck. She looked at his reflection in the mirror. "Okay, Gary, how much?"

"Just a half inch, no more than that," he answered.

Running her long, red fingernails through his hair, she glanced at his reflection and then refocused on his hair. "You show up without an appointment, wait an hour, and all you want is barely a trim? That doesn't make good sense."

"Actually, I'm looking for a place to take my son." He needed to think of something she would buy, and she looked like a sucker for kids.

Her eyebrows raised in a way that demanded he tell her more.

"He gets made fun of because he is half Vietnamese, and I'm looking for a place where he will feel comfortable." It was a stretch, but she seemed to be buying it.

"What's your son's name?" She worked a comb through the tangles that had formed when he drove with his windows down.

"Loc," Garrett answered. Too many lies would surely backfire on him.

She combed and trimmed and quizzed him about Loc's age and interests.

Diverting the conversation, Garrett asked, "Do you have any children?"

"Naw, I never married. Me and Betty just share Abi."

"Is that who you mentioned earlier?" Garrett asked.

"Yep, she's our baby. I haven't seen her, though, in a month of Sundays. Betty, let's call Abi up and tell her to get herself over here. We're behind on what's going on with that gal."

"That's a good idea," Garrett said spontaneously. Betty shot him a quizzical look, so he added, "You can never spend enough time with your kids. My son is only six, but he'll be driving before I know it."

Vince making the newspaper and Betty refusing to talk about it worried Garrett. Urging Betty to check on Abi felt like a step in the right direction. Hopefully his suggestion would not backfire on him or Abi.

\*    \*    \*

## March 17, 1973, Saturday

Close to dark, Vince and his dad faced each other over a blazing campfire. They had some trouble getting it started, so the grease was just now getting hot enough. Daddy was in charge of frying fish while Vince tended the fried potatoes. This was their second day camping, and their first meal of fried fish. Vince had never cooked in his life. Thankfully, Daddy seemed to know what he was doing.

Vince remembered going camping with his dad as a boy and having Daddy all to himself while Mama stayed home with Bea. Back then, they fished most of the day. Then they cleaned what they caught, and if they had been lucky enough, they ate until they were miserably full. So far, they had not had that problem. Neither one of them seemed that keen on fishing—or talking. Daddy was probably waiting for Vince to apologize. Hell would freeze over before that happened.

Leaving town was the last thing Vince wanted to do, but it was the only option his dad gave him besides staying in jail. From the minute his folks showed up at the jail, Vince knew Daddy was taking Abi's side. He wouldn't listen when Vince tried to tell him he smelled another man on her. And when Mama tried to speak up, Daddy said he wouldn't hear it. His dad was stern, but he had never known him to be this hard-headed.

After Vince went over to get his clothes for the trip and saw what he had done to Abi, he understood why Daddy thought the worst of him. At least, he had an open mind about the gun business. He agreed it was wrong for Abi to make up a story like that. The one issue Vince couldn't let go of was her screwing someone else. Daddy wouldn't discuss the idea, but Vince knew she was. Every time she was around Buck, she gave him that moony-eyed look. Ever since she started that damned school, she had been coming home later and later. He remembered holding her from behind and smelling that pretty-boy cologne on her. More than that, he had smelled cum. She was fucking someone. He knew that better than he knew his own name.

"How are those potatoes coming along?" Daddy asked.

Vince poked at them with a long handled wooden spoon. "I think they're just about done."

"Take them up on that plate." He pointed to a chipped plate on a large boulder they were using as a table. "Check that can of beans and see if they are bubbling." He scooped fish fillets out of a pan of grease. "I think we are about ready to eat us a feast."

"Good, my belly and my backbone are bumping," Vince said.

The flames of the campfire lit up Daddy's smiling face. "Where'd you get that one?"

"Abi says it sometimes," Vince had to admit, although he didn't want to talk about her.

Daddy set a plate of fried fish on the boulder. "Yeah, that Abi, she's something."

"Yes, she is." Vince doubted they could agree on what that something was.

* * *

Sunday morning, I lay in bed when I heard a car pull into Thelma's drive. Through the window, I saw Martha Hasselmeyer knocking at Thelma's front door. Thelma came out dressed for church, and they left in Martha's car. In the bathroom, I examined my body with a hand-held mirror. Prominent bruises still crisscrossed and overlapped each other on my back and legs. The swelling in my face had gone down, but my black eyes seemed more conspicuous than ever. Intending to go to school the next day, I experimented with make-up.

Finally feeling strong enough to work on it, I pulled out my better mouse trap project and finished it, so I could turn it in Tuesday when I went to class. Late that afternoon I sat studying in bed. It felt good to have the house to myself, but I couldn't quit worrying about what would happen after Vince and Papa Martin got home. The phone rang, and I answered, pretty sure it was Mama, wanting to know why I had not come to see her.

"Hi, Baby. Aren't you coming over today?"

"I've got a lot of studying to do."

"You sound funny. Is there something wrong?"

"No, I just have some allergies." My nose was still swollen. "I made all A's on my mid-term tests."

"Great, I knew you would. How's Vince?" She must know something.

"He's gone fishing with his dad," I replied.

"Really? When will they be back?"

"Next Sunday. A week from today."

Mama hesitated before speaking. "We saw in the paper where Vince had been arrested."

"What did the paper say?" Getting arrested was big news in a little town.

"It said he threatened to shoot Christi's husband, Buck."

"That was just a silly misunderstanding." Given the option, Buck had probably pressed charges.

"It says he spent two nights in jail. Is everything all right now?"

"Yeah, everything's fine." I tried to sound nonchalant.

I wanted to tell her the truth, but my throat tightened as I remembered the first time Vince beat me and both of my parents had told me in their own words, "You made your bed, now lie in it."

We talked for a few more minutes before she hung up.

Monday morning, I stared in the bathroom mirror and wondered if the dark glasses out of Bea's give away bag didn't look more obvious than the black eyes they partially concealed. I parked across campus from my usual spot, knowing Garrett would look for my car. When I got to class, I sat in the back away from Lucille who had been smart enough to get rid of her husband. Fellow students asked me about my bruises, and I said I had a car accident. During her lecture, Dr. Horton kept looking at me like she was trying to figure out what was wrong.

After class, she stood by her podium until I walked past. "Ms. Martin, I'd like to talk with you."

I ducked my head, trying to hide the obvious. "I really need to go. Can it wait until Wednesday?"

She didn't respond.

I looked at her concerned face. "Is that all right?"

"Yes, of course," she said with more softness than I expected from her.

In my art class, I told people who asked the same thing I said in history class. Because the weather was so nice, Dr. Cole told us to draw outside. I found some interesting sculptures far from everyone else.

On the way to my car, I took my usual short cut through the social science building, which took me past Dr. Posey's door. Typically, I stopped if I had any excuse at all to talk to her. This time I looked the other direction, which put me directly in line with her walking toward me.

When I tried to walk past her, she grabbed my arm. "Abi, my goodness what happened to you?"

"I—I've got to go." I could have said I had been in a car accident, but if she saw Garrett and told him that, it would only make him more concerned. Eventually, I would face him, but I needed more time, and a better story than I had come up with so far.

She kept a hold on my arm. "Abi, would you like to come to my office and talk?"

"No, no, I've got to go." As I hurried away, I glanced back and saw the revulsion on her face. Why had I been so stupid, coming this close to her office? I would see her tomorrow, but by then I had hoped to look better and have made up a story to go along with my appearance. For now, I had to get off campus before Garrett saw me. I desperately wanted to talk to him, but I couldn't face the possibility that he would be repulsed by my appearance, or, worse, unmoved to action by what had happened to me.

*   *   *

When Garrett got out of class, he scanned the parking lot that Abi usually used. He had done that when he first got to school, but he had not spotted her VW bug. Thinking she might have gotten there later than usual, he looked again. Abi once mentioned that she often stopped to talk to Mariam Posey. Garrett decided to gamble that they had spoken. He needed someone to assure him that she was okay.

Like nearly every other time he had dropped by her office, Mariam was bent over a pile of papers. Seeing him, she motioned for him to come in. "Have a seat if you can find a place."

"Thanks. How was your Spring Break?" He cleared a tall pile of papers from the only other chair.

"My husband and I went to London. What did you do?"

"I spent most of my time worried about Abi." A direct approach might yield the most information.

She put the cap on her pen and took a deep breath as she sat back in her seat. After a moment, she checked a nearby coffee cup and laughed softly to herself. "It's grown mold in my absence."

The fact that she refused to broach the subject told Garrett she knew something. "What's going on? What's wrong with Abi?" he asked, again hoping his openness would produce something.

"I don't know what's going on in Abi's world, but I do know that interference can only exacerbate the situation." She tossed her pen on the desk.

"Exacerbate?" He gripped the arm of the chair to keep from jumping out of it and shaking her. "If you don't know then how can my *interference* make a difference?"

She flexed her jaw and then picked up her pen. "I've already said more than I should."

"I care about Abi. I want to know what's wrong. Apparently, she said something to you. Please, tell me what I can do to help her."

She studied Garrett. "If you want to help, leave her alone." She returned to her grading.

He got up and walked away, totally perplexed by Mariam's desire to protect Abi from him. He loved Abi—even if he had not had the courage to say that to her face.

\* \* \*

Stirring from the drug-induced sleep of Papa Martin's pain pills, I awoke to darkness, the sound of my name, a hand on my sore shoulder, and the silhouette of someone crouched by my bed.

"Bird," he whispered and shook me again.

I had to be dreaming, but his touch felt so real. My fingers found his bearded face. "Garrett, what are you doing here?"

He held my hand and kissed it. "I had to see you."

"It's not safe. Vince will kill both of us." I ran my fingers through his curly hair and drew him to me. It had been too long. This was only a dream, but I needed to pretend Garrett was really with me.

"When will Vince be back?" he asked, his warm breath against my chest.

"Sunday. He's gone fishing with his dad." I puzzled over how a dream could feel so real.

He crawled onto the bed and wrapped his arms and legs around me, holding me tightly. The pressure was excruciating, but I needed him too much to tell him. It was only a fantasy, though. I could endure anything imaginary if it meant having him with me—if only in my dreams. We lay entangled for several minutes.

In the darkness, we kissed. When I began unbuttoning his shirt, he slipped my gown over my head. I thought of the bruises, but in the darkness, he couldn't see them. Plus, he was not real; the pain pills were picking up where my thoughts had trailed off as I drifted to sleep.

My hands moved slowly over his warm body. Even in a fantasy, I wanted to be a good lover, good enough that he would want to marry me. "I love you, Garrett," I whispered.

He pressed his chest to mine, penning me to the bed. "Oh, Abi, I love you."

Fueled by his response, I said, "I love you so much."

"I love you more than there are fish in the sea," he answered.

I laughed. "I love you more than there are tumbleweeds in Texas."

"I love you more than there are stars in the sky." He kissed me, stopping the exchange.

Even though hearing those words verified I was truly caught in a dream, I still savored the feelings of joy that swept through me. We made love more slowly and gently than ever before.

The next morning, I opened and shut my eyes, allowing the sun-filled room to wake me slowly. The sensations and feelings that accompanied my dreams of Garrett floated in my thoughts. Behind me the sheets rustled. I rolled over and saw his shocked face staring back at me. The fog of sleep lingered with me, and I puzzled over how the dream could still seem so real. His hand inched toward my face where he barely touched my cheek and the bruise below my eye. Realizing he was actually there, that I wasn't imagining his presence, I turned my back to him and drew the sheet over my bare shoulders.

He lifted the sheet and ran a finger along the rows of bruises on my upper back. Then he pulled the sheet down and exposed my lower back, butt, and legs. "Oh my god. Why didn't you tell me?"

I wanted to say I was scared he would find me grotesque. Instead, I said nothing and stared at the picture of Papa Martin and Thelma that hung on the wall.

"Of all the things I've imagined, I never once thought of this. And yet it's so obvious." Garrett's fingers lightly traced the blue stripes that fell in an uneven pattern all the way up and down my body as if trying to convince himself that they were real.

Finally, he asked, "When did he do this?"

"Tuesday night."

"Does he know about me?"

"He thinks I'm having an affair, but he thinks it's with someone else, my best friend's husband."

"I don't understand." He pressed his lips to my back.

"I got home late that night. You remember I fell asleep?"

"Yes, I knew you left later than usual, but I had no idea this had happened. I had an overwhelming feeling that something was wrong, but this—oh, God Abi, I never imagined."

I turned to him and ran my fingers through his beard. His green eyes met mine, and I told him about the policeman bringing the gun back. As I described Vince's vicious attack on me, his brows gathered in a knot.

When I finished talking, he tenderly drew me to him.

"Oh, Abi, what are we going to do? What can I do?"

*Ask me to move in with you,* I wanted to say, but the words had to come out of his mouth.

We lay together as long as I dared. But if I didn't go to class, Thelma would want to know why, so I slipped out of bed and went to the bathroom. When I stepped out of the shower, I saw a note written on the mirror in the shower steam. "See you at my place."

Using the same response I had used the day before, I got through my psychology class, and took advantage of Dr. Posey talking to another student to avoid another encounter with her. After I got out of my at class where I delivered my mouse trap project, I drove to Garrett's apartment.

In response to my knock on his partially open door, Garrett called, "Come in."

He sat at the kitchen table, hunched over the classified section of a newspaper. Red, oblong circles accented the newsprint. The phone, whose long cord had been stretched from the living room, sat in the middle of the paper. Garrett held the receiver to his ear and said, "Yes, I see," periodically to the party on the line.

When I approached him, he looked up and smiled, but his thoughts seemed occupied with what he was hearing. I sat down and began reading the circled ads. *One-bedroom efficiency. Clean. No pets. $100 a month. Close to UP. Share with three others. Utilities paid. $95 a month. One-bedroom duplex. Clean. $105 a month.*

He said good-bye to the person on the phone and hung up. Our eyes met, and a wave of fear washed over me. Garrett had no intentions of offering me a place to live.

"What are you doing?" I asked, knowing all too well.

"I'm looking for a place for you to live. We've got to hurry and get you moved before Sunday."

I slowly shook my head. "I can't make it on my own."

"But you have to." He threw the pen on the table.

"What would I do? How would I support myself?"

Garrett folded his arms across his chest. "Ask your folks for help. I can't believe they've let you stay there. Do they know what he did to you? This probably isn't the first time."

"No, it's not, and they don't know—not this." I pointed to my face.

"Tell them, Abi." He reached across the table to grab my hands, but I pulled them away.

"My mom's done all she can. Without her support I wouldn't be going to school."

We stared at each other, and I understood that I was on my own. None of his solutions included him.

I stood up. My voice quivered as I said, "Thelma watches every move I make. I should go home."

"If you get there early, she'll be suspicious. Keep to your pattern." He spoke with the same dogmatic tone he used to drill me on my notes.

"I need to leave." I turned and walked toward the door.

His chair scooted back, but he did not follow me. "If you stay with him, I can't help you."

I grabbed the doorknob and turned to face him. "Unless you're willing to get involved, you don't have anything to offer." I wished he would walk across the room, hold me, and say he loved me like he had last night. More than that, I wanted him to ask me to be his wife and let him take care of me.

He sat down. "It's your decision, Bird. You're the one that has to leave him. You're in control."

His words hurt worse than any blow Vince had ever dealt me. Refusing to give in to my tears, I forced myself to smile. "I just realized something. You and Vince wanted the very same thing from me—sex . That's all I'm good for, just a sweet piece of ass."

His face twitched as if my words stung him, but he remained seated. "You know that's not true."

"Oh, I do, huh? I think I'm right on the mark. When it comes down to it, that's all I've been to either one of you." While I wanted to run away crying, I stood there, hoping and praying he would come to me.

He closed his eyes and worked his dog tags from side to side. Finally, I let myself out. As I drove out of the parking lot, I looked up at his apartment. In the past, he always waved to me as I left, but not this time.

# Chapter Sixteen

*Bolder than a brass spittoon.*

**March 21, 1973, Wednesday**

*A*fter dark, I sat at the kitchen table studying when I heard a knock at my front door. Thelma always used the back door, and she never knocked before entering. My car out front and the lights on in the house said I was home, but I had already dressed for bed and my injuries were still evident, so I prayed they would take a hint and go away when I did not answer.

On the other side of the door, I heard Mama and Charlene speaking to one another followed by school-girl like giggling. They knocked again and both called in unison, "Abi, we know you're in there."

As I swung the door open, Charlene and Mama greeted me, "Surprise!"

Stepping back to let them in, I prayed the dim light would soften the shock of my grotesque face.

Mama reached to hug me, but she stopped at arm's length. "Baby, what's happened to you?"

"I had a little car accident," I said for the hundreth time.

"Lord of mercy." Charlene flipped on the overhead light. "When did this happen?"

"Last week," I said, knowing they would want more details than that.

231

"But why didn't you tell me?" Mama grimaced as she examined my face.

"Say, girl, your car looked all right. Or were you in Vince's truck?" Charlene quizzed.

"No, I was with a friend," I answered weakly. "I should have worn my seat belt."

Mama grabbed my shoulders and pulled me to her, patting my back like she did when I was a child.

I winced with pain.

"Betty, better lighten up. I think you're hurting her," Charlene cautioned.

Mama stepped back. "Where else are you hurt?"

"Just bruises." I tried to smile reassuringly.

"Let me see." Mama reached for the front of my robe.

I crossed my arms over my chest. "It's nothing really."

She stared at me in disbelief and shook her head.

"Betty, can you believe this? It's just like Gary said." Charlene jabbed Mother's shoulder with her index finger. "This very afternoon, he sat in my chair and said you should go see about Abi. It's like he had some kind of sixth sense."

"Who?" I asked. "Who told you that?"

Mama stood dumbfounded, staring at my battered face.

Charlene popped her gum. "Gary. Not your usual drop in. He came last week and then again today. Last week, he said he was looking for a place to take his son for haircuts because he's Vietnamese, and he gets made fun of." Mama didn't say anything so Charlene continued, "He's got the longest, prettiest mop of hair you ever hope to see and a beard, too, which looks pretty good, although I generally don't care much for those hippie types. Today he immediately started up talking about a friend of his that he was worried about."

As soon as she said Gary, I suspected she was talking about Garrett. When she said he had a mop of long curly hair, I was certain. "You say he has a son?"

"Yeah, today I saw his picture. Cutest little Vietnamese kid you could ever hope to see."

Mama cupped my face in her hands. "Gary said I needed to see about you? How did he know?"

"What exactly did he say, Mama?"

"We were talking about our families, and he asked me when I'd seen you," Mama said, her eyes locked onto my blackened eyes. "It was almost like he was trying to tell me about this."

"That's a little spooky. What do you know about him?" I asked.

As usual, Charlene took over the conversation. "Like I said, he's showed up twice—both — times without an appointment, and both times he only let me trim a tiny bit off that mop of his. Today when he opened his billfold to pay, I saw he had a picture of him and a woman and a kid. So I asked him if that was Loc, which is what he called him the first time he was there. He started sidestepping, but I reminded him about what he said about Loc being sensitive on account of his nationality. Then he said the woman was his brother's wife." She gave me a knowing wink. "Which was a bald-face lie. Why would she get her picture made with Gary and his son? I think he's the one who's sensitive about them being Vietnamese."

"So that was his son?" I asked, still trying to sort out what felt incomprehensible.

"You could see it clear as day," Charlene answered. "He's got Gary's green eyes."

"Sort of a family trait," I said. Garrett's explanation about the child who had drawn the picture had gone from his nephew, and then it became his friend's child when I pressed him. My skin crawled.

I invited Mama and Charlene to sit down, but I hadn't cooked in over a week, so I didn't have anything to offer them except water. We talked about Vince going fishing with his dad, what was going on at the beauty shop, and how my semester was shaping up. I still had questions about Garrett, or rather Gary, but I forced myself not to ask. They had volunteered more painful truths than I could begin to absorb.

After they left, I thought of the pictures Garrett had given me when he asked me to draw my portrait, and I wondered if the negatives were still in the envelope. From the depths of my school bag, I pulling out Garrett's copy of *As A Man Thinketh* where I had hidden the pictures. When I held one of the darkened plastic strips up to the light, I couldn't make out the details. Then I remembered the magnifying glass Vince bought to look at maps, so I rummaged in the kitchen junk drawer and found it. Using it, I saw a boy holding a present and sitting in front of a Christmas tree. In the next one, I made out a woman with the boy, no doubt the woman in the picture that Garrett carried in his wallet. A dozen negatives in all showed the boy, and or the woman, and several had Garrett in them, smiling for the camera.

Twenty-five years of working in the Beauty Box had honed Charlene's ability to read people like a book. In two visits, she knew more about Garrett than I had figured out in over two months' time. What a fool I had been. What a complete idiot.

*       *       *

The phone rang just as morning light started shining through the curtains. Garrett had been awake most of the night, worrying about Abi. After stumbling to the living room, he answered, his voice raspy.

"Will you accept charges on a call from Abigale Martin?" the operator asked.

"Yes, of course," he responded. "Abi, are you okay?"

At first she didn't answer. Finally, she said, "I need you to tell me the truth."

"About what?" She knew. How could she not after his botched visit to the Beauty Box.

"Your wife and child," she demanded.

He opened his mouth to speak, but Abi cut him off. "Stay away from me and my mother."

"Is that what you really want, Abi?" he asked gently.

"Yes, that's all I want." Her voice quivered.

"Can't we talk about this?" he asked, hoping to keep her on the line. "Abi, come to the apartment when you get through with class today." He wanted to explain to her in person about Loc and Trang.

"No, absolutely not. That's how I got into this mess."

"I won't touch you," he promised.

"Right," she scoffed.

"I love you, Abi. God, I love you." He wished he had told her the truth from the start—not only about Loc and Trang, but the fact that he loved her. It wouldn't sound so hollow now.

"No, you don't. If you loved me, you would never have lied to me, and you would do more than line up apartments I can't afford. If you loved me, you'd ask me to marry you. Oh, but you can't because you're already married. I understand. I understand completely."

"Abi, come to my place and let's talk," Garrett pleaded.

The phone clicked in his ear. She had hung up. Going to the Beauty Box had not helped his relationship with Abi, but at least Betty had seen her, whether Abi was with honest with her or not.

\*   \*   \*

I stumbled through the next few days, dreading Vince's return and mourning the loss of the only man I had ever loved. Both weighed on me for very different reasons.

Sunday morning, Thelma called for the first time since A.V. and Vince left. "Martha's taking me to church. She wants to know if you want to ride with us."

"Yeah, when are you going?" I answered, glad for a break from studying.

"Nine forty-five," she said, sounding surprised I had accepted her offer.

As I dressed, I noted my blackened eyes. Though the bruises had faded, they still clearly showed the results of Vince's temper. Sensing the power I gained in displaying them at church, I did not attempt to camouflage them like I had for school.

When I saw Martha's car in the drive, and Thelma getting into it, I walked outside.

"Thelma said I could ride with you two," I said as I got into the backseat.

"Sure." Martha glanced at me and did a double-take. "What happened to you?"

My gaze shifted to meet Thelma's, and I silently dared her to say anything. She looked away.

"A little accident," I said. The pause had been too long and the answer too vague.

All the way to church, Thelma remained quiet while Martha and I discussed our long drive to school and work. When Martha mentioned meeting for lunch, I told her I study in the library at that time. Martha kept insisting that we get together, so I finally agreed to meet her at the cafeteria. I immediately regretted it, knowing Thelma would use Martha as her spy. Then I reminded myself I no longer had anything to hide.

I sat with Thelma and Martha at Sunday school and church. When people asked about my eyes, I hesitated before answering, "A little accident." I could feel Thelma's anger building every time I responded this way. Anyone that knew Vince could put two and two together and come up with the truth. After Martha took us home, Thelma and I stood side by side and waved as Martha backed out of the drive.

Still waving, Thelma said, "Don't think you can get away with that *accident* stuff. You'll pay for that."

"Why, Mama Martin, did you want me to tell them Vince beat the crap out of me?" I asked timidly.

As Martha rounded the corner, Thelma turned on me. "Nobody shames me or mine."

"For all I care you can go to hell. And take your son with you." I walked to my house. At my front door, I watched her waddle home, head bowed and her stumpy arms swinging at her side.

\* \* \*

Vince and his dad broke camp at daybreak. They had a six-hour drive ahead of them. Ideally, they would get back to Quits in time to put away their gear, do something with the fish, and get to bed early enough to go to work tomorrow. The fishing and the companionship had gotten better as the week progressed. Other than the occasional comment, Daddy hadn't said much about Abi—until last night. He'd been saving up.

As they sat by the campfire after supper, Daddy asked Vince how things were going to be different between him and Abi. Vince shrugged his shoulders and said he didn't figure he could stop her from going to school if she wanted. For him, that had been a big deal since that was exactly what he wanted to do, but Daddy had specifically said when he bailed him out he had to let Abi go to school as long as she wanted.

Daddy stirred the fire. "If you ever hurt that girl again, I'll tell my boss to put you on a different crew." He gestured toward Vince's pickup. "And I'll take the keys to that truck." Now, that was hitting below the belt.

"But she's messing around with somebody else," Vince had protested.

After poking the fire, he looked at Vince. "If someone had done to me what you've done to her, I'd be looking. You better count your lucky stars she's willing to stay with you. And you better start being the man she wants to live with, or you will lose her."

Nothing was said after that, and neither one of them had spoken this morning. Vince wasn't about to break the silence. Saying something would be the same as agreeing to his dad's ultimatum, and Vince couldn't do that. He could not believe what Daddy said about supporting Abi even if she was unfaithful to him.

It was overcast and rainy as they drove toward home. When they stopped for gas, Vince offered to drive and Daddy agreed. Once they were back on the road, Vince tuned the radio to a rock station to make the miles go faster—and to let Daddy know that at least he could listen to what he wanted in his own truck. Daddy, who was trying to sleep, turned it off.

As they entered Quits, Daddy stretched. "Well, my backbone is ribbing against my stomach."

Vince was hungry too. He wondered if Abi would go back to cooking, or if she'd go off on some women's lib tangent and think he should scrounge up his own meals.

As soon as they pulled into the drive, Mama came out of the house. She hugged Daddy first, and then she gave Vince her usual bear-hug. That's when he saw Abi looking out their bedroom window.

While they were still hugging, Mama whispered in Vince's ear, "I got stuff to tell you about that little she-dog, but not now. She's looking at us." Mama nodded toward his house.

"We'll talk later," Vince whispered back.

In no time, Abi sashayed her butt onto the drive. "So the fishermen return," she said all chipper.

Everyone looked at her, but Daddy was the only one who responded. He raised his arm, and Abi saddled up to him like she always did.

"Catch anything?" she asked.

Daddy chuckled. "The big one got away."

Vince glared at Abi, and she stared back at him, confident that Daddy would always be there for her.

"Looks like we're going to get a break in the weather," Daddy said. "If you girls will round up some grease and meal, Vince said he'd fry us up some fish."

"Do we have enough for Bea and Chuck?" Abi asked.

"Well, sure, that's a great idea," Daddy agreed.

"Let's use that big old kettle that's out in the shed and do it here in the drive," Mama said. "I don't want my house smelling like fish for a week."

"Only way." Daddy headed for the backyard shed.

Mama left saying she was going to call Bea. Vince and Abi carried camping gear into the detached garage that sat behind and between the two houses. As they worked together, neither one of them spoke.

Then Abi helped Mama cook until Bea and her family arrived. Chuck shook Daddy's hand, and Vince recruited Chuck to help build a table out of a sheet of plywood and two saw horses they got from Daddy's shed. Bea and Abi spread the table with a red-and-white-checkered tablecloth.

The wind kept blowing it off, so they weighted down the corners as they brought out coleslaw, condiments, and a pitcher of lemonade.

When everything was ready, everyone gathered around the table. Instead of his usual prayer, Daddy said how wonderful it was to have his family all together. The adults stood around the table while the kids sat on it between Bea and Chuck. They filled their plates, and Daddy told about the one that got away. Vince couldn't help but join in. Abi laughed along with the rest, but she was careful not to look at Vince.

They were well into the meal when Chuck asked, "Abi, where'd you get those shiners?"

"Yeah, tell us about that," Bea chimed in. "You said in the kitchen you had an accident."

"What happened?" Chuck asked.

"This guy ran a stop sign. I braked really hard and my face hit the windshield. I should have worn my seatbelt. Thankfully, I didn't mess up my car," she explained calmly—a real expert at lying.

Chuck shook his head and resumed eating. When Bea looked at Vince suspiciously, he ignored her.

Mama pointed to the fish platter in the middle of the table. "Better eat this up. Fish don't keep."

Daddy grabbed another piece, and everyone else followed suit.

Afterwards, Vince stuck with the men while the women cleaned up. Bea and her family were driving away when Daddy pointed out the colorful sunset. He seemed happy to have everyone together, and he probably thought he could intimidate Vince into letting Abi get away with her shenanigans. For now, Daddy held the upper hand, but with time, Abi would hang herself.

\*   \*   \*

### March 26, 1973, Monday

When I got out of class, I hurried to the cafeteria and found Martha Hasselmeyer waiting for me. We claimed a table in the back corner, and

I sat down while Martha went through the food line. As soon as she got back to the table, she asked me why I brought my lunch instead of buying it since we had agreed to meet. When I told her that Vince handled all the money, and I had forgotten to get any cash from him, she made a face and asked me if that didn't aggravate me to have to ask for money.

I shrugged my shoulders like I didn't care. "Vince is sort of old fashioned. He doesn't want me to worry with stuff like that."

"Really?" Martha asked innocently.

"Oh, yes. He wants to make my life as easy as possible." I smiled, knowing every word I said would go back to Thelma who would report it to Vince.

Her face broke into a nervous grin. "That's great."

Martha grilled me with questions about my schedule throughout the week, which I answered vaguely.

After we separated at the steps to the student union building, I walked to the library. Drawn to the third floor and the tiny room where Garrett and I had studied, I approached it and saw a figure with long, golden hair hunched over the desk. An empty chair sat next to him. Before he had time to turn and see me, I moved away. I found a desk on the same floor, but in a remote corner. As much as I despised what he had done, I could not hate him. Through knowing him, I had discovered too much about myself.

\*   \*   \*

Monday evening Vince arrived home from work, grabbed a couple of beers from the refrigerator, and sat in his chair in the living room. The phone rang, and he answered. He spoke in hushed tones, so I figured it was Thelma. When I finished cooking supper, I sat down and ate by myself. After Vince hung up the phone and walked back into the kitchen, he hesitated when he saw my half-empty plate. Still not uttering a word, he filled a plate and took it to the living room. I got out my history book and read while the TV blared in the other room.

That night we went to bed with our backs turned to one another like we had the night before. I was grateful he had decided to punish me with silence, but I wondered when and how it would end. In the past, Vince's calm exterior hid an explosion waiting to happen.

*    *    *

## March 27, 1973, Tuesday

When Trang and Vinh got home from class, Vinh asked Garrett if he wanted a ride to the airport, probably because Garrett had opted to go back rather than spend the night the last couple of weeks. Garrett told him he needed to talk to Trang, so Vinh gave him a snaggle-tooth grin and a thumbs up before he prepared his bed, which consisted of rearranging the throw pillows on the couch.

Garrett suggested he and Trang talk in her bedroom. It felt too intimate given what he wanted to discuss, although there was no place else to carry on a private conversation.

Once Trang had settled on the bed, and he had positioned himself standing against the wall, he asked, "How far along are you?"

She stared blankly at him.

He used his hands to create a mound over his stomach. "When will the baby come?"

Trang's mouth spread into a large grin, and she nodded, saying, "Baby."

"You want to keep the baby?" he asked slowly, over enunciating each word.

Her brows bunched in confusion. "Yes, I keep."

It was Garrett's turn to answer by nodding. The idea of an abortion was out of the question. Since she had purposely gotten pregnant, there was no way she was willingly giving it up. When Garrett turned toward the door, she patted the bed next to her leg.

"No, I'm not sleeping with you." He grabbed the doorknob.

"You baby's father," she said as though trying to convince him.

He didn't want to argue, so he left the room without answering.

As he settled in the bed next to Loc, he thought of Abi. After Abi called, asking him to bow out of her life, he told himself it was all for the best. Loc needed him, and Trang sure couldn't get by on her own with one child much less two. Still, he couldn't quit thinking about Abi's blackened eyes and the striped bruises that ran down her back, buttocks, and legs. If she stayed in her marriage, Vince would eventually kill her, but she wasn't going to leave unless Garrett begged her to move in with him. He couldn't do that without putting an end to his marriage, which felt impossible at this point.

*        *        *

Over the next few weeks, Martha insisted we eat together every few days. Each time, she grilled me with questions like why Vince didn't give me money and what did he do that really irritated me? Surely there was something because after all he was a husband, and they all did something. It became a challenge to figure out the most creative way of saying that I was crazy about him and there wasn't one thing I would change.

Everyday Vince and Thelma talked on the phone or stood out in the yard together, but neither spoke to me. My silent war with Vince included total abstinence. On Friday and Saturday night, he cleaned up and left the house without an explanation. Well past midnight, he returned smelling of alcohol and perfume. I was glad he found someone else to satisfy his needs. Sex was sex, but true intimacy, albeit short-lived, was the one thing I had found with Garrett that I had never experienced with Vince.

The end of March came and went and a calmness I had never known before settled over me. With one month of school left in the semester, I spent my time studying. My thoughts often centered on Garrett and my undeniable desire for him, but I pacified myself with a reminder that to find peace I had given up something I never really owned—a man who had his own family.

A week later, my newfound serenity turned to pure anxiety. My earlier calmness had grown into a drug-like state leaving me tired and listless throughout the day. My breasts felt full and mild nausea threatened every time I got hungry. I was a week late starting my period.

Seated at the kitchen table, I studied my personal calendar where I noted my period each month. I started keeping it when Vince and I were working at getting me pregnant. On it, I verified for the umpteenth time that my last ovulation fell within the week following Vince's attack. I thought of Garrett appearing by my bed in the middle of the night—the last time I had sex. Garrett's child grew inside me. Something I had spent years praying for, now felt like a curse—the very worst thing that could happen.

It now made perfect sense why years ago Vince blamed me for being infertile and refused to let me get a second opinion. He was sterile, and he would kill me when he realized I was carrying another man's child.

*     *     *

Garrett was walking down the hallway of the psychology building and noticed Abi walking in front of him. Since their last conversation several weeks ago, he had trailed her all over campus. If nothing else, he had to make sure she had no new injuries. When she walked into Mariam's office, he stood outside in the hall and leaned against the wall, his head bent low and a book open in front of him to avoid making eye contact with anyone he knew—out of Mariam's sight, yet close enough to hopefully eavesdrop.

Abi said something about the spring weather and how nice it was that the sand and wind had quit blowing for a change. Then Mariam answered with something Garrett couldn't understand, and they laughed.

After another brief exchange, Mariam asked Abi to sit.

"I don't know what to do," Abi said, her voice strained like she was trying not to cry.

"What's the problem?" Mariam asked.

"It's so complicated. I shouldn't saddle you with my stuff." She sounded even closer to tears.

"So it's not about school?" Mariam asked.

"I'm doing well in my classes. It has to do with a lot of other things, personal problems, stuff that there's no easy answer for." She sniffed and then blew her nose.

"I was really worried about you after Spring Break when you came to class with both eyes blackened."

"I knew you were, and I appreciate that," Abi said.

"Garrett came to see me, and he was also concerned about you."

Based on how tight-lipped Mariam had been, Garrett was surprised she mentioned him.

"Yeah, we talked," Abi admitted, "but Garrett's not in a position to help."

"I'm not sure I understand," Mariam said. "What's the issue, Abi? Is it money or a place to stay?"

"Both, and a whole lot more." From the change in her voice and the sound of movement, Garrett figured she was getting up to leave. He needed to do the same, but he could not tear himself away.

"Like I mentioned to you before, there's a great counseling service right here in this building."

"Yes, I've already filled out the paperwork." Abi sounded close to the doorway.

Garrett tiptoed away. His eavesdropping had not alleviated his concern for Abi. In fact, he was more worried than ever.

# Chapter Seventeen

*There's never a good time*
*to have your gun jam.*

**April 11, 1973, Wednesday**

"*L*et's see, you're pregnant, and you're sure this is not your husband's baby. But you don't want to tell the biological father. Is that right?" Valerie Smith sat back in her chair after doing a damned good job of summarizing what a mess I had made of my life.

"That's about it," I said, amazed I had spilled my guts to a total stranger.

"Why not tell Gary about the baby?" she asked.

"He's married." I used the name Gary because Valerie might know Garrett since they were both graduate students working on counseling degrees.

She grimaced. "That does complicate things, but shouldn't he know? It is his responsibility too."

"I guess so, but ultimately I'm the one who needs to decide what I'm going to do."

"Well, what are your options?" she asked.

"I can't stay with Vince. He'll kill me when he realizes I'm pregnant by someone else."

"With time, he might understand what prompted you to...to be unfaithful," she suggested.

"Actually, he would kill me. This past December he came close to it." It felt strange telling someone about something I had spent a decade hiding.

"What happened in December?" she asked.

I explained about wanting to go to school and how I had started cleaning houses without him knowing about it. Then when he found out, how getting to go to school had been born out of all that.

She took a deep breath. "Back to my original question, what are your options?"

I thought about it and finally admitted, "I don't think I have any."

"Actually, you do. Choosing to do nothing is an option, and with time, things will work themselves out one way or the other," she concluded.

"Yeah, Vince will kill me if I stay with him."

"Then what else can you do?" she prodded.

"I could ask Gary for help." I mentally rejected the idea, although it was a possibility.

Valerie nodded. "Is there anything else?"

"Getting an abortion is out of the question."

"It's legal now since the Roe versus Wade ruling," she offered hopefully.

"That would take money, which Gary might give me." I thought about the time we talked about abortion at the beginning of our relationship, only a few months ago, although it felt much longer than that. "All my married life I've tried to get pregnant to make Vince happy, but now that I am, and I shouldn't want it, I can't imagine wishing it away." I studied her thin face and short hair. She was about my age. "Do you have kids?"

"No, but my boyfriend does, so I see them a lot." She checked her watch. "We're out of time. Before next time, I want you to think about why you married Vince and what prompted you to have an affair."

"That's a lot to think about." I got up from the chair.

"It may help you to decide about your future." She walked me to the door.

I stuck my hand out to her. "Thanks for your time and for listening. When can I see you again?"

She held my hand in both of hers. "Tell the receptionist I want to see you again as soon as possible. We're close to the end of the semester, and you've got some hard decisions to make."

*   *   *

## April 18, 1973, Wednesday

Garrett had trailed Abi to the cafeteria before where she ate a sack lunch with a woman close to her mother's age. This time Abi was alone, so Garrett approached her table, holding out the envelope he intended to give her and then calmly walk away.

She looked up and momentarily smiled before hissing, "What are you doing here?"

Garrett knew Abi would balk, but borrowing money against his car and making her take it left him focused on that—not dealing with Abi's lunch partner who sat her tray on the table next to Abi.

"Hi, Martha," Abi said, obviously perplexed with the situation.

He thrust the envelope toward her, saying the first words that popped into his head, "This is for that book I got from you."

Her gaze shot to Martha, who was settling herself in her seat. "Sorry, I'm not interested." Turning her back to him, Abi propped her elbow on the table as if building a wall against Garrett's intrusion.

"I think he's trying to give you money," Martha said, clearly interested in Abi accepting it.

"Martha, that's just a come on. I've never met this guy. Just ignore him, and he'll probably go away."

Martha looked at Garrett expectantly, which told Garrett he needed to get lost. He sat at a table out of their vision, but one in which he could see when Abi left the cafeteria. About thirty minutes later, he saw Martha and Abi leaving. Deciding to follow her and corner her once she was alone, he trailed them. Martha stopped to talk with the man behind the counter at the newsstand, and Abi walked past her into the restroom. Garrett scooted outside and waited for Abi behind some bushes at the base of the stairs.

A few minutes later, he saw Abi come down the steps and grabbed her arm as she started to walk past him. "Abi, I've got to talk to you."

"I can't, not here," she blurted out.

Garrett looked beyond Abi and saw Martha who stood at the top of the steps. Her expression said she had heard and seen their exchange. Abi's gaze followed Garrett's to Martha, whose pouty little mouth had spread into a satisfied grin.

Fully aware of his major screw up, Garrett froze. Abi hurried away. Knowing it would make matters worse, he dared not watch her go. Instead, he walked the opposite direction.

*       *       *

When Vince had gotten home from work, he saw that Abi's car wasn't there. Then straight-away Mama called, saying Martha had seen Abi refuse to take money from some long-haired guy while acting like she didn't know him. But when they thought Martha wasn't looking, she said, "No, not here." Martha said the creep put his hands all over her. Finishing his third beer, he got another one. Eventually, she would come home, and he was ready for her.

He finally heard the putter of her little car as she pulled into the drive. Through the living room screen door, he saw Abi walk toward the front porch. She usually came in the back, but this worked for him since he needed to keep her from seeing his setup in the bedroom. As she approached, a hot car drove past, a red Charger. He couldn't see the driver, but it reminded him of the car he saw a while back at the intersection with a hippie driving it. Martha said this guy Abi talked to had long hair, but the odds of him driving past and Abi walking in at the same time were too coincidental. They couldn't be that ballsy. He kept going, so Vince figured a teenager was showing off his new wheels.

While Abi trudged up the steps, Vince sat in his chair, his eyes focused on the news that was blaring at full volume, a good cover up for the noise he expected Abi to make.

When Abi opened the screen door, it squawked. Vince didn't dare look at her. The oscillating fan stirred a breeze through the room.

She stood inside the door for a few seconds like she expected him to say or do something. Finally, she said, "Vince, I'm leaving you."

His jaw worked with a steady rhythm as he glared at the newscaster. He had not expected that, and he sure as hell was not going to let her sashay her little butt out of here without getting what was coming to her. She needed to get farther into the room though before he made a move; otherwise, she would run outside.

"I just came to get a few of my things," she said, trying to sound matter-of-fact, but her voice was squeaky and scared. She started toward the kitchen.

When she reached the center of the room, he lunged for her, saying, "This time, I'm doin' it right."

She pivoted toward the door, screaming.

He grabbed her shirt and yanked her back, holding her from behind. To shut her up, he cupped his palm over her mouth. With the intention of gagging her, he pulled a bandanna from his back pocket. Before he could get it around her head, she bit the hell out of him. When he instinctively jerked his hand away, she squirmed out of his hold and headed for the front door. He tackled her to the floor.

Clawing at the carpet and dragging both of them, she screamed, "Help!"

Vince grabbed a wad of her hair and pulled. She shrieked like a stuck pig, kicked him in the gut, and managed to get loose again. Then she scrambled toward the front door.

Leaping to his feet, he stumbled toward Abi and grabbed her hair again. This time holding it more securely, he slammed the door shut.

She turned on him and clawed at his face, so he grabbed her wrist. With her screaming and kicking for all she was worth, he dragged her toward the bedroom. As they passed the kitchen table, she hooked her foot on one of the chairs, but he yanked her free. At the bedroom doorway, he shoved her against the closed door and inside where she fell in a heap on the floor. She looked up at the bed where he had laid the ropes to tie her and a cup towel to gag her. Then she glanced at Vince, her eyes wide with terror.

He unbuckled his belt and slipped it off. "We got a little score to settle."

Keeping her eyes on him, she panted and slowly got to her feet. "I'm just here to get a few things."

"You ain't going nowhere. Matter-of-fact, it's going to be a long time before you leave this house again—if that ever happens." He doubled the belt and popped it to let her know he meant business.

"You can't do anything to me without your dad finding out." She spoke slowly as she backed toward the bed. When she got there, she leaned against the mattress.

He couldn't believe she was making it this easy. "That's right, Abi-girl, you just lay down there and take what you got coming to you." He stepped toward her.

Quick as a jack-rabbit, she jumped onto the bed and stood up. Seeing what she was going after, Vince stepped toward her. She grabbed his gun out of the rack, swung it around, and pointed it at his head—the barrel end of the rifle not more than four feet away. They both breathed heavily.

Vince leaned toward her with his hand extended. "Give me that gun, Abi-girl."

She cocked the hammer, the mechanical click surprisingly loud against the background of the television. He paused, and the floor boards creaked as he shifted his weight. If he was going to do something, he had to do it before she panicked and pulled the trigger. He put his weight in his front foot and began to take a step.

"Step back, or I'll shoot." Her voice trembled.

With his leg in motion, he figured how far he needed to reach. The barrel of the gun was almost within his reach when she jerked it up and immediately fired. The explosion made Vince step back.

She shifted the gun back to his face. "Next time, it'll be you instead of her." Abi gestured toward the wall behind him before she cocked the gun and rested her finger on the trigger.

Vince glanced at his parent's picture that now hung crooked. Damn, if she didn't shoot right through Mama. "You'd go to jail, Abi-girl," he warned.

"I'd rather be there than here with you." She kept the gun trained on his face.

Vince was weighing the odds of her following through on her threat when the backdoor flew open. Daddy hurried into the room while Abi kept the gun trained on Vince. Finally, Daddy would see for himself what Abi had become.

"Is there a problem here?" Daddy asked cautiously.

"Yes there is." She pointed the gun at the ropes and towel and then at the belt in Vince's hand.

He had forgotten he was holding it. Everything had happened so quickly. Vince slipped on the belt. "Abi and I are having a little disagreement. You can leave now, Daddy. This is between me and my wife."

"I thought you understood; you're not to hurt this woman again," Daddy said in his sternest voice.

Vince faced his father, flabbergasted. "She's been lying to me. All this time, she's been lying."

Daddy took in a long, ragged breath. "I can't believe you're my son. You make me sick."

Mama appeared in the doorway, holding her heaving chest. "That she-dog should be shot."

Daddy turned to face her. "You think I haven't heard you putting crazy ideas in his head. You've fanned the flames 'til neither one of you can think straight."

Mama pointed a finger at Abi. "The truth is she's a whore."

"She lied to me," Vince pleaded, sounding pathetic, but desperate to make Daddy see reason.

Daddy looked from Mama to Vince. "Abi's guilty of one thing—trying to survive."

"Tell us the truth about this man friend of yours," Mama demanded. "Or are you going to lie again?"

Abi lowered the gun and looked into Vince's eyes. "He is a friend, a dear friend. And he cares about me...more than anyone else ever has."

"See there, I told you," Mama shouted with satisfaction, having exposed Abi.

Daddy looked around the room until his eyes settled on the portrait of him and Mama, the one they had given them last year for Christmas. It now hung lopsided and Mama's hair done up in curls was all that was left of her. Nearly smiling, Daddy said, "Abi, you're a damn good shot - or awful lucky."

Vince worked his fists in and out, mad as hell that Daddy was passing out complements instead of admitting he was wrong. What Abi owed him he couldn't begin to put into words.

After taking a deep breath, Daddy asked, "Well, Abi, what do you want to do?"

Damn it to hell. Vince could not believe Daddy was once more taking her side.

"I'm leaving," Abi said with determination. "I just need a few minutes to pack a bag."

Daddy nodded. "I can't say that I blame you." He turned to Vince. "Give her all the cash you've got."

Vince watched with amazement as Daddy slipped his wallet out of his back pocket and pulled out all the cash he carried, which was only a few one dollar bills. Vince wasn't about to hand a penny over to Abi.

Daddy laid his money on the bed, and then he glared at Vince. "Don't try me, or I'll take that belt off of you and whip you like you've done to her."

Working his jaw back and forth, Vince considered how far he could push Daddy, which wasn't very far. Finally, knowing Daddy meant business, He took out his wallet and pulled some of the smaller bills.

Damn, he had nearly all of last week's paycheck in there. He wasn't about to give her all of that.

Daddy watched him with a steely gaze, and when Vince started to close his wallet, he barked, "I said all of it." Then he turned to Abi. "Does he have any money anywhere else?"

"No," she answered. "Not that I know of."

"You can't expect me-" Vince started to protest, but Daddy gave him that look that said he needed to back down.

Mama opened her mouth ready to say something, but Daddy turned on her, so she walked away.

Vince opened his wallet again, emptied it, and threw the money at the bed. Most of it fell on the floor.

"Now get out," Daddy ordered, looking at Vince and pointing at the door.

Not sure he could take further humiliation, Vince stared him down.

"Move!" Daddy shouted and flailed his arms like he was herding cattle.

From the kitchen, Mama screeched, "Daddy, you can't treat Vince like that!"

"Both of you get out of here," Daddy said in his no-nonsense way.

Vince strode out of the house with Mama behind him. In the backyard, he gawked at his house. How had she done that? He had been ready to fix her little red wagon, and now she was leaving—with Daddy's blessings and Vince's money. He wished like hell he had grabbed that gun. Even if she had shot him, it would have been better than this.

\* \* \*

After following Abi out of town and down a country road going 20 mph for thirty minutes, Garrett pulled around her and slowed to a stop. When she parked behind him, Garrett got out and walked to her car.

He folded his arms and rested them in her open window. "You okay?"

Abi nodded, but she didn't take her eyes off the tail-end of his car.

"Where did you go?" he asked. "After I scanned all the campus parking lots, I drove to Quits. Your car wasn't at your house, so I waited for you at the intersection outside of town. It was the only way I could think of to see you when you came home."

"Yeah, I saw you when I came by," she said, finally looking up at him.

"Why didn't you stop? And why did you go back in that house after I—well after I stuck my foot in my mouth." He couldn't believe he had been such an idiot.

"I went to your place, and when you didn't come home, I sat in the parking lot and thought. Finally, it dawned on me that I had to tell Vince I was leaving. That's why I went in there." She smiled wistfully.

"You can't imagine how much I wanted to stop you. And then I heard that gunshot. What happened?"

"Vince was ready for me—like I figured he would be, and we did have a showdown so to speak. But thankfully Papa Martin showed up." She gazed at the flat horizon, a far off look in her eye.

"You want to talk about it?" he asked gently.

"No," she answered with finality.

After a time he asked, "Where you going, Bird?"

"I'm not sure," she admitted.

"That's evident. You've gone ten miles in thirty minutes." He paused. "Come home with me."

She studied his face. "I'll see if Mama won't put me up for a night or so."

"Are you sure?"

"If it doesn't work out with her—or them, her and my dad, I'll go somewhere else." She ran her index finger along the steering wheel. "If I have to, I'll get a motel room."

"Let me give you that money I tried to give you earlier."

She shook her head. "That would officially make me a whore."

He understood her reasoning, but it didn't change his desire to help. "So if I put it in your car when you're not looking, which is what I should have done, you're going to hate me forever."

She looked at him for a long moment. "How could I hate somebody who gave me wings?" She was smiling, but her eyes were full of tears.

"There's a thousand dollars in that envelope. You can go somewhere and start over. You're strong now. You can do it."

She stared at the horizon again. "I need time to think."

"If you'll come home with me, I'll tell you everything you want to know about Loc and Trang."

"I'm not ready for that right now." She glanced at him. "I'll call you when finals are over."

That was over two weeks away, which seemed like an eternity. Garrett stuck his head inside her car and kissed her cheek. "If you need me before then, don't hesitate to call or come to the apartment." He squeezed her arm, walked to his car, and drove away. It took all of his strength to leave her there alone. But like Abi said, she now had wings, and she needed to use them.

*   *   *

I knocked at my parent's front door, and then let myself in. "Mama, it's Abi."

We met in the living room. She had a cup towel over her shoulder and held up her hands caked with flour and dough. "Baby, I'm surprised to see you. Everything okay?"

"I'm leaving Vince," I said, determined, yet terrified.

She blinked as if trying to make sense of my words.

"I need a place to stay…just for a while." Daddy would object, but I felt obligated to ask before I moved on to "my other options," as Valarie would have termed it.

Mama glanced around the living room like she was looking for a place to park me. "I'm not sure you should stay here. You know how your daddy is." She met my gaze. "Can I call Charlene?"

"Sure." She and I both knew Daddy would insist I go back to Vince—no matter what.

Charlene immediately agreed to host a slumber party for the two of us. After Mama walked me to my car, I started backing out of their driveway, eager to leave before Daddy got home.

"I'll come over and talk to you later this evening," Mama promised and waved as I drove away.

Five miles away, on a dirt road, I parked at Charlene's house. She was out her front door and coming toward me before I had turned off my car. While I grabbed my book bag out of the front, she opened the passenger door and pulled my suitcase out of the backseat. We walked arm and arm up her sidewalk.

"So we're going to be roomies," she said. "Ain't that a kick?"

Inside the house, she stepped into her spare room right off the living room and set the suitcase by the bed. "Here you go. I already opened the window to give you a breeze. And you're just in time for tuna salad."

I followed her down the hall, and stopped at the bathroom to wash my hands. In the mirror, I studied my tired face. So much had just happened. I could not begin to get my mind around it.

When I joined Charlene in the kitchen, we sat down and filled our plates.

She had not taken her first bite when she blurted out, "Did Vince give you those black eyes?"

I stabbed a chunk of apple and nodded.

"Has he done that before?" she asked indignantly.

"Yeah," I admitted.

"You done the right thing," she said with conviction.

God, I loved her spunk. How I wished Mama had said the same thing—in spite of what Daddy thought.

We talked about school and the beauty shop. Then I said, "I've got some money. Let me pay you for staying here."

"Abigale Marie," she scolded. "Me and Betty are closer than sisters. You think I could take money from you? No way."

"There are only a couple of weeks of school left. After that I'm not sure what I'll do." I laid my hands on either side of my plate, feeling I needed to hold myself up.

She patted my arm. "Honey, you're welcome here as long as you can put up with my big mouth."

Later in my room, I unpacked my bag and set up a study area. As a child I had played in this room and wondered what it would feel like to live here. Exhausted and still dressed, I flipped off the light and lay on the bed. Now I had an adult body and a child grew inside me.

The phone rang, waking me from a sound sleep. Soon after that, I heard a car park outside. Charlene met Mama at the door within earshot of my bedroom.

"How's she doing?" Mama asked in hushed tones.

"I think she's still sleeping," Charlene answered.

"Did she say anything?" Mama asked.

"It's just like what Gary said about how many women are beaten by their husbands every day. Abi's one of 'em. Don't it just make your skin crawl?"

"What did she specifically say about Vince?" Mama asked.

"Those black eyes were on account of him, and that wasn't the first time. Her face looks a little puffy to me. I bet he hit her today. If we could check her body, we'd probably find bruises all over that baby."

A few minutes later when I walked into the kitchen, Charlene and Mother sat at the table with sweaty glasses of iced tea in front of them. They both turned and looked at me.

"Well, Sleeping Beauty, did you get a little nap?" Charlene got up to fix another glass of tea.

Mama's eyes followed me as I sat at the table. "I told your father you're here. He wanted to come over and talk to you, but I asked him to wait."

"I'm not going back to Vince," I said.

Mama glanced at Charlene who had her back to us. "Maybe we should take a drive." She got up. "Charlene, we'll be back in a bit."

We got into Mama's ten-year-old Chevy.

As she backed out of the driveway, she said, "Abigale, there's not much I can do to help you."

Her calling me Abigale made me feel like a child. "I'm not asking you to do anything."

She drove slowly down the dirt road. "Is there any way you could make another go of it?"

"You want me to put up with the same life you've had for the last thirty-seven years?" I asked angrily.

Without responding, she stopped the car and turned off the lights. The smell of fresh-turned earth drifted in through the open windows. Dots of light an eternity away lay in a straight line marking the horizon.

"Daddy's getting ready to plant. We've had some good rains. He's hoping we'll make a decent crop." She paused. "That means we'll have money for your tuition this fall." There it was—her bargaining chip for getting me to go back to Vince. I couldn't go to school if I was working full time to support myself.

"First I've got to get through this semester," I answered, knowing it would be my last one at UP.

"Baby, I don't know what to say," she said, sounding frustrated.

"I don't either." I studied Mama's silhouette and wondered what she would have done in my situation. Of course, she would never have done what I did, get pregnant by a married man who already had a kid.

"What can you do to support yourself?" Mama asked.

The night air ran a chill through me. "I'm not sure."

"Jo Kelly found a pretty good job in Oaces," she said hopefully.

"I'm not staying here." My heart felt heavy at the idea of leaving all I'd ever known. "I need to know the world doesn't stop when you get to the edge of the Caprock."

"You can't take off without a job or a place to go."

I thought of the money Garrett tried to give me—a thousand dollars. That sounded like a fortune.

"Do Vince's parents know you've left?" she asked.

"Yeah, they do," I admitted.

She looked in my direction. "Things look bleak now, but in a couple of days, you'll be ready to patch things up, and Vince will too."

"I finally got strong enough to leave, and I'm never going back. I can't."

"So you had a little fight. Marriage is like that," Mama argued.

"I know. You and Daddy taught me well." I forced back tears. "I watched him beat you for eighteen years. Maybe that's why I thought it was okay when Vince did it to me."

I felt guilty for what I'd said, and her stony silence told me my words had cut deep.

As we drove back to Charlene's, I thought about the child who grew inside me. My mother would never know it. She couldn't. If Vince ever found out about the baby I had conceived while married to him, he would somehow take it away from me. It was the one thing I had left, and I had no intention of losing it.

# Chapter Eighteen

*She stuck to it like a
June bug to a screen door.*

**April 19, 1973, Thursday**

The next morning, when I walked into the kitchen, Charlene stood at the stove with a spatula in her hand. "I'm getting ready to fatten you up, gal."

I swallowed, willing my nausea to go away. "What's cooking?"

"Spanish omelets." She folded the eggs over. "George and I had these in Santa Fe last month."

"So you're still dating George?" I poured two glasses of orange juice. Going on an out of town trip and not married was pretty scandalous, but Charlene did what she pleased, and nobody challenged her.

"Yep." She took the glass I offered.

"You two ever going to get hitched?" I asked.

"Shoot no. I'm still sewing for my hope chest." She poked at the eggs with her spatula.

"Why not? He's crazy about you."

"What do I need a man for? Somebody to clean up after? No thanks. I make enough money to pay my bills." She scooped up the omelet. "I wish Betty would smarten up."

I set the table, wondering how much Charlene knew about Mama's marriage.

"Your mama is the one that makes the money in that house. And what does she get?" She looked at me squarely. "Not much by my way of thinking."

"I agree, but I think she feels stuck."

"Given her mind-set it may be too late for her, but it's not for you. You got a right to be happy." She wrapped her free arm around my shoulders. "I don't know everything that's going on between you and Vince, but if he's hurting you, don't go back—that just gives him license to do it again and again."

Wrapping my arm around her waist, I rested my head on her shoulder. "Thanks. I needed to hear that."

*   *   *

Garrett put Loc to bed early and was waiting for Trang when she got home. He had told Vinh before they left for class that he wanted to talk to Trang alone, and asked if he would stay in his car. None of this bedroom stuff again. It would be hard enough to make her understand what he wanted to tell her.

"Will you talk with me?" he asked, pulling out a chair for her at the kitchen table.

Smiling, she sat down. "What you want to talk?"

He sat across from her. "Several weeks ago you said I had a girlfriend."

"I think so," she answered, watching him closely.

He moved his water glass in a circle on the table. "You're right, I do."

Tears filled her eyes, and her voice was tight when she said, "Trang no like that."

"I'm sure you don't. And I regret not telling you sooner. I've known her since January, right after I moved you and Loc down here."

She silently counted on her fingers. "Four months you have girlfriend."

"I haven't seen her in a while, at least not in that way."

"You make baby with her?" Trang asked.

Garrett wasn't sure if she was asking if they had had sex or if Abi was pregnant. That was beside the point. He had one thing to tell her. "I love Abi. I want to marry her."

Her tears spilled down her face. "You make baby with me. You daddy to Loc. You marry me."

"Yes, I know that. And I'm going to continue to take care of you and Loc. I'm not going to let anything happen to you." He took a deep breath. "But I love Abi."

"You no love me?" Now the tears were falling from her eyes in a steady stream.

"Not in that way." He pulled a handkerchief from his pocket and handed it to her. "You took care of me when I was hurt. Without you I would not be here, but I do not feel the same for you that I feel for Abi."

"Her American?" Trang asked in an accusing tone as she dabbed at her eyes.

"Yes, she's an American."

Trang sniffed and mopped her face. "What you do?"

"When school is out, I'm going to do my internship in Houston as planned. I'd like to live here if it's okay with you. I'll sleep on the couch."

"What about your girlfriend?" Trang snarled.

"I'm not sure what she'll do. When I talk to her in a couple of weeks, I'll ask her to move down here, or I'll help her get an apartment in Oaces, whatever she feels comfortable with."

"What she feel comfortable with," Trang echoed indignantly. "What about me and Loc?"

"I will continue to take care of you," he repeated. "I'm not going to abandon either one of you."

"You send me back to Vietnam?" she asked.

"No," Garrett declared, clear that Trang held the high trump card—Loc.

"You leave me and marry her, I take Loc. We go to Vietnam," she countered.

"Trang, there's nothing there for you—or for Loc."

"What life for me here if you marry girlfriend? What I do? Don't know English. No job."

"But you're learning, and like I said, I'm not going to quit taking care of you." She had not brought up her pregnancy, and he dared not ask. If she was, he would be obligated to tell Abi when he asked her to marry him. From what Abi had said about babies, he knew that would be a deal breaker.

"I no like this." She stood up.

"I'm sure you don't."

"When you tell Loc?" She scooted in her chair.

"Let's wait. I don't want to upset him before we have to," Garrett suggested.

"I no tell him. I no hurt him like that," she said in a loud whisper.

"When the time is right, I'll sit down and talk to him. If you want to be there, we'll tell him together."

She walked down the hall and quietly shut her bedroom door. Garrett heaved a huge sigh. The truth had been too long in coming.

\* \* \*

### April 20, 1973, Friday

During the first few minutes of my therapy appointment, I brought Valerie up to date on my leaving Vince and staying with Charlene.

"Why aren't you with your parents?" Valerie asked as she wrote on a tablet in her lap.

"My dad wouldn't allow it."

"What does he think you should do? Go back to Vince after all he's done?" she asked indignantly.

"Yes, that's exactly what he thinks I should do."

"Does he know that Vince hurt you?"

"I told them the first time, but after that, I kept it to myself because when my dad gets upset he takes it out on Mama."

"So your dad hits your mom?" Her eyes widened.

I nodded.

"You and your dad don't have a very good relationship then," she concluded, still writing frantically.

"No, not at all." I thought about telling her about the memories I had of my dad trying to get me to touch him. My recollections felt so bizarre, and they still made me feel slimy just thinking them.

"Psychologists are starting to see a pattern of women marrying men who are similar to their fathers, especially in abuse cases. Some theorists think it is a subconscious desire to heal the relationship; in other words, if you have a negative role model for a father and then marry someone who has similar characteristics to your father, the mind is trying to fix the old relationship by making it work with someone else, someone they can link subconsciously to the man they always wanted to love them."

I nodded. Her psychological theories fit, but they weren't helping with my current problems.

"So what are you going to do?" she asked.

"I have to leave, and I can't tell anyone that I'm pregnant—not anyone who might tell Vince."

"You're keeping the baby then," Valerie concluded.

"Having an abortion was never an option for me. Whether or not I tell Gary is my biggest concern."

"You said you were afraid he couldn't support this child as well as take care of his wife and son."

"Maybe he could, but I couldn't do that to him."

"Do *that* to him?" she echoed.

"If he knows I'm pregnant, he might divorce his wife."

"But you said you love him," she argued.

"I do, but I don't want to destroy his life."

"He's as much as destroyed yours," she countered.

I thought about what Garrett had been to me. "Gary helped me find the courage I needed—to leave my marriage. Without him, I would have kept on doing what Vince and my parents expected me to do."

"Why did you marry Vince? What attracted you to him?"

"When I was a senior in high school, a lot of my friends were engaged and planning weddings for the week after we graduated. Vince and I met in January, and by Valentine's Day he gave me an engagement ring." I looked at my naked ring finger of my left hand. "He never asked me to marry him. He just sort of assumed we would. By then we had already had sex, so I felt like I had to—because I wasn't a virgin anymore."

"So Vince ramrodded you into marriage," Valerie suggested.

"At first, he was really charming, and I was flattered that he wanted me. I guess that's why we had sex so quickly, but once we did, I felt obligated to marry him because I wasn't sure anyone else who would want me."

"You really believed that?" Valerie asked sadly.

"A part of me still feels that way. The whole time I was having an affair with Gary I kept thinking I couldn't leave Vince until Gary wanted to marry me. I didn't leave Vince until I got pregnant with Gary's baby."

"It sounds like your guilt about having sex led you to marry Vince. Do you now feel guilty about having sex with Gary?" she asked.

"Sort of. I grew up thinking I wouldn't have sex until I got married, but then I did, which made me feel like I had given away whatever I had of value. Over this past semester, I've realized I'd never be happy with Vince, but having an affair with Gary wasn't the way to change things. Still I'm not sure I would have been strong enough to leave my marriage if I hadn't. And even then it took getting pregnant." I propped my elbows on my knees and dropped my face into my open palms. "I still don't know what I'm going to do."

Our conversation felt like a circle that kept spiraling back on itself.

\*　　\*　　\*

## May 4, 1973, Friday

As Garrett walked past the counseling center, he met the receptionist, Sally, in the hallway. She smiled and spoke. They had gotten acquainted when Garrett did his clinicals. Sally walked into the lady's room, so

Garrett walked behind her desk to check the appointment book. He scanned the page and found Abi's name under Valerie's column. She had seen her six times in the last three weeks. Aggressive therapy, probably since it was the end of the semester, and Abi has some major issues. Garrett and Valerie had had some classes together, and she would tell him every detail of Abi's case. Valerie was finishing up a session in a few minutes. He decided to hang around in the hallway and just happen to bump into her.

A few minutes later, she came out of the counseling office.

"Hey, Valerie, is that you?" Garrett said as he approached her.

"Oh, hi, Garrett. Aren't you on your way to Houston?"

"I've started packing. How are you doing?" Was she aware of his connection to Abi, and if so would she play ignorant to get more insight into Abi by talking to him, which was unethical, but he and Valerie were friends. He had talked about his clients, and she would too, especially if she knew he had a personal interest.

"How about a cup of tea or coffee?" Garrett asked.

"Great idea." She walked with him toward the elevator. "How's your semester shaping up?"

"Fine, I only had two classes, stats and anthropology of the family. I managed to pull a B in both, which is a miracle considering the garbage in my life."

"Really what's happening?" she asked.

"I had a friend who's having a lot of difficulty. She has an abusive husband, the whole nine yards."

"God, I have a client like that. She started coming several weeks ago. Such a sweetie. I want to take her home with me, but all I can do is encourage her to take care of herself."

"Sounds like my friend," Garrett commented, knowing she was talking about Abi and feeling guilty about intruding on Abi's privacy. He had overstepped his bounds with her before, and he needed to back off.

"Hey, you know what, I just remembered something I've got to take care of. Let me take a raincheck." He gave her a brotherly hug and they parted ways. In the past, he had been unethical concerning Abi, and he was determined to change all that—starting now.

\* \* \*

## May 11, 1973

My last final fell on Friday morning. I was the last one to turn in my test. After I placed it on top of the stack, Dr. Horton said, "I've enjoyed having you in my class this semester, Abi."

"Thanks. You'll never know how valuable it's been to me."

She smiled and seemed to understand without asking for the details.

I drove to Garrett's apartment, but he wasn't there. He could have already left for Houston. On the way to Dahlia, I wondered if I would ever see him again since I had promised myself I would leave as soon as I finished the semester. If we did talk, he might ask me to marry him, which is what I had yearned for—before I found out he was already married. Now I didn't know what I wanted.

\* \* \*

Again, the Beauty Box was surrounded by cars. Garrett found a space, parked, and peered into the rearview mirror, taking one last look at his hair and beard. He needed to do this, but knowing it and doing it were two different things. His internship started next week, and he had to make a good impression. Taking a deep breath, he opened the car door. Like before, he would get in line and keep his ears pealed for anything that was said about Abi. Hopefully either Charlene or Betty could work him in.

When he opened the door, Charlene, called out, "Gary, how you been?"

He tried to hide how pleased he was that she remembered him. "Great, how are you, Charlene?"

"Just fine. You ready to take the big plunge and take it down to the scalp?" she teased.

"Not quite that close, but I'm going for what some might call 'acceptable.'" He glimpsed at his reflection in the mirror. "Oh, yeah, and the beard has to go too."

Betty, who had been standing with her back to him, turned when he mentioned cutting his beard. "Now, we're getting serious. What's the occasion?"

"Got to look presentable," he answered, curious if Abi had told her about him.

"Presentable for what?" Charlene asked as she continued ratting the hair of her current customer.

"I'm starting my internship in Houston next week."

"Internship?" Charlene echoed. "In what?"

"I'm finishing up my training to be a psychologist," he said.

"A shrink, huh?" Charlene quipped.

"Yeah, a shrink." He picked up a magazine and began reading about the National Organization for Women. It seemed so removed from this Panhandle town where all the women did what their men told them to do—except Abi had left Vince, and if Garrett had his way, she would soon be setting up housekeeping with him.

He was halfway through the article when Charlene motioned to him. "You're in luck, Cowboy. Gracie Dane is late again, so I'm gonna slip you in and make *her* wait for a change—when she finally gets here."

Charlene tied the cape around his neck, her gaze trained on his hair while she worked. "So we're going for that professional look. Shall we save your hair to donate?"

"Sure, if you think there's enough." He liked the idea of a cancer patient benefiting from his loss.

Without hesitation, she pulled it back in a ponytail and put a rubber band around it. Then she began cutting through it on the scalp side of the rubber band. "Damn you got a lot of hair," she said, flashing him a toothy smile in the mirror. After she cut through, she held it up like a trophy. "Kiss these locks good-bye."

She was kidding, but he was going to miss his hair since he had not cut it since he got out of the air force. Charlene laid his detached hair on her workstation, pulled out an electric razor, and turned it on as she approached his head, looking like a lady with a mission.

Garrett turned to face her. "You're not really going to the scalp, are you?"

Charlene laughed. "Relax. I'm going to have you looking like you were born with a briefcase in your hands." She swiveled his chair, so he couldn't see what she was doing.

Betty glanced over periodically and teased, "Charlene, I'm not sure you should do that."

When he tried to turn his head to see what Betty was talking about, Charlene caught his face between her palms. "I want you to be surprised. If you don't like it, no charge." She gave him another charming grin.

He liked this woman, but he didn't totally trust her.

Before she would let him look, she snipped off his beard, lathered his face, and shaved him with a straight razor, the whole time kidding about how few people had died by accident in her chair. While she worked, she randomly started telling the shop at large about her new roommate, Abi. She bragged about Abi studying every night, what good grades she was making, how helpful she was around the house, what great company she was, how they ate popcorn and watched TV nearly every evening. Betty was quieter than usual, even though Charlene was talking about her daughter.

Finally, Charlene turned Garrett to the mirror. Someone he did not recognize stared back at him.

"Wow," he whispered.

"Pretty darn handsome," Charlene remarked.

"Is George in trouble?" Gracie Dane asked. She had come in after Charlene started working on Garrett, and she like everyone else in the shop seemed to enjoy the show.

"Naw, I think this one's taken." With her back to everyone else, she gave Garrett a knowing wink.

That along with all she said about Abi told Garrett she understood what had motivated him to come to Dahlia all three times. "Thanks, Charlene. I really appreciate everything." He gave her a tip bigger than he could afford, but he wanted to express how much he appreciated her taking in Abi.

She followed him to the porch and shut the door behind her. "I'll make sure Abi knows you came by."

"How did you know? Did she tell you?"

Shaking her head, she smiled. "Dr. Freud, a woman knows. Even when she don't think she knows, and you don't think she knows, she knows. Bear that in mind."

Like many things she said, there seemed to be great wisdom in her words. "Thanks, I will." Since no one could see, and he wanted to, Garrett gave her a hug, his nose even with her chin.

"Too bad you're moving to Houston. I'm gonna miss you." She opened the door, and as she stepped inside, a chorus of hoots and hollers greeted her. Charlene threw back her head and laughed. "Jealous, I reckon," she sang out, shutting the door behind her.

He would miss her too, but hopefully he would see Charlene when he brought Abi home for a visit.

* * *

After supper, Charlene and I watched television as usual. During a commercial, she said, "Remember that Gary-guy that Betty and I told you about?"

"The one with long hair?" I asked.

"Today, he came in the shop and asked me to cut that all off." She got out of her chair.

"Really?" Garrett had been at the Beauty Box when I went by his apartment.

"Beard too," she added before going to the kitchen.

I followed her. "Why did he do that?" It was hard to picture him without his long hair and beard.

She pulled a skillet from the cabinet, lit the burner under it, and covered the bottom with popcorn kernels and oil. "Said something about doing an internment."

"You mean an internship?" I suggested.

"Yeah, that's it." She put a lid on the popcorn. "In Houston."

"Really? When?" I got out the wooden bowls we used for popcorn.

"He said he was leaving Sunday."

When the corn finished popping, we returned to the living room and watched television while we ate. I couldn't quit thinking about a short-haired version of Garrett. The phone on the table next to Charlene rang. She answered it, and then handed it to me.

"Hello?" I said.

"This is A.V. Martin," he said softly.

"Papa Martin, how are you?" I asked, surprised to hear from him.

"Your mother said I could reach you here," he explained.

"Charlene's one of Mama's friends." It felt awkward admitting I was staying here.

He cleared his throat. "How have you been?"

"Fine. I finished my finals today."

"How did you do?" he asked.

"Good, I think."

"I'm proud of you," he said, sounding like he meant it. "I've been getting some money together for you. I figure it's best to give you what's yours before something happens to it."

"That's great. I plan to leave town pretty soon."

"I'm sorry to hear that." He cleared his throat. "But under the circumstances I understand."

"Thanks, Papa Martin." Hopefully, he did not fully understand my situation.

"Will you join us for Sunday dinner—so I can give you the money, and I know Bea wants to see you?"

"Won't that be awkward for you?" I asked.

"Don't worry about me. You need to get what you can use—cooking stuff, linens, towels."

"I can't carry very much in my car, but I do need to get my stuff. Plus, I would like to see Bea."

"Good, I'll tell Mama to lay a place for you, and I'll let Vince know."

"If you can, don't tell them." I hesitated. "No need to torture them ahead of time. Besides, I'll be just about as welcome there as an outhouse breeze."

He chuckled so faintly I could barely hear it. We said our good-byes and hung up.

"You need to get you a lawyer. Don't settle for what your father-in-law sees fit to give you." Charlene chewed vigorously on a mouthful of popcorn.

"Papa Martin will be fair."

"He'll take care of his son. That's what parents do." She smiled to herself. "Unless they're too busy taking care of their husbands." After pulling a phone book from the shelf under the table next to her, she tossed it on the floor. "Call a lawyer and find out what he can do for you."

Later, in bed, I blindly leafed through the yellow pages. I didn't have the money to pay a lawyer, and there wasn't much to fight over anyway. Plus, I wasn't waiting around long enough for him to come up with a divorce agreement. After I turned out the lights, I lay awake, picturing Garrett with a crew-cut. I worried about whether to go by his apartment, and how much to tell him if I did.

# Chapter Nineteen

*It's time to paint your butt
white and run with the antelope.*

**May 12, 1973, Saturday**

*A*fter Charlene left for work, I drove to the Flatland Public Library
and looked up the current divorce laws. It took me hours to wade
through all the legal mumbo-jumbo. Closing, the last thick book I looked
at, I vowed I would never let Vince know about the child I conceived
while married to him.

All afternoon, I did laundry and cleaned Charlene's house, anything
to occupy my mind and hands.

That night after supper, I approached Charlene who sat in her chair
watching television. "I'm going over to see my parents. Then I'm leaving
in the morning."

"Well, Chickie, you know you're always welcome here anytime you
need a nest to light in."

"Thanks. I appreciate that more than you can ever know."

When I got to my parents' house, I knocked. My father got to the
front door first, followed by my mother. He pushed it open. "You need
an engraved invitation to come in this house?"

"No, I didn't know how welcome I'd be."

He gave a muffled grunt and returned to his chair while my mother
slipped her arm around my waist. She and I walked to the couch and sat
next to each other. I wanted to turn off the television, but that would

275

aggravate Daddy. Plus, I didn't know what I would say in the void that followed. Instead, I blindly watched while trying to decide how to say good-bye.

During a commercial, Mama asked, "You want me to trim your hair, Baby?"

"Sure." I trailed her to the utility room where she kept a stool and a pair of scissors for drop-ins.

She draped me and immediately started trimming the dead ends.

"Let's cut it off—even with my chin," I said.

"You sure?" She was wondering what Vince would think, and frankly, I was too.

"If I don't like it, I'll grow it back," I said, braver than I felt.

Mama shampooed it and then she began cutting. I watched with fascination. When she finished, I swung my hair from side to side and marveled at how lighter I felt.

When the news ended, my father passed by the doorway behind us. "Well, folks, I'm going to bed."

Still planted in the chair while Mama snipped at renegade hairs, I called to him, "Just a minute, Daddy. I need to tell you something."

He returned to the doorway.

I swiveled around to face him. "I'm leaving tomorrow, and I'm not coming back."

Daddy sniffed. "You'll be back—after you run out of money." He sauntered down the hall.

"He doesn't mean to hurt you, Baby. It's just his way." Mama continued combing and snipping.

"I meant what I said to Daddy. I'm not coming back."

"You got to come home—eventually." Her voice had thickened, although she kept snipping.

"No, I don't."

"Why?" She watched my face in the mirror.

"I can't be this close to Vince." I stared at her reflection. "But I love you, Mama. I always will."

She slapped her comb and scissors on the counter and grabbed a wad of toilet tissue from the mud room behind us. "Damn allergies," she muttered, and blew her nose.

Smiling through her tears, she finished the hair-cut. Then she wrapped her arm around my shoulders as we slowly walked to the door. "Good-bye, Baby. Let us hear from you soon."

I kissed her cheek and held her close, savoring the familiar smell of perms and hair coloring. Without a backward glance, I hurried to the car, so she wouldn't see me crying.

The next morning, I ate a huge breakfast since I doubted I would eat much for lunch. Then I dressed in my loosest jeans and blouse, which were starting to get snug. Charlene's vow to fatten me up had worked. After I finished packing my bags, Charlene helped me carry them to the car.

"Abi, you been a super house guest," she said as we loaded my things into the backseat.

"Thanks, you've been the hostess with the mostest." We hugged. She had been there for me when I could not count on anyone else.

Breaking away, I said, "After lunch with Vince's family, I'm heading out."

"Which way you going?" she asked as I got into the car.

"Not sure. I might go through Oaces and see a friend before I leave town."

"That sounds like a prize winning idea." She gave me one of her toothy grins.

"Thanks for everything, Charlene. You're the best."

"Don't you forget it." She waved as I backed out of her drive and puttered down the dirt road.

Only five minutes away, I stopped at Christi's place, a small farm house on the outskirts of Dahlia. When her first son, an eight-year-old bolted out of the front door wearing a white shirt and black slacks, I realized they were on their way to church. From the end of the drive, I watched as the other two kids and then Buck filed out and headed for the car. I got out.

"Hey, Ab, you doing all right?" Buck asked on his way to the car.

"Yeah, I'm fine. I just came by to see Christi for a minute."

"She'll be right out. As usual, we're running late." He opened his car door. "Catch you later."

"Yeah, later," I called to him.

Christi hurried out the front door, zipping her zipper in the back of her dress and smoothing her hair. When she saw me, she made a beeline in my direction. "Well, look what the cats dragged up. Abi, you are a sight for sore eyes." She wrapped her arms around me, folding me in a tight embrace.

When we separated, I held her at arm's length. "And look at you, all gussied up."

"I'd make you go to church with us, but Brother Bill would probably have a heart-attack if you showed up wearing jeans." She laughed.

"I know you're in a hurry. I just want to tell you thanks for everything."

"I heard you finally did it. You flew the coop. Good for you." She gave my shoulder a playful slug.

"How'd you know?" I had thought of calling her, but I would end up telling her things I shouldn't say.

"Dahlia's small and Charlene's mouth is big, so put the two together, and everybody knows everything." She shook her head as she looked me up and down. "You look good. Damn good."

"Thanks." I hesitated. "Thanks for everything." I hoped she knew what I meant by that.

"You're welcome."

"And I need to tell you good-bye."

"Where you going?" She laced her fingers into mine.

"I'm not sure." Our interlocking hands reminded me of how we held hands as teenagers.

"You going to be okay?" she asked gently.

"Sure, A.V. said he had some money for me. I don't know how much, but I'll get by. Remember, you're the one that told me I could do it?" I mentally took a picture of her smile for safe keeping.

"Listen now, you stay in touch. I want to know where you are and what you're doing."

I hesitated. "Thanks for all you've done. You'll never know how much you mean to me."

"That sounds too final, Ab. You're coming back, right?"

"I may not." I swallowed hard. Her image blurred with my tears, so I grabbed her and held her tight, whispering in her ear, "I love you."

"I love you too," she said.

Buck tooted the car horn. We smiled at each other, and then she ran to the car and got in. Buck backed out, and they headed down the road, leaving a trail of dust behind them.

On the way to Quits, I parked beneath a lonely elm tree beside the road where I waited for the Martins to get home and start lunch before I showed up.

*   *   *

Vince was well into Sunday dinner when he heard a car pull into his driveway next door. It sounded like Abi's bug, but he couldn't imagine her showing up here—not after the shenanigans she pulled. A minute later, someone knocked on the front door. Bea jumped up and hurried to answer it.

"Abi, you're the last person I expected to see," Bea shrieked.

They walked into the dining room arm in arm. Abi's hair had been cut short, but she still looked like a knockout, which Vince hated to admit—even to himself.

"Look who I've got," Bea announced.

Vince avoided looking at Abi until she said, "You're here. I didn't see your pickup, and I thought…." Her voice trailed off like she was putting it all together.

Grinning from ear to ear, Daddy got up and gave Abi a big hug. Vince looked at Mama who was glaring at Abi—just as pissed and shocked as he was.

"Got an extra plate?" Abi asked with her arm still wrapped around Daddy.

"Sure," Daddy answered, heading for the kitchen because he knew Mama wasn't about to get it.

As soon as Daddy was gone, Mama hissed, "Did you come crawling back?"

Abi met Mama's gaze and smiled. Mama's face turned red, and she was about to speak, when Daddy walked back in the room. Vince figured Daddy was the reason Mama had been so tight-lipped since Abi left.

Daddy put the place setting in the empty spot next to Vince, and then Abi sat down as if nothing had changed. This was Daddy's doings—inviting Abi here so he could rub it in Vince's face that he had sold everything Vince owned. When his money ran out, she'd come crawling back, especially once her boyfriend got tired of her frigid ways.

Bea's kids were gawking at Abi.

She laughed. "Don't worry; I'm only here to say good-bye."

"Well, we're glad you could accept my invitation," Daddy said like he was hosting a damned party.

Mama opened her mouth, but Daddy gave her a look, so she started eating again. Vince did too.

Daddy handed the roast to Abi, and then he ordered everyone else to pass the rest of the food to her.

When Abi had finished filling her plate and was eating, Daddy asked, "So your final tests went well?"

"I made straight A's this semester," she bragged.

She had done a lot more than go to class and study for tests.

"Are you going back to school in the fall?" Bea asked while she fed Tiffany.

"Yeah, but I'm not sure where," Abi answered.

Vince had intended on keeping tabs on her, but if she moved off that was going to be a lot harder to do.

"Going to keep that a secret too?" Mama asked.

"I really haven't decided," Abi answered.

"Your boyfriend leaving you like you left Vince?" Mama smirked while she ladled gravy on her meat.

When Daddy cleared his throat and gave her a warning look, Mama smiled to herself.

"Abi, I love your hair," Bea said. "Where'd you get it cut?"

"My mom did it." Abi ran her fingers through it, which made Vince think of the many times he had done that. She turned her head from side to side, so her hair swung out. "I felt like I needed a change."

Bea and Daddy kept passing food to Abi, and she ate like Vince had never seen her chow down before. The three of them talked about what Bea was doing while Vince waited for a time when he could leave.

When Abi finally finished her plate, Daddy said, "Abi, would you do us the honors and get dessert?"

She got up and sashayed her little butt into the kitchen, and then she came back carrying a pie in one hand and a stack of saucers in the other. Like she had countless times before, Abi cut the pie, put it on the plates, and handed them out, making sure Daddy got the first and biggest piece. She was closer to Daddy than Vince had ever been. Even after what she did, Daddy still couldn't see her for what she was.

Daddy stood up, and everyone looked at him while he pulled a thick envelope from his pants pocket. Vince's money no doubt.

Holding it with both hands, Daddy said, "Abi, I've loved having you as a daughter. I hope this helps you start a new and better life." He leaned over Vince to hand the envelope to Abi. Watching Daddy give that little bitch everything Vince owned was harder than anything else that had happened. He wanted to grab the goddamn envelope and run out the door, but what would he do after that? He didn't own a vehicle anymore.

"Thanks," Abi whispered, all sappy.

Vince gritted his teeth to keep from saying anything. Daddy had warned him to keep his mouth shut if Abi ever showed her face around here again. As usual, Daddy was thinking ahead.

Mama glared at Abi while Bea sat there smiling.

Then Daddy got up and walked to the hall closet, pulled out Vince's gun, and returned to the head of the table. "Vince wants you to have this."

That was the final straw. When Daddy hadn't given it back to him, he assumed Daddy sold it. As Vince stalked toward the front door, Mama called after him, but he ignored her.

"Vince," Daddy said, stopping him in his tracks. "You need to steer clear of your house for a while. Abi will be getting what she wants out of there.

The screen door slammed shut behind him as Vince walked out. He needed to go somewhere and cool off. Seeing Abi again had gotten him all stirred up. As much as he had told himself he did not need or want her, he now felt that emptiness in the middle of chest that hurt so bad he thought he might die. He could not imagine the rest of his life without her. Worse than that, he could not imagine her with someone else.

*     *     *

Tiffany and Chase's eyes were riveted to the gun in Papa Martin's hands. Noticing their fascination, he returned it to the closet where he had gotten it. After we finished dessert, I started helping clear the table.

"Don't worry with that," Papa Martin said, "Go over to the house and get what you want. I'll send Bea over with some boxes."

"What about Vince? I sure don't want to be alone with him," I said, stating the obvious.

Papa Martin kept his eyes on his empty plate. "I think you'll be okay."

I wanted to remind him that he had told me that before, but I decided to not challenge him since he seemed to have everything under control, and he had always been my only real advocate.

As I walked into the house that I once called home, I marveled at how empty and hollow it now felt. So much had changed in the last five months. From the kitchen and bathroom, I picked out my favorite dishes, cooking utensils, towels, and linens, trying to take only what I needed and the things that Mama, Charlene, or Christi had given me over the years. I weeded through my clothes, taking only what I liked best along with Bea's old maternity clothes. When I found Vince's Christmas present hidden in the bottom drawer of the dresser, I held it up and laughed out loud.

Bea appeared at the doorway about that time. "Going to take that with you?"

I smiled and threw it in the reject pile.

Bea helped me carry out four full boxes. We crammed them into my small car along with the bags that were already there. I walked back to the house by myself and strolled through the rooms. Papa Martin had apparently sold anything of value—including the three TV's and Vince's new pickup.

In the living room, I caught my thumb on the pages of the Bible and let the pages fall until I found my dried blood. I thought of the events that led up to that day and what Garrett's kisses had meant to me at the time. The red blotch now turned brown on those onionskin pages had served as an indictment of my sins. Now, I saw it as the beginning of finding the strength to walk away.

The back door opened and heavy footsteps came through the kitchen. My heart pounding, I put the book down, ready to defend myself if I needed to. Vince walk toward me, not with anger or malice but slowly and calmly—like he had something he needed to say.

"You ready to go?" he asked, using a tone that had once charmed me.

"Just taking a last look," I said.

"You got plenty of gas? I'll take it down and fill it up for you." He held out his hand for the keys.

I glanced at his open palm. "Do you remember the first time you made that offer?"

One side of Vince's mouth lifted in a half-smile. "The night we met. I wanted to make sure you got home okay. I knew then that I was going to marry you."

"And you did," I agreed.

"Abi-girl, I was wrong for doing what I did, but I do love you." This was his version of an apology and a proposal to try again.

Phrases about how he had never considered my wants or needs came to mind, but what would they buy me other than even more resentment? We stared at each other, and I realized there was absolutely nothing left to say. As I turned to walk away, I saw the open Bible and the stain. Outside, Bea and Papa Martin stood by my car and the gun lay on top of the boxes in the back seat. We hugged and exchanged take-care-of-yourself farewells.

As I backed out of my driveway for the last time, Vince stepped onto the porch. The weight of the large open book that he held seemed to be too much for him because it tipped downward, showing the blood stain. Papa Martin and Bea looked back and forth from me to Vince. While I drove away, I waved at Papa Martin and Bea, not caring one iota what any of them made of the situation.

# Chapter Twenty

*Independent as a hog on ice.*

**May 13, 1973, Sunday**

When he spotted Abi's car in the drive below him, Garrett stood at the head of the stairs with a heavy box of books in his hands. "Bird," he called, and hurried down the steps. He loaded the box into the last possible space in his trunk and wiped the sweat from his brow with the length of his arm as he walked back to her.

She nodded toward his car where both doors and the trunk stood open. "Looks like you're about as full as you can get."

"Yeah, I'm glad you got here before I took off. Charlene said she would let you know I was moving."

Abi shot him a surprised look. "She specifically told you she would tell me?"

"Not exactly, but you know how she has a way with words." He needed to help her unpack before he took off. "When you didn't come by, I panicked and drove to Dahlia."

"So you decided to get your head shaved while you were there?" she teased.

He raked his fingers through the short strands, still not used to its length. "No, I'm starting my internship Tuesday, and I wanted to make a good first impression."

She evaluated his hair for several seconds then announced, "I don't like it."

"I like yours," he said, trying to penetrate her defenses.

"Yeah, but I didn't cut off *all* of mine," she countered.

He studied her face. "You'd look gorgeous without a hair on your head."

Fighting a smile, she shook her head. "Comments like that are what got this thing started."

He leaned into the window to get closer to her. "Park, and I'll help you unload before I have to go."

"I'm just here to say goodbye before I head out." Her voice quivered.

His chest tightened. "I had hoped you'd stay here—in my apartment. I'll have the same job, just originating in Houston." Delaying her for a few hours could turn into the rest of their lives.

"You want me to be your mistress," she said, clearly detesting the idea.

"No, I just want to see you." He wanted to ask her to marry him, but he had to ease into that gracefully, not as an appeal to keep her from leaving.

"I can't live like that." She reached for the gear shifter.

Instinctively, Garrett gripped her other arm. "Bird, let's talk before you go."

She rested her hands on the bottom of the steering wheel, closed her eyes, and took a deep breath. "If I don't leave now, I'm afraid I'll lose my courage."

"If you go without talking one last time, you'll always wonder what could have been."

After what seemed like an eternity, she admitted, "You're right."

She parked her car while he closed the doors on the Charger. As she was getting out, he noted a gun lying on top of the boxes in her back seat.

"Abi, you do realize you have a rifle in your backseat, don't you?" he asked cautiously.

"My father-in-law gave that to me. Actually, he said Vince wanted me to have it." She gave a half laugh like that was the farthest thing possible from the truth.

"I bet he does." Garrett gingerly lifted it from its resting spot. He had not held one of these things since he was in Vietnam, and even then they made him nervous. "How about we hide it under some clothes or something? I would hate for some kid to see this and think it would be a cool reason to break into your car."

While they shifted the boxes around and created a space in which to camouflage it, Abi told him the details of Vince's shocked face when she shot his mother's picture. "Luckily A.V. stopped me from shooting Vince. Things could have gotten really messy. I mean with a trial and everything."

Garrett studied her short hair and her confident manner. She was not the same demure lady he had run into five months ago in the bookstore. "Even though you're the cutest little Annie Oakley around, the court would not have been sympathetic if you killed him. You'd have ended up in jail."

"You're right, they'd ignore everything he did to me." She patted the coat that now lay on the gun before she shut the door and locked it.

They walked to the apartment, not arm in arm like he would have liked, but she had stayed. On the balcony landing, Garrett waited for Abi to step into the apartment he hoped she would inhabit. Inside, she immediately walked to the kitchen and examined his images in the pictures she had drawn. "I thought you'd take these with you."

"I left them here for you." He couldn't tell her how hurtful they would be to Trang if she saw them and realized who had drawn them.

"When are you leaving?" she asked.

Garrett hesitated, not wanting to rush her. "I have my orientation Tuesday, so I need to get away as soon as I can." He had told Trang he would reach Houston by midnight, which meant he would need to leave now. He joined Abi in the kitchen. "How about a beer?"

"No, thanks. I'll just stick with my regular," she said.

"Sure." He drew a glass of water for her, glad that he had left his dishes for her. He grabbed a beer from the refrigerator for himself. "You want to sit down?"

She sat in her usual chair.

Garrett sat next to her, thinking how right this felt, but when he looked at Abi, she was frowning. "Would you rather I sit across from you?"

"Yes, I'd feel more comfortable with that." Her tone was cool, almost cold.

Garrett scooted his chair around to the other side of the table. Neither of them said anything as he drank his beer, and she sipped her water. He longed for the time when they had laughed and played and made love. It felt so long ago. This was a make it or break it conversation—but neither one of them was saying a thing.

"I love you, Abi," he confessed, setting his empty beer can on the table.

"You have nothing to hide, but your eyes tell me it hurts for you to admit it." She moved her glass aside and then picked up the can and rolled it between her hands.

He worked his dog tags back and forth. "It does hurt, because I'm afraid I may have lost you."

"I told you I was married, so you never really had me," she replied defiantly.

"You're right, I didn't," he conceded.

"Why didn't you tell me you were married when we met?"

"I should have, but I couldn't. I was attracted to you from the minute I saw you in the bookstore."

"What about your wife?" She squeezed the beer can and folded it. "What were you thinking about her while you were charming me?"

He closed his eyes and pinched the bridge of his nose.

"What about now? What do you want from me, from her?" She twisted the can back and forth like she needed some place to vent her energy.

"I love you; I want you to marry me," he said, regretting this was so different than the way he had fantasized asking her.

"Where does that leave Trang; that is her name, isn't it? And your son, Loc? What about him? What will happen to them?" she demanded.

"She left her country and gave me a son. I can't abandon her, but that doesn't mean I have to stay married to her." He started to say more about his commitment to Trang and Loc, but her face was beginning to crumple with emotion. He needed to keep his mouth shut.

"Why . . .?" A sob caught in her throat, her fingers gripped the beer can that much tighter, and she struggled to speak. "Why did you make me love you when you were married to someone else?"

His eyes lingered on the mangled can in her hands. "I told myself you needed me." He looked up and held her brown eyes with his. "I needed you. And to be honest, I wanted you."

"And I wanted you." She let the can fall to the table. "I still want you."

While they stared at one another, his mind raced through a montage of scenes with Abi and him together over the last five months, studying in the library, making love, studying here at his apartment, making love, hiking in Palo Dura Canyon, and making love. "I have some things for you."

Grabbing her hand, he led her to the bedroom where a cardboard box sat in the middle of the bare mattress. Garrett knelt on the bed and opened the flaps. He pulled out his new copy of *As a Man Thinketh* and handed it to her. She leafed through it, revealing margin notes on every page and a pressed rose.

"Everything I've written in there is about you, Bird. That rose is from your birthday."

"Our birthday—or is that a lie too?" Her chocolate brown eyes drilled into him.

"No, they're the same. March 6, 1943." That in itself sanctioned their union.

Abi sat on the bed and peeked inside the box at the black satin sheets. He pulled them out, uncovering a white gift box. She opened it and pulled out her negligee, stretching the arms out like they were wings.

Not able to stop himself, his hands stretched toward her. "I want so badly to hold you."

She laughed. "Don't you dare touch me . . . unless you plan on making love to me."

Shoving the box out of the way, he enfolded her in his arms. "Oh, Abi, Abi, my dear sweet Abi."

She clung to him. When they separated, she reached up and wiped tears of joy from his face. "Big baby," she teased and laughed.

\*   \*   \*

Being there with Garrett felt so right, too right. After a while, I sat up, looked inside the box again, and found candles, a bottle of bubble bath, and the envelope of money. I held it up. "How much am I worth?"

"It's not how much you're worth. It's all I could get together." He ran his hand up and down my back.

"I don't want your money. Vince's dad also gave me an envelope full of cash." I pulled it from my back pocket. "See? I'm rich."

Garrett emptied the envelope onto the bed and counted over six-thousand dollars. "He out did me by a long shot."

I was surprised by the amount. "Well, you have to figure that represents twelve years of marriage."

"Twelve hard years," Garrett corrected.

I nodded in agreement and shoved his money across the bed at him. "Keep this for your wife and son and to pay for your divorce." Even as the words came out of my mouth, I could not believe I was saying them.

"So you'll marry me?" Garrett asked hopefully.

Purposely ignoring his question, I stood and surveyed the bare mattress as I put Papa Martin's envelope back in my pocket. "Get up," I ordered playfully.

Garrett frowned.

"I want to put the sheets on. We're not making love on a bare mattress."

He helped me spread the satin sheets and tuck them around the corners. While I drew a bath, Garrett lit the candles and placed them at the four corners of the tub. With the last candle in place, he flipped the light off, faced me, and slowly slipped his arms around my waist. I pressed him to me, wishing I could somehow stop time and live in that moment forever.

We undressed each other in the wavering light of the candles, and I was glad that he could not see the circle around each of my nipples had darkened with my pregnancy. Naked and facing each other, on impulse I reached for his dog tags and started to pull them over his head.

His hands caught mine. "I've never taken them off—since I got them back from Trang."

I smiled wickedly. "All the more reason. I don't want anything to come between us."

He slipped the chain over his head and dropped it on the tank of the commode.

After reverently soaping and rinsing my entire body, he helped me stand and dried me with one of his thread bare towels. After I bathed and dried him, we walked to the bedroom hand in hand, and made love. As our bodies moved in unison, I savored the moments, determined to cling to him while I could. Afterwards, we lay together, sweating and spent.

Once hidden by his beard, I stroked a scar that ran along his jaw bone. "How did you get this?"

He closed his eyes. "In Nam my plane was shot down, and I was badly hurt. A group of villagers found me. Trang set my broken leg and took care of me for over a month, nursing my wounds and feeding me."

"So you owe her your life?" I stroked the smooth, white line of his scar.

"I wouldn't be alive if it weren't for her," Garrett admitted.

"And you saved my life." I rested my head on his arm.

"Why do you say that?"

"My life with Vince was a living hell, but it took meeting you to realize I could have anything else. Even then it took me a long time to understand what you were trying to tell me." I reflected on all he had given me. "Knowing you has helped me find a part of me that I did not know existed, an inner strength."

"You can do anything you want," Garrett whispered.

"I love you," I whispered.

"And I love you," he returned. The words now seemed to come so easily.

I wonder how things might be different now if he had said it when I wanted him to. Still, that would not erase the fact he had a wife and a child. He was willing to divorce Trang, but he owed her too much. He owed her his life. And I credited Garrett for saving mine.

His lips found mine, and our bodies intertwined as we kissed and talked and laughed and made love.

\* \* \*

It was midnight, and Garrett was still struggling with how to end his letter to Abi. She was sleeping, and he needed to get on the road. He reread his pleas for her to marry him, fully aware that she had avoided the question earlier. After explaining that it would take him around six months to get everything in order, he said he wanted her to move to Houston when she was ready, and that he did not think he could live without her. She was his other half, his soul mate—their common birthdays were proof of that.

After signing his name, he added the phone number at the Houston apartment and the address. He wanted everything to be open and above board. If she needed to contact him for any reason, he wanted her to have the means to do so. Folding the letter, he told himself that she would not leave Oaces; she would be here when he got back Tuesday night.

He left his apartment key and the envelope of money next to his letter.

For ten minutes or more, he stood in the doorway of his bedroom and watched the shadow of her sleeping form. He yearned to kiss her once more, but he knew if he did, he could not tear himself away. From the first day he ran over her in the bookstore, she had held him captive. With a heavy heart, Garrett walked out of the apartment, shutting the door behind him.

\* \* \*

I rolled over as soon as the front door shut. It had taken everything I had in me to keep from going to Garrett and kissing him one last time, but I knew if I did, he would linger, and I would let him, unable to resist. I got up and walked to the window where I peeked through the curtains and saw his taillights disappear as he pulled out of the parking lot.

On the table, I found a letter, the envelope filled with money, and a key. I sat down and read his letter. It was the answer to my prayer—just not when I had asked for it. A part of me wanted to do exactly what he was proposing, stay here and marry him once he had gotten a divorce. If I did—I wondered how he would react to my pregnancy—if he would say he was thrilled even if he wasn't—or if he would truly welcome another child and more responsibility.

Something I could not ignore kept me from seriously considering staying. Once I was visibly pregnant, someone would see me and news of that would get back to Vince. After that it was only a matter of time before he demanded to have rights to the child that I conceived while I was married to him. At that point, it would not matter what A.V. said. Vince would be within his legal rights, and he would make my life and my child's life a living hell. The idea of going to another city occurred to me. Couldn't I have it all, Garrett, the baby, and freedom from Vince? Then I thought of Garrett's wife and son. My mind kept coming back to them. If I were Trang, how would I feel, how would I react to another woman robbing me of my husband?

Garrett had said he did not love her, but he owed her his life. He had brought her to this country; he had made promises and commitments to her. Of course, I loved him, and he loved me. I had no doubt about that, but it was impossible to have what I wanted if it meant destroying the lives of two other people.

From the very beginning, Garrett had encouraged me to be strong, to be my own person, to be willing to fly. Now I needed to try my wings.

*   *   *

## December 8, 1973, Saturday

The announcer beamed from the television screen. "Good morning, Austin and surrounding communities, here's the news for December 8, 1973. Today is Gerald Ford's first full day as our new Vice-President."

My roommate still slept, so I cut off the sound, but the date stuck in my head as I marveled at the tiny creature in my arms. Exactly one year ago, I lay in a different hospital bed in Flatland, Texas. When Papa Martin asked Vince about me going to school, I had cut a deal with God, thinking I could manipulate fate if I was only good enough—except my definition of good enough had changed dramatically.

"...man is the master of thought, the molder of character, and the maker and the shaper of condition, environment, and destiny." James Allen's words echoed through my head, and I pictured Garrett. This is where my mind nearly always went.

From my billfold, I pulled out Garrett's letter to me. I knew the phone number by heart, but I wanted to make sure I got it right since I had never called him. When the hospital operator answered, I asked her to make the connection.

On the second ring, he answered, "This is Garrett Clay," sounding either irritated or in a hurry.

My heart pounded. I clutched his dog tag that hung around my neck and silently waited.

"Who's there?" he asked, his voice more gentle.

"Bird," I said so softly I doubted he heard.

"Abi! My God, I've been half crazy. I looked everywhere. Where did you go?"

I smiled, pleased he had tried to find me. "I'd rather not say."

"I thought we were getting married."

"I wanted to, but I couldn't do that to you, Garrett."

"Do what to me, Abi?"

"Destroy your family."

A young boy's voice called out, "Are you coming, Dad?"

"I'll be there in a minute," Garrett answered him.

A door slammed, and Garrett said to me, "That sounds like you, Abi." He paused. "I've worried about you. Charlene and your mom have no idea where you are."

"Did you tell my mom about us?"

"Not everything. But I told her we were good friends, and that I wanted to know when she heard from you. Since she has never called, I guess, you haven't contacted her."

"No, I haven't."

"You ought to—for Christmas." A silence followed his suggestion, and he added, "Are you alone?"

"I got a roommate yesterday—Morgan."

"Morgan? That's my middle name," he remarked with obvious fascination.

"I know. I've seen it on your dog tag."

"I noticed you took one," he said, sounding pleased. "Tell me about your roommate. Male or female?"

"Does it matter?" I chuckled, pleased by his jealousy. "We're actually already very close," I said, unable to keep the dreamy affection out of my voice.

"That's wonderful." He paused. "I'm glad you have friends."

I could tell he was saying what he was supposed to say. "Besides your dog tag, I found your leather hat and vest in the closet, so I took them as well, sort of keepsakes since you were wearing them when we met."

"I hadn't missed them. They don't exactly fit my work attire." He used his snooty voice, the one that always made me smile. "But you should mail the dog tag back to me. The air force may ask me to return it."

"So you can see what city is on the postmark?" I laughed, but his remark about his current life being different made my heart ache with the truth that we could never go back to what we once had.

He laughed too. "You're too quick for me." Then he paused. "You sound sleepy,"

"I was up late last night."

"Did you go to a Christmas party?"

"Sort of. I was the center of attention."

"Really? That's not like you."

"It was sort of my coming out party, the new me." I examined the precious baby in my arms. "My whole life changed last night."

"In what way, Abi?"

"I finally understand what you were trying to tell me with James Allen's book. My life is made up of my thoughts. And every thought I have somehow changes my life. Everything that has happened since I met you is a reflection of that."

"That's right, Bird. You're in charge." When I didn't respond, he asked, "Do you need money? You didn't take the envelope. I can wire it to you."

"No. I'm doing all right. I have a job working in a café, and I've made some friends. The older couple I rent a garage apartment from are sweet. They live in the house, and they kind of watch out for me." I didn't dare tell him I had decided to go on to Houston to find him when I stumbled onto the job and apartment in Austin, both in the same day. It seemed like an omen to stay there and see if I couldn't make it on my own.

"Are you going to school?"

"I've taken a few art classes. Finals are next week, but that just means showing the paintings and drawings I've done. Guess who they're of?"

"I'm guessing me. I don't know how you do that."

"I've got your image in my head." Drawing it repeatedly had insured I did not lose it to the eraser of time. I would need to show our son what his father looks like.

"Thanks for leaving your pictures. But you still owe me a self-portrait."

"Someday," I said teasingly and laughed. "How's your internship going?"

"My partner, the person I co-counsel with, Delthea, has been great about listening to me go on about you." He paused. "I needed someone to help me understand what had happened, where you must have been with all this. Do you mind?"

"No. I've told Morgan all about you."

A long silence hung between us before I said, "I'll let you go. I just needed to hear your voice."

"Call me again, Bird."

"I can't." My voice broke. "It hurts too much."

I heard him breathing into the phone, and I could almost feel the warmth of it on my neck. "Bird?"

"What?"

"Don't forget I love you," he said softly. "Don't ever forget."

A cat like meow erupted from Morgan, so I carefully hung up the phone and gently cradled our tiny son, swaying him from side to side and studying his prune-like face.

"I love you too, Morgan Clay Barker."

# Living with Abi

Ten years ago, Abi and her infant son, Moa, fled her abusive husband, Vince, by escaping Texas and settling in New Zealand. Now, Abi is facing certain death due to ovarian cancer. Moa is not Vince's child, but she dare not contact Moa's biological father, Garrett, because Vince would somehow find out and claim Moa as his own. Moa cannot imagine losing his mother. They have been everything to each other.

Garrett, who does not know Moa exists, is a psychologist and author. He has just returned from a book tour, and is enigmatically obsessed with finding Abi his lost lover of ten years earlier. He is also suffering with inexplicable abdominal pain. His quest to locate Abi does not make sense as he is happily married to Delthea. Still, he cannot shake his growing need to find Abi and relieve the pain in his gut.

Delthea felt attracted to Garrett when they started working together - right after Abi disappeared and he was married to Trang. She was there for Garrett when he lost Trang and their child in a car accident. After dating and marriage, Garrett first convinced Delthea to postpone parenting, so they could both get their PhD's, and then so he could write and promote a book. Finally, her time has come.

*Living with Abi* tells the mystical story of how these intertwined lives come together across time and distance, bridging the gap between life and death.

Turn the page for a sneak peek at Pat Grissom's next book
*Living With Abi* - a sequel to *Call It Quits*.
Set in Houston, Texas and Jacob's Springs, New Zealand,
*Living With Abi* takes place ten years after *Call It Quits* ends.
Once more Abi and Garrett
are drawn together by a matter of life and death.

To read the rest of the story, purchase *Living with Abi*,
now available in eBook or hard-copy.

# Living with Abi

# Chapter One

A thick fog lingered in Abi's head. The high ceiling and pale green walls didn't look right. Where were her paintings, her books? Oh yes, she had checked into the hospital yesterday - immediately after she saw Dr. Cook. He wouldn't let her go home, birthday or not. This morning before dawn, a nurse apologized for waking her, not that Abi had slept, so somebody else could shortly put her back to sleep. On the way to surgery, the nurse who pushed her trolley commented on the oddity of Dr. Cook scheduling a surgery so early in the morning.

Movements at her side made Abi gaze at the three people she loved most in the world. They stood next to each other, nervously grinning at her.

"*Kia Ora. Tena koutou tamariki ma,*" Moa asked, giving her a Maori greeting and inquiring after her health, which was not good, but how bad she did not know.

Abi flopped a deadweight hand toward Moa, her nine-year-old son, Takahe, her best friend, a tall, dark-skinned Maori, and Colin, the sailor who had rescued her and Moa and brought them to New Zealand from the States. Takahe, rubbed her nose against Abi's in a traditional New Zealand greeting.

Abi chuckled, which awakened the newly sutured muscles of her abdomen. Takahe had welcomed her to Birdsong Inn, a bed and breakfast in New Zealand, with that same gesture when Abi still carried Morgan in her arms, before Takahe dubbed him Moa, before she took them in and treated them like family.

Through parched lips, Abi whispered, "Have you talked to the doctor yet?"

Takahe moved her face from side to side, shaking her dark, wavy hair, now prominently streaked with gray. "The nurse said he would be around soon." She poured a glass of water and held it to Abi's mouth.

It helped, although the dryness in her mouth felt permanent.

"We brought your sketch pad like you asked and a surprise." Gripping her fingers, Moa pointed to a chair where a cake sat. Something Abi couldn't read from her perspective had been written in the icing. She attempted to raise her head, but shooting pain stopped her.

"You picked a hell of a way to celebrate your fortieth birthday," Colin said.

Abi held his calloused hand. "That was yesterday. You missed the party." Since bringing her to New Zealand, Colin had drifted in and out of their lives, pursuing his love of the sea, but always returning to Birdsong Inn for short visits.

"Afraid you're the one who wasn't there." His broad, tanned face broke into a mischievous grin. "So we had to celebrate without you."

"I wouldn't have it any other way." She kissed his scarred knuckles.

The door opened, and Dr. Cook walked in, his expression more grim than yesterday when he spoke of possible ways to put this cancerous growth in check. Takahe and Colin introduced themselves and Moa.

Dr. Cook, American by birth, shook hands with everyone, ending with Moa, who was small for his age. Bending over, his head was level with the boy's. "What grade are you in?"

"I'm not, sir. Me mum teaches me at home," Moa answered.

"And why is that?" Dr. Cook asked.

"There aren't very many children in our village. 'Sides, we can't find a teacher to come to Jacob's Springs," Moa said. "I don't know why. It's the best place in the world."

The doctor chuckled affably as he straightened. Takahe and Colin followed suit while Moa looked pleased with himself. Moa was everything to her, absolutely everything.

Abi stroked Moa's mop of curly, golden brown hair. By the thickness of the folder under Dr. Cook's arm and his seriousness masked by forced pleasantries, Abi suspected the worst. "Colin, would you mind taking Moa for a walk while Takahe and I talk to Dr. Cook?"

"Not a problem." Colin wrapped an arm around Moa's shoulders and guided him out the door.

Moa poked his head back in, his green eyes glimmering. "We'll make it our mission to get milk to go with the cake."

"Good idea." Abi blew him a kiss.

He caught it, high and outside, exactly where she had thrown it. Clutching it to his heart, he disappeared.

"He's a fine young man," Dr. Cook stated, his somber tone asking what would become of him when the awful thing that had invaded her body had run its course.

"Give it to me straight." Abi braced herself.

Her request seemed to catch her doctor off guard. "I wish you had come earlier, when you first started feeling the pain." He had expressed this sentiment several times yesterday when he was evaluating the test results.

"So you didn't get it all?" she asked, avoiding the dreaded term for the demon that slowly consumed her.

"You have to remember it's the elglitics. Advancements in treating cancer are being made every day. A colleague of mine in Houston, Texas is showing amazing results in arresting ovarian cancer. Since you're from Texas, perhaps you'd like to go there and. . . ."

"No," Abi snapped. Dr. Cook had no idea what had forced her to flee Texas, but that didn't stop Abi from remaining terrified at the prospect of ever going back.

Dr. Cook's brow wrinkled, and his mouth gathered in a pout.

"But I don't have *just* ovarian cancer, do I?" she observed.

"No, you don't. Chemotherapy is still an option. While I can't make promises for a full recovery, we can slow it down."

"You mean prolong my death."

"Give you more time—with your son and your friends." He glanced at Takahe's grave face. "You'll need to get your affairs in order, determine a guardian for your son, make sure your will is up to date, all of that.

Maybe spend some time with your mother. You said you hadn't seen her in a while."

"How long do I have?" Abi asked, drained by the prospect of putting a timeline on her remaining days.

"A year at the most—with treatments," he replied.

"And without?" she prodded.

He glanced at his closed folder as if he might see the answer on the cover. "It's hard to say. Six months, perhaps more. There's no way of knowing."

Loud footsteps slapped on the tile floor outside, Moa's tennis shoes. He never went anywhere quietly.

Before he had time to charge back inside, Abi pasted on a smile and touched Dr. Cook's sleeve. "Thanks. You've done all you could. I prefer to proceed without intervention." Her words sounded so rational, like she knew what she would do with Moa, like she had a goddamn plan.

"You don't have to decide now. Think about it," Dr. Cook urged.

"I have," Abi assured him. She had also thought about the fact that Moa's father, who didn't know Moa existed, was married and already had a son. Worse than that, as far as she knew, he still lived in Texas, a big state, but obviously not big enough for Abi to get away from Vince, the monster Abi had been married to. When Moa was only a few weeks old, Abi had made the mistake of calling her mother and telling her she lived in Austin. Before Abi could get off the phone, Morgan started crying. Mama must have put two and two together and came up with a grandchild, which she sent Vince to find.

When Abi started feeling abdominal pain three months ago, she tried to ignore it. That didn't work, so she willed it to go away. After that, she prayed and bargained with God. Now she must face it—and what to do with her nine-year-old son.

\* \* \*

Garrett blinked and tried to focus on the red digital numbers of the clock that sat at the far side of his office desk. His damp forehead rested on the blotter. He felt wet all over. After he passed out, he must have started sweating. He dragged his arm that felt like it had weights tied to it toward his face, feeling for the negatives of Abi that he had been examining. The narrow strips of plastic, his only concrete proof that Abi had existed were still there. Thank God he had thought to lock his door before he pulled them out and lined them up on his desk, an insane, yet compulsive habit he had acquired in recent days. Delthea, his wife, would die if she walked in and saw them lying there.

How long had passed since he blacked out? He couldn't remember what time it had been when he couldn't hold up his head any longer, and he had felt himself collapsing onto his desk, much like a child falling asleep in his highchair. When he began feeling drowsy, he wondered if it had something to do with the constant discomfort in his gut that had gradually intensified over the last three months.

When he regained consciousness, he still felt bad, although his abdominal area felt semi-numb like the sensation that remains for hours after getting a tooth filled. It was nice to lack sensation in the area that usually pained him, but while he was unconscious, he had emptied his bladder and his bowels, so he needed to get cleaned up — if he could muster the strength to do so. Luckily, Judy, his secretary, and Delthea, his co-therapist and wife, were leaving him alone. Delthea probably told Judy not to disturb him since he had been listless yesterday when he arrived back in Houston after a month long book tour. By now his wife had left the office to prepare for his birthday party.

She wanted to surprise him, and he had played along, never mentioning the messages he heard on their home answering machine when he called from hotel rooms and checked it. He had not given Bud Anderson his home phone since he dared not let Delthea know he had hired a private eye to find Abi. Bud was touted as an individual who pulled information out of thin air, things like phone numbers. Supposedly, he could find anyone, even a mistress who had disappeared ten years ago.

\*   \*   \*

Delthea glanced at her watch. Then she tossed a roll of black crepe paper to her sister who stood on top of a stepladder. "Can you move a little faster? We've still got balloons to blow up and posters to hang. Garrett will be home in less than an hour, and the guests will be here any minute."

"Don't get your panties in a wad, Deli," Elaine drawled while she fiddled with a roll of tape. She had an infuriating habit of moving at a snail's pace, yet somehow working circles around Delthea.

Frustrated from a day full of setbacks and delays, Delthea threw her arms in the air and marched into the kitchen. Even though the caterer had spelled Garrett with one 't' on the cake and brought the wrong brand of champagne, he *had* arrived. She couldn't say as much for the piano player who had promised to come an hour early and warm up on the newly tuned baby grand. Neither Delthea nor Garrett was musical, so this seemed like the perfect opportunity to actually utilize an extravagance bought simply to fill that corner of the living room.

While Elaine puffed on balloons, Delthea emptied the refrigerator of serving platters piled with a variety of cheeses, boiled shrimp, and vegetables and fruit cut into decorative pieces and assembled into recognizable shapes like birds and fish. She laid out her china, silverware, and linen napkins, none of that paper stuff for this special occasion.

When people responded to the invitation, they said how eager they were to see Garrett since he had been away so much promoting his book. Delthea hoped his schedule had finally slowed down some. At the beginning of their relationship, Garrett delayed marriage until they both finished their doctoral degree in psychology. When they finally married, Delthea was ready to start a family, but on their wedding night, Garrett convinced her to help him manifest his dream of a successful counseling practice before they had a child. As soon as their business had taken off, her dear, sweet husband plunged into writing a book. Now it was her turn. More than anything Delthea wanted a baby.

Garrett looked and sounded so tired last night. He fell asleep wearing his traveling clothes. Jet lag, she supposed. Who wouldn't be tired after thirty cities in as many days? He didn't have another book tour on his calendar. At last, they could finally enjoy being together. She had turned down several speaking engagements in lieu of spending time with her absentee husband, preferably in bed.

After finding the perfect spot for a bouquet of long-stemmed red roses, Delthea glanced out the window of their fifth floor condominium and noted the profusion of pink azaleas.

March in Houston. Spring came earlier, and it got hotter here faster than any place she had ever lived. Still it was a lucrative city, and if you didn't go see your shrink once a week, you had "not arrived." Delthea hoped those with disposable income, continued to think that way. She had sacrificed her most fertile years to help Garrett start a practice and then to keep it all going while he followed yet another of his dreams. Now he could see their patients while she took time off.

Oliver Matthew's car pulled into the drive. He had been compulsively punctual since the day she and Garrett both showed up to start interning at his psychology clinic nearly ten years ago. From the very beginning, Delthea fell in love with Garrett's green eyes, his short, muscular frame, his caring demeanor, his confidence, wit, humor, everything—except his marital status. Neither ethical nor prudent nor wise, Delthea had hopelessly fallen in love with a married man.

Although Garrett openly admitted that he remained with his wife out of obligation, having brought her and their child from Vietnam, he was indeed taken and a father to boot. On top of that, Garrett was recuperating from a failed affair. His mistress, Abi, had disappeared about the same time Delthea met Garrett. A year later, Garrett seemed to be coping with losing Abi when his wife and child died in a car accident. Delthea's willingness to listen and comfort Garrett through both ordeals eventually brought them together.

The phone rang and Delthea answered it. She told Milton, the doorman, to admit Oliver and anyone who mentioned they were here for Garrett's birthday party. She asked Milton to give her a warning call when Garrett arrived. As she hung up the phone, she shouted to Elaine, "The first guest is on his way up. Let's change our clothes."

She prayed Elaine didn't plan to put on that purple dress she had worn to Garrett's first book signing. What little there was of it fit too snugly in what Elaine would consider all the right places. Elaine was well endowed; Delthea couldn't argue that, but she was also thirty pounds overweight.

Soon the apartment teemed with friends and colleagues. Delthea, now wearing a long, black evening gown, circulated among them, smiling, offering more wine, and periodically checking her watch. Noting the phone remained disturbingly quiet, she picked it up to make sure it had a dial tone.

Oliver cornered Delthea and asked if she still planned to cover for him in October. At first she drew a blank. Then she remembered their telephone conversation about his inadvertently booking two speaking engagements for the same night, one in Austin with the Cattlemen Convention and the other in Houston with a group of dermatologist. Once she assured him that she wouldn't think of letting him down, he asked her which she preferred. She opted for Houston since hopefully Garrett would be home. Besides, she doubted her ability to meaningfully engage a herd of cowboys.

An hour after she expected Garrett, Delthea sought out their secretary and pulled Judy aside. "Was Garrett at the office when you left?"

"Yes, he said through the door that he was going home soon." She winked at Delthea. "I nearly said I'd see him when he got here—of course, I didn't."

Good thing Garrett had been out of the office most of the last month. Judy used no discretion about saying things on the telephone loud enough for anyone to hear or leaving notes on her desk about so and so RSVPing.

Across the room, Elaine chatted with a group of prospects for husband number three, their enraptured faces all spellbound by her skimpy, purple dress and candid stories of life as a nurse in the ER. Invariably she repeated that hideous story about the three-hundred-pound woman who was dropped off wearing nothing but a gee-string. Delthea hated to see Elaine embarrass herself with junior high humor, not to mention how her behavior reflected on Delthea. When Elaine paused for air, Delthea grabbed her elbow and guided her to the kitchen.

"Hey, Deli, what's the big idea? I was just getting warmed up?" Elaine protested too loudly.

Delthea pulled her sister toward the pantry, out of sight and earshot of the crowd. "I need you to drive to my office and see if Garrett is still there."

"You go. I'm having a good time." She shrugged off Delthea's hold on her. "Anyway, I've drunk too much. I can't drive."

"I thought you were doing a night shift later." Elaine had agreed to help with the party but made it clear she must leave by nine to go by and check on her sons before she went to work. "What about Kent and David?" Delthea reminded her.

"Who's that?" Elaine laughed and tipped her empty glass to her lips. "Call Garrett and tell him to get his butt home."

Delthea grabbed the wall phone and punched in the office number, certainly not because Elaine had told her to. It was simply the most logical thing to do. The phone rang until the machine answered. Yes, she had an emergency, but the number the recording said to dial wasn't going to help her find Garrett. She slammed the receiver back onto the cradle.

"I'm driving over there," she announced to Elaine who looked none too steady. "Make some coffee and sober up."

"Maybe he had an accident," Elaine offered grimly, probably reflecting on what she saw wheeled into the ER every night.

Delthea grabbed her purse from the pantry. "Call the office again in a few minutes. Garrett might have gone to the john. If anyone asks, tell them I've run out for ice."

"Right," Elaine affirmed with little enthusiasm. "And if I reach Garrett, should I tell him there's a house full of people here waiting to celebrate his fortieth birthday?"

"No, just—just tell him to get his butt home." Delthea rushed out the door, ignoring the questioning gazes that followed her, the woman who had planned a party for three months but had failed to make sure the guest of honor would show up.

To read the rest of the story, purchase *Living with Abi* now available in eBook or hard-copy.

# Acknowledgments

When Hurricane Harvey destroyed 80% of my business inventory, *Texas Commission on the Arts* offered a grant for artist who had been significantly impacted. As I reflect on Abi's struggle in *Call It Quits* and my own challenge in recuperating from the storm, I am eternally grateful that the right people, resources, and ideas show up when we need them the most. Thank you, *Texas Commission on the Arts* and the *Andrew W. Mellon Foundation*, for providing funding to publish this book.

My everlasting appreciation goes to my long-time critique partners, Marsha Harris and Debbie Sanders (now deceased), for holding my hand throughout the initial formation of this novel over twenty years ago. Our collective encouragement for each other to "Never Give Up!" reverberates with me still.

Another debt of gratitude goes to the various readers who have given me feedback through its several iterations: Mary Bishop, Myrethia Wood, LaVern Watters, Kathie Yates, Reagan Grissom, Therese Clemens, Dorthy Edwards Hawkes, and Cody White. Finally, heart-felt thanks goes to Yvonne Vermillion of *Magic Graphix* for her expertise in graphic setup and cover design. Please, forgive me if I have overlooked someone as this novel has taken its time finding its way into the world.